BROKEN
Love &
FOREVER
Bound

Layla Stevens

Broken Love and Forever Bound

Broken Love and Forever Bound Copyright © 2014 Layla Stevens

Published by:

The Scilicet Group, LLC
4139 South Nolan Drive
Pearland, Texas 77584

Edited by: Lynn Palmer

This work is a work of fiction. Names, characters, places, and incidents either are a product of the author's imagination or are used factiously, and any resemblance to actual persons, living or dead, business establishments, events or locales is entirely coincidental. Confidentiality Notice: This e-mail message, including any attachments, is for the sole use of the intended recipient(s), and may contain legally privileged and confidential information. Any unauthorized review, use, disclosure, or distribution is prohibited. If you are not the intended recipient, please do not read, copy, or use it, and do not disclose it to others. Please notify the sender of the delivery error by replying to this message, then delete it from your system, and destroy all copies. Thank you.

ISBN-9781941839201

Looking Back…..

"Love yourself and everything else falls into line. You really have to love yourself to get anything done in this world."
---Lucile Ball

The bell rings and the students of King Junior High embark on another casual Friday as the crowd narrows the halls. The over-achievers rush to their honors classes, making sure they arrive early in order to be prepared for their next subject. While other students, like athletes, goof off and push each other into the lockers. Some locker doors are open so horny, teenage couples can enjoy a make out session before their next class. Kids sneeze and wipe their snot on their shirts because the overused, nasty, mildewed text books they carry have been around for centuries.

Kayla Ashby, a shy, quiet twelve year old girl, shuffles down the hall with her nose stuck in a *Goosebumps* book. She glances over her black rimmed eyeglasses at the blue-eyed fraternal twins, Garrett and Wyatt Winters—the cutest boys in the eighth grade. Kayla ducks her face behind her mousey, brown hair and continues to read her book.

"Kayla, Watch out!"

A hand grasps Kayla's shoulder before she bangs her head on one of the open locker doors. She peers up at the boy who saved her from what could have been an embarrassing moment because in junior high, everything can be an embarrassment. Garrett's eyes seek her pale green eyes.

Why?

It's feast or famine among the cliques. You're either cool like the Winters Brothers or considered a nerd like Kayla. Therefore, the room of embarrassment comes in spades—with one of the cool kids making fun of the less fortunate. An uproar of laughter breaks through the hall.

I will not cry…I will not cry…

Repeating the old saying over and over again, Kayla hugs the book and removes the butterfly barrette from her brown hair—concealing her face. Yet, her emotions fail her and tears protrude from the corner of her eyes as they gloss over.

"Are you okay?" Garrett tips her chin with his right index finger and wipes away some of the unwanted tears. "I didn't want to see this pretty face of yours get bruised because of an open locker."

"Huh?" Words escape Kayla as she stares into his sapphire blue eyes. "Umm." Her mouth dries. "Thanks."

Oh, lord, I could look into those eyes for days. The way his irises sparkle, I wonder what they would look like especially at night. Drool much Kayla? Stop gawking at him…

She tugs on her loose, blue T-shirt that covers her large breasts—which seemed to appear overnight. While other girls wear daisy dukes and tank tops to tempt the boys, Kayla covers her whole body in order to push them away. She never shows skin because of the ugly and angry scars branded into her chest.

Garrett starts to chit chat, and Kayla tries to pay attention to him, but her thoughts run away from her. Garrett Winters is the hottest boy in the eighth grade. His black wild hair covers a scar on the edge of his forehead.

His scent…it's cedar from the woodland areas. I'm so in heaven…I could stare at him for hours. He is just…Dream worthy.

"Kayla, are you listening to me?" He asks. The crack in his voice sends shivers over her body. "I was wondering if I could walk you to class."

"You want me to walk with you?" she stutters. Kayla covers her folder so Garrett's eyes won't see the two pink hearts and initials G.W. and K.A. written all over. "Really?" Taken back, Kayla's eyes wander to left and right, looking to see if one of the 'Plastics' are nearby.

No Barbie wanna-be's near me. He must have lost his freaking mind, but I won't complain. Being in the same space as him makes my heart flutter.

"I'm talking to you and no one else." he says, a dimple appears on the left side of his cheek—bringing out his smile. Garrett relaxes his left hand in his jean pocket and offers the other.

Shyly, Kayla accepts it. Weird sensations enter her lady bits as butterflies flutter all over her. Chicken pimples, or what normal people call goose bumps, pop up on her arms.

This must be love, isn't it? Like I would know, no one has ever shown me any type of love. Just hell...

Throughout the day, Garrett spends as much time with Kayla as possible. She may be a geek to others, but in his eyes she has natural beauty. From her delicate skin to the way her green irises shine with yellow specks in them, making them look like she has tiger eyes. Nervously, he rubs the back of his black hair and continuously rambles about anything he could think of. Just so that he can spend time with her.

Instead of listening to what he is saying, Kayla stares at his physique, picturing him in his tight, ripped blue jeans and white tank tops—also known as wife-beaters.

At lunch time, Garrett and the guys from the baseball team brag about their games and scores. Each trying to out-do the other by arguing over who had the winning run. All the "pretty girls" sit around eyes fixed on the team, pretending to be interested in the conversation hoping that one of the boys will throw a crumb of attention their way. Kayla sits picking at her Salisbury steak with her fork just trying to blend in.

God! This gravy smells like shit and it's making me ill. Reminds me of Millie Stanton's god awful cooking.

Kayla rests her hands on her stomach while it does somersaults. She watches Garrett's every move—from his emotions to his hand gestures. She imagines what it would be like if his hand touched hers. One of the best love songs, *Emotions* by Mariah Carey, pops in her head— after all, she's in love.

I can't believe God's gift to teenage girls is into me. If this boy only knew he has invaded my dreams, and his face has brought me comfort—especially after dealing with my screwed up pretend family.

"Why would you think a guy would love you? You've been beaten with an ugly stick so don't bother. You are nothing but a screwed up cunt. You're just damage goods." Distressing voices float inside Kayla's mind, interrupting her moment of bliss. She zones out thinking of the hell hole she calls home with the Stanton's.

Oh yes.

Senator Seth and Millie Stanton portray themselves like an ideal couple with two *well-to-do* identical twin boys-- Edwin and Elijah. All they need to make their portrait family complete is Kayla—the Orphan Annie. With her, they are thought to be the *All American family*. This family, however, is far from perfect. The amount of physical and mental abuse behind closed doors would have Child Protection Services breaking the door down. Kayla called them only once, and after the social worker left the house, there was hell to pay. She was beaten to a pulp, and her brown hair burned to a crisp. Kayla never tried to seek help again.

Millie Stanton is far from being a mother. She turns a blind eye and often ignores her children. Her husband, the senator, sleeps around with any short skirt and high heel there is—the younger they are, the more turned on the guy gets.

"I'm broken…" The lost words slip out of Kayla's mouth—her lips tremble. An unwanted tear slips down her cheek. She wipes it before any more falls down her face.

"Baby, are you alright?" Garrett's gentle touch on her lap startles Kayla. She almost jumps off the damn bench. He then brushes his knuckles across her soft pink cheeks.

"Fine." She bites down on her lips and sulks back into the chair, trying to control her emotions. She looks over to her best friend, Violet Palmer, who has been there for her since day one. Violet questions Kayla as her big blue eyes soften.

Kayla shrugs her shoulders and wipes her sweaty palms on the white *Guess* jeans she borrowed from Violet.

"We need to talk," The blonde bombshell mouths to her.

"Not now VI," Kayla pleads.

Violet shakes her head and turns her attention to Wyatt, flicking part of the blonde hair falling on the side of her face. Garrett's twin winks at Violet, strands of his short light-colored hair cover his eyes. He then grabs Violet's knees, and she giggles. Kayla watches them and twirls a strand of her brunette hair around her finger.

Every boy wants VI and every girl is either afraid of her or envies her. Just ask one of the plastic bitches, Reagan Woodrow. VI ripped the girl's hair out for trying to fight me. I wish I had an ounce of the bombshell's luck. Violet Palmer doesn't need luck. She not only has a sense of style and a bitchin' attitude when it comes to protecting her friends, VI's family is what some call the 'elite'. Granted, they go to all of those stuck up charity events and contribute to society, but this family has their own uniqueness. The Palmers are warm and loving with their Yankee traditions and their northern sense of humor. Since VI's family lived in Baltimore, her father insists she learns self-defense so he takes her to the shooting range every weekend. He firmly believed wealthy or not, a girl should know how to protect herself. He even offered to take me shooting, but the douchebag, Millie thought it would hurt Seth's reputation, and she is not too fond of their northern ways. God forbid I learn to protect myself and ruin the good ole' senator's rep.

"Kayla, did I lose you?" Garrett's soft voice draws Kayla back from la-la land, and she stops playing with her hair.

"What?" She drops her hands into her lap and gawks at him. "I'm sorry," Kayla gazes down at their hands caressing one and other. The pain she goes through on a daily basis, creeps up to her throat. She clears it and says, "I just get lost in my own thoughts."

"I understand." He stares at her with his beautiful blue eyes like he's seeing her damaged spirit. "If you need to talk, I'm a good listener."

God, please don't let anything happen to him.

Chapter ONE

The Past...

"Life is what happens while you are busy making other plans"--- *John Lennon*

    Massive rough hands shove me into the pool house. I scream bloody murder. His left hand smacks my face as his knuckles dent my cheeks and there's a metallic taste that seeps to the corner of my mouth. The horrible predator slams me into the wall and his hands wrap around my throat. I start gasping for air, losing what little breath I had. His grip tightens and my vision starts to blacken around the edges. I know I only have moments before I lose consciousness.

    "Shut up, you fucking cock teaser." The disdain in Edwin Stanton's words are of pure hatred. "Get the fucking zip ties."

    "Please," I shout, praying for the Lord's help.

    "Go ahead and scream bitch, we love it when you fight us," Edwin says as he grits his teeth. "Just so you know the more you scream, the harder things will be for you." The baritone sound vibrates through his voice leaving me numb and scared shitless.

    Tears gush down my face and onto the damp grey carpeted floor. "Please don't!"
The room silences for a second until devilish laughter surfaces.

    "Please...don't," I mutter it again.

    "We all have to make a sacrifice for this family, superstar," Elijah, Edwin's twin, whispers in my ear and then licks it.

"Kayla, are you with me?"

I blink as I watch the setting sun over Birmingham's skyline. "What?" I slightly budge on the plush grey couch.

"Just what I thought," Dr. Patrice Doyle says with her strong southern accent. She peers down above her red rimmed Sally Jessy Raphael glasses as they rest on her perfectly sculpted nose.

Patrice is the fifth psychologist within the last three years. Her informal ways and rock star attitude, plus the fact she could be a cross between a motorcycle mama and an ex-play boy bunny, gives me comfort and hope. Unlike the others, who thought I just went through some teenage drama, Patrice is the only psychologist that actually gets me. She is like a tornado, feisty and full of spunk. I just know that she's going to be the one to fix me. She reminds me of what I perceive my birth mother to be.

"You've got to forgive, not forget Kayla, but forgive," she lectures like a mother.

"I'll try to forgive the douche canoe and the cunt that are my so called parents," I say fighting back the forsaken tears. "But the other pussy ass Fucktard, I will never forgive." I suck the corner of my lip then bluntly state, "Well, one day I will get my revenge and like other frozen things, revenge is a dish that is best served cold."

"Kayla you know I don't like that four letter word, even if it fits the description," Patrice's stare made me squirm on the couch like I was a child in the principal's office.

"Yeah, but not if you're telling the truth about the individual's personality," I shrug my shoulders.

"Darlin' you'll hate yourself more if you resort to vengeance." She rises from her desk and walks over to her comfy red office chair. Dr. Doyle then pulls it towards me and takes a seat. She leans forward and rests her hands on my knee.

"As a doctor, I have to empathize with all God's creatures. But as a human being—some of them, well they just need to be_stuffed. Like the two dickheads, I'd like to see mounted_on my den wall. They would jazz up the place quite nicely." she chuckles.

As Patrice continues her lecture, I grunt and zone out thinking of ways to injure the two as monkey's. I could brand them with an iron with my initials on it or tie up their hands with cable ties to a maple tree—just watch fiery red ants eat the flesh off of them. "I'm just tired…"

"Of the nightmares or the fact that you hide from any type of relationship?" The doctor breathes and exhales, probably trying to figure out the words to say. "When you first walked through those doors, you were lost," she continues, "You're alcohol abuse and your self-medicating drove you to the edge. You were at a point that if you didn't do something we would have lost you. You came through my door and you were high. I knew you were on something other than pills." With her index finger, Dr. Doyle lifts my head towards her dark chocolate brown eyes. "It's time to go home."

"Go home?" I rub my temples with my two index fingers. "So Seth and Millie can just write me a check like I was another damn scandal." I wrap my arms hugging my chest. "How can I go back to the place that made me into the train wreck that I am?" I wave both hands slowing, showing my body. "I'm broken because of them."

"Kayla, there is an old saying about a victim and a survivor." Her eyes burning into mine, pulling at my inner thoughts. "A victim, who becomes broken, choses to. She or he fills their emotions with regret and self-pity. Making horrible decisions that reflects their life—one mistake after another until they feel the emptiness inside of them. Now, a survivor pushes through the rough times and rises above all else. The survivor is strong and falls back on the one thing that brings her peace and serenity."

"That's deep Patrice," I scratch the top of my head with my index finger than ask, "What is the one thing?"

"Faith, Kayla," Patrice states. "The one thing that no one can ever take away is your faith. You can lose everything else in your life, but your faith is something that no man or woman can ever take from you. As long as you believe in faith, you will always have someone and something in your corner backing you up."

She continues, "You have friends and a man who you left behind. It's time to forgive and to put your life back on track. Yes I said forgive not forget."

"I want to go home," hypnotically, I repeat the words.

"Remember, when you decide to go home, I'm only a plane ride away." She taps my knee and strolls to her desk. "I'm available anytime day or night and Kayla, before you go did you do your assignment that I asked of you?"

I nod my head in a yes fashion, and I take the piece of paper out of my back pocket, and I unfold it. With shaking hands I tell her that it's a poem by **Julie Mishler Called "The Woman in the Mirror"**.

As I look in the mirror

At the face staring back at me

I see a shell of a woman

Or the woman I am meant to be

Not the real me

I want so much

I need to feel

I want it all

But can I?

Can I be that woman?

I close my eyes and ponder

The smell of your skin

The way your hands peruse my body

Grabbing my hips

Swaying to the groove

Grinding into me

My fears rule me

Control what I do

The passion and desire

That burns within me

Ignites my thoughts

Fires my dreams

Could I?

Just let loose

Reach up

Wrap my arms around your neck

Yes I can!

Free my soul

Let the music take me away

Follow my dreams

Let my passion flow

I open my eyes

Looking into the mirror once more

I see a beautiful woman

A passionate, desirable woman

And loudly I say

Yes, yes I will be the woman in my dreams!

"Kayla, that poem is beautiful, I think that she captured how you feel one hundred percent," She says with a wink.

I wipe the tears from my face, and head to the door, one last question before I leave, "Dr. Doyle do you think my mother is okay?"

"Kayla, that question came out of left field," she replies and taps her pen.

I turn away from her, so that she can't see my face, because I know if she sees me she will know --- more of my dark secrets from the past.

"Kayla, dear, I think your mother is fine and she is proud of you wherever she is." Patrice smiles.

"I hope one day that I will meet her. That's my only dream other than dealing with my demons, I want to know her." I hug my chest.

"Honey please remember that she did what she thought was best for you at that time. Please think about what we've talked about and let me know if you are indeed going back home." She hands me a script.

"Yes, ma'am! I will, and thank you for everything that you have done for me." I take the script and sigh.

"I will always do anything for you Kayla; remember to keep your head held high, you are no longer a victim." She places her left hand on my right shoulder and gently squeezes it.

I haven't been back to Seattle in seven years. I spent my time getting my degree in engineering and I'm one of the best damned architects in the south. I've seen all varieties of life and travelled as much as I could. Even met some amazing people, but the ghosts of my past still haunt me. Driving ------ home, I keep going over this therapy session in my head. "It's now my aim, my goal to face my demons head on. I have no other choice, it has to happen, maybe then I could move on and smile once more."

Automatically, I flick the blinker heading towards my studio apartment. "I have to forgive them, so I could forgive myself. Does it scare the hell out of me? Well I would be a liar if I said no that it didn't, because it scares the shit out of me."

The smell of Chrome cologne mixed --- with bourbon taints my skin. My voice is hoarse from screaming. I shiver and whimper as two naked bodies slam into me, taking away my innocence.

Shrieking, my eyes pop open and my chest screams for air. I scramble to sit up, messing the cream colored silk sheets— frantically, running my hands over my face as tears drop on to the canopy bed. These nightmares have become more vivid since I returned back home to Seattle.

"Relax, Kayla. No one can find you or get you." Calming my breathing before I move, I tug the damp sheets to my chin— wishing they would protect me from my dreams. I read that the green numbers on the alarm clock say 1:30 AM through blurry eyes. I blink and rub my eyes from the fog. "Shit" I utter harshly realizing I still have my contacts in knowing they're going to be a bitch to get out.
I close my eyes. The fierce grey-blue eyes with murky yellow tints appear along with the smell of stale cigarettes and expensive cologne ----.

I jump and snap my eyelids open. "Seven weeks since I'm back and now my anxiety sky rockets," I sigh. "Really? Did you expect it to be different, Kayla?" I mumble. "You knew coming home would be hard."
Since I'm blessed being a whopping 5ft 4 inches tall, I scoot over to my right side by the little set of steps I had built so I won't fall

flat on my face. After stepping down, I lean over to the right side of the bed and snag the wooden baseball bat that Garrett gave me at one of his victory games in eighth grade. The fact that I still have it after all these years still amazes me.

Slowly and carefully, I head to the big oak front door and make sure all the locks are in place, including the deadbolt. "Okay, I typed in the code… so the system's on."

I inhale and exhale sharply.

Sneaking around the house, I check every nook and cranny. My fingers find their way up the wall in the pitch dark to the light switch. I flip the switch as the light flickers on, I inspect each state of art appliance and making sure that it is in its rightful place with no extra fingerprints on the stainless steel fridge.

"Kitchen is checked." I loosen my grip on the bat and lean over to the dining room wall and flip a switch. Every piece of furniture from the oak table to the designer high back chairs are intact. No sign of entry. I swipe my fingers along the table as dust attaches to my pointer finger, then wipe it on my pink boxers. "I really should entertain or invite people over for dinner. This room needs to be used."

Exhausted, I carry myself to the living room, and lifted the heavy burgundy curtains with the bat. Of course there's nothing there. You really need to sleep, Kayla, or you're going to lose your mind.

As I peer out into the Seattle skyline, thousands of lights from the city, give me serenity. "I am a survivor not a victim," I whisper as I peer up at the sky, a shooting star crosses over the bridge. "The only wish I want is happiness."

The curtain slightly budges.

"Bastards!" I pivot quickly with my eyes shut, swinging the baseball bat at the empty air. I pause and drop the bat to my left leg. "Get a fucking grip, Kayla."

I plop down on one of the black leather couches and kick my feet up on the glass top coffee table. After I reach for the remote, I turn on the television that's mounted above the fireplace.

There is no place like home. Immediately, the scene from The Wizard of Oz comes on, when Dorothy taps her shoes and repeats these famous words over and over. There's no place like home, there's no place like home.

This home is what I have wanted ever since I was a little girl. A place that shouts Kayla Ashby. The old warehouse with the high ceilings and open beams that settles in the heart of town called to me. The best part about it is that I'm in the middle of Pike Street market and not far from Mt. Rainier. For a bonus, my favorite restaurant, Ivar's is close by, when I need a quick dinner.

With hard work and determination, I was able to buy it, gut it, and design the old warehouse to my exact specifications—it's everything a girl like me could ask for. An actual home to live in, but it's still missing something. Then it hits me like a lightning bolt. It still needs a mother's touch. A tear slips down my cheek as I think of her and questions stir in my head. Does she think of me? Does she know that I'm alive? Does she ever miss me?

I close my eyes and softly say a small prayer for her and wipe away the tears. God, I know she doesn't know me but please protect her, make sure she's okay. When the time is right, please place her back into my life.

My eyes flicker to the light of the video monitor and I see no movement on the screen. Maybe a hot shower will do me good.

The moonlight dances across the cool cedar wood floors in the open living room, I walk into its path and see my shadow as I check the locks on each window and door, one more time. Then I head up the spiral staircase to the corner of the master bedroom.

As I walk in the lights ---- come on automatically while the tile warmer heats the floor. I stroll to my seven divine shower heads and turn the knob to the hottest setting possible watching as the water sprays at all different angles.

I love this bathroom, with the double sinks laid in with silver granite tops ---, and a mirror above the counter that reaches to the ceiling and cabinet. I turn on the cold water as I peer into the large oversized but completely necessary mirror. "My god, I look like death warmed over."

Beady eyes and puffy cheeks, all do to the late night drawing of plans for a client. "Now I have raccoon eyes. Oh, that's attractive. Good thing I live by myself. Because Lord forbid a man see me like this, he'd be scared off. All though, if I could make the Stanton twins run that would be a fuckin' dream come true in itself."

I splash the cool water over my face and dab it with a soft pink cloth. Then I drop the cloth into the sink while turning the tap off.

I scuff my tired aching feet over to the glass doors of the shower that's in the opposite corner of the tub and climb in. The water beats down on my tired shoulders. It feels so good to wash off the nightmare, until the heat of the shower scalds the scar lines on my back, making them stand out. The nightmare replays in my head. Every motion, every mark made by these two men—not to mention the sensation of their bodies invading mine—breaks through the darkness from my mind.

The hot relaxing shower turns into a torture chamber and a pair of hands grab hold of my throat—forcing me to hit the shower wall.

"You have the best fucking cunt I have ever had," Edwin growls. His hands grip tighter around my neck, leaving his indentations. Tears protrude, again as the word "Superstar" slams into my head.

After the torture, Elijah's arms comfort my naked body. So tired and exhausted, my head rests on his chest. "I'm sorry, Superstar. Edwin can get out of hand. But he's right about one thing."

I peer up to Elijah's grey eyes.

*"Your birthmother left you here for a reason," he whispers. "You **are** ours. If you ever fucking leave, or try to look for your birthmother again, I will find you and hunt down everyone you love, including the little piece of shit, Garrett." He gently lifts my chin and wipes the tears. "You belong to us and no one else so don't you ever fucking think of running."*

Too tired to do anything else or even talk, I just nod.

I shake my head to loosen the memory. Realizing I have been crying yet again I face the water to wash the remnants of snot and tears from my face.

I wash up and shave all my bits before turning off the water and opening the slider door. I reach out and notice in my distracted state I forgot a towel.

I step out from the shower as water drips down my naked body. I open the cabinet door and grab a huge pink fluffy towel and securely wrap it around me. Once I grab the pill bottle for my anxiety from the medicine cabinet, an eerie feeling comes over me. "It's nothing."
I close the cabinet door quickly.

Grey eyes stare at me in the mirror.

I spin around bracing my palms on the sink. No one's around, just the steam from the shower. I uncontrollably giggle and snag the medication in the other hand. "Well, no use trying to sleep now."

As soon as I reach the bathroom door, I stop and make sure the coast is clear. Years of paranoia have finally made me feel like I'm losing my mind.

I throw up my hair in a messy bun, put on a pair of

comfy jeans and loose pink shirt. Then head back down the stairs to my small but well equipped office just on the other side of the living room. The stained glass doors are a welcoming sight. I slump down on my black office chair and twirl the medication bottle in my hand.

"Speak it, believe it, and live it!" That will be my motto. "One day, I will be free from all of this." I throw the bottle in the wastebasket. I sit and watch the clock for a minute—wondering if I made the right choice by tossing it, but for now, I want to do things completely sober. For the first time in years, I don't want to be high.

I flick on the desk lamp and seven text messages appear on my phone from McKenna-- my somewhat ex-girlfriend.

"Oh, great." I scan it. "Bitch, whore, slut, cunt face. You think you can break up with me." I click erase. "Okay, I don't need to go there."

My so called relationship with McKenna Ramsey was just sex. She was married and well I was never looking for a relationship—especially with a woman; well not that one. I mean it wasn't like we were serious and hell, we had only slept together a few times, and each time was when I was drunk or high other than the first time on the green sofa at our dorm. I don't have a type when it comes to sex, man or woman, because GOD knows there are some sexy ones. I'm attracted to the person. It never mattered to me the color of their skin or the shape of their eyes. To me it's all pink in the middle. And because of my past, I don't know if I will ever truly be ready for a man. I'm not even sure I would ever be ready for the only one who I ever loved. Women are safer, period.

After countless hours of sending designs out to get feedback from the hot pink HP laptop, a message from Myspace pops up. It's from VI. The message is dated almost four months ago. Even though it seems like I haven't been on Myspace in forever, because it's the dinosaur of social media, something told me to browse it. Really Kayla, time to update and jump into the

Facebook, Instagram, and even Twitter era, I chuckle.

As I rock back in my chair and read Violet's message, I bawl. Out of everyone that I walked away from, Violet and Wyatt are the two people who I missed the most. "I wonder if she's online, now."

I scroll down and her name pops up. I hesitate in a response. What should I type? Will she react like the same Ol' Vi or did she change? How do you just type SURPRISE, I'm alive and well, not dead and laying in a gutter or in jail, but hey I'd love to catch up with you.

I stare at the screen for a couple of minutes—tapping my finger on the desk. Nervously, I open the chat box and simply type Hi! Just two little letters, to let her know I'm still around.

Instant letters appear.

HELLLLLLLLLLLLOOOOOOOO!!!!! Flashes across the screen.

"Okay Kayla breathe. She responded and didn't cuss you out." My heart is beating so loud I can hear it. Before I chicken out, I give her my number and within seconds my cell vibrates.

"Gutterslut, about time you got in touch with me...Jeez, I thought I'd never hear from you again," Her voice is unusually peppy.

We both breakdown and spit out nonsense to each other. Once we catch our breaths, I explain to Violet that, yes, I have dated, mostly girls and really didn't want to explain my relationships. She in returns elaborates that she loves being single and has no intentions on getting married. But her parents on the other hand want grandkids. Violet remarks that someday she'll have babies, but right now she's not ready to be a mom. I, on the other hand, can't wait to have them once all my shit settles.

"You know, I'm not the only one who's been trying to track you down. Wyatt has too," Violet's voice becomes ridged.

"How is he?" I ask. Besides Violet, Wyatt was one of my best friends. He's the brother I wished I had. Whenever Edwin or Elijah were out in public with me, Wyatt made sure he was nearby. He never trusted the two of them. The day he saw one of my scars, fire burst into his eyes. I had a feeling he knew it was them but he never said anything--I guess he was waiting for me to bring it up.

"He's good babe. Still drop dead sexy, a real ladies man," she giggles. "He can have any woman he wants, and probably has."

"Ha. Ha." I switch the phone to my right ear.

"I missed you two so much. I've done a lot of traveling and I wish you had been a part of it." I sigh and rest my phone on my forehead. "Can you please tell me what's so important that Wyatt is needing me for?"

"We've always needed you, Kay. A lot has happened to all of us in the last seven years," she lectures. "But I'll torture you with all of that later. Let me flip through the messages on my cell, so that I can tell him who I'm talking to. He'll be thrilled." Violet chats as she finds his last message on her cell. "Found it. Let me type in a few words and send it. Done."

"Well, you found me now love bug and we have lots of time to make up for." I put my feet on my desk, getting nice and comfortable. "I promise that you will never lose me again. So now spill the beans woman, what does Wyatt need me for?"

"He needs a contractor. And you are a contractor aren't you?" she asks.

"A contractor, for what? Why in the hell would he need a contractor? Actually, I'm an architect, but how does he know that I do that?" I quiz her.

"I have no idea. He just said that he has a project and he needs someone he can trust." Silence takes over. "Ah, found it."

"Why did he think of me? Aren't there architects in

Seattle?" I ask while I cross my left leg on the desk.

"Really, Kayla?" Violet taps her phone. "Have the brain cells ---- rotted out of your head when you went on your hiatus? He thought of you because you're still our best friend." A sound buzzes from Violet's phone. "Oh, here he is."

"Am I the topic of conversation between you two? And why are you texting him this time of morning? He may have a girl over at his house bumpin' uglies." I scratch my head.

"When you left us behind, Wyatt became, well, he lost his best friend." Her voice cracks. "So forgive me if I give you shit for a while, because you put us through hell when you left without saying good bye," she sobs. "I mean would it have killed you to call and say I'm leaving?" VI clears her throat. "But nooooooo. You just took off and didn't even go to graduation. Imagine our surprise when they called your name and you're nowhere to be seen. It was like Bam! You're here one minute and gone the next."

"Shut it Vi. I know I hurt y'all and I'm sorry." I search for a Kleenex on my desktop and dab my eyes. "Everyone was preparing for graduation, so it was the perfect time for me to leave." I wanted to tell her I --- bought the one way ticket two months prior to graduation and prayed like hell the whole way to the bus station that I wouldn't be seen. Luckily, I was able to leave without problems.

After a sniffle and finding the right words to say, I continue, "All I can say is I am sorry, there will never be enough words in the English language for me to express my true feelings to you or to Wyatt. I love you both and I never, I mean it, -- never wanted to -- hurt you. That wasn't my intention."

"I won't say that it's okay, because I'd be lying. But I'm glad you're home where you belong." Violet throatily laughs. "Wyatt just responded. It says, 'Umm hello, do you know it's after midnight." She snickers and responds to his message out loud. "I know but I have news...SHE'S BACK!" Then she speaks to me in good spirits. "I'll give him a few minutes and I bet he's calling or texting me."

"Dang, stuck on yourself, much?" I grumble and sigh.

Violet laughs her ass off while I hold the phone away from my ear as the delightful sound echoes through the phone.

"Nope, not conceited, I'm convinced because conceit is an imperfection and well… I'm PERFECT." She then drops the phone and quickly snags it. "Guess who is texting me as we speak?"

"Ummmmmmm let me guess, it's the pope," I sarcastically answer as I tap my chin.

"No, better than the almighty. It's Wyatt and this are his remarks not mine. "OMFG. Also, please have her call me." She taps into her phone. "I just asked him if he had his ovaries in check, because he said, omfg."

"You two are turds," I giggle as a genuine smile appears on my face. "Tell him I will call." Hesitantly I ask, "So do you see him a lot?"

"Him or Garrett?" she ponders. Her inquisitive voice saying Garrett's name, sends uncontrollable shivers up my arms, just like the first day he and I held hands in the lunchroom.

"I didn't…" I try to conceal my happiness.

"You don't have to," she states. "Any time you think of him, it reflects in your voice. It gets raspy." She snickers. "Wyatt hears from his brother from time to time. Last I heard, Garrett's living in Pensacola, Florida with his bitch of a fiancée."

"I couldn't care less about who he dates or marries." Even though at the moment I have a sudden chest pain that rips into me. I wonder who his fiancée could be. Yeah Kayla, keep telling yourself that and keep acting like it's no big deal.

"You're a damn liar, Kayla Ashby," VI snaps. "You can tell yourself or anyone else that, but I know your ass still has a thing for him. Remember who the people watcher is and can read faces...that would be ME. You would lose at poker because your face is easy to read. When it comes to Garrett Winters, my friend, you have love written all over you. I saw the way you two used to talk to each other and it was more than just friends having a conversation."

"I won't lie, Vi. I always wondered what it would be like to be in his arms, but he's getting married, so I'll just have my dreams about him instead. I will always love him. But everyone deserves to be happy and if he's getting married..." I breathe deeply as my throat tightens and tears form, "then he's happy and that's all I ever wanted for him." I cough then say. "What about you? Have you given into Wyatt's mojo yet?"

"If you must know, I could go for a long ride on his hog," she brags.

"OMG, you two have totally hooked up. I had a hunch you two would be together."

"No, babe. We have never played hide the sausage, not that I haven't gotten off from his mental images, on many occasions. I'd love to screw him thirty ways from Sunday, but as of right now, I'm just a friend. Even though I could really show him what a real woman is." Like a giddy school girl, Violet continues, "Wait till you see him sis, he was hot in school, but now he's like a damn walking orgasm."

"I've missed your sense of humor," I burst into tears from laughter. "You're killing me Smalls."

"Damn, really Kayla? I miss my carefree friend," she adds. "So you know if Wyatt's a walking orgasm...his twin is sure to follow. I think you may be surprised. Garrett, may want to see you or talk to you."

"Yeah well I'm not a home wrecker. I may be a lot of things, but home wrecker isn't one of them."

"Kay, you used to not care. We were all friends when we were younger. What's happened to you?"

"Life happened, love. I will not be that woman who ruined a happy home."

"Touché, I understand where you are coming from. It's not fun to be the other woman, believe me I have been her and well, it sucks balls. I was told he was leaving his wife, and his family for me, and one weekend I saw him with her. I knew I was being played for a fool." My best friend clears her throat before saying, "but that is a story for another time when there is a lot of red wine involved."

"I'm sorry VI, do I know him?" I ask.

"No, he's someone I worked with, no one special," she grumbles. "Should I ask how Millie and Seth are doing?" Her voice hesitates when she speaks their names. "I know how you feel about them, but they are the only family you have. Though you have never been silent about your feelings for them."

"I don't want to talk about them, VI," I bluntly say and change the subject again. "Let's make plans to meet sooner than later. I've been without my best friend for long enough."

"Hey now, I'm not the one who left remember? I have been in the same city, so all you had to do was call my parents and they would have given you my digits." Abrupt and hurt by the tone of her voice, she goes on, "I do expect an explanation, Ashby. You can't just leave and expect me to be okay with it. I felt that you did a Mexican hat dance with my heart."

"Yeah, I know, I did, but I'm back now and I intend to make up for lost time. You name the time and the place and I'll be there with bells on."

"Done. We need to get together tomorrow and have your famous homemade lasagna with Mr. Fine Ass Walking Orgasm on his boat."

Omg, is VI getting off on his image right now…

"Boat, Vi?" I questioned.

"Yes, darling, a boat," she answers. "He took up fishing in order relieve his stress."

"So, your bony ass needs to get to the pier by five tomorrow for an evening cruise and homemade lasagna." She snickers. "We missed you and your food."

"I know we have a lot to catch up on. I do have a spare room, so feel free to bring some stuff to put in there. I love you and miss your face," the smile disappears as a lump in my throat catches my tongue, I stutter, "I'm so glad that you got in touch with me."

"I love you too. I miss my sista' from another mista'. I always knew you would come back, I had faith." She utters and sniffles.

We both say our goodbyes and end our calls.

I stare at the rising sun out my office window as the red and yellow rays shine on my skin and let out a breath I didn't know I was holding in. Thank you Lord for keeping her safe in my absence.

Chapter TWO

Old friends....

"It is one of the blessings of old friends that you can afford to be stupid with them."--- Ralph Waldo Emerson

After cleaning my house, I snag my favorite black and pink Coach Poppy small tote and pink flip-flops. I head out the door to my black SUV—custom made to my standards. *Oh, yeah, black with hot pink accents and best of all, eyelashes on the headlights. It's every girly girl's dream. You would never know what my favorite color is...*

Before I get into the black beast, I clutch my purse and glance to the right and left. "Jeez, Kayla, paranoid much?"

I love driving this truck. Especially, while I listen to Reba and Luke. Let me tell ya' Luke Bryan can *Shake it for me* any time he wants-- I promise I won't mind. I wiggle my butt to the music and a natural smile appears. *Everything's coming into place. I'm actually rebuilding my life. From the purchase of the SUV, and building my house, to talking to VI and seeing Wyatt with her tonight, God I miss them so much, it hurts. I feel like a kid in a candy shop.*

"I finally did it," I utter. "It's about damn time, Ashby."

Whirlwinds of emotions set in, creating ugly tears as I cry. The song *Sisters* by Reba plays and I think of Violet. "I know that eventually I will have to tell them why I left. Knowing

Wyatt and VI, they won't give it a rest. Especially, how I blew off graduation and everyone around me," I shake my head. "Right now I don't want to think about the past." Letting out a breath, I blow part of my brown hair out of my face. "How am I going to explain this to them, anyways? Hey guys I love you and the reason why I left was the fact that the "perfect" Stanton boys made me their sex slave." I tap on the wheel "and it gets better. Millie and Seth wrote a check and asked me to leave before a scandal happened," I mutter. "Yeah, that's going to go over like a fart in a church.

I drive into the parking lot of the supermarket. "I don't want them to see the pain that I have endeavored. It'll crush them. I'll see it in their eyes and that will destroy me."

I pull into the vacant parking space. I breathe deeply then snatch a tissue from the purse and dab my green eyes. "You're going to forget about this crazy idea of telling them. You're going to walk into that store, grab the ingredients that you need for your homemade lasagna, and you are going to enjoy your life, starting by having dinner and a decent conversation with your best friends."

I drop down the visor mirror and reach into my bag for my natural pink lipstick. Making an oval out of my lips, I apply.

"Looking good Ashby." After, I pucker my lips then giggle. *Garrett always told me that I don't need make up for my pretty face.*

I climb out of my beast, lock the doors and set the alarm. I then scan the perimeters of the parking lot to make sure there's no sign of the Stanton boys. *Coast is clear, just a huge chain food store, shopping carts, and new and ratty old cars…Phew.* I let out a deep sigh and let in the crisp cool air of the city.

Every city and providence I visited, I've always had a feeling I was being watched. ---Now I'm back on *their* turf. I constantly look over my shoulders wondering when I will run into them, and if I do the question I have is this... Will I be strong enough to stand up to them? Will I be able to forgive them? Or... Will I succumb to their predatory behavior and submit?

I fluff my hair and hold my head up high then stroll into the newly painted historical building—hoping and praying that I'm strong enough to stand my ground.

I wait in line at the counter of the --- PCC which is the local organic grocery store. I know it can be a drag just simply going into the store. Waiting in line while an extreme coupon hoarding woman finishes her order is downright torture. While the annoying lady in front of me gives the cashier a hard time, I glance around the place and see a fine piece of specimen in back of me. "Holy, fuck."

Nice abs, and not to mention his black pants show off his appealing package—actually all of him is a present just waiting to be opened. I would love to run my fingers through his shiny black hair and look into those baby blue eyes. Damn yummy and sexy all in one gift....wait a sec.... he looks like an older....shit....shit....shit.... it's not that he looks like, but he is.... Garrett Winters.

Frantically, I grab a magazine from the stand and flip it up like a tent as it covers my face—pretending to read it. Slowly, moving it down—taking a peak at him.

Double Shit he looked at me....

I flip it back up not paying attention to what the total was on the bill.

"Miss, you're total is four hundred and eighty three dollars." The cashier gently pushes the magazine down.

Shocked, I peak at the gingerly grandma' looking woman. *What the hell did I just buy?* I quickly give her my debit card.

"A lot of pop." She giggles as she swipes the card. "And the gentleman you're purposely ignoring has been trying to get your attention."

"Huh?" I ask as heat rises up to my face.

"Don't worry dear," she says as she hands the card back and taps my hand. "If it's the right fix, it'll happen."

"Umm, thanks? Ahh..." tongue tied, I draw a blank on what to say next.

"Betty, dear," she answers.

"Betty," I nod. *I can't believe a senior citizen who's a cashier in a supermarket gave me advice about the man of my dreams. But it seems like she would know. The smile on her face warms my cold heart.*

Being juvenile, I squat down to the food carriage and take wide strides out of the store hoping he can't see me like everyone else in the line did. Laughter and giggles spread throughout the lines. "Yep, Kayla, you have proved once again that you can be a god damned idiot."

I load the groceries in the back of my SUV and jump into the beast. Fumbling through my purse, I take my keys and drop them in my lap. I then grab my *Gucci* shades and throw them on.

"Oh," I mumble. "Can this day get better?"

I grab the keys and start the engine. I peak into the rearview mirror and there he is, *again*. He's staring right at me. My chest tightens. "Why do I feel like I'm in the fucking Twilight Zone?"

His gentle smile warms the blood that flows through my veins, making my heart pound out of my chest. Then he waves me to come over. Not knowing what to do, I rev up the engine and barrel out of the parking out like I was *Mario Andretti*.

On the drive home, I gaze out the windows just looking at my home town. God, I love this town. The hustle and bustle of the city life, plus all the small mom and pop shops to the elite stores, like *Armani*. The best part of the city—on any given day, the sweet smell of the rain and mist lingers in the air. *Hmm home.* Did I do the right thing by coming back? Is this fate? For once, is God actually letting me have happiness in my life?

Everything is happening so fast, contacting VI and now her and Wyatt on the boat tonight, not to mention seeing Garrett. And that cashier being like a grandmother, she made me smile. Is that a way a grandmother is like when it comes to her granddaughter? I just don't know. I have no clue about my biological family. I don't even have my mother's birth name.

Again, stomach pain enters my abdomen.

I need to clear my head. I hit the button on my steering wheel, and it automatically goes to the one number that I know the person on the other end will listen, without judgment.

"This is Dr. Patrice Doyle speaking'. How may I help you?" she answers. *Oh thank God she's there.*

"Hey, Patrice, how are you?" I ask, my voice trembles.

"I'm good, Kayla." Caution in her voice rises through the phone, "Are you okay?"

"Well, yes and no." I pull over to the side of the road. My nerves act up and my throat tightens. "I'm nervous about being home."

"Breathe in and out through your nose and count to ten like I taught you," she instructs me. "That's understandable, sweetie," she kindly answers. "You're taking a huge step in conquering your demons." She pauses then says, "Maybe, I should come out there so we can talk in person."

"No, I'm not there yet." I take in a breath and exhale. "I just needed to hear a familiar voice, and you said that if I was having a difficult time for me to call." I close and open my hands in order to release my anxiety, "so, I'm calling."

"Well tell me what's going on, so I will know what to help with," she gently orders. "Do you have the pink band I gave you on your wrist?"

During one of my many episodes, Patrice gave me on those a pastel pink rubber bands with the words faith engraved in it. She said she got it at a breast cancer charity event, but she thought it called my name.

"Yes, I have it and it helps, but it's not the same as

having you close by. I've been home for a few weeks now, and it's seems that everything's falling in to place. My dream house is done and it's like a piece of heaven, I love my work." My breath quickens, "and now I've gotten back in touch with my two best friends, VI and Wyatt and I'm making dinner for them tonight. I even saw Garrett or at least I think it was Garret," my voice begins to tremble, "and this woman at the food store reminded me of what my grandmother could be like. Is God playing a nasty trick or...."

"Slow down, Kayla," the good doctor's kind voice eases my emotions. "You found your two best friends and saw the love of your life, so what's bothering you?"

"Well, to be honest, I really don't know," I garble the rest. "Something just feels....*off*."

"Like what?" she asks. "Kayla, I can't help you unless you talk. You can't clam up and shut me out, I'm here for you, always."

"I don't know if it's paranoia or if I'm being watched." I suck my bottom lip and continue, "I've installed two separate security systems and my house is on video surveillance. I just can't help feeling that they know I'm here," I ramble on, "and if they know I'm here, Elijah and Edwin will make sure my loved ones suffer. Especially, Garrett. They already hurt Wyatt before and I'm sure that if they have a chance, they'll do it again."

"Have you had any interactions with them or your parents?" she asks. "Does anyone in that family know you're even home?"

"Patrice, please stop referring to the cold hearted bitch

and the ass wipe as my parents," I annoyingly say. "Anyway, that's a big *hell* no. I don't want to see the two scumbags that screwed up my life. I did call Millie and Seth, but of course they were out of town and will be home in a couple of weeks due to the election," I snap. "The ass is planning to run for the presidency. God help us if he becomes the next leader of the free world."

"Does that bother you" She asks.

"No, I don't care about them; well I do," the tone in my voice deepens, "but I don't, they're not what's bothering me." I let out a huge sigh. "I'm just nervous. I just have this God awful feeling like something bad is going to happen. I also had another nightmare last night."

"Are you taking your meds?" she sternly asks.

"I don't want to be on anything," I answer. I clench my heart and shudder. "I have to learn to accept my fate here. I'm just scared."

"Kayla, remember what we've talked about; they may have hurt you, but you're not a victim, you're a survivor," she talks to me like a mother again. "I have *faith* in you, sweetie. If you ever need me, I'm just a plane ride away."

"Thanks, Patrice," I utter and finally calm my senses as my pulse rate slows down and my teeth stops chattering. "I just needed some motherly advice and you were the only one I could think of calling. Your words always seem to help."

"Kayla, I'm here for you no matter what," she states. "Call me later this week and let me know how dinner went."

"Okay." Tears drops fall onto my lap. "Thank you. It means a lot that I can call you when I'm having a hard moment. I know it won't be easy, but each new day is an adventure, right?"

"Yes, Kayla, life can be an amazing adventure when you open the door to it," she kindly says. "Just remember that you are more than capable of handling your own life."

Turning into the parking lot of the pier, I see Violet and Wyatt waiting for me. Wyatt leans on his blue 1969 mustang. His hands rest in his faded blue jean pockets while Violet talks to him. I throw my SUV in park and jump out of the beast. I hear *Gutterslut* and I just want to laugh. I turn ---- and there they stand right in front of me.

Violet looks exactly the same since the last time I saw her. She's gorgeous with her baby blue eyes and long blonde hair. The only thing that's different are the electric blue tips at the end, not to mention she's sporting the latest *Abercrombie* fad. Always put together and beautiful.

Then I peek over to Wyatt. He's always been good looking, but now he's hot as sin. At 6'3 and two hundred fifty pounds of pure muscular bliss, with tree trunks for legs and arms that can wrap around you, keeping you safe and warm, he's every girls erotic fantasy. And thanks to the ink gods, tattoos cover his olive complexion. Plus, the Mr. Clean look that I love (although I miss the blond). And from what Violet has mentioned, he has piercings all over his body including his shaft which I have been informed it's has pearls under the skin, making him the eighth wonder of the world.

He's stunning. Now I know why Violet wants to take a ride on his hog. Damn he must be great in bed. I shake my head and smile. *The man is a walking, talking orgasm just waiting to happen.*

"You little shit. You've been here for how long, and you just told us." He crosses his arms playfully glaring at me.

I just stand where I am and stare at them without blinking an eyelash. *Are they going to forgive me for leaving?*

"Kay?" Violet asks as her face softens.

"Are you going to say something, Ashby, or just stand and stare?" Wyatt's eyebrows narrow as the piercing in his right brow shines.

Damn, they're both beautiful. My eyes fog up and tears fall from them. I run into my best friends' forgiving arms and we all embrace. Uncontrollably tears fall down my cheeks. This is my family and no matter how long we have been apart, we will always be there for each other.

"Shh." Wyatt gently plays with my hair and kisses my forehead. "There's no need to cry baby doll. Suck it up princess, we're here. No worries, no tears."

As much as I wanted to, I couldn't let go. They loosen their holds and I grab their arms tighter. I mutter over and over how sorry I was for leaving. After hugging each other for what seemed like hours, we break apart.

"You forgive me?" I ask, wiping away my tears from the corner of my eyes.

"Of course we do, we love you Kay," Violet snaps as she opens the back of the beast. "We would love you even more when you make that homemade lasagna that I've been craving."

"I was never mad at you, Ashby," Wyatt says as one arm drops on my shoulders. "I do want to know why? Unlike, the blonde bombshell over there who's drooling over food, I won't make you talk. I want you to tell us when you're ready to buttercup. I'm just happy to have my little sis back."

"Would you guys help me with the food?" I lean on Wyatt's shoulder. "We have a lot to catch up."

The Grady White 28- footer anchors in the middle of Green Lake. As the white and blue rimmed boat gently rocks, Wyatt casts the lines and sets the dark green rods in their holders—waiting for a nibble. I open the white cooler and pulled out the chilled Chamblee wine for Violet and me and a Sam Adams for Wyatt. I also reached in and open a container of fresh bruschetta.

"I hope I used your oven right, Wyatt." I pass the container around and give the Sam's to Wyatt. "It would be my first time cooking on a boat."

"Ah, my dear Kayla," he says and takes an appetizer. "This is not just a boat, it's a home away from home."

I sit next to Violet on my soft pink beach towel and hand her the bottle of wine.

"Who are you kidding?" Violet reaches into her bag and grabs two red solo cups. "Besides the cabin downstairs and your pricey Captain seats with whatever gadgets drilled into on the top of your council." She pours the wine and hands me a cup. "This is not a home, it's just a man's toy. The bigger the size the bigger their manhood."

"Those gadgets Vi, are for depth and navigation. I learned my lesson from my last experience—never go anywhere without them." He clips the cap of his bottle with one of the sharp edged of the boat and lifts his drink up with his right hand and says, "Cheers." Then takes a swig. "I don't need a large toy to help with my manhood love. This package is the real deal."

Time passes by as the sunset brings out a beautiful display of pastel yellows and oranges along the lake. We reminisced about college experiences and life in general while we indulged in bruschetta, lasagna, and white wine. It comforts me as I giggle to Wyatt's stories and Violet's wit. *God please don't break us apart, ever again. Because this time I don't think I can make it.*

"Do you know how much you were missed, Ashby?" Wyatt as he casts another line. "If my idiot brother didn't have his head up his ass, he would have found you years ago."

"I'm nothing special, Wyatt." I lower my head wiggling my toes. "I'm just a geeky girl who chose to wear loose baggy clothes to hide…." I pause and stutter, "My body."

"I don't know what you're complaining about," Violet says as she files her nails. "You have a body like a *Sports Illustrated model*. And you need to flaunt it more."

"You're something Kay. You're the most attractive woman I ever laid eyes on, not to mention having a heart of gold," he states. Wyatt then rests on the edge of the boat, his left ankle on his right knee. "I don't ever want to hear that come out of your mouth again."

"She should know it by now, but words of confidence don't sink into her head." Violet sips on her wine then waves her hand. "I want to know what's happened to that luscious twin brother of yours, Wyatt."

"Nothing to tell, he ran off with a bitch and I only talk to him once in a while." The line tugs and he begins to reel it in. "He doesn't even talk to our mom or step dad. He went his way after high school and I went mine." He yanks the line. "Vi, I need the net" He then says, "I would occasionally see him on the holidays when we were off on breaks, but it was never without *her*. I swear the bitch has him wrapped around her pinky."

"Do you blame him for cutting the apron strings?" Violet interrupts. "You both didn't have the perfect childhood." She sips her wine again then looks at the nets. "I just don't understand why he went for *her*, out of all people." She scratches her head. "Which one?"

"We had an alcoholic dad who liked to put a fist where our skull was," Wyatt mutters, his voice rumbles. "Mom finally kicked him out and we found happiness. My brother, did I mention he's the idiot twin, can't see his past his own ego. END of discussion, Vi." He keeps reeling in the line. "The one next to the pole."

"Okay. Okay! Don't get mad at me because he ran off with a trollop bitch." Violet places her cup down and rises up-fixing her hair and then points at two nets that are next to the pole. "Which one would that be?"

"Either one," He grunts. "I'm catching trout not bass."

"Okay." She grabs the net and hands it to him. "What's the difference?"

"The size." He yanks the rod and leans his right hand over the edge of the boat and snags a line. "Hold the net up and stand there looking pretty."

Once he caught the line, Wyatt carefully held the line as the wiggly colorful trout drops in the net. Drops of lake water fall onto Violet's pedicured feet.

"Eww," she jumps on her tiptoes and quickly moves back to her towel and wipes her feet.

"Come on, Vi," Wyatt tries not to laugh. "How are you going to get your sea legs if you can't stand lake water? I'm mean you're acting like a queen bee."

"Correction, I *am* not a queen bee or your brother's queen bitch." With attitude, Violet moves her index finger from side to side. "I *am* my own starlight."

"Yeah, Vi, you are definitely one of a kind." Wyatt measures the fish. "Too small," and dumps the trout back into the lake.

My best friend's blue eyes bulge as she taps her right foot watching Wyatt shake the trout from his net.

"Who's the bitch?" I ask, dismissively and giggle.

"What?" They both stop and stare at me like I had five

heads.

"Garrett's fiancée," I answer. "You guys talk to her like you've known her for years."

"Oh, you know her, *very well*," she mutters. "I kicked her ass in the school for messing with you."

"No." I gasp as my fingers touch my lips. "You mean to tell me…"

"None other than the insatiable witch with a capital B, Reagan Woodrow." Violet burps then gently touches her chest. "Excuse me, good food. It was so much better than frozen."

"Thanks." My heart sinks and a tightness creeps into my chest. "At least he's happy."

"He's not." Wyatt nudges Violet. "He tried to find someone to replace you, Kay." He slams the fishing rod back into its holder. "And the fucking gold digging whore clawed her way into him. I mean the guy who used to love casual clothing and cooking. *Hell,* I used to call him *Mary* because of it. Now he dresses like he's an *Armani* model and spends money left and right on extravagant dinners."

"Garrett's always been lost without you Kay." Violet plops back down next to me and pours more wine into her cup. "Even though you two never had anything except friendship, he still cared about you."

"Oh, I wonder why he was at the grocery store." My mind starts to ponder again about fate. "He was wearing black pants, I wouldn't consider them Armani."

"Garrett, huh?" Wyatt's lip turns into a wicked grin. "The prodigal son returns."

"WHAT?" Violet coughs and spits out some wine. "Excuse me." She continues then taps her chest. "Are you serious? Did you talk to him? What was said?"

"I didn't." I slouch back laying my hands on the towel,

"because you said he was getting married."

"Getting married and married are two totally different things. Girl, haven't you heard the song *put a Ring on it?*" Violet waves her ring finger and continues, "You should have said hello at least."

"VI, I told you before and I'll say it again, I'm not a home wrecker. I mean, seeing him in the store and looking like the same boy next door..." I shake some hair out of my face and let out a sad pathetic sigh. "Can we talk about something else?"

"Alright, I won't press it," The blue eye girl says. She pushes her blonde hair back, creating an up do. "I was sure he was the one to pop your cherry."

"Really Vi." I squint and mumble, "More like I *wish* he was the one."

"Girls, come on." Wyatt tugs on his collar of his graphic T. "Do we have to go into the first time we had sex?" His mouth devilishly curves up "unless, it's with a woman."

"You perv." Violet hits him with one of the red cups. "What if she has?" Violet smirks, recalling our phone conversation.

"I did and it was fucking mind blowing." My lips curve up to a crescent moon.

"Wait, you Ashby?" Wyatt's blue eyes darkens as they shine. "I never thought...I always thought VI would play around with her sex, not you."

"Hey." Violet angrily stares then says. "Never said I will and never said I won't, but Kay? Hell I'm still in shock."

Shyly, I slink back has my shoulders drop. "Thank you for making me blush." I wink.

"Now, I need to hear this." Wyatt scurries over and sits next to me, like a boy eagerly waiting to hear about the birds and the bees. He rests his head in his fists. Violet leans in to hear what I have to say.

"Alright, I'll tell you." I tap my foot on the towel, "but promise me, you won't judge me."

"Kay, you should know by now we love you no matter what," Violet snaps.

"Okay, it happened during finals at ASU. Her name was McKenna—a hot bisexual who loved to experiment with sex."

The words pour out of my mouth as the story unfolds bringing back to the small room we shared. *"McKenna was in several of my classes at ASU. We got into an argument about what station to listen to. I of course wanted country and she wanted a rap station. Horsing around, we both played with the remote control on the old green leather couch and tried to change the channels. Well, she had won of course. I let her win.*

At that moment, she settled on top of me, I giggle in defeat. She played with the ends of my hair and slowly lowered her lips to mine. Soft and tender, her tongue skimmed my mouth—making wet trails along my n lips. After, McKenna leaned on her arms as her blond hair relaxed to the side. Her teal contacts connected with my eyes and she leaned forward again. The diva clasped her fingers with mine and explored my mouth, gently touching my tongue as the muscles inside our mouths danced with each other. Soft moans came from her throat.

She continued her enjoyable assault as our bodies melted together. The black skin tight leather pants stroked against all the right places and I could feel how wet I was getting her touch was soft yet aggressive, worshipping me like I was a queen. Hell, I loved it. I kept thinking—how is this possible? Does this make me a lesbian because I kissed a girl? At that moment "I kissed a girl" by Katy Perry ran through my head. I let out a chuckle.

McKenna's face softened as the teal in her eyes tear up. She scooted off of me and placed her right elbow on the couch's arm and broke loose of our hold. She stared at me waiting for a reaction like I was about to go off on her with my broken filter. It was awkward, but I wanted more…. I just didn't know what to say or do. As soon as she was about to rise from the couch, I snatched her hand.

"Please, don't." I massaged her fingers. "I've never done this before. It's new and exciting for me."

Her luscious lips smirked and her hand trailed along my neck and down my pink tunic. She ripped it off quickly and unfastened my black lacy bra. McKenna snagged it off and threw it across the room. She grunted when my soft mounds pressed against her chest. She began to massage each breast. Both nipples hardened as her subtle lips kissed them. With her mouth gently pressed against my nipple, she began to nibble—while her other hand founded its way down to my jeans.

The button popped opened and her hand slid down to my sweet spot.

"Boxers?" She muttered and tugged on my hardened pierced rose bud—making it so much more intense.

"Yes," I groaned and whined. My body rose and fell on the sofa cushions. She circled and patted my clit, while sucking and circling her tongue around my tender areola. She then caressed my throbbing nipples, molding and reshaping them to her satisfaction.

"McKenna, I think we have too many clothes on," I moaned with every touch.

"Well, I can fix that," she replied.

In a matter of a nanosecond, she whipped our clothes off and flung them across the room. She laid me back down on the green couch and continued. Her sweet blush colored lips opened as her mouth gently sucked on my breasts then she spread my right leg around her hips and kept going down to my wet core never missing a single lick. Her pink tongue teased as it gently licked my treasured area. She looked up at me through hooded eyes as I moaned and groaned. I grabbed the couch cushion and she took hold of my moist lips.

She dug deeper into my core and damn fireworks appeared behind my closed eyes. Her teeth jerked on the fold and nipped at the piercing on my most sensitive spot. Her left hand reached toward my tit—squeezing the nipple and pinched it.

This woman was in complete control. I kept building and building until I came undone as cum gushed out of me. She growled at the exact moment my juices flowed and my body bucked—then I squirted. My body heat rose through my body—feeling redden. I snatched a cushion and laid it on top of my face.

"Hey! She grabbed hold of the cushion and tossed it. "Don't hide that was the fucking hottest display I ever have seen," she smiled then she rested her head on my stomach.

"HOLY FUCK, ASHBY! I may need the bathroom for a few minutes," Wyatt mumbles. "Excuse me." While he holds his zipper of his blue jeans as his goods peak out.

Violet nudges my arm and nods to his direction.

"Go right ahead Wyatt, just know this, I will not clean up any spunk. That's all you." I smirk.

"Awwwww, what's the matter Kayla, you don't think you can handle this?" He says as he stands and adjusts himself.

"I'm not even going try babe. I've heard stories about your sex-capades. From what I hear, you are the master of the bedroom and I'm not giving up control in any aspect of my life. Been there, done that and got a damned T-shirt because of it." I hide my chest crossing my arms over them.

"When you want a threesome ladies, I'm always available." Wyatt smirks as he taps on his package. He starts taking down his jeans.

Violet and I look at each other then take our solo cups and throw it at him.

"What? Seriously, I have to use a bathroom so the lake is the next best thing. I'm not a perv. I do have swim trunks underneath," he laughs. He whips off the jeans and throws them at Violet. "I'll be back to talk about plans for the club." With a quick wink he dives into the lake.

We ended the night down in the cabin at the small white table next to the stove. We discuss the drawing plans for the club. I tell him that I would be honored to design it for him and it should be up and running in six months.

"Yes!" Wyatt slaps the table with his right hand and scoops me up in his arms. "Kay, I'm so happy you're home. And I'm honored that you'll be doing the project."

Chapter THREE

The Club....

"I was born to make mistakes, not to fake perfection"---
-Drake

Club Fuchsia is now opened and Wyatt's in hog heaven. He didn't reveal the name till opening night. Six months of planning, delegating, and the freedom that he gave me to create it. The club is a dream that finally came true for Wyatt. He even asked my opinion on names. After hard work and dedication, the egotistical men at my firm made me partner. I'm now the youngest and only woman partner in the firm. Thanks to Wyatt's dream.

Drained and tired from working my ass off for my best friend, I head upstairs to my bedroom and crawl into bed for a cat nap before I go out with Violet. I stare at the twinkling lights and the holiday decorations along my street. Including my delicate display of a winter wonderland outside my home. This Christmas, I'm going to make it count.

I then drift into a pleasurable sleep of a faceless blonde.

I remove the blonde's hair tie—releasing her long locks. It flows down the contour of her naked, creamy white back. With one smooth motion, I ran my hand gently up her soft skin.

Reveling in her sex kitten curves, I slide my hands to the nape of her neck and forcefully end up with a handful of hair.

She growls in the depths of her throat—letting me know she's even more enthralled than I had imagined. Tilting her head slightly to one side, I trace soft wet kisses down her neck and across her milky white breast. With each breast entering my mouth, I allow my tongue to play with her areola. Tugging the nipple with my teeth and sucking it with my mouth like I was taking milk.

My tongue travels each side of her curves then stops just above her hip bone. I lean over to the night stand and reach into a glass of ice cubes. I pop the cube in my mouth and drop it on her belly button—sucking the cube with it. After I lick down the crease of her leg, showering her with sweet kisses along her beautiful thick thighs, her body sings as her enjoyment drips from the nether lips of that lovely pussy.

I run my cool tongue up the center of her sex. I consume and breathe in her sweet succulent creamy liquid. Her back bucks as it leaps off the bed. The taste of her is so good, as I tantalize in the moist treasured pearl of passion, captivating and drawing me in like I'm bringing her into heaven.

Caught in the joy and excitement of this woman, I reach a place I never been—complete and total lack of control. The need to slow down is lost at this moment when my fingers reach their full depth, I climax uncontrollably. This woman has an effect on me that I never experienced before and I'm still inside her, massaging that wet gorgeous sweet spot. Holy Shit! I play with her clit and finger the inside once more.

After, I remove my strap-on from the drawer in my bedside table. I have her sit on my face. I lube my cock as I continue to tease her clit with my tongue. Before I know it, I have her flipped around so I can insert my cock inside her—never missing a lick. Her moans are euphoric.

As her labia stretches, I stroke my cock in and out of her warm wet delicate hole—sucking and tugging on her treasure.

Her head jerks up and she flips back waving from side to side. She holds on to my head pushing me further into her.

Unable to remove my hand from this gorgeous body, I rub a small portion of lube on my fingers and slowly insert my index finger in her ass.

The combination of my dick being inside her, my mouth sucking her dry, and licking every fold of her pussy, she hums. Then my finger dances in her anus—moving to the same rhythm of pure blissful fullness. She whimpers but I continue the erotic torment.

In a loud scream and mind numbing full body spasm, her climaxed soaks me. Her face appears....

Omg, its VI!

Slowly, I come to from this dream and soaked my boxers. I groan. Ah what the fuck? Wet dreams about my best friend? I really need a good lay and fast. I glance over at the alarm clock. I reads eight forty in the evening.

"Oh, fuck, I'm supposed to pick up VI in an half an hour." I rise and stretch with a smile. "At least I didn't have a nightmare." I rush to the bathroom, wash up really quickly, and rush back to the bedroom to grab my clothes for the club tonight. I race to my walk in closet and snag my hot pink fuck- me heels off the shoe rack. I then search around for a pair of black tight ass jeans that have the sides open down the pant legs, and see through black and pink lace top with a black lacey bra to wear underneath. "This should do." I huff and dress myself under ten minutes.

I call VI, "Hey, Gutterslut, I'm on my way."

The hottest club in Seattle sits on the corner of 6th Street and 5th Avenue, with a line that wraps around the building. Awestruck, I gaze up at the black and rose color sign that stands out as the crowd talks about the name and what it's like inside—also how this is the hottest club in Seattle. Even reporters flash their cameras at it.

The vibrations from the music inside vibrates along the curb as we approach the door. *"Roar" from Katy Perry* plays. I dance and sing along to it with Violet as we wait to get in.

Violet looks at me and laughs her ass off.

"What?" I ask as I jiggle.

"I have never heard you sing like this out in public no less," she says, her teeth chattering. "You've got some pipes."

I roll my eyes and keep dancing. Since its a few weeks before the Christmas season comes upon us, the temperature dropped down to the cool forties—making a chill in the air and it's a bit breezy. The small shops already have their Christmas displays out for their upcoming sales event. I start mentally making a Christmas list.

Violet's fire engine red lips shudder like she's going to freeze to death. "You're such a sissy la la."

"It's too damn cold," she states as she rubs her arms.

"Well, it doesn't help that you're wearing a black leather mini skirt and a mini shirt to match it. Which by the way pushes your girls up." I point out as I stuff my hands into my long black coat. "Don't you have a longer coat?"

"Shut up," she snaps and hops in one place. Violet could easily be labeled a hoe because of the way she dresses, however, her no nonsense bitch of an attitude would never let any man treat her like she's lower than them. "I need to get inside and warm up. Maybe up to Wyatt."

"Vi, this is nothing," I state as my eyebrows rise, then shove her with my shoulder.

She laughs. "I can't wait to get inside." My best friend fixes her girls and searches her purse. "Okay, emergency essentials." She thumbs through her purse. "Lipstick check, condoms double check, gun triple check."

"VI, I don't know why you carry that gun with you all the time." I peer up to the line in back of us.

"I carry this gun because it's a part of me," she mutters. "It makes me feel safe and I'm a female. If I ever get mugged, then the poor bastard will get some lead in his ass." With confidence, she shuts her purse and straightens her posture. "Something my friend you need to learn."

"I know. I know. How many times are you going to tell me that I need to learn to not only hold a gun but shoot it as well?" I say then I nudge my head. "Look the line is moving. Will you please stop taking glamour shots of yourself," I snatch the phone from her and then I take a picture of us together. "You know you can make any guy's bulge spring forth. Thanks to your father's pioneer efforts, no asshole would ever get the best of you.

"Why, Kayla Ashby, you know how to make a girl blush," she says in a deep southern accent. Her fingers gently touches her chest as her dark eyelashes blink.

"Whatever, Scarlet." I snicker.

The hair on the back of my neck rises when I hear a distinct voice in the background.

"Oh my god, finally the damn line is moving," the man's voice in the back of us makes my knees weak. And not sweeping me off my feet kind either.

I think, no I know that voice and if so—I'm in for one hell of a night. "Vi, would you look at the guy in the back of us. He's about seven people behind." I move closer to her, "tell me what he looks like."

"Why are you hunched down trying to hide?" She asks as her fists smacks her hips. "Kayla, what is with you lately?"

"I don't want to argue about this, please just look," I plead. Like a shy kid, I try to hide behind her.

She throws her hands up in the air and rolls her eyes. Then, she scans the line. "You're losing it girl. There's no guy there, only jealous bitches."

"Are you serious?" I ask. I peek and there's a group of

girls giving us the stink eye. After I shake it off. I know I heard that voice. The dark raspy voice that haunts me to this day. Why do I have that awful feeling that something bad will happen tonight? Call it intuition, but something's off and I can't put my finger on it.

"Kayla, we need to talk," Violet lectures as her eyebrows nit. "You've been downright irritable lately," she continues, "You haven't been eating. You're up all hours of the night." She taps one finger at a time on her right hand, "and now you're hiding from a man who I know nothing about. What the hell happened to you?"

"VI, can we talk about this later," I say as I open and close my hands on the sides of my pants. "I don't want to spoil a good night."

"All right," she mutters. Then my best friend twists her mouth. "But you owe me an explanation."

Just like that our conversation is forgotten as we head toward the bouncer. Like seeing the color of the sea in his eyes, the drop dead sexy blue eyed bouncer sits on the stool in his tight black shirt and black jeans that look like they were put on with butter. He asks us for our ID's with a thick southern accent. Damn he looks like sex on a stick. More like a yummy raspberry Popsicle waiting to be licked.

"And what's your name?" I can't help but gaze down at his pants—running my tongue on the top of my lips.

"Hello, sweetheart my name's Micah." That must be the most fuckin' sexiest accent I ever heard. The song Save a horse ride a cowboy by Big N Rich rushes to my mind. If this guy asked for panties, women would seriously whip them off and throw the damn things at him.

Shit, I'm starting to get wet.

"Nice to meet you, Micah. I'm Kayla and this firecracker is my best gal VI," I introduce Violet like she's God's gift to men.

"Hey," he mutters—checking out her breasts and her long delicate legs.

The girls are on guard as Violet sticks her hand out to shake his. The cowboy then leans toward her and whispers sweet nothings in her ear as he gets a good view of her tits. Then he dives his face into them –feeling her up by doing what I call a "motorboat gesture."

"Oh, you are bad." She slides her phone out and takes his picture. "Thank you big boy." She taps Micah's package and gives him our business cards. "Call me sometime."

"I just might do that." He laughs and opens the velvet rope to let us in.

Gutterslut kisses his cheek and struts her ass as she walks in the club. Got to love Violet. She gets attention whether she wants it or not. Hell, half the guys in line tried to talk to her and their dates kept giving her the death stare.

As I follow suit, the bouncer tugs me back and presses his body up against mine. His erection pulsates against the ass of my jeans. He reaches around and sneaks his hand up my see through black shirt. Then playfully cups under my black bra and tugs my pierced nipple.

My head leans on his black fire tattoo on his neck and smell his panty dropping cologne. I softly moan to his assault and all I want to do is explore his tattoo—and find out where it leads to.

"I didn't want you to be left out, Darlin'," he whispers in my ear.

Fuck me, I'm aroused by the sweet succulent word 'Darlin'.

Then he releases me from his hold as if nothing's happened. Quickly, I jog or at least attempt to jog in fucking heels to catch up to Violet.

"What took you so long?" She impatiently asks.

"Really Vi, it's not my fault that your legs are like freaking five feet long," I snap trying to put myself back together. "I was getting felt up by the hot ass molten lava bouncer."

"No fucking way," she giddily says and looks over to him. She then flips her hair and blows him a kiss.

The cowboy catches it and then pockets it. After he fixes his huge ass erection. "I can't believe I missed the action." She pouts.

"See good things come to those who wait," I tell her. I yank her through the heavy club doors that have a big capital F on it.

"Girl, I can't believe you have a dirty mouth," she teases. "Maybe Micah can help tame it."

Even though my eyebrows narrow, I can never be mad at her. She cracks me up and always puts a smile on my face, and no matter how old we get, I still amaze her by my no filter mouth.

"I want the deets," she demands.

"Really, it was nothing." I shrug my shoulders as we walk to the coat closet.

"I call bullshit; you get felt up by that hot ass man and you don't want to tell me." She eyes me, waiting for me to crack.

"Bullshit? Are we reverting back to being eleven years old?" I ask like a grade school teacher.

"Spill it, Ashby," she impatiently replies, tapping her black Louis Vuitton heels—of course they're the ones with the red under bellies that scream I'm a shoe hoe.

"He just pulled me back and pressed his hard as a rock dick into my back and played with my pierced nipple through my bra," I explain as my palm rises. 'Seriously, VI, it was nothing to write home about."

"Nothing to write home about?" She sharply asks as she check our coats in. "Girl, you need a good piece of ass and being with a female doesn't count." She fluffs her hair. "You have been home for six months and I haven't seen you with any guy. Now if you don't take that bouncer home and give him something-- other, than your nipple to play with, then I'm forced to find another piece of ass for you tonight. You need a good piece of pipe to lay. It is in the best friend handbook."

"Wow," I comment as our heels clack along the marble floor to the bar. "Just because you have a regular piece of ass on standby doesn't mean that I'm out searching for my own. My B.O.B. takes care of me just fine."

"Not if it's a good one; now that'll make you smile." She winks. "By the way, too much info on your battery operated boyfriend," she answers. Her voice rises as the beat of the music changes, vibrating the floor. "It'll help take the edge off," she says at the top of her lungs. "All I'm saying is that you don't know what you're missing. And your book boyfriends don't count. I don't even want to hear what is on your kindle that keeps you up at night. Even though I have read *Fifty Shades of Grey by E.L. James,* and it was defiantly hot, but you need a real man Ashby not some man you read about in a book. Because they are not real babe. Just fictional characters who were invented for our reading pleasure."

Yes, I know they are not real you ass but I can still pretend they are real. "Come on, let's get drinks." Scanning the place, things pop up that I had not noticed when doing the walk thru just a week ago. Every piece of item has pink in it, which is my signature (you have to love *Steele Magnolias*), and the stage up front for live bands one night a week.

Since Wyatt is a huge fan of the old school rock and roll, he hopes the group **Last Moment** will come around Christmas time in between their tour dates. He's been in touch with the group's manager Amber, who reminds us of an older Janice Joplin. If he's able to pull this off, his club is on the map state wide. I ran into the lead singer Alex when I was in D.C. For a meeting not too long ago.

People huddle up to the bar in every direction which gives them access all the way around the club. I immediately see my favorite men waiting for me to devour them—Jack, Jim, and Jose of course. The endless alcohol bottles are neatly stacked on the shelves. Wyatt even spent extra money to have my men on tap. And the display of beer and wines are a consort's dream come true. You did it, Wyatt.

As I wait to see my favorite bartender, I observe several places that are considered the lounge; the white leather couches with black and pink accents making it girly, yet manly at the same time. Plus the extra high bar tables that are along the wall give it an open feel as it surrounds one of my favorite places, the dance floor. The big ass dance floor with pink lights shooting up from it looks like fireworks going off—waits for me to arrive and party the night away.

I look upstairs to the VIP lounge which is also known as my baby. No one can see through from this angle because of the glass that I designed in the prints to be put up there. It's like glass from the police station's interrogation room. If you are in the room the window changes colors, to a bluish-purple color, letting you know that it is occupied. What can I say, the idea popped in my head when I was watching my favorite show, SUV.

I also take account the back door to the deck as smokers enjoy their breaks.

"I love the way all the pinks are subtle and yet still very in your face." Violet's in heaven as her eyes wander at everything and every man to hook me up with. "You did me proud, girlfriend. I could never imagine the ideas that you had for this place." She glances at the bar. "The lines are sleek and sexy at the same time." With her head held up high looking upstairs, she confidently smiles at me. "How hot would it be to have a private party for you in the VIP section? You know you have a birthday coming up ma'am."

Yep, her mind is on overdrive as the wheels turn in her head.

"Hell, yes. I may need to get on the VIP list." I laugh.

"You know all you have to do is bat your eyes at the person who handles the VIP list and you would be on that list, sweetie." She tilts her head.

"Or you could just do Wyatt, VI." After I made the little comment with one word attached to it, VI jumps up and down like she won the lottery or lost her mind, either way she is freakin' killing me.

I see that spark in her eyes...Great she must be thinking of Magic Mike. I've got to tell her yes or I'll never hear the end of it. When this girl is in her party planning mood, watch out. Knowing her, she has dirty thoughts and how big the celebration's going to be is running through that head of hers. All because of the years we've been apart.

I just agreed with everything she says as she animates the whole set up. While she gabs, I imagine how hot it would be having sex up there. Damn, that would be a dream come true— black and pink leather panties along with a riding crop whipping a girl, like VI or Garrett...

"Kayla, are you hearing what I have to say?" Her voice interrupts my thoughts.

"Yeah," I shake off the fantasy. "Do you want to find a table while I grab the drinks?"

"Sure thing, Gutterslut." She dashes off to find one of the vacant tables by the dance floor.

Eyes stare at me like I'm the last female alive all around the place. My instincts kick in as hair rises on the back of my neck again as if someone is watching me at the corner of the dance floor. I glance at the general direction of the floor. Nothing.

"Hello, Gorgeous," Wyatt calls to me as he finish pouring vibrant pink cocktails.

"Hello yourself, handsome," I acknowledge as I climb up on the stool, pressing my breasts into the hardwood of the bar.

"Lean over and give me a hug?" He playfully demands.

I reach over him and squeeze the incredible bulk to no end. A whistle comes from behind and Wyatt's head jerks up. Scowling, he searches to see where the whistle came from then releases his hold. "Sorry, Kay, we have idiots tonight."

"I'm not surprised. I'm so happy to see you." I say. It seems like it's been ages since I have seen Wyatt. My demands at work sky rocketed and with him opening the club, it's been forever. "Wyatt dear, can I please have two drinks?"

"Two, Ashby?" he questions. "Why the hell do you need two drinks? Did you finally get the stick out of your ass?"

"Well, one for me, silly and the other for a friend of mine." I blink my eyes flirtatiously. "Believe me if there was something up my ass, it would not be a stick."

"I didn't know you're into anal play. Jeez, girl I'm getting a hard on just thinking of it. Would it be a man or a woman with a strap on? Cause my offer still stands. Anytime you want me to watch or join—let me know. That would be fuckin' hot." He winks as he grabs the drinks. "I would love to see the playmate."

"Wyatt, you are funny at times. But you know I wouldn't want to share you," I flirtatiously say. "Besides the playmate is Vi. And to answer your other question, I will never tell what goes on behind closed doors."

"Really, now? If I thought you were serious, I'd take you and her in my office right now and do very bad things to you." His voice deepens.

"Oh maybe one day, Wyatt, and it would just be me. But right now…" I shyly shrug my shoulders. "I need those two drinks."

"Damn, I'll have to use my imagination on the anal business. But for the drink order," he scratches his chin then snaps his fingers, "I'll make you two one of my specials, Fire and Ice. If you like it, I'll make it the house special."

"You know I will love any drink you make." I can't help but stare at him and jokingly lick my lips to get a reaction. "You're a kick ass bartender."

"Kay, be careful. You out of anyone should know if you play with fire, you're going to get burned." He settles the drinks on the counter. "So have you eaten, yet?" He asks like a concern father.

"Yes, Dad," I sarcastically say. "Why the hell would you ask that? You know I'm a grown ass woman and I don't need to be watched."

"Easy killer. I'm just looking out for you," he answers as he wipes the bar. "Like I said before, there are loser men here tonight and I don't want anything to happen to you. I would hate to kick some guy's ass because they laid a finger on you." He takes my hand.

I smile at him and playfully tap his face. "I love you Wyatt. Thank you for looking out for me."

"You're welcome, buttercup. Besides if you shimmy on the dance floor the way you're dressed, I might have to take care of you." He takes my hand. "If you ever want your headboard knockin' just call me and we can rock like we're in Bedrock."

"Rock like we're in Bedrock?" I bust out laughing. "Honey, I don't have the eyes for you. Not like…" I cover my mouth quickly with my two fingers.

"Like who?" He smiles and wiggles his eyebrows. "Spill it."

"Vi wants to ride you into ecstasy." Fuckin' ay. What did I just say? Now, there's going to be trouble.

"Well then, tell her the package is here and waiting for her." He taps his package. "All she needs to do is ask." He snickers. "Well buttercup I've got to tend bar. Drinks are on the house."

Damn, really Wyatt. You just smacked below your belt. This is so not good. My two best friends want to bump uglies with each other. As I shuffle back to our table, the hairs rise again on the back of my neck. I turn quickly but there's no one staring at me. For some damn reason, I can't shake off this feeling, like one of the Stanton boys are here to torture me. This is all I need, a big ass scene at Wyatt's club. I check every area. Then I sit next to Violet.

"Kay what is it?" She asks.

"I feel like I'm being watched," I say as I play with the pink band. Sudden shivers follow rising up my arms.

"Yeah," she speaks slowly. "It's Friday night and we're at a fucking club." Violet grasps one of the drinks. "Kay, what's going on?"

"Nothing," I snap. I quickly change the subject before she grills me. "We came to party, right?" I ask. The high pitch in my voice breaks. "Let's dance."

"Fuckin' hell, yeah." She chugs her drink and escorts me out to the dance floor.

Being in our own element on the floor, we grind with each other to warn off any predators. I love getting down and dirty with VI and any gorgeous man who wants to cut in and dance in the middle of us. I enjoy watching the shows that are being put on as Blurred Lines play in the background. Whoever's spinning is doing a fantastic job, all you see are bodies pressed up against each another—which is actually turning me on. It's like I'm on a set of a porn movie. Oh lord, what the fuck is wrong with me, I'm thinking about sex in the middle of this club. VI's right, I need to get laid.

"Kayla, this night is fucking awesome." She leans in as the loud music vibrates on the floor. "I'm going to make rounds and snag another drink. Maybe, get a taste of our favorite bartender's ass."

"Don't make me sick," I say. "I'm going to keep dancing, so don't flake out and forget about me," I sternly lecture as I jokingly wiggle my ass. "I don't want nasty boys to get this."

"Okay." Violet playfully smacks my bottom and laughs. "I'll be right back."

She walks away and throws up her blond hair as the blue ends shine with the lights.

The music slows down to one of my favorite songs, *Yeah* by Usher. I lift my brown hair up and close my eyes— pretending to dance like no one's front of me. Then all of a sudden, I felt a chest press up against me.

I open my eyes and felt the mystery man's jeans and the soft shirt rests on my back. It's like a fucking instant orgasm just dancing with him. However, my inner voice inside my head majorly screams and the hairs rise up on the back of my neck.

I am not drunk but I have a good buzz, I grind up against him. His arms wrap around me as I lean my head close to his neck. The dragon tattoo on his neck with my initials engraved into it stands out. Shocked, I gasp for air as my body becomes rigid.

He kisses my cheek as the chrome cologne insults my nose.

"Hello Superstar," he whispers and kisses the back of

my neck.

I froze with fear.

Chapter FOUR

Scared....

"The only way the devil wins is if you let him."---- **Author unknown**

Elijah flips me around and I slam up against his chest. His erection hits my core. The grasp of one of my hands and the grip on my back makes it impossible to move.

"Just smile politely and dance with me," he demands. His piercing green eyes gaze down into me—drawing fear. "You don't want another incident to happen like it did before with Wyatt."

I shake my head no. My eyes glisten with tears just waiting to make their appearance, I slow my breathing and count down.

"Baby, there's no reason to cry." He gently wipe away my tears. "I missed you and I'm glad to see you finally came home. You know this is yours." He takes my hand and places it over his crotch. "It missed you."

The floor spins and I push the rising bile down from my throat. Elijah clutches me tighter so I won't fall.

"I've been trying to track you down for years Kayla and spent money on bounties to try to find you. And the sex Gods delivered you to me." He nibbles on my ear. "It'll be fun getting you back into our house and into my bed," the asshole continues, "You were more than a perfect lay."

"Perfect lay? Is that what you called being raped? I

didn't have much of a choice, now did I?" I snap and fucking fume as adrenaline overcomes me and the pulse rises in my body.

"I do recall you enjoyed it when I went down on you. Especially when both of us were in you," he cockily brags as the grip tightens. "Do you have any idea how your tight cunt felt around my dick? The way it would milk us both." His green eyes fill with sexual desire. "There's no one like you, Superstar. There has never been. You are truly one in a million."

"Quit fuckin' calling me that, you bastard," I hissed and grind my teeth. "I hated that name when I was younger and I damn sure hate it now."

He laughs and twirls me as my backside faces him. His massive dick presses on my ass. He pushes away some hair and taunts, "Keep it up and I will have you here and now while people watch. You know I would love fucking you this way. Listen here and listen well, I'm not a bastard for I know my parents name. Remember, you were the little bitch who was dropped off on our stoop and we took you in, Kayla?" He digs his nails into my wrists. "Superstar?"

Tightly, I shut close my eyes and cringe. The predator draws his hands down my back and inside the back of my jeans—reaching around till he plays with my labia. Of course no one is of the wiser. I whimper and try to move out of his reach, but his damn hold is like steel chains.

"Please stop, Elijah. I beg you to stop," I cry.

"You owe me," he tantalizes me and kisses my cheek. "You left without saying goodbye and for the years you have been gone. No submissive leaves me until I've had my fulfillment with them." He sucks my neck and licks it. "I will never get enough out of you, my dear girl."

How the fuck am I going to get out of this? I glance at Wyatt as he talks to a guy with jet black hair whose back faces me. As soon as he glances over, I see his blue eyes. No, Garrett. It can't be him. He can't be here too. Wyatt eyes me then says something to the young bartender. He then gradually walks to the dance floor.

This can't be happening, this can't be. Shaking with fear for my friends and Garrett; the room keeps spinning and if I don't break away from Elijah's hold soon, I'm going to pass the fuck out while horrid memories come back in fuckin spades. The predator embraces me like he's making freshly squeezed orange juice. Now, I reverted back to the frightened twelve year old and I just want to run and hide.

"Kayla, I'm glad you found someone to dance with," Violet interrupts with pure lust in her blue eyes. "Aren't you going to introduce me to your friend?"

I barely shake my head, I try to mouth help, but Elijah put on his charm. His strong arm wraps around me—gripping the left side of my waist. I wince. I'm going to have lovely black and blue bruises tomorrow, right on the side that I sleep on, that bastard.

"I'm an old friend of Kayla's," he politely says. He brings her right hand up to his mouth and gently brushes the back of it with his lips. "You must be Violet. Superstar has told me so much about you."

"Well, I hope all good things." As pink appears on her tan cheeks. "When were you going to tell me about this conquest?" Violet's blue eyes twinkle as she checks him out with excitement. "You do look familiar."

VI sober up will you and take a hard look. He's my foster brother. I silently wish we could talk to each other without words being spoken like in one of those old star track movies.

"I have a recognizable face." He shrugs his shoulders, then whispers in my ears, "Act naturally and no one gets hurt."

"How romantic," she blurts and gawks over him. Girl wake up will you? He's molested me on the dance floor.

Nervously, I smile at him. "I need to cool off and get some air." Clumsily I scuff my heels towards the backdoor as Wyatt comes towards me. I signal him—letting him know I'm okay. The over protective friend that he is, grunts and strides back to the bar.

One step away from the door, and a hand snags my wrist. My back slams into Elijah.

"I'm not a very patient man tonight, don't make me wait. We do have unfinished business to take care of." He sniffs my brown hair. It sends unsettling chills up and down my spine. He mutters. "Remember you are mine and I better not catch you dancing with another man, especially Garrett Winters, or shit will hit the fan really quick and I hate to ruin the other pretty boy's bar. Especially after he has worked so hard to build it."

My chest pounds and fatigue creeps in. How the hell did I get myself here after all these years? Why the fuck do I let him get to me like he does? How can I be strong with someone who will always scare the crap out of me?

"Give me two weeks." I softly touch the side of his face and chastely kiss him.

"Two weeks and counting. Don't play with me." He draws his mouth along the side of my neck and whispers, "I have a big plans for you. Now that you're home, we can have fun." He yanks on my hair.

I cry out.

"The way you left us has been extremely annoying." Elijah yanks it one more time to etch fear into my face. He then snags my chin and has me look into his eyes. "You know when I'm mad, I like to cut and bleed bad little girls," he grumbles as he checks Violet over. "It'll give me great pleasure to inflict pain on your friend because of your selfishness. Maybe I'll record it and then let you watch it."

After his taunting words, Elijah vanishes like a ghost.

Teary eyed and nauseous, I'm left holding my stomach.

I want to scream and call him the rapist that he is, but I choke and race outside—tripping over my heel, I collapse on the deck of the smoker's lounge.

Chapter FIVE

Guy's night out....

*"Open your eyes, look within. Are you satisfied with the
life you're living? ----Bob Marley*

*"An editor from a small publishing company Garrett
Winters had just bought...the channel changes....Garrett
Winters now known as Forbes 500...the channel flips...Winter's
Inc. has brought in...."*

"God I need to take this flat screen down from the wall.
The annoying voice of the reporters echoes through the damn
place and it really pisses me off." I flip the mute button and toss
the damn remote across the room as it lands on the black sofa in
the corner of the office.

Straightening out the stacks of paper on my glass top
desk, I glance outside the glass windows to my twin's club. The
steeple peak sends me a vibe that I should get my ass out of this
dump that I'm in and enjoy a night out. "Yeah, right."

I sulk into my black leather chair and position the
monitor in my direction. I then pull on the panel underneath that
has the keyboard on it and start typing. "In order to keep being a
successful financial analyst, I need to stay focused."

Then I see the old Goosebumps book that Kayla gave me
laying on the side of my old photographs. I pick it up and flip
through it.

The cell vibrates out of control. Todd and his claim to
texting. Seriously, the guy could pick up the phone and dial.

Todd: Hey, Gar, what's up?

Me: Not much. Cutting off loose ends and getting ready for the next meeting.

Todd: You need to get out and sow some wild oats.

Me: Is that an offer?

Todd: Funny, but no you're not my type. You need to get out instead of dicking around in the office.

Me: Fucker, don't start on me man.

Todd: Okay, calm down. Two words. Club Fuchsia.

Me: Dude, two words, not interested.

"Idiot. The guy thinks more with the head in his pants than in his head on his shoulders." I shut off the cell and toss it, landing it softly on the sofa next to the remote.

Hours seem to drag by as I finish up what I needed to do for the meeting...My mind becomes fried and I break away and stare at the background of my favorite photo of Kayla and me at my eighth grade baseball tournament. My mind wonders back to the first day I laid eyes on the girl of my dreams.

Goofing off, the eighth grade boys from the team at school, we played baseball using playground rules. Meaning there are no rules. Our mound was a red clay sandpit and crumbled pieces of tar. If the boys skid along their sides, they ended up with a nasty third degree burn, or a trip to the hospital so that the ER docs can remove the rubble. Man we were fuckin' idiots.

In the midst of pitching, a young girl cussed like she had a sailor's mouth. Entranced by her voice, the baseball passes by me almost knocking me unconscious.

"Gar, will you get your head back into the game and not

the girls," my twin yells. Wyatt then slammed his blue baseball cap on the ground.

"Fight," one of the geeks called out. Like a herd of elephants, the eighth grade class swarmed to the swing sets. Pieces of blond and brunette hair flew all over the place while Reagan Woodrow pounded on the poor girl. It's the goddess, I mean girl next door to me… she's not doing a bad job holding up her own against a bitch like Reagan.

The girl next door might have been on the ground, but she blocked the mean girl's punches and then peered up at me. Her tiger eyes struck a chord, with me as she turns her attention back to Reagan. While an electric current of some sort races through my whole fucking body. Hell, I felt a hard on coming just staring at this brunette beauty.

Violet Palmer pushed her way through the crowd and took hold of Reagan's fair hair. Like superwoman, the blonde haired wonder yanks Reagan's hair hard and flung her off of this girl.

Regan then rolls on the ground and hunched over — breathing heavily. Violet then glared at the audience. "Don't y'all have something better to do than to watch two girls making fools of themselves?"

No lie, every single student scattered quickly or slowly shook their head as they walk away. For it's a known fact in this town that no one messes with a Palmer kid, because their father taught them self-defense and how to use fire arms.

Regan's brown eyes narrow as her face turned ugly.

"Back off douche canoe." Violet's blonde hair whipped around and her fists smacked her hips and glared at the ugly tart.

"That bitch was talking' to my guy," Reagan sneered at her. "I had every right to go after her."

"Says who Twatwaffle? It's a free fucking country,"

Violet glowered. She must be pissed off to no end because the girl has a major case of word vomits. "She can talk to anyone she wants to. News flash hoe, you don't own him so Suck it up Bitch!" Violet stomped her foot to the ground. "You come after Kayla again, I'll personally see to it that your eighth grade life is a living hell."

New girl's name is Kayla. God, I love that name. It just rolls off my tongue, K-a-y-l-a.

"Whatever, Vi," Reagan rose up and wiped the off of her designer clothes. "Just keep her away from Garrett, he's mine." She wrapped her arms around her chest. "You're a fucking brat Kayla Ashby. Some of us aren't a charity case and have a senator for a daddy."

The bitch did not just say what I think she said. God I hate when Reagan says shit like that to girls. Especially to Kayla.

"Vi, what's going on?" I ease my way to the scene.

"Your cold hearted jealous bitch of a girlfriend came up and slapped Kayla for talking to you," she snapped like she was a rattle snake spitting out venom—waiting to strike her next victim. "Garrett, you may tolerate her being a Twatwaffle, but I will not let her disrespect me or anyone else."

I have to admit Violet got a chuckle out of me.

"Reagan, I'm not yours." I narrowed my eyes and gave the death stare to the conniving witch. "You can be such a bitch and I don't appreciate you slapping anyone." I walk by her. Reagan mumbled obscenities and stormed off. The witch then yells, "It's not over, Ashby. You won't always have Violet around to protect you."

"Well, that was pleasant." I sigh and kneeled down to the tiger eyes brown hair beauty. "Kayla, are you okay?"

"Fine." Golden yellow appeared around her soft green irises. Tears form from the corner of her eyes. "I'm used to this."

"What, fighting?" I held out my hand and pulled her up. As soon as her body leaned on me, my heart pounded—wanting to come out of my chest. I leaned and pressed my chest tightly to hers. "Sorry cutie. Reagan is just jealous of anyone prettier than her."

"Ah, yeah." Kayla shyly stepped back and looked at herself frantically.

I scratched the back of my black hair. Is it something I said? I mean she has to know how much of a babe she is. Wait a sec... Holy shit! I know what's she's doing. Wyatt and I do the same thing, when the old man slams us into a piece of furniture or his fist knocks into our chest—leaving us short of breath. I'll fucking kill the bastard who has hurt my Kayla. I'll do what it takes to protect her from the asshole who's hurting her. Jeez, what the hell is wrong with me; I'm branding her already.

"*Every rose has a thorn...,*" Violet taunted us with songs from Guns and Roses and *Tears* from Clapton, she laughed. "You two need a closer look at each other." She then puckered her lips and made kissing noises.

"Shut up." Kayla bumped her shoulder. "Thanks for breaking up my first fight."

At that moment, I knew their bond was strong like steel and they would be friends forever....

A silly grin crosses my face. I stretch back, relax my hands around my head, and kickback as I gently place my black converse on the glass top. "Kayla, Kayla, where could you be?"

The intercom buzzes.

"Yeah," I answer with a drawl.

"Miss Woodrow is on the other line," my assistant Sean answers.

"Take a god damn message," I reply.

"Mr. Winters," he hesitantly says. "She won't let up on our intern."

"Jesus, Sean," I snap as I angrily smooth my face. "You can sweet talk any woman for a one night stand. I even heard that you can charm the panties of a celibate nun, but you can't handle my ex and get her off my line. I thought you were better than that?"

"She's not a naïve cutie or a nun," he mutters. "She's a straight up bitch."

"Don't hold your feelings back Sean, but I can't disagree with you on that one. She's a bitch with a capital B. Fuck, put her through." Annoyed, I turn the speaker phone on and walk around my office as my shoes echo on the black and white marble floor. "If I'm still on the phone after three minutes then interrupt me and hang up the phone. If you don't, I will make you work every weekend from here till hell freezes over."

"Yeah, yeah. I got it. Dang, you are so touchy lately." He presses hold then answers. "Here she is Sir."

"Hey, Baby," she answers. "I miss you."

"I'm not your baby. You screwed any chance you had of that when I barged in on your gang bang activity." I stare back at Club Fuchsia's Peak.

"I gave into temptation," she snarls. "You didn't have to send one of them to the hospital. Oh, Mason's testicle retrieval was a success in case you wanted to know."

Leave it to my ex fiancée to make me feel like shit for what I did, all because I walked in on her being double penetrated by two men and with their balls deep in her.

"What the fuck do you want, Reagan?" I sigh and tug on the pink collar of my shirt. I then crack my neck.

"I want you back," she whines. "Wasn't one of your

fantasies having two women at once?" she moans. "Now's your chance."

"Not with you, Darlin'," I smugly say as my eyes wander to the lights of the Ballard Bridge.

"If your threesome's not with me....hmm...who could it be with?" She teases. "Are you thinking of that slut Kayla Ashby?"

I don't say a word and rest my hands in the pockets of my pants.

"Babe, the girl's twisted," vainly, she accuses my Kayla of being a hoe. "Rumors have it that she slept with her foster brothers."

"You know Rea, this is one of the many reasons why I like to cut you off." I stroll to the speaker.

"Because I tell the truth," she barks like a Chihuahua.

"You really are one conceited bitch, aren't you?" I blurt. "I would never cut anyone off who is truthful, but I will cut someone off who's a gold digging bitch that will lie, cheat, and claw her way into high society." That stupid grin pops up, thinking of my goddess. "Kayla Ashby is far from it."

I press the off button and end our conversation. Then, I hit Sean's extension.

"Mr. Winters," he stutters.

"From now on, take messages." I crack my neck again to loosen the tight knot near the nape.

"Before I say yes," Sean sputter.

"Sean, I don't care if it's the Messiah himself sending me a god damned blessing," I sarcastically remark. "Take a damn message." I lean back in my chair and turn on the search engine. Nervously, I type in Kayla Ashby. Immediately, several things pop up. She attended ASU and got her degree as an architect—

I'm so proud of her, she accomplished her goal. What's this… a Myspace page? I start to laugh. Oh Baby, technology has changed.

"Mr. Winters?" Sean asks with concern in his voice. "Are you alright?"

"I'm fine Sean." As I scroll down the screen. Happiness invades my heart, I don't realize how loud I am. "Just take messages. End of discussion." My left index fingers edges to the speaker phone.

"It's your brother," he quickly rambles.

I immediately stop. I know my brother quite well, he never calls the office unless it's urgent. "Put him through," I answer. I stare at Kayla's name on google.

"Hey, bro instead of messing around with your computer and work, you need to get your ass over to the club. It's been open for how many weeks and I haven't seen hide nor hair from you," Wyatt demands.

"I'm not," I trip over my words. I then pick up the receiver "messing, it's called work."

"It's called escaping. Look, there's someone here who's better than Wi-Fi" he states. "She might spark an interest." The snap of his fingers that echoes through the phone—piercing my ear.

"Sorry about that. The offer still stands. Go through the VIP entrance and meet me at the bar," like usual, my twin orders me around like a father.

"Wyatt, wait I'm…"

"You're not busy, Gar," he states. "Stop playing the sucker and embrace life."

Silence crosses over the phone and then the automated voice comes on.

Someone one who would spark my interest. Could it be Kayla; my Kayla? I reach up, stretch my back and head towards the sofa. "Hell, I'm not doing this alone."

I grasp the phone from the black cushion. Getting comfortable, I straighten out my pant legs and tie. I ease down on the sofa and text.

Me: Change of heart, meet me at Club Fuchsia.

Todd: Hell yes. I heard that the place is bad ass!

Me: Yeah, Yeah, bad ass. Meet me there at ten.

Todd and I make small talk as we walk up the sidewalk to the VIP entrance. While he rambles, I ignore most of it. Don't get me wrong, Todd and I go way back. We both went to Oklahoma University and managed to pull each other out of many fights. But Todd likes himself way too much, and instead of - being a grown up, Todd plays around and parties any chance he gets. The man is pretty much a twenty eight year old teenager.

"Garrett, dude, I'm so fuckin' glad your brother opened this bad ass club. Look at all the honeys that are dying for us to get in their pants." Todd winks at every single woman that passes us by as he rubs his hands.

"Holy shit the line's wrapped around the block." I analyze how many people are waiting. "Wyatt told us to go straight up to the front. I'm on some kind of VIP list." As we pass by the crowd, there are all sorts of people waiting to get in.

"I wonder how much he's charging for cover." Todd waves his hands. "Look at this. The guy's making bank. Thank God, we can get laid and not have to bring out the check book."

"Why the hell are you so damn cheap? Speaking of money. It's like your wallet creeks as you walk," I say searching the crowd, hoping to find my goddess out for fresh air. "Before we see my brother and get into whatever mischief, my family knows that I bought a company but they don't need to know I'm part of the fortune 500. We never had money and I don't want to brag about it especially, to my family."

"Damn," he grabs my shoulder. "Gar, you need to tell your family. You make more money than Midas," he says. "How long have I known your family? I know they won't go after your money. I mean your mom always sends you care packages. Hell, she stills sends me goodies in the mail like her famous chocolate chip cookies. Dude, you have a family who would do anything for you, unlike my jackasses that I should call family. My dad who plays golf and his secretaries, instead of actually paying attention to his wife and kids."

"Todd I really don't want to reminisce tonight on how bad our childhoods sucked. I love my family, especially my mom. I'm just not ready to tell them yet." I loosen the god awful gray tie. If it comes down to suits or jeans and a tank top, I prefer the jeans. "I know that you have loose lips when you're drinking the hard stuff. Remember Asshat, loose lips sinks ships, so zip it tonight."

"Very poetic." He claps as we walk into the club. "I hate to tell you this, but you're going to need to tell them fast. Because once mainstream gets wind that you bought Scilicet Publishing," he sighs. "The phones are going to light up like a Christmas tree." He then looks at the red head hottie in the corner. "By the way, I'm sticking with beer tonight. But it will always be ladies' choice." Pointing at the variety of women in the bar, he licks his lips.

"What's the difference from this night verses every other?" I ask. Relaxed, my thumbs skim the top of my gray pants as my unbuttoned jacket hangs loosely.

"Very funny, man," he annoyingly answers as his eyebrows pinch.

"I know, I'm a fucking comedian," I mutter. Then I see her. Brown hair and an hour glass figure that can turn many heads in the club, including mine. She's stunning. I have to find out who she is, tonight. If it's Kayla, she will be in my bed by the end of the night----. Jeez, I'm hanging around Todd way too much.

"What the fuck dude. I have been talking to you for like three minutes now and you're just fucking ignoring me." Todd shoves my shoulder. "Gar, are you really thinking about work while we're out? Seriously, loosen up, bro."

"I swear to you that I wasn't thinking of work." I scan the dance floor again for the mystery woman. "Shit, where did she go?"

"Yeah, who?" He asks as looks around. He scratches his head.

"No one that you're interested in," I growled. "I mean no one."

"Damn Garrett, you sound like a dang blasted female. Do you need a tampon or some Midol?" He nods at the red head cutie and scratches his chin. "If you want to be a Mary, can you go to the bar and get me a Sam's."

"You really are fucking incorrigible," I cursed. "Yes, dear. I'll be back with your beer. Do you want it up your ass or in a glass? What do you think I am, a god damned waitress?"

"No, they're sexier than you are!" He laughs his ass off as <u>he</u> strolls over to the red head <u>and</u> starts to dance with her. The white boy can't dance to save his --- life. As I walk over to the bar, I see her again.

God Damn, she looks familiar. It has to be that girl from the supermarket. She hauled ass before I got a chance to talk to her. I have to find out who she is. I mean Kayla is the only one who can get me unraveled, but this woman, she's more than easy on the eyes.

The brunette walks by me as the smell of a fresh clean linen tingles my nose and heightens my senses. This forces me to check out how her ass curves in those jeans. Oh my god, she could make any man here stand at attention. I need to know her, in more than just a friend or a friendly way. Damn! Garrett get yourself together you have been single for too long. You're seriously looking at this woman like you could eat her for breakfast, lunch and dinner.

I finally get to the bar and wait at the corner for my twin. Lost in deep thought, I gaze at the little vixen as she saunters to the dance floor. Those long legs, I'd love to have them wrapped around my neck, while making her scream my name. Damn, I'm in heaven just watching her.

"Hey Gar, it's been a long fucking time. Where have you been ass wipe?" Wyatt calls out across the room. A wet towel smacks me in the face. Leave it to my brother for making my wet dream fade and manages to humiliate with one breath.

"Shit, Wyatt, why are you such a dip shit?" I mutter.

"You needed to cool off." He hands me a dry one and laughs. "So what the hell? You don't write, you don't call..."

"Well, you know work." I grunt then throw the dry towel back at his face.

"Yeah, I would be too after I bought out my supervisors," he leans on the table. Girls that are next to me on the bar stools, drool over his tattoos and piercings.

"Yeah, The Scilicet Publishing Company is among the Fortune 500 fastest growing companies. Got it for a damn good price and I couldn't pass it up." I shrug my shoulders like it isn't a big deal. "How did you know? I didn't tell anyone. Not even Mom."

"Really, bro?" He sarcastically replies. "Just because I'm a bartender, does not mean I don't watch Fox <u>Business. You</u> know I went to college for business and I do have that shiny piece of paper that says I have a business degree on it. It also happens to hang in my office." He snickers. "So I do keep up with the happenings in the business world." He pats my head like a dog. "Anyways, I'm so proud of you."

"Would you cut it out? No one knows and I like to keep it that way." Irritated, I whack his left hand away from my head. "How is the club doing? I'm sorry I didn't come on opening night or been around in general. It's been a long couple of weeks."

"What can I say? I landed a gold mine. I have a fantastic staff and a great crowd," he says. "When you're known as the manager and not the owner, you get more out of the place." He winks. "That's why I want to stay incognito, if you get what I mean."

"I see you have secrets as well as I do," I answer.

"I do it for business sense. You do it, well because you're an idiot." Wyatt scratches his chin. "So about the folks, she worries about you Gar. We had no clue you were even back in town. How long were you going to hide in that office of yours?"

"Long enough for my brother to call or barge in." I eagerly scratch the back of my neck. "I know I need to see them. I just don't want to answer any questions. You know it's still unsettling to hear them talk about what could've been."

"Man, Garrett, you're the older one of us, but at times I think I was supposed to come out first." His blue eyes darkens, which means he's either really pissed off or wants to lecture. Wyatt not only had grown up fast and become a father figure, he has and will always feel like he needs to protect mom and me because of the drunken ass of a father that we had. The hatred the old man had between Wyatt and I was downright evil. The man used to torture the crap out of me with his fist. If it wasn't for Wyatt, I would have been in a wheelchair or worse.

"No buts this time around bro, this isn't a woman who you can give to charity. It's Mom. Hell we got shit, but she took it the worst," he continues. "Remember, she left him for us—leaving us without a dime. She also worked her ass off for us so we could go to college and have a better life. We did alright afterwards. She met a guy who I like to think of as my dad, so she'll always ask that question, especially since the drunk bastard passed away not too long ago. So please just do me a favor, stop by and see her once in a while, it would take the heat off me. Deal?" He punches the counter then says. "I'm not an only child. It's our turn to take care of her. We owe it to her. So, get your ovaries in check and go by there and check on her."

"Can I think about it?" I ask. Great it's a long ass lecture that will go on for ages.

"It's a start. It would mean a lot to her, Gar. She misses you a lot." He rolls his eyes then says. "So what can I get for you tonight? I have everything you can imagine. So let me hear it. Wait let me guess?" He plays with his temple like he's reading my mind. "Let's see Captain and coke."

"I never thought coming to a bar would entail therapy and a drink." Wyatt can never stay mad at me. Even though we haven't talked in what seems like forever, since I have been consumed with work and a stupid bitch, it will never change how tight we are. "The womanizer is with me tonight and he would like a Sam's and forget the Captain, just give me a double shot of Jose, and keep them coming."

"Will do, on the house. You do know there's a five drink max, right?" The bold man flips the towel over his shoulder and reaches in the ice bucket. He grasps onto a glass and pours the Sam Adams out from the draft.

"How are you making money, when you have a five drink policy and you give away free drinks?" I glance around the place and stop in my tracks again to the goddess who I want to take home. "Forget about your policy, who's that woman? She gave you a hug earlier." I begin to fantasize about being wrapped up in her legs and squeezing that ass of hers.

"Hey, dip shit, don't make me pour water over your head instead of throwing a wet towel." He places the glass of beer on the counter and waves his hand in my face. "Yep, you got it bad. I knew it."

"Knew what?" I blink and lean, paying attention to the way the brunette moves her hips while she dances. "Seriously, who is she?"

"You really don't know who she is?" He shakes his head and reaches for a shot glass of Jose. "You have been sheltered way too long. That woman you've been drooling over and that you're referring to, is none other than the one and only, Kayla Ashby."

"You're kidding." My mouth drops to the floor as my heart sings to her name.

"Why would I kid, I love the girl. Not only is she my best friend, she was my right hand when it came to designing this club," he says like a proud father and smacks the back of my head. "Hey Gar, shut your mouth before you catch flies."

"Shut the fuck up? She's here and she's an architect?" I act like I had not googled her just a few hours ago. My heart feels like an electric jolt starting it up on turbo. "Why didn't you call me, I don't know... when you found out I was back in town? You knew, I've had the hot's for her over a decade now."

"Because you would have been too chicken shit to say or do anything. --- Besides you were busy pretending to be an Armani playboy with someone who's superficial. I will never, I mean never, put Kayla in a position where her heart would be ripped out. You know if it wasn't for Todd calling me to tell me no more Reagan, I wouldn't have called you," he snidely remarks. "Really, Gar? Reagan? What the hell was that all about?"

"I don't know." That stupid grin appears again as my palm rises up. I keep watching Kayla on the floor and all I can think of was eighth grade and how I rescued her from running into the locker. She had her nose stuck in that damned book. She was cute back then. And now, she's what I always pictured in my dreams. A total knock out.

Wyatt says my name but I ignore everything he's saying because, I'm lost in my own thoughts of Kayla Ashby.

His fist hits my shoulder to get my attention.

"Ow," I sneer and rub it. "You Fucktard!"

"And the reason why I called you tonight is not so you can watch Kayla dancing." He places the drink on the counter. "Stop gawking and just ask her out." Wyatt tries to hold in his laughter, even though he's doing a piss poor job of it. "You know, go up and say something, even if it's, Hi. You would be surprised to know that she saw you at the grocery store a few months back."

"You see. Shit like that, Wyatt, pisses me off. You knew she saw me at the grocery store. And you never called me. I was at the grocery store. That would have given you a damn sign, I wasn't with Reagan." I glowered. "For your info, I tried to talk to Kayla, but she hauled ass out of the parking lot."

"Gar, you're stalling." I want to punch that incorrigible grin off his face. "She's here and you're here. So go and talk."

"I will," I squeak and clear my throat. "I mean, I am." I grab my drinks quickly from him, and start back to where Todd is on the floor.

Got to hand it to the guy, he has a cutie showing him some moves. Thank God, because he has no rhythm. I raise the beer to him and he smirks. He lifts his head in acknowledgement. I rest them on the table. I sit on the stool watching my goddess dance, thinking of what to say to her. I feel like I'm back in junior high, again.

A blonde haired woman that has auburn streaks drags me from my seat onto the dance floor. She may be cute, but my mind's set on Kayla, tonight.

"Garett, you owe me a dance." The thirty year old tries her best to twerk on my body and I seriously want to laugh. I don't understand why older woman try to be like Beyoncé or Miley. I can't keep my emotions in check, I chuckle.

"I'm surprised you're amused." She shakes her big ass in front of me. "You used to love it when I was down and dirty."

"I did?" I ask like a dumb ass, knowing what will happen next.

"You don't remember me, do you?" She stops and taps her heel. Her tongue pushes out her left cheek. "I should have known."

"I ah," I stumble the rest of my words. "Of course I do."

"What's my name?" She stares me down like she's going to draw a damn gun.

Oh shit, now I'm done for. I puff some air out of my lungs and shake my head, no. "Heidi, no Staci. No wait Maci?"

"Bella," she answers. Her arms wrap on her chest and she smirks. Then a hard kick went straight to my junk and I nearly double over. I'm really having an off night.

"May I ask Bella, out of all places to hit, why did it have to be my package?" My voice becomes a soprano. Leaning over, I hold my left hand on it and try to be calm. "Did I do something to you?"

"Oh you did something, Garrett. More like we both did something." Her fists tightened to the sides of her waist. I hold my junk before she aims at it, again. "We have slept together several times. Apparently, I wasn't good enough for you." Her face burns red with anger. "You're a male slut, you two balled bitch." Bella tries to hide the tears in the corner of her eyes and she flings her hair and storms away.

I count down from ten, just trying to relax. Man, I am out of it. How could I not remember that I slept with her? Too many drunken nights since I caught Reagan. I barely remember the days of the week much less, who I let get my rocks off.

Todd jogs up to me. I stretch and tap my breast pocket. Yes, I remembered them. My lucky cigars. They weren't so lucky now, but I have to have one right this instant.

"Garrett, dude, are you okay?" Todd rests his left hand on my right shoulder.

"Just being my charming self with the ladies," I mutter.

"If that's the no one you told me about earlier," he eyes Bella like a hawk. "Damn, you're losing it." He crocks his head. "Look at her. She's pouting in the corner." The famous smirk rises from his face. "I think I may need to cheer her up."

"Go right ahead Romeo and have my sloppy seconds," I say. "I'm going to get some fresh air. Enjoy whoever you decide to pick up, Nasty Bastard. Just make sure your ass wears a love glove, because you don't want something A-jax can't wash off."

"You know I can never leave my rocket uncovered," he jokes.

"Rocket? Really? You are delusional, do you know that?" I snip and pat my jewels.

"Awwwww, are we a tad jealous?" He pinches his right index finger and thumb together.

"Fuck you, Asshat, I have no problem with my goods." I crack my back. "I really need a cigar right now. Stay out of trouble, no fighting in my brother's club."

He checks Bella over and waves to me. "Yeah, yeah, I got you. No fighting."

Once I step outside in the "smokers lounge", I bite off the end of the cigar and light up, breathing in the sweet scent of vanilla and clover—thinking about the gorgeous tiger eyed woman inside. A giant grin rises up and my heart hammers against my chest.

Chapter SIX

The Kiss....

"The most important thing is to enjoy your life."---
Audrey Hepburn

Crying out of control, I breathe in and out to calm down my nerves like Dr. Doyle taught me. I play with the pink band. And I remember a poem that was my first assignment from Dr. Doyle. It is another one by Julie Mishler and it's called:

"Would You."

Would You

Would you notice

If I wasn't there?

Would it matter

Do you even care?

Putting myself out there

Day after day

Trying so damn hard

Putting on a fake smile

Acting like everything is okay

I want this void

I feel inside

To be filled again

My heart to be full

My smile to be real

The happiness I once felt

To exude from within

Just like it did

When I was with him

I miss so many things

Especially all the little things

The ones that meant so much

Like "Good morning sunshine" or "Good night"

How much they really mean

Knowing the bond we once shared

But I took for granted

"I Love You"

Or "You are amazing!"

You never realize

Until they are gone

What I would not give

To feel special again

Was strong again

You might not notice

Or even care

But every day

This void I feel inside

Yearns to be filled

Thrives to be happy

Longs to be whole again

I think back to when I found this poem, and I wipe a tear from my face. "Get your shit together, Ashby."

The low beats to the music vibrates the deck and I become lost in my own thoughts. Why is this happening? The only time I see the man of my dreams is of course the only time that the forces of evil show up. It's like some cruel joke that keeps playing over and over. I hate the Fucking Stanton's for what they did to me, especially Edwin and Elijah. Is it wrong to wish revenge?

The door opens and I don't even care to look.

"Kayla?" Violet's sweet voice comes from the behind. "Are you okay?"

"Yeah." I use my sleeve and wipe away my tears. "Just crying. Nothing new."

"What happened?" She asks curiously. "Did your friend that you were with do something to you in the past? Come on Ashby, I have been patient, I know something is going on. How can we help you if you won't even talk to us?"

"Vi, I can't talk about it." I flex my hands controlling my breaths. "I promise you when I'm ready, I will."

"Why can't you?" She shrieks, the even keel in her voice becomes rigid. "Kay, I'm worried about you. You vanished into thin air then just reappeared, not that I'm mad that you came home, because God only knows how much I freakin' missed you, but you've changed. Now you're crying on top of it. I know that you're hiding something. Please just tell me."

"Vi, when she's ready, she'll tell us." Wyatt holds the door to the club. "Come inside and give her a moment."

She grumbles underneath her breath and shakes her head as Wyatt escorts her back inside. I watch them head in. I then turn my body and lean on the banister. I don't know what time it is, as I blink my dark lashes.

I then hear muffled conversations and even someone panting like they're having sex out here. It's dark enough so no one would be of the wiser and the panting is turning me on like there's a damn fire burning inside of me. Jeez, I need to get some relief soon or I'm going to explode.

I snap my head at the dark corner by one of the entrances. "I'm now going senile. I see shadows in every dark corner, watching me." I turn my head to go back inside and I see someone right in front of me who l least expected.

Garrett Winters stands and stares into my eyes. He wipes away tear drops that still rolls down my cheeks. After his animal instincts kicked in as his blue eyes grow wild. He pushes my body against the side wall by the door and kisses me.

Holy shit, he's kissing me like I'm the last female alive. My mind tells me to push him away, but my heart and body betray me—it's so fucking electrifying. What can I say? He's a god damned itch that I can't scratch. I surrender to his assault.

The gentle movement of his hands cover every inch of my breast, making my nipples hard like diamonds. His skillful silk tongue possesses my mouth as my core wets and cum seeps through my jeans. Just by this one kiss. A kiss that sends shooting stars in the back of my eyes, more like fireworks on the 4th of July.

"What the hell is your problem?" I break away quickly, before I change my mind and do anything and everything with him that I'll regret. "Have you lost your mind?" Agitated, I push my hair back. "You just don't go up to someone who's broken and kiss her. You come at me with nasty ass cigar breath, really? Try a breath mint."

Before I know it, my heels turn away from him and I

hightail it into the club—leaving him dumfounded with a confused look on his face.

Once inside, I frantically search for Violet or Wyatt so I can get advice on what to do with the guy who I'm uncontrollably in love with and know that I can't have him. God why does this kiss have to be the best kiss I ever have had.

As I search down the hall by the service entrance, I hear some kind of noise. "I wonder what that noise could be."

Walking on my tip toes, I sneak closer to the bar's storeroom to get a closer peek. After I check the doorknob and of course it slightly budges. I gently push it open. "I need to tell Wyatt he's got to fix this lock."

Moaning and slapping sounds that could be mistaken for a man who's balls are deep inside the woman's core. "You've got to be fucking kidding me." Curiosity gets the best of me and I stay to hear more. "This is the hottest thing I ever heard. All I need now is Porn music playing in the background."

Hey I'm not a prude, I have read several adult books on my Kindle, my favorite being *Kendall Gray's Hard Rock Harlots Series* and I fucking love it. But it's different when you can watch it live. Not going to lie, I have used those mental images on more than one occasion, but now I'm going to see it first-hand I fucking can't wait to see it up close.

Snickering, I creep in the room to find out if it's an employee.

"I know Wyatt. He would fire them on the spot."

Muffled words, like dirty little bitch and nasty slut along with moans and groans echo through the room. All this sex talk is making me need an old fashioned orgasm. I become a peeping tom and peek through one of the stacks of beer cases.

My eyes wander to the distinctive voice. To my surprise, Wyatt and Violet are going at it like two dogs in heat. Getting turned on at the site of my best friends having sex, I unbutton my jeans and let them slip over my hips, until they encircled my thighs. I lean back on the wall and lift my leg on one of the red wine cases—giving me just enough space to reach my clit. Lightly, touching the delicate part of my breast and then my two fingers of my right hand dance their way to the sweet spot. I close my eyes and skate over it—thinking of Garrett.

"Fuck me, Wyatt." Violet cries out in a husky voice. "Fuck me hard."

Caught up hearing them, I continue to tease my g-spot with my fingers and dip into pure bliss with my left index finger. Hard and fast as I hear Wyatt slamming Violet from behind.

As they scream into ecstasy, I find my own climax and tilt my head back softly—moaning in enjoyment.

After, I breathe heavily and pull on my tight ass jeans— feeling satisfied but not content or happy. I'm about to walk out when I see a shining piece glass struck me. ---

I glance down at it. It shows my best friend sucking Wyatt's massive cock. "No wonder she was moaning like that. Hell, I would scream like a damned banshee if I had that in me."

Mesmerized, I stand watching Violet indulge as Wyatt fucks her mouth. Her greedy blue eyes find mine and she nips the top of his cock, then points to me.

Stunned, my legs don't budge, and she continues her assault on his shaft—never breaking her suction. She's like a *Jenna Jamison*, sucking his dick as he holds onto her hair and tilts his head in the air. "She's getting skull fucked in the process," I mutter.

Wyatt's face changes dramatically from the puffed out cheeks to a lean very pleased face as he closes his eyes and deeply moans. He shivers and shakes as he releases. Violet just swallows his load, licking her lips for left overs-getting every single drop.

She takes it like a fucking champ. My best friend, the cumguzzling bitch. Afterwards, she rises from her knees and kisses his mouth.

"Now, that's fucking hot," I mutter as I blink my lashes furiously.

They both laugh as they stride up to me. At this point of embarrassment, I want to hide my head in the sand like an Ostrich.

"Holy shit," is all that comes out of my mouth.

"You're so innocent when it comes to certain things." Violet wipes her tears from laughter. She side glances at Wyatt. "Call me sometime big boy and we can repeat a great therapy session."

"I just might do that and Kayla can join in." Wyatt raises his eyebrows. "Kayla, did you like what you saw? I told you anytime you want your bed rocking come on knocking or give me a call." Still smiling like a cat that ate a canary, Wyatt chuckles as he fixes himself while he lifts up his jeans.

"Wyatt, you need to get that door fixed, I came in here because I heard noises. I thought it was one of the employees." I ramble and twiddle my thumbs, so I don't look at the two of them. "I mean do you know how uncomfortable it is to see two of my best friends bumpin' uglies and not being able to move because you're too interested in what they are doing?"

"Kayla, slow down. You're sounding like you're hopped up on caffeine." Wyatt touches my back. "If it makes you feel any better, I'll have door fixed. He then kisses Violet's hand. "Thank you Hot Lips. Later." Wyatt then saunters outside— shaking his ass at us.

"He does have a nice ass." Violet peeks at it. "It's firm and tight."

"Can I leave now and escape my sorrows." I grumble and perch my lips to the side.

"Shit, you <u>know</u> what we did was hot," Violet smugly brags a she wraps her arms in front of her chest and with attitude moves her head.

"Ah, I ah, ah." I tap my foot. "Can we please get a drink?"

"Bitch." I nudge her shoulder like I use to when we would come to a disagreement. "Come on. Wyatt will buy us drinks." We snag a stool at the end of the bar and ask for the house special. After smoothing her back, I look up and there he is. I hunch over as my hair falls into my face.

"Kayla, what's up with you? You look like you've seen a ghost," Violet asks. She gently pushes back some of my hair.

"Oh I'm fine, just the boy of my dreams since the eighth grade and I made a fool out of myself." I slouch trying not to be noticeable.

"You're hiding because he's staring right at you." Violet made a face like I have a screw loose then combs my hair with her fingers out of my face. "Will you stop acting like an eighth grader and pull this mane of yours back? There's chemistry between you two and you need to embrace it." After her motherly lecture, Violet nudges her head to Wyatt.

"What was that all about?" I curiously ask.

"Uh, what?" She quickly responds. "Nothing. You know the ladies room is calling me." She jumps off the stool and fixes her skirt. "I'll be right back."

"Vi wait," I blurt and reach for her arm, but she's faster than me and shuffles at a rather fast pace to the ladies room, while Wyatt talks to Garrett and tilts his head my way.

Garrett rises from the stool and heads toward me. My legs don't move, again. My heart beats fast and furious, while goose bumps spread all over my arms. So I do what comes naturally… hide behind my hair.

Chapter SEVEN

Seeing Red....

"I'm selfish and a little insecure. I make mistakes, I'm out of control and at times hard to handle. But if you can't handle me at my worst, then you sure as hell don't deserve me at my best."-Marilyn Monroe

"In order to get a girl like Kayla Ashby, you have to show what you got in here and here." A quote from my twin. After Wyatt taps my head and points to my heart. "She's more than one of your ladies you like to escort."

Then he leaves me like I'm a helpless teenager as I watch Kayla hide through her silky brown hair of hers. I snicker. <u>In the past I've had any woman I wanted in the a blink of an eye, but --- the only woman I've ever loved was always a heartbeat away but never in my arms.</u>

Okay, Gar, the man said use your mind. Let's see what you can do?

All night I imagined myself between her legs or pressed up against her on the dance floor, and now it comes down to this....small talk.

Automatically, my legs and feet find their way towards her. How can one woman make you want to forget your damned religion? Making me want to bury <u>myself</u> balls deep inside her and brand her to be mine and no one else's? If she would just give me a chance, God, <u>I'd</u> show her I could love her. To tell her that I have loved her for years. Even when I was preparing to marry Reagan, Kayla was the one I saw at the end of the isle.

I take a seat next to her and brush back her brown hair, then lift up her chin. "Is this seat taken?" I nervously ask. My hands shake, hopefully she doesn't notice.

"N...no...," she shyly stutters as those tiger eyes gaze into mine.

"Thank you." After relaxing on the stool, I turn my head towards her. "I think we got off on the wrong foot."

"So trying to fuck me with my clothes on is called starting off on the wrong foot?" She asks as she rolls her tiger eyes and chews the inside of her right soft cheek.

God, that's hot.

"Yeah, hmm." I slightly itch my nose. "Sorry about that. I've wanted to do that with you ever since..." Stuttering, I clear my throat. "Let's start over." My hand reaches out. "Hi Kayla, I haven't seen you in years, and by the way, I'm sorry for the cigar breath."

"Hi." She giggles as she rubs her small hands on her jeans then shakes mine. "It's nice to see you again. What's your name? I'm not sure I remember you."

"Garrett," I answer. She waves her hand, telling me to finish. Yep, I knew this would be humiliating. "Winters." I slouch on the stool and reluctantly let go of her hold.

"Oh." She sips her drink and continues. "I think I might remember some guy by that name that I went to school with. Let me see if it's you." Her index finger brushes against her mouth then she says," I remember you following me to my classes and you also had a girlfriend. Oh what was her name?" She dramatically touches her chin. "Oh, yes. Wasn't her name, Reagan?" She snaps her finger. "I just can't think of her last name."

"Woodrow." I slouch and sulk even further down on the stool like I hit a wall.

"Yeah that's the one." Her look could kill the way her green eyes look directly into mine. "She's the one who I got into a fight with over you. Now, I hear that you're marrying the trollup bitch. Excuse my colorful words but she was never one of my fans, and I never knew why."

Ouch. That's harsh Kay. Man she's tough and I saved her delicious ass more than once. All she can say is I would follow her around like I was a puppy dog. Out of all the things she could remember the most about me was my involvement with Reagan. But her smile tells me she's playing hard to get. *Oh sweet*

Kayla, two can play at this game of cat and mouse Trust me, baby, I will win.

"She was." I undo my tie letting it hang loose on my shirt. "Look, Kayla. I want to make things right. There's a lot I want to make up for and I was hoping for a date." I take my glass. "Just two people getting to know each other." With a heavy sigh, I continue. "If you want to change your mind, I'll be over in my corner. If you're interested come see me. If not..." My face softens. "Well at least I can remember the sexiest kiss I have ever had, not to mention the most cherished."

Slowly, my feet scuff along the floor to my corner. I could hear her giggle. Which means I made some kind of progress. I have to say, I do love her giggle. I pull myself up to the bar and raise my glass to her as she does the same.

It seems like an eternity as we both look at each other then turn our heads in different directions. The club is shutting down and the bar is only opened for last call. So it's pretty much just the staff and a few regulars.

She waves the bartender, who could look like a Hollywood superstar, over to her and ask him something.

The bartender pours out of the tap and hands me a dark lager.

"From the lady." He places the napkin on the counter

and the glass. The foam rises neatly to the top—making it just right.

"I like to buy her whatever she's having," I say. "From the top shelf." I wave.

"Yes sir." Hollywood chuckles. He fills one of the cocktail glasses with ice and presses one of the buttons on the soda tab.

"You're laughing because?" I glare at him.

"She's having soda water on tap sir," he indicates.

"Oh well soda water with a cherry in it." I take a napkin he handed me and reach inside my pocket. "If you mind giving her this note, too." I scribble on it and fold it. "Tell you what...I'll give you fifty for a tip right off the bat." I snatch the old leather wallet that I carry around with me every day. Kayla had given to me, in fact it's the only gift she gave me, since high school. "And here's another fifty if you don't blab to the other employees and don't read the note." Arrogantly, I flip the two bills on the table.

"Understand?"

Greedily, the waiter shakes his head yes.

"Good." I smirk. "Run along now and get her the drink, Hollywood."

Straightening myself out. I wait.

I look over to her while the waiter points at me and hands her the note and soda water, then walks away. He shakes his head and cleans the bar area.

The goddess opens the napkin like a school girl and belts out laughing. She waves the waiter back over to her. He gives her a pen. She writes something down on the same napkin and gives it to him. He huffs then stalks over to me.

"You know, the tip was just to deliver the message, no to go back and forth with like I'm an errand boy." He places the napkin down. "If you two are interested in each other, my suggestion. Get a room." He dismisses me like he's royalty.

"Thanks Hollywood," I reply. He makes a face and went back to his business. I open the note to my invite and her reply.

It read:

Anytime you want your pop, I'm sitting in the corner, panting. Always yours, Garrett

What ever happened to getting to know one and other, first?

XOXOXO ~Kayla~

I chuckle. I raise my head. Kayla raises her glass and winks. I pocket the note. I know it's a Mary move but if it's the only note I ever receive from her, then I will cherish it.

"It's now or never, Winters." I smooth my pants and rise.

One of the idiot Stanton twins angrily marches over to Kayla's side. Her eyes grow wider with fear. I slowly move toward her direction. Stanton's hand gently caresses her face and she smacks it away from her. He touches her breast inappropriately. That ass. What the hell does he think he's doing? I mean she couldn't be interested? Could she? Was Reagan right? She had a thing with the Stanton boys? They were the most popular kids in town and at school. "Fuck a duck, lick a moose and screw a damn cow," I mutter to myself.

My chest begins to hurt as I smooth it. I'm about to bail when I hear her distress call from her delicate voice and that's all I needed.

Like time flies backwards, Kayla looks like the girl I first met, scared and <u>alone</u>.

"Edwin, cut it out," Her voice shrieks while it strains. "You've got bourbon on your breath."

"You have two weeks to get back where you belong, bitch, in my bed or else." Edwin slaps her and then wraps his hands around her throat. "Back in my bed where I own you. I will fuck you and then I will fuck you again, you stupid cunt," he growls. "Superstar, do I make myself clear? I want that tight ass pussy of yours, because I own you. I will always own you."

"Stop!" She beats on his arms to let her go. But she couldn't break free. Her eyelids open and closes. "Stop," a whisper comes through her soft sweet lips. Kayla's face turns beat red as her eyes seek mine for help.

"You know I love it when you fight me." He brushes her lips.

She bites his lip. Growling, he reaches and tugs the back of her hair. Then slaps her face again, blood spatters on the counter and trickles down the side of her beautiful lips.

The fucking piece of shit is not going to see the light of day after I get through with him. The fire inside me explodes as rage inhabits my body.

I politely tap his shoulder. The dumbass release his hold on her and turns his head. "What?"

My left fist slams into his nose. He wobbles backwards, knocking over a couple of bar stools. Then the asshole balances himself. He wipes the dark red blood that seeps from his nose. Then he narrows his green eyes and smirks like a jackal waiting for his next pray.

"Someone, get Wyatt," Hollywood calls out.

Commotion starts to happen in the club, bouncers start rushing left and right. While Kayla's weak body falls to the ground. I squat down to check on her. I move her hair back. She holds her arms on the floor to balance herself as blood and tears mix in—running down her face.

"Kayla, baby?" as I check her neck, marks from his finger nails that he dug into her soft skin, produces a small amount of blood. This is the tip of the fucking iceberg. The rage has now taken over my body and all I see is the color red when I glare at Edwin Stanton.

"You want to play for keeps, Winters?" The bastard grunts. "Let's play." He storms his way and tackles me to the bar like a football player. My body cracks on the edge. His fists jabs into my sides with a damn class ring. I'm going to feel it tomorrow. I feel a sharp pain in my side, but I don't pay any attention to it. I see him pocket a knife and I know the bastard has fucking cut me.

He clenches my neck and pushes it to the side. Adding pressure from his elbow as it digs into my carotid, Edwin tries to cut off the blood flow. He then dips his hands into a glass full of bourbon. After, he presses the alcohol on his fingers to the cut that he made on my ribs. The burning sting is unbearable.

I bite my tongue in agony. Look over to see Kayla, covering her ears, bawling.

"Call 911," Wyatt yells to the bartenders. "Guys leave this fucking prick to my brother. If anything happens it's on me," he barks orders at the bouncers as he rushes in with his bat in hand. "Violet, take care of Kayla."

Violet then screams for Kayla to come to her. But Kayla does not move. She is sitting there rocking back and forth screaming "This isn't happening, this isn't happening." The pleading words of my sweet baby.

"Don't worry, Kay." Violet slides over to her, cradling her like a mother. "You're safe," Violet utters and again and she kisses Kayla's forehead.

"The bitch belongs to me," Edwin cackles as he spits in my face. "How does it feel to want something Winters? You will never get her. She's no one else's but mine."`

"The hell she is." Once I'm able to maneuver my knee, I jam it into Edwin's stomach. I rip his blond hair as I take hold of it. He squirms as he screams bloody murder. What a fucking Mary. "She is no ones for the taking."

I pound his face and let him drop to the floor. "When she's ready, I will have her and love her. So take this as a fair warning Stanton. STAY THE FUCK AWAY FROM HER!!!"

He then topples to the ground while cocktail glasses break everywhere. I crack my neck and my shoulders. I am now bouncing around like a boxer. As adrenaline takes over, I pounce on the rat. Blood splatters all over the place. I just keep pounding. Every time I look into Edwin Stanton's crazed eyes, I see my old man, which angers me even more to think he touched my Kayla.

"Take it easy killer," Todd calls out to me. I don't care at this point, for no one, I mean no one, lays a hand on Kayla Ashby without paying a price.

"God Damn it, Garrett." Todd lifts me off of the guy and drags my across the floor. "He's not worth the five o'clock news." He tightens his grip. "Remember who you are, man. You can take this guy in the courts."

"Gar, get your head into the game," Wyatt's deep voice eases me as I look up at my twin. "Todd's right, the prick's not worth jail time." He then squats down. "Todd, you can let my brother go. Security is taking Stanton up to the office while they wait for the cops."

Todd releases me. Wyatt then pulls me back up and pats my shoulder. I touch my black hair. Blood stains and sweat covers my favorite pink shirt. Oh shit...well as long as Kayla's safe. Or is she?

"I thought you left?" I glance over at my friend.

"I had my fling and came back to check on you." He scratches his nose. "Lucky I did." He glances over to the bar. "So was this no one that concerns you worth fighting for?

"More then you'll ever know," I blurt. All that pops in my head is the fear in Kayla's eyes and my adrenaline spikes even more. Fists anchor to my side as I scan the bar, making sure the other asshole Elijah Stanton doesn't get his grimy fucking hands on Kayla.

"Todd, let him cool down and I'll get you a drink,"

Wyatt waves him to the bar. "Gar, wash up and go see Kayla. She needs you more than ever." He points two fingers up at Hollywood. "Chuck, two Jose's and tell Meg, to wear gloves while she cleans. Also, make sure the mess is disposed of properly."

"Mess?" I question then I look at the floor. There is blood, clear liquid, pieces of glass and broken bar stools scatter everywhere. "What the fuck did I just do to my brother's bar?"

I don't remember ever being this mad before. Stanton brought out the beast and if he ever goes after Kayla again, I will do more than messing up his ugly face.

Chapter
EIGHT

The Truth Shall Set Her Free....

"The truth is you don't know what is going to happen tomorrow. Life's a crazy ride, and nothing is guaranteed."----
Eminem

Violet cradles me on the soft grey couch in Wyatt's office. The spotless area smells of lemon pledge, especially on the newly polished furniture. Wyatt even has old black and whites of his childhood and college days. Next to his degree is a beautiful black and white photograph of a mother and her daughter and they are holding umbrellas in the rain at Oregon State Park. The love in their eyes as they both stare into the camera. Hmm...I wonder why he has a random photograph like that. It don't look like anyone I know, but hell I have been gone for seven years so it could be anyone.

Just like St. James Cathedral, this place is like a sanctuary for me. I keep glancing at the photographs and see all of us when we were younger. The picture brings tears to my eyes. It was the senior banquet and we were dressed in evening wear. That was the last night I was with them before I disappeared. Garrett stands next to Wyatt but gazes at me.

I never noticed how he looked at me, so carefree and in love. Damn, I was dumb. I wipe away a tear.

"It was a matter of time before they found me," I mumble under my breath.

"Kayla," Violet lifts up my chin. "Honey, you need to tell me exactly what happened to you in the past."

"I don't know if I can say the words out loud, VI," I whisper and my left index finger wipes underneath my eyes. I tried to bury these demons for years, but they keep popping up."

"Kay, you need to tell me," Violet urges. "You should know by now, I'm not going to leave you."

"Okay, the two men you saw tonight," I state. My teeth chatter in between words. "Do you remember who they are?"

"Yeah, one was extremely hot," she answers. "And the other was a monster." Her face drains. "OMG, the Stanton twins," Violet gasps. "Oh Kay, I'm sorry. I should have remembered. I didn't even think they would be here. When I asked you if you had talked to them you told me you didn't want to bring any of the Stanton's up."

"Well there's more to the story," I explain. "I was raped at the age of thirteen."

Violet's blue eyes glisten. "Please let me tell you all of the story before you say anything, because I won't be able to finish if you interrupt me. This is going to be really hard on me VI and I need to know that what I tell you, you'll be strong enough to listen. I look over to her and she <u>nods</u> her head confirming that she will be ok.

So I continue....

"Growing up with the Stanton's wasn't like living with Daddy War bucks, Violet. I remember Winston Avenue where the orphanage was and the Stanton's home. The old colonial house stood out from the other with its well-manicured yard. I still can hear Millie snapping at the gardeners not pruning the red rose's right and the star gazing lilies taking over the flower beds. Man she gave me a migraine."

'But nothing compares to the wrap around porch that had the grape vines neatly decorated throughout the railings. The porch was my favorite place, it was out front of the house so I knew I was safe. They wouldn't want to hurt their precious reputation, Lord forbid that the truth be told."

"We can't forget about the family pool area out in the backyard with the pool house for our guests to sit and relax like a lounge. Yeah, more like a mating place for Senator Stanton and his slut internists or administrative assistants. There was always a parade of women. Though I use that term loosely, none of them ever looked like they were over the age of eighteen."

"I always made myself at home on the white wicker swings as I drew patterns of a house of my own. I see Garrett from the corner of my eye with Wyatt riding bikes or playing catch. It put a natural smile on my face since they always played ball with their shirts off. VI, Garrett was and still is one the sexiest guys alive. Hell, even the sixty year old women on our street stated he was easy on the eyes."

"But to Edwin and Elijah, Garrett was a bug that needed to be squashed. They didn't like the fact that Garrett tried to spend time with me. Even if we were just talking outside. Nope, the gruesome twosome made his life a living hell by almost running over him with their motorcycles or nailing him hard when they played football with him and Wyatt. I always knew when it was going to happen and there was nothing I could do to prevent it. I could see the look in their eyes, it was like they were possessed. Even if Garrett and Wyatt just rode by and said hello, either I caught hell or Garrett and Wyatt would.

The day Millie and Seth left Elijah in charge was the worse day of my life. It's the day my innocence was taken from me. Seth and Millie had left for the last tour of the campaign trail, they were trying to get the last little bit of votes.

Since the unbearable heat and humidity struck our town, I decided to lay out by the pool jamming to one of the hair bands on my Walkman. "*Signs, Signs, everywhere is signs,*" I sang out loud as my pink toes wiggled and my feet moved to the beat. What I didn't notice is my cleavage from the blue two piece bathing suit Millie bought me was too revealing.

A hand gently removed the headphones. Startled, I jumped up and leaned on my hands. I curved my shoulders to hide my mountains—hoping they wouldn't notice. My suntan lotion began to glisten with perspiration. I was starting to turn a shade of pink, and I felt the tingling sensation from the sun.

"Was I too loud?" I hesitantly asked.

"No baby, you weren't." Elijah squatted down and leaned forward. "That must be the most sensual voice I ever heard. Isn't that right, Edwin?" He peers up at his twin. Their green eyes glower at each other.

"Yeah it is. We need to make sure the Winters boys don't come over here and make obscene gestures."

Edwin was so close to my face, I could smell his nasty bourbon breath on me.

"I don't think they would do that." I quickly sit up. "I'll just leave."

"You don't have to." Elijah searches every inch of my body. "I'm sure you're hungry because you haven't eaten breakfast this morning," he lectured. "You need to eat Kayla for what we have planned." He sounded like he was dominant, controlling and frightening. "In the game room."

"I'm really not hungry, Elijah." I folded my arms to my chest. "I just want to lay out and get some sun. I was hoping to look like a sun kissed goddess. Well maybe not a goddess, but more like Vi's color."

"Now that's original." Elijah laughed out loud. "Baby, you are not a goddess and I hate to tell you, no one, not even you can compare to Violet Palmer. She's a Filet Mignon and well you're just a cube steak."

"Let me get you that sandwich, sun kissed goddess." He shook his head and strolled off to the kitchen.

"You're a fucking cunt, do you know that?" Edwin knelt

down and leaned over. He whispers in my ear, "There's no way that you'll ever be a goddess. You're nothing but air. Your mother couldn't look at your ugly ass face so she left you on the steps of that orphanage." He yanked my hair. Edwin's green eyes darkened with lust. "If it wasn't for our parents taking pity on your stupid ass, you'd be rotting in that place. And how do you repay them?" he asked as voice tightened. "By hanging out with Garrett Winters."

"Listen Edwin, I didn't ask to be brought into this family." I snapped and whacked his hands off of me. I looked at the water and ignored him.

"Time to pay the piper, sweetheart." His words circled the air and sent shivers up my arm making me nauseous.

"Please don't." I couldn't get those words out of my mouth. It seemed like the cat caught my tongue. Edwin then lit up a cigarette and puffed away, making smoke circles.

Gradually, I crawled to my knees and gathered all of my stuff. And before I knew it...

He clunked me in the back of my head with his fist. I tumbled over and peered at the water.

Like a caveman, he dragged me to the pool house. As soon as I was aware of my surroundings, I tried to fight him, but he was too strong. I could not do anything but dig my nails into him and claw at his eyes. He forced himself on top of me and burned my chest with his lit cigarette. The burning tobacco cuts into my breast and created marks.

Every time I fought him, more marks showed.

"Stupid ass cunt." He slapped me so hard that I thought my teeth and eyeballs were going to pop out of my damn head. He continued to drag me on the red tile floors kicking and screaming, I tugged on my hair to release from his hold, but I lost momentum and dark red liquid flowed over my back, matching the tile on the floor.

I whimpered and cried. Hell, I even screamed the last time. He tossed me into the game room of the pool-house like I was yesterday's trash. My limp body rolled. I laid on my back, stunned and mortified to what would happen next. Edwin snapped my hair toward him and ripped it as he lifted me up. I felt like the roots were coming out of my head.

"Scream bitch, no one will help your ugly ass." He sneered.

"Stop it!" I stomped on his right foot.

"Ow, you fuckin bitch. You'll pay for that." His left hand smacked as his knuckles dented my cheeks. As blood seeps from the corner of my mouth, he then slams me into the wall. His hands wrapped around my throat. "Shut your fucking trap, you cock teaser."

"Edwin, enough!" Elijah's booming voice echoes through the hall.

"Please, Elijah," I shouted. "Help!"

Elijah strolled up to me, soothes my cheeks and grabs a hold of me.

"Edwin, get the rope cuffs," he bluntly said.

"Why do I have to get the damn cuffs?" Edwin asked as he swayed.

"Because I said so," Elijah's face was full of malice. "Now."

Edwin snagged a purple rope that had hoops at either end from one of the drawers their father kept his sex toys.

"Please," I shouted and collapsed in Elijah's arms.

"Go ahead and scream, bitch, we love it when you fight us," Edwin said as he grits his teeth. "Just so you know the more you scream... the harder things will be for you." His voice vibrates through his throat.

"Please." Tears gushed down my face onto the damp grey carpeted floor. "Please don't."

The room silenced for a second until devilish laughter surfaces.

"Please....don't," I muttered it again. "Elijah please, I know you have a heart in there somewhere, please don't let him hurt me."

"Shh." Elijah pushes some my brown hair out of my face and wipes away my tears. "We all have to make a sacrifice for this family, Superstar, and this is how you can repay us for you getting time with our parents." Elijah whispered in my ear and kissed my cheek.

My body immediately seized and I felt the air squeezed out of me. While, Edwin's hand tightened around my throat, Elijah cuffs my hands to the bar that hung for wet towels with the purple rope. Even though it was made of silk, the more I moved, the more they cut into my wrist. I open my eyes slightly as the blood drips from my wrist.

"Don't fight them, Kayla. It'll burn and hurt more." Elijah muttered as he pulled my hair to the other side of my neck, he kissed every inch of it and then proceeded to circle my nipples—they became hard. He knelt down and sucked on them. Tears ran down my cheeks and I wished for this to be over.

Edwin fingered my labia rough and fast, touching himself. Something happened to me as I screamed, I squirted.

"Yeah bitch, that's what I'm talking about." He then smacked my core hard with his hand. "I need the flogger."

"Not on her first time." Elijah made a direct order. His chest brushed up against mine, like he was protecting me. "She's not ready, Edwin, we don't want her dead or beyond damaged. Do you really think it would be fun when she's almost dead?"

"Yeah, but I love the way she screams," Edwin stuttered and licked his lips at me. "It turns me on."

"You touch her by laying a mark or wrap your hands around her throat like you just did," the darkness inside Elijah's voice scared the shit out of me and it stopped Edwin dead in his tracks. "I will kill you myself. She is and will always be ours, dear brother, but not the way you like it." His green eyes quickly turned to gray as he glowered. "Understood?"

Edwin slightly nodded. By the expression on his face and what he mumbled under his breath, Edwin was not happy with what Elijah said.

"Good, now Superstar, it's time." Elijah's lips brushed against mine then he unbuttoned his jeans. His cock stood out as it smoothed against my anus. "Don't worry, you'll enjoy it."

Oh lord, I prayed. They're going to rape me. Please take me away so I don't feel this. Tears keep rushing down my face.

"I'll be good," I pleaded. "I won't be a cock tease and wear only jeans and shirts. I promise."

"Shh," Elijah's index finger reached my lips. "Baby, I don't think you're a cock tease. I'm just making you into a woman."

I no longer felt my body. I tensed as he grabs my shoulders. My bent ankles become uncomfortable and hurt as the cable ties cut into them. I then felt oil on my ass. After, something big forces its way into the small hole—I shriek so loud that my voice became hoarse. I can't believe I was just ripped open. My vision goes black. Then Edwin's huge cock rammed into my backdoor.

"Forgive me, Lord," I squealed bloody murder as Edwin smoothed and slapped my ass.

"You're so fucking tight, Superstar. My dick's so hard because it responds so fucking well to you." He continues his torture.

I couldn't think, I just cried and shook my head. I thought the worst would be over, but I was highly mistaken

Elijah then reached down and opened my legs.

"Aaggh," I cried out.

"Shut your," Edwin then stopped as Elijah enveloped me into his arms.

Elijah's Adam's apple rose and fell. He then squatted down and licked my core. His tongue penetrated inside of me as he nibbled and sucked my pussy. His brother moved in and out of me as he claimed my ass.

The warmth of the blood ran down my legs.

What's worse, Elijah had risen and met my eyes. The rage on his face told me that I was in hell and there was no way out. Then all of a sudden his dick then slammed into my front ripping into my vagina. He claimed my virginity.

I cried and muttered nonsense, I swear I thought my soul left my body. I wished I was dead, instead of seeing a pool of blood under my feet. I lean my head towards Elijah, with a silent plead. He kissed my head and uttered. "Baby, I love the way you feel. It'll be over soon."

"Yeah, you like it rough, bitch," Over and over again, Edwin banged the inside of my ass—making it swollen.

Too spent, I couldn't yell or call for help as they found their own pleasures. The whole time I was smacked around and being sexually abused for pleasure, I kept asking God for forgiveness because I was heavy chested and for being a tease.

Then darkness took over and my body was numb. Once I felt my hands and feet free, I collapsed right back into Elijah's arms. He gave me a warm cloth to wipe the blood off of me and wrapped one of the grey blankets around me. As he carried me over to the flowered couch, he gently wiped my tears away. "Superstar. I didn't know you were a virgin. I thought for sure you had given yourself to Garrett."

Speechless, I shook my head. Horrified, I just stared at

the bloody carpeted floor. I could barely keep my eyes opened and my body told me to rest, I passed out in his arms. Waking up every few minutes with a warm rag on my lady parts. As Elijah's grey eyes always watching me—wanting to say something but he never does.

It became a ritual when Seth and Millie left Elijah in charge. The more Edwin tried to physically abuse me, Elijah would protect me only so he could torture me with whips and floggers at the pier and in the cottage. My body would always betray me and sing to him, Violet. That's what scared me the most."

After telling this horrific story, Violet doesn't say a word or move from where's she's sitting. Tears roll down her chin. Various stages of grief wash over her face, from denial then anger. I catch her muttering to herself, as she tries to bargain in her head as her hands flip side to side. Only words I could get, "If I wasn't too wrapped up in boys," or "I should have noticed the signs."

After, debating with her own conscious, she cries uncontrollably, then she smacks herself. "I don't have to accept this shit of not being there in the past, but I am here now."

"Vi?" I ask and gently nudge her. "You're not saying anything and it's scaring me."

"Kayla Ashby, out of all the secrets to keep," she states in horror. "This one you could have told us. My dad would have taken you in and you would never had to be around those awful hateful people again."

"It wasn't that easy." My hand becomes jittery and I move up from the couch and finger brush my hair.

"Elijah told me that he would hunt down anyone who I care about, including my birth mother." I pace around the room.

"Don't you get it? He's the worse one out of the two of them. He makes a threat and follows through Just ask Wyatt."

"What happened to Wyatt?" Violet's curiosity got the best of her.

"Wyatt knew the boys were abusing me in some way." I let out a large breath. "He confronted Elijah on the football field and the bastard smashed his ribs in while tackling him at practice." I choke and continue as my voice becomes hoarse. "Elijah came home that day and beat the hell out of me thinking I said something. I swear on my life I never told anyone. "The beating" was for my own good or at least that was what I was told. Yeah, this beating was horrible.

I had to strip down into my panties and kneel in front of him. Elijah undid his black belt and whipped me. The black piece of leather slashed every inch of my body. But that wasn't good enough for him." I wave my palms up in the sky like I'm speaking to the Lord himself. "He snagged one of Seth's back whips with the spikes on it. He whipped me so hard, VI that I had broken ribs. He proceeded to burn off my hair in order to see my face at all times, so he could tell if I was lying or not. You always wanted to know why I cut all my hair off. Well now you know I had no choice."

"I tried to tell Millie, but she of course turned the other cheek, told me a little sibling fighting is normal. You asked why I never wear shorts, or shirts that show off my body, well there are your reasons. I'm a god damned freak! I look like Frankenstein. I even have the scars to prove it and also a friendly reminder of my horrible past." The tears slide down my face.

My best friend pops her lips, she then taps her right hand on the couch. I gradually walk over, plop down, and relax my arms.

"When are you going to learn that the people who love you will go to great lengths to keep you safe," she utters as she reaches for my hands. "Especially, your best friends."

A knock from the door startles me and I squirm. Garrett leans on the door cleaned up in a jacket and wife beater. Holy hell, I should be in heaven! He's beautiful and for the first time.... I notice him as a man. The wounds around his knuckles ooze, and dried blood from his swollen lip to his jaw, makes me want to kiss every inch of him and make the pain and anger go away.

I just hide my face in my hands, sniffling. Violet wraps her arms around me then she whispers, "You need to tell Garrett what you just told me." She then kisses my forehead like a mother and straightens herself out.

"I'll give you two sometime alone." She walks over to Garrett and mutters, "Give her time, but listen to what she has to say." She winks at me then leaves.

"Okay." He jokingly scuffs his feet towards the couch.

I don't budge and hug myself while more tears followed.

He kneels down in front of me and grabs my hand— gently tugging them away from my chest. My eyes wander the other way, I just can't look into his serene blue eyes after what he witnessed or seeing me like this... weak and broken.

"Kayla, I need to see your lovely face. Please look at me and talk to me. I want to protect you, if you let me," he pleads as his sapphire eyes dance.

I slowly raise my head and smirk, however, my lips tremble. "I'm ready to tell you my story." I tilt my head and stutter. "Remember how we used to meet at the church so I could help you read?"

"Yeah," he answers as he plays with my hands. "Because of your kindness and patience with helping me read." He gently touches my forehead. "If it wasn't for you Kay, I wouldn't have stayed on the right side of the tracks or become a publisher."

"Well there's more to St. James than meets the eye." I

utter. "I'm going to tell you the story how you and I became close friends, but first I'm going to tell you the story of the reason I snuck out at night and ran to the only place I felt safe."

Every day after Elijah and Edwin took my innocence, I would sneak out at night to St. James Cathedral off of 6th Avenue. I would stare at the antique golden stone building that looks like a castle, with the black and white stain glass of Jesus holding his arms out for the lost on the top of the entrance way.

Tears poured down as I wiped my cheeks. I walked into the church as the open ceiling's light shine white. I stroll to the end of the pews and dropped to my knees in front of Mother Mary and baby Jesus. Shakily, I lit a candle then prayed to our Lord to forgive me for my sins and asked for a miracle to take place.

"Kayla?" A friendly voice from behind gave me hope.

Has my miracle been answered?

"Yeah?" My palm wiped over my eyes as Garrett plopped down next to me.

"What are you doing here?" He asked as smiled. "I wouldn't picture you in a place like this."

"Why? Because I don't have a filter." I eased on my knees. "For your information I was praying for my mother to come find me."

"I could understand," He says. His blue eyes peered up at Mary. "It must be hard being a debutant."

"That's what you think of me?" My eyes fogged up. "I'm a princess. There's a lot more to the story than I like to share." I rose up to leave.

"Please wait." Garrett snagged my arms. "I didn't mean to say it like that. It's just being around someone who's like a goddess."

He cleared his throat. "Please sit."

Getting lost in his eyes, I sat down and glanced over at the book he was reading.

"Utopia?" I asked.

"Oh, this," He stuttered and scratched the back of his head. "I'm trying to read it, but I ah…"

"Having trouble with it?" I looked at him through the corner of my eye—hiding behind my hair.

"Yeah." Like he usually did when I like to hide from people, he pushed away the hair from my face. "I have a hard time reading."

"Oh." I bit down on my lips then said. "I could help."

"I'd like that." He handed me the book.

"This is actually one of my favorites." I flipped through the pages as he moves closer to me. Fascinated by the book, I spoke to him like he was Wyatt. "I would love to have this in my family life, a world of peace and serenity, not. Full of malice and hatred."

"Wow." Garrett's voice squeaked. He cleared it, again. "You're very good reading this stuff."

"Oh, it's not stuff," I answered as my eyes gazed up at Mary. "A book can take you away from the hardship of your life, into a world of fantasy and love, where dreams and wishes come true."

"Do you believe that dreams could come true, Kayla?" He asked as his hand reached over to mine.

"There's always hope," I answer as my eyes fogged up again and I sniffled.

"You see Garrett, the reason why I went to that church was for my sanity and hoping that some kind of miracle would happen, hoping to take me away from that miserable place. What's worse was before graduation, I tried telling Millie and Seth what the boys did to me and do you know what the bitch said." I wipe the snot and tears with my sleeves. "I shouldn't have provoked them with my behavior or wearing slutty clothes." I angrily sigh and look Garrett straight in the eyes. "The Fucking cunt Millie and Douchedog Seth decided to write me off and wrote a check just to 'shut me up.' He then asked me to leave everything behind and vanish so this secret can be well hidden." After I went through the horrible details of Edwin and Elijah, I wrap it up with the lovely Senator and his wife, I take a couple of breaths and say, "Why would anyone want someone who's broken?"

Garrett reaches up and plops down next to me on the couch. He gently grabs my face and stares into my eyes. He whispers close to my mouth. "Kayla, survivors are never broke or weak." He then kisses my forehead and the tears keep trailing down my face. "You are the bravest woman I have ever met and I'm in love with you." He smirks. "I think I always have been. Wyatt was right, I was too chicken shit to say anything, but tonight, when I saw the fear etched into your face, I knew." He places my hands up to his chest as his heart pounds like a base drum. "I had to protect you." He then brushes his lips against mine. This kiss is the sweetest kiss I have ever known. I wrap my arms around his neck as Garrett places my head on his chest. "I will protect you, Kayla. I swear to you, you won't have to go through this alone. I will be here for you as long as you let me. I will never leave your side."

"Garrett, please don't promise me the world when you can't protect me from it," I mutter and sniffle.

"You are right Kayla, I can't make promises like that, but I'd damn sure try if it would keep that stunning smile on your face." He whispers in my ear, "I would offer you the world."

I look over at the photograph of Wyatt and his mom playing catch and more tears roll down my face. "What a mother should be," I state as I peer over to the photograph of the mother and child, again—the love and protection in her eyes, made me realize, I may not have it, but I have a different love. I will have to protect my loved ones from the Stanton's. I look back at Garrett. "Garrett, I can't let you take the fall for this, if anyone gets in trouble for this, it needs to be me."

"Ashby, do you really think I would let you take the fall for anything? We're not teenagers," he utters and presses his chin on my head. "Besides, the only ones who are in deep shit are the Stanton assholes. I will make them pay dearly."

"All I want Garrett, is the amazing kiss I just experienced. Please just kiss me again. Like you did outside, I want to feel all your emotions again, with just one kiss." I gaze into his crystal clear blue eyes again, and smirk. "I want you to kiss me like I'm the only woman in the world."

"Oh, baby, that'll never be a problem." His fingers move to my mouth and skim my lips. "You have always been the only woman in my world." He leans in and claims my mouth.

"It's about damn time," Violet leans on the doorframe. She then calls over to Garrett's twin. "Wyatt, they finally made out."

"It's about bloody time." Wyatt walks in with a huge smile on his face. "Babe, let's give them some time to themselves." Like a gentleman, he escorts Miss. Violet Palmer out of his office with his arm around her waist.

Garrett and I both smile at each other as our foreheads meet.

Chapter NINE

The Phone Call....

"If you're going through hell, keep going."----Winston Churchill

The annoying ring from the land phone wakes up a grumpy Senator Seth Stanton from a dead sleep. He slightly pushes up to a sitting position and his hand clumsily glides along the nightstand and turns on the lamp. He then grabs his glasses and flips them on.

"Why the hell is the phone ringing at this god forsaken hour?" Millie mutters and gently stretches. She opens the drawer to the other nightstand next to her bed and takes out a mirror and hot red lipstick. She then glides it across her mouth trying to look like she has just stepped out of a salon even though it's four in the morning.

"I don't know, Millie, that's why I'm going to pick it up and answer it, Lovey," the senator grumbles. "Someone better have dropped out of the fucking race." Seth screams into the phone as he grinds his teeth, "or dropped dead."

"You have a collect call from Edwin Stanton," the automatic voice states. "At the Seattle Police Department: to accept these charges press one."

"Son of a bitch." Seth runs his right hand through his salt and pepper hair. "Damn it, Millie, your son has been arrested again. It had to be one of them. Not something else like a scandal on Senator Brown, so that I can be in the lead." His gray eyes stare at his wife. "Noo. It has to be one of our kids."

"Seth, stop being such an asshole that you normally are and just accept the god damn call." She puckers her lips then says, "They are still our babies." She fluffs up her hair and places the mirror and lipstick back into the drawer...

Seth mumbles under his breath, ignoring his wife like she's the family dog. Angrily, he presses the number button hard. "What the hell son, you know we're in the middle of a god damned campaign," Seth scolds and immediately let into him. "I can't afford to have any bad publicity."

"Yeah dad, love you too," Edwin says with sarcasm. "I know about your campaign, but this time, it wasn't my fault."

"Edwin you always blame the person next to you. Who is it this time? Gandhi? Your mother? The preacher down the street? You just can't ever behave." Aggravated, the senator rubs his face with his left hand. "God, you're such a fuck up."

"It was Kayla Ashby's fault," his son stutters.

"That's original, I fixed that problem years ago,' he scribbles on his paper. "Because of you two asses and all of your fucking sex antics."

"Yeah well, Dad, your problem's back and I've seen her," Edwin states. "You know, I do know what she looks like."

"Yes, son," Seth mutters. "I'm sure you know her figure quite well." The senator's mind ponders as he taps the pencil on the notepad. "If this is possible, which it shouldn't be because she left us when she was eighteen, I need to make sure she clams up and I mean clams up." His blood pressure spikes, "or I'm screwed."

"Seth, honey what is he saying?" Millie shoves his shoulder. "Is my baby okay? Talk to me. What's going on?"

The senator presses the cordless phone on his chest. "Kayla's back. Twiddle Dee and twiddle dumb ass are trying to see her." He brushes his hair hard like he's going to rip in out of his roots. Seth then taps the cordless phone on his forehead.

"This is all your fault." Millie shuffles off the bed while throwing on her red silk robe. She paces the bedroom. Her voice cracks. "Everything you do in the public eye, they watch. Such as the little vixens you like to spank." She hysterically bawls her eyes out. "No, this can't be happening. She never was supposed to come back," she mumbles. She points to Seth, "Fix it now."

"Dad, did I fuckin' lose you?" Edwin yells through the phone. "Hello, I have only one call."

"No your mother's having a nervous breakdown." Seth lets out a deep breath and answers, "You need to hold on before I let your ass rot in that cell."

"Well tell her to take a Xanax or better yet, take the shot of scotch setting on the nightstand," his ignorant son suggests.

"Millie, calm down and just pray like you're in the fuckin mission," the senator demands then speaks to his son as he grits his teeth. "What the hell are you in there for?"

"Assault and Battery," Edwin questions himself as his voice drops.

"Oh, Christ's sake," flabbergasted, Seth yells into the phone. "Out of all the woman you could easily lay your hands on, you had to go after Kayla Ashby? Do you know the term 'let sleeping dogs lie?' Your brother does, why not you?" He angrily asks. "She's not worth it!"

"Dad, remember your blood pressure," Edwin grunts. "Just come bail me out of this dump."

"You do exactly what I say," Seth orders. "I'm going to get your sorry ass out of jail. I'll call my attorney, Dennis Dewey. Do not say another word until we all get there. And DO not GO anywhere **NEAR KAYLA ASHBY, UNDERSTAND ME**. I need to find your DAMN brother and tell him as well."

"Elijah, knows about her pops he's seen her as well."

"Why can't you two just leave her the fuck alone, no

pussy is that fucking good?"

"Well there goes the luxury, Millie." Seth abruptly slams the phone on the charger and lies down in his sleigh bed. His arm rests on his forehead. "I don't know how I'm going to pull this off."

"No baby, we are not going to lose everything." Millie crawls onto the bed and relaxes on his shoulders. She massages his chest. His arms move as he moans. "You'll have your press conference and you will negotiate your way out of this, like you always do. Starting with the Captain." Her red painted nail skims his chin. She then takes hold of it, "and you are going to find a way to get Kayla Ashby out of the picture and this is time it needs to be permanent, or I will do it myself."

"Millie you are the antichrist," Seth shrieks at her. "You don't have the balls to pull the trigger."

"Watch your mouth, Seth." She folds her lip then continues, "Remember I know your dirty little secrets."

"Are you threatening me, Millie?" He laughs. "That's rich. You know I don't deal well with ideal threats."

"Seth, I can promise you this. It's not a threat. Get rid of her, or I will take matters into my own hands." She chastely kisses his lips. He grunts as he becomes hard. "Don't let the pearls fool you dear, I can ruin your life in a matter of a minute." She kisses his neck. "With just one." Then she nibbles on his ear then whispers. "Phone call."

"You are more than a spawn, Millie. You're Satan himself." He lifts her head and brushes back her hair. "Just remember if I had stayed on the right side of the tracks, you wouldn't have been able to climb the ladder." He pushes her off of him and rolls out of bed. He snatches the phone and walks over to the large cedar walk in closet—snags a suit and places a call on his cell. "Dennis, Seth. I need you to do me a favor. I know it's four in the morning, but one of my sons found himself on the other side of the law. Meet me at the Seattle Police Station in fifteen minutes."

Dennis grunts, "Seth, do you think we can…"

"Dennis, I don't want to fucking hear it, get your dick out of the whore's pussy you have it in and meet me there… **RIGHT FUCKING NOW.** End of discussion." Seth slams the end button and throws the phone on the bed. "Millie, get dressed and wear something presentable. I'm sure there will be press."

"Yes dear, as you command." She bows to him and goes straight to her side of the closet then pulls out a navy blue pantsuit with matching pumps.

"Don't show your ass, take your meds and be charming," he instructs.

"Why of course dear, I wouldn't think of being any other way." She shakes her ass at him. He playfully hits it. "How is it that Kayla Ashby can cause so much trouble? What does she want? I mean we took her in, for God's sake, and this is how she repays us. I always knew she was trouble."

"Millie, I don't have time for fifty fucking questions." He dresses. "I'll handle her."

"Okay, Seth, I trust you." She sighs.

"Good, now let's get a move on. We have until eight am before the press has a field day. And when we get into the car, keep your mouth shut, I don't want to have your annoying voice in my head while I come up with answers for the god damned vultures." He looks over at her as he tries to do his tie.

She kindly strolls up to him and fixes it, then nods.

What a draining, emotional night. Not only did I just spill my guts to Violet and Garrett, I told Wyatt and he rocked back and forth on his heels holding his bat. He then swung his bat across the bar, breaking the top shelf liquor. Thank GOD for Violet and her soothing voice, cuddling him. I never seen Wyatt lose it; never mind breaking down and falling into a million pieces. All I want to do is go to bed and put this this night behind me.

"Babe, why don't I stay with you tonight?" Garrett wraps his arms around me and kisses my cheek. "Let me get the truck."

"Okay," I answer shyly. Garrett kisses the top of my forehead and heads out the door.

I drop my head as my hair falls into my face. "Wyatt, I'm really sorry for what happened, I was trying to protect all of you."

"Ashby." Wyatt lifts my chin. "You're not going to go through this alone. Violet and I will stay at the house too. These demons will pass." He embraces me with a huge bear hug. "I love you kid. You are part of my family. And I like to protect my family. Just don't ever do something fucking stupid like you did to us again."

As I wait for Garrett on the barstool, I find myself nodding to sleep.

Men and women stroll in an atrium. The stones that protect the exotic plants have engravings on them. As I walk towards the stones, I peer at the unique plants-- Dumb Canes, Ficus, Peace Liles, and orchids. The river in the middle trickles down a pebble stone path to a small pond where different color fish swim around. The bottom of the pond has SVP engraved in it. They head into this new sex Club called ~ S'il Vous Plait~ which means Please in French. The medieval halls had a familiar smell—the smell of sex and money. The dark halls echoed as my pink stilettos tap on the smoothed maroon rock floor with the color black swirled into it. I browse at the white lit candles that are hung by the torch wall sconce.

Rowdy, a 6'4" man who's completely naked expect for a diamond cut black dog collar around his neck, walks by me. When he glances in my direction all I can see is a batman mask covering his face.

Even though I never met the man, I know his name.

I don't know whether to turn and run, or stay and play. Being very curious, I continue my steps toward the small candle lit hallway with what looked like bedrooms on either side. "I wonder why the rooms have their own color scheme."

I slow up my pace even more as I head to the room directly in front of me.

Tommiesina--the beautiful dominatrix—appears in front of me. The fiery red head has subtle breasts that make you wish you were a baby breastfeeding on one of them. The tattoo of throngs curves into knots that are shaped like roses covering her hour glass body. Each rose has an initial in them. She motions her index finger for me to follow her to the room. As we enter the dark lit room, my wardrobe suddenly changes to black lace panties and stockings with four-inch black heels.

I'm in fucking shock.

My mouth waters and my darkest desire inches its way to the service as I scan the room. The pale green sex room has every toy possible neatly spread on a marble end table. My eyes fixate on the riding crops and floggers hung with care along the wall. Next to the swing is an open bathroom with a drop in tub. The tall flaming red candles surround the floating bed. A woman with legs for days has black hair and is handcuffed to the headboard and footboard.

Tommiesina attaches a strap on and crawls onto the bed. She saddles the dark haired beauty and inserts the strap on. Her perfectly tattooed hearts that are just below the hip line, points to the freshly shaved pussy—waiting to be pounced on. Fast and hard, she slams into the opening of her soaking wet pussy.

The dark haired beauty delightfully hollers.

Was I seeing this right? Oh wow could I do that? Would she?

"Me next" I blurted like I'm an eager honor student trying to get a high grade. I couldn't help it, the words just flow out of my body.

Oh, shit. Did I really just say that out loud?

"Come join us love," The deliciously enticing women involved asks in a raspy voice.

I froze. My eyes looked to the door for an escape route and to the bed. My mind ponders as I think of the poem the one road Less Taken. If I leave, I'll always wonder what I missed out on. If I stay, oh L the passion of erotic ecstasy.

The tattooed beauty then removed her strap on and casually strolled toward me. She licks my lips then, smoothly and exquisitely gently sucks my ears and neck. After, she brushes my lips and removes my black lace panties.

She moistened two of her fingers inside of her mouth and flips me so my back side is showing. She pushes my hair to the right side of my neck and slips her wet fingers inside my now dripping pussy as her other arm wraps around my waist. Slowly, she slips her fingers in and out. I moan as my head leans towards her left shoulder.

"It's now or never," she utters.

"Yes," I grunt.

While she was working her magic with her two fingers, she leads me to the bed. After, the dominatrix reaches the marble table for another strap on. She kisses every inch of me while gently pushing me down on the bed. The tattooed woman gives the strap to the dark haired beauty and continues dipping her fingers and penetrating my center core.

Their mission is now very clear, as they both begin to touch and caress me. My whole body becomes their playground and I'm unable to control it. As their hands massage my breasts, they both take turns sucking on them and her tongue circles the harden nipples. She straps on the cock while Tommiesina's fingers continue their delicious torture.

My mind has left my body and before I know it, my arms reach up to the beautiful woman wearing the strap and yank her towards me, pleading for my body to be filled by her... The tattooed woman lifts my legs high as the other woman moves around her to fulfill my request.

The tattooed beauty passionately and seductively kisses me while whispering softly in my hair to control and calm my breathing. The other woman delves into me with waves of pleasure that I felt my body leave the bed.

With my eyes closed, I enjoy the gentle kisses and forceful fucking that I asked for. I groan and feel my spirit leaving my body. I suddenly feel a different sensation; warm, sweet, and moist but very different.

I opened my eyes to my surprise the sexy tattoos I had been admiring were now right in my face. How the hell does she expect me to eat pussy? Her clit waves in my face waiting for me to indulge.

Well it's worth a shot. I slightly lick the salty taste of cum after I circle the tongue around the moist folds. Then my mouth takes over—sucking and nipping her clit. The moistness of her pussy drips down my chin.

She penetrates me, she pushes my legs up to reach the back of the tattooed woman sitting on my face. Tommiesina turns her head slightly and claims the dark haired beauties mouth.

I'm fucking enjoying this torture.

My face and cleft are so wet and pulsating and I let out a loud but muffled moan! "OH PLEASE!"

All at once the brunette works the cock harder, deeper, and faster and the tattoos above my head are bouncing to the same rhythm, and cum drips off my chin as my body convulses.

The damn alarm rings again, the pink satin sheets cover parts of my body, showing my legs.

"Why can't I have a dream about Garrett for a change?" I toss my pillow on my face punching it.

It's been a living hell since "fight night" at Club Fuchsia. Scared shitless and not able to get a good night sleep, Violet and Wyatt took over and have been staying with me while Garrett's out of town on a merger—making sure I'm taking care of myself. Well, in Wyatt's case making sure twiddle Dee and twiddle dumb don't invade my safe place. Hell, I even sleep with the bat in my bed now.

The only time I have been able to get shut eye and I dream of being a submissive to women. God, I refuse to be one of those women who jump or curtsy on command. Unless, I get to play Dom. Kayla, get that idea out of your damn head.

My cell rings.

"Hey, Baby checking in," Garrett's sweet voice is what I need.

"Hey," I hug the soft white down comforter pillow with my right arm, wishing he was here. "I'm okay. I miss you."

"I miss you too," he utters. "I'll be home before you know it." Silence reaches through the phone, then he clears his throat. "Kay, have you decided on what we discussed?"

"Gar, a great deal," my voice trails off. "But, I can't give into them and leave my home." I hug my pillow tighter. "Even, if I can have my happily ever after living with you."

"I just…" his voice scratches. "I don't want anything to happen to you. I know you love your place and you have state of the art alarm systems, he continues choosing his words carefully, "but it's not enough. At least at my apartment, there's stronger security measures and no one will be able to get in that aren't warranted."

"I know." A smile reaches from ear to ear, knowing and loving that he cares about my safety. "This is one of the many reason's I love you." I glance at the clock. "Shit, it's late." I rush out of my bed and race into the closest—holding the phone in one hand and whipping through clothes for today. "I have get to the police station and drop off plans at the office."

Rushing down the stairs, I button my jacket and grab my

Vera Bradley messenger bag and plans heading out the door.

"Hold on Gutterslut," Violet orders.

I spin around and snap, "What? I'm late."

"Kay." She hands me coffee and a scrambled egg burrito that Wyatt made. "You forgot something."

"Yes, Mom." I roll my eyes. The pink Vera Bradley messenger hangs on my right lower arm as I grab the burrito. "Will you two stop being parents?"

"We will when you start taking better care of yourself," she lectures like a mother.

"Whatever." I say then I take a bite... "This is so good." I take another bite. "It's like an orgasm in a wrap."

She laughs uncontrollably. "See," she says. "You needed something to eat."

"Hey, Kay," Wyatt calls, he comes around the corner. "Hungry, are we?" His eyebrows furrow.

"She's having oral sex with her breakfast." Violet smirks and leans on the door frame. "Someday, I'm going to find how you became an unbelievable cook, Wyatt."

"I'll never share my secret." He chuckles. "Listen, Ashby, I have a huge shipment coming in today for the club, so if you need me I'm a phone call away."

After wolfing down my burrito, I take the coffee Violet gave me and nod.

"Swear on it," he demands.

"Yeah, yeah, I swear. I got what you're saying but its day time. I'm just going five blocks up the road to the office." I announce. "Hell, I might even walk it."

"The fuck you will," screamed Wyatt and VI at the same time and it echoes through the room.

"Okay! Calm down, I'll drive," I reach for my messenger bag and lift to my shoulder. "I'm the one who is paranoid y'all and you act like it's you. " I open the front door and sip my coffee. After I wipe my mouth "oh, after you bump uglies, make sure you both lock the all the doors and set the alarm before you go."

"Okay, buttercup go do what you need to do," Violet shoos me along with her hands. "We will lock up."

"Make sure you guys wash up and stay out of my room. I mean it. I don't want sperm juice on my bed. I will knock the shit out of both you," I lecture. After I walk out the door as they laugh their ass off. Glad my comments are amusing.

I get into the beast and put the keys in the ignition. I stare out the window. Being in the silence I gather my thoughts, rest my head on the head rest of my seat and close my eyes. I send a prayer out to God, the universe or whoever would listen.

"Dear God, I come to you today to make me a strong woman who does not let the hardships of my life tear me apart. And with this strength that you give me, please help me accomplish what I want even though I may be torn apart. I really need your help. Amen."

I buckle my seatbelt and turn on the ignition. I don't turn on the radio, I just roll down the window and listen to the world passing me by.

Since it's a weekend morning, I'm able to sneak in the office, grab what I need and send out the plans for one of the firm's big clients. Best part about it, no one was in the office to ask ten million questions.

I get back into the beast, start the ignition.

"It's now or never, Kayla," I whisper. "You have to put these ghosts behind you." I pull out of the office parking lot, making my way to the dreaded police station.

Each step I take, I say a silent prayer looking at the glass building of the Seattle PD. As I open the heavy glass doors, I spot an image of two people having small talk with one of the Captains on the force. This is an image I didn't expect or want to see.

I stroll up to the glass counter. The sound of my flats makes a hollow noise that you could hear a mile away. I press a black button. I look around the hall. Buckets are on the side collecting donations for Wounded Warrior projects; old cell phones are put in another donation box for the soldiers overseas and a second hand clothes box for families who are in need. Paintings of Police Captains who served in the past proudly stands out.

"May I help you," a voice disrupts my thoughts.

"May I see Office Jernigan," I ask.

"And who might you be?" the tired frosted hair receptionist asks. The wrinkles on her skin make it look like she has been here since the Stone Age.

"I'm Kayla Ashby, and I need to speak with him about an incident regarding me and Mr. Stanton," I calmly explain, but my adrenaline is at its peak and my hands begin to shake.

She pressed a button on one of the intercoms. "There's a Kayla Ashby here to see you," She grunts. "Okay." She peers at me. "Please have a seat. He'll be right with you."

I take a seat on the old stained wooden bench. Of course I'm under the domestic and sexual abuse posters. Can it be more humiliating?

Watching the built in gold clock, the second hand moves like a turtle. Fidgeting, I pull out my phone and earphones. I hit play and start my notes on the high rises I've been working on.

Deep in concentration, erasing mistakes and using the phone as well as a calculator. Dark shadows appear from the corner of my eye. I peek up and there they are; the two people who brought me into the hell hole that I escaped from. It's Senator Seth and Millie Stanton.

They have their noses up in the air as they casually walks toward me. Being like the cocky arrogant snake in the grass that he is, he slithers up to me looking so regal. God he makes me sick. Of course Millie, who's dressed to the nines with her perfect hair up in a French twist!

"Well, look who is back in town. You have not been home for very long and you are already causing a ruckus," says Seth. He straightens his tie.

"Seth, look I am not here to have a debate with you or cause trouble." I look him straight in the eye, showing no fear. "I am here to talk to the police about your son."

"Yes. About that," He says like his the king of the city. "The charges will get dropped and the world will never know." Frustrated, he runs his fingers through his salt and pepper hair. "So let's just drop the charade, and just tell me how much it will cost me this time."

"Look here you slimy bastard." I jerk my head and narrow my eyes. "I never wanted your god dammed money." Gripping my notepad to my chest, I continue, "You paid me off to keep my mouth shut, but this time there are witnesses. So it's not just me."

At that moment, an overweight forty year old officer walks out and asks, "Who is Miss Ashby?"

"That would be me," After my steady glare, I eagerly remove myself from the bullshit that rests with the Stanton's and walk down the hall with Officer Jernigan.

"Oh, Kayla, dear. Please come by the house sometime, we miss you." Her artificial tone of caring hit a nerve and my shoulders tightened.

There she goes like she's the queen of the state. You got to be fucking kidding, they're actually holding hands.

The officer has me sit at one of the desks as we go through the paperwork.

"Officer Jernigan I don't have a lot of time and I'm sorry that it has been a few days, but I had to gather my thoughts," I mutter as I hunch over fiddling my fingers in my lap.

"It's ok Miss Ashby, we understand." He gently smiles. "I want to let you know before this goes any further that what you say will be recorded; it's in your best interest as well as the stations." He moves his seat to get comfortable. "Are you ok with that?"

"Yes sir," my voice is almost at a whisper.

"Miss Ashby," he begins.

"Before we go any further please call me Kayla." I itch my nose. "I am not old enough to be a Miss anything."

"I understand. Kayla, so please tell me your side of the story, as I have heard from the others," he states as he leans back in his chair.

"Well, I don't remember much as I try to block out when there is anything to do with the Stanton's," I stutter. I hear my heart beat as it pumps loudly. "Especially Elijah and Edwin."

"Just take your time." His soft voice helps my pulse to slow. "Tell me as much as you can remember."

"Okay, I was at the club and I was having a good time dancing and drinking. I had the five drink limit," I express as I speak with both my hands.

"Five drink limit?" Officer Jernigan asks.

"Wyatt Winters, the owner of the club; its strict policy." I utter and shrug.

"Oh?" he sighs. "Continue, please." He nods his head and writes down notes on his yellow legal pad.

"I was still very much aware of my surroundings." I

squirm in my seat. "When out of nowhere Elijah was behind me I did not know it was him on the dance floor and he assaulted me. His dragon tattoo even has my initials in it on his neck. What's worse, he called me superstar which is a name I hate and told me to act natural and no one will get hurt." Tears stream down my face as he hands me some tissues. "Thanks."

"It's okay Kayla," he pauses the recorder. "You don't have to do this today. You can always come back."

"No I need to." I blow my nose and continue, "He told me that he missed me and that I had made a mistake when I left town."

"Do you mind telling me why you left?" The officer folds his hands on his desk.

"Well, I'd rather not if it has nothing to do with this case." I let out a deep breath. "So later on that night I was up at the bar and Edwin Stanton showed up. He grabbed my throat and slapped me. Then told me I was a cunt and a whore," I continue, "The rest was a blur. I just saw Garrett saving me and Violet taking me into Wyatt's office, while Edwin was taken to the security office in the front of the bar."

"Kayla," He reaches and stops the recorder. "I have been dealing with domestic assaults for years." He peers into my eyes. "Each one comes down to one thing." He holds up his index finger.

"What's that?" I ask.

"Trust" he bluntly says. "When you're ready to tell me why you left your home I'm here to listen and to put your demons to rest."

"I'm not ready." I fold in my bottom lip.

"I'll tell you what." He rises up from his chair. "I will be leaving the case open." He walks over and rests on his desk. "I think there's more to this than meets the eye."

"Thank you." My eyes wonder up to his gentle green eyes as I rise from my desk. "Is Edwin Stanton still in jail?"

"At this time he is but I know his lawyer has been here and so has Senator Stanton," he angrily mutters. "Off the record, the Senator has been schmoozing up to one of our Captains, so it seems that the case will be dismissed." He smirks. "But it doesn't mean I can't go through another avenue." The grandfather like man chuckles and hands me his card. "There are always a way around a politician," he says. "If you're ready, I'm here to help."

"Will do," I slightly smile. "I just want this shit to be over."

As I'm getting up to walk out the door, my phone goes off. I know that tune. I stop short. Trembling through my messenger bag. I peer down to the text.

It's the alarm company.

"Sir," I shakily say. "My alarm is going off at my house."

"Wait, Kayla." He waves a couple of police officers over to us. "Let me get a patrol car to follow you."

I haul ass out to my truck. I have the button pushed to call Violet.

"Vi?" My voice cracks. "Are you still at the house?"

"No, what is up?" She asks.

"My alarm went off and --- I was at the police station, so they are right behind me." I hit the gas pedal hard.

"Kay, don't do anything stupid." She has a nervous tick in her voice. "I will be right there; do I need to call Garrett?"

"Yes please, but I don't know if Garrett is back from his meeting but please call Wyatt too." I choke.

"Okay, no worries love," she replies. "Don't do anything until one of us or the cops get to your house.

I know it's fucking them. How in the hell did they get in

to my sanctuary, my home? Those bastards.

I finally pull into my parking space. I fly out of the car and rush into my house. I hit the number to my floor. "This is taking fucking forever," I grumble.

I made it to the floor and walk into the place.

"It's destroyed." My face softens as walk around.

Broken glass is spread from the kitchen to the living room. The television is ripped out the wall. My office is completely destroyed. The desk is flipped over and holes burnt into the plans that I have worked hours on and photographs smashed. There is even some dried blood circled around Garrett and me in high school.

Dreadfully, I walk into the bedroom and slowly glide to the bed. The cops call out my name and I answer.

Officer Jernigan, hustles behind me and said, "Kayla, please get out of the way so I can look in here."

Stunned, my index finger automatically points to the note on the bed...

"Kayla, I need you to step away from the bed." He walked over to the bed, and puts on the latex gloves, and picked up the note.

After he picks up the note. He then calls dispatch. "Shelly, we have a ten/ninety."

In big BOLD letters, it said:

BITCH YOU ARE GONNA DIE.

Chapter TEN

Demons....

"Believe in yourself! Have faith in your abilities!
Without a humble but reasonable confidence in your own
powers you cannot be successful or happy."---Norman Vincent
Peale

"Kayla?" sinister laughter whispers into my ear like the air. "You're dead bitch. And so is your fucking piece of shit boy toy."

I pop open my eyes, I push myself up and scan my room. Scratching noises come from the outside. I hesitantly grab the bat in my hand then head to the window. After slipping the bat under the curtain, I peak outside. The melted snow drops from the window screen.

"I've got to get a grip." I wipe the back of my hand. Someone envelopes their arms around my waist.

Forcefully, I shove the predator away from me and ready myself to swing the bat.

"Jeez, it's me." Garrett's palms surrender.

"I can't get their voices out of my head." I drop the bat and then fall to my shaking knees. He plops down next to me and caresses my back. "I'm so sorry."

"Babe. I am sorry, I didn't mean to scare you. But you look so exotic holding that baseball bat, I couldn't help myself. Maybe we need to go to the cages and just take out all the aggression. It's good for the soul," he jokes at my expense.

I snicker and lean closer to him. I want to be cherished and safe. He pulls me in, tighter. My head rests on his sculpted chest and I draw in his woodland scent. His mauve shirt hangs to the side as I try to wrap myself in it-- protecting me from the nightmares that have invaded my thoughts.

"I got you," he whispers. "Sleep baby, you're safe."

Hours pass, and the dreams disappear. All that went through my mind are colors of red, yellow, and orange. I blink my eyes as my head lies on his chest and his heart beats slow and steady. His fingers gently play with my hair. I look up at Garrett and brush his lips with my fingers.

"How long have I've been out for?" I ask.

"A couple of hours." He draws me closer to him, wrapping his love around me. "I carried you to bed, but I couldn't leave; I had to make sure you were safe." He chuckles "from your dreams."

"That's so sweet," I utter. My eyes glisten.

"Let's get something to eat." He rises from the bed. "I'll let you get ready."

"You know you can always stay in my bed at night." I lay my chin on my right hand "and do other things."

"Not until those asses are found and locked up." He kisses my forehead. "I have to think about the other things, because once I get a taste of you I will never want another." He taps my butt before he leaves. "Get changed."

"All right Garett, I'm horny as hell and you're being way too much like a gentleman." I slowly move and put on my robe and show some leg and flip my hair. My nipples are hard and standing at attention begging to be touched.

I walk out to the living room and strut by him. He peers up at me on the couch smiles then looks back down on his laptop while on his cell.

"Listen, Wyatt, Dr. Doyle's flying out today," Garrett says as his rub his jeans. "If you could let the cleaning crew into my condo."

"Gar, I'm going to take a bath." I lean on the doorframe to the bathroom relaxing my right leg over my left.

"Kay's fine" he types away. "She just needs someone to talk to other than us."

Did he just ignore me? Well Winters you have another thing coming. Nonchalantly, I turn my back to him and slip off my robe as it gracefully drops to the floor. Water flows gently into the claw foot tub as steam rises and the lavender smell of the bath gel calms my senses. Carefully, I place one foot, then the other, followed by the rest of me while water splashes. I lean back on to the plastic pink pillow and close my eyes.

Reba McIntyre's Somebody's Chelsea plays in the background.

Hmm. Garett must have turned on the stereo. This bath is what I needed to release unwanted stress.

Tears roll down my face, not because of the bullshit that's happening around me, it's all because of this one man who stole my heart with just a blink of an eye. I don't bother to wipe them away, I just let them go. It's at times like these I wish I knew my birth mom.

I picture her in my head, looking like me and her arms wide open for an embrace. I would tell her about the amazing friends I have and about Garrett.

My arm drapes around my forehead. The smell of woodlands hit my senses and I notice the water ripples, and it brings a sincere smile on my face. I open my eyes. Garret's eyes twinkle has they starve for my compassion.

"Hey," I utter.

"Hey," he utters. "Come here."

I slide over as he pulls me into his arms and I ease into his chest. Then he wipes away the droplets from my cheeks.

"Kay, talk to me." He massages my neck. "What's wrong?"

"It's nothing really," I moan. "I've been thinking with all the things that have happened." I sigh. "I wish knew my birth mother. I'm in such a messed up place right now that I don't think I can get out of this."

"I understand that baby, but I'm here. I won't let anything happen to you." He brushes his lips against mine then continues, "So let's take it one step at a time and see what we can eliminate."

"Okay, for starters, there was a lot of damage to Wyatt's club and I need him to know how really sorry I am."

"Kay, stop." He places two fingers on my mouth. "It's been taken care of and no you will not pay me back. I was the one who was the ass, not you."

I take his two fingers away. "How can you say that? If it wasn't for Edwin and Elijah, it wouldn't have been destroyed." I rest my head on his chest. "Then there's Millie and Seth. They just want to pay me off, again. I just want to tell them to shove it up their ass. I shouldn't have taken their money the last time. They did this. I should have stayed and fought, but honestly when you are eighteen and there is an offer of over half a million dollars to disappear that is what you do."

"Listen, you were only trying to find a way out," Garrett explains. "You were also protecting your friends and me." He squeezes me tight. "Kayla, it's the bravest and yet stupidest thing anyone has ever done for me and it's one of the many reasons why I love you." He drifts off and stares at the bathroom mirror. "You need to tell the cops everything, baby."

"I'm scared to," my lips tremble. "I want this shit to be over but I'm still that shy little girl inside."

Garrett lifts my chin and passionately kisses me while his manhood begins to swell. The water laps as his erection grows. The very essence of my womanhood comes alive. I'm like his personal vice as he controls every sensation in my body.

His blue irises darken and shine as he gazes through long dark eyelashes. God he is the most beautiful man on this earth. I flip around and gently kiss his chest. He growls deep from his throat after he lifts me onto his cock. I easily sink down, his cock continues to grow as my sex fills with his manhood inside of me. My voice vibrates along with his steady moan. Seductively, his lips touch my neck and make their way to the barbell on my breasts. He gently tugs them with his teeth, I shiver with joy. No words are spoken as we explore each other. Our eyes never leave each other...

"I have wanted to do this since the first day I laid eyes on you," he whispers and moans. He then takes control and lifts me. I'm barely on top of his cock. "If I knew how much love I had for you then, I would have looked for you a long time ago."

"Garrett, I need this, please don't leave me empty," I utter. "I want to feel you completely inside of me."

At that moment he slams into me. Moaning and hissing, I melt into his arms as we make love. This is where I want him to be, inside me, always. I didn't know that it could be like this because the only thing I have to compare it to is Edwin and Elijah. They were never gentle.

Garrett touches places that I did not know even existed. We rock back and forth, holding each other close, with all of the love and passion that we have bursting from within us.

After the first time making love with Garrett, I lay on his chest while we are still in the bathtub—becoming prunes. His heartbeat steadies as his pulse quickly races through his veins. He caresses my back while we come back to earth.

"Kayla, I'm just going tell you that was the best time I've ever had in the bathtub," he says with a nerdy smile.

"Yeah, it was supposed to be relaxing and refreshing." I snicker. "I'm both but, I'm really dirty and need a shower." I smile. "I don't know if I've got chills because of the water is now freezing cold or because I'm in love with the way you made my body sing. I'm tingling in all the right places, Garrett, but I really need to get in the shower and warm up because I'm freezing to death."

"Hmm." He kisses my forehead. "We need to fix that." He rises and turns on the shower. I of course admire the view. I place my arms on my hips as I look at God's gift to women kind. The muscular structure of this man is just amazing. One of my favorite parts of him is his suggestive shoulders. Those shoulders look like they could carry the weight of the world with no problems. Plus he's hung like a freaking horse too and he's all mine!

His blue eyes fixate on mine as he extends his right hand to help me out. I rise and he examines my body for the first time. His eyes run across the scars of the burn marks along my chest. He clears his throat and his Adam's apple rises and falls, dramatically. I gaze up him through my long lashes, my hair falls across my face --while a tear slides down.

"Don't cry baby, the scars make you more exquisite." He pushes back my hair. His arms become ridged. His forehead touches mine. His eyelids slowly shut.

"Don't say that." I take his hand and squeeze it. "They are an ugly part of my past. I have thought about laser surgery to try to remove them."

"Don't." His eyes pop open as he peers down and whispers in my ear. "You have a body of a goddess,

Kayla," His hoarse voice deepens. "I knew something was going on. I saw the signs," he clears his voice again and continues, "but I didn't know it was this bad." Then he drops to his knees and hugs my body as his face softens resting on my chest. His eyebrows rise when he gazes up to me. "Can you ever forgive me?"

"Forgive you for what? You did nothing wrong," I utter. "Umm. Hmm." I then take his other hand and swing them. "It was me, I made it possible to happen."

"NO," his voice rumbles. "You were an impressionable child and they took advantage of it." His body trembles. "Hell I know what abuse looks like ..."

"Gar?" I ask holding him closer.

"Wyatt and I didn't grow up with wine and roses." He gently rises up on his feet and brushes my forehead. "But that is a story for another time." Garrett then lifts up my chin. "I promise once we deal with all the demons of your past. I'll tell you mine." He reaches the cucumber and melon shower gel and face cloth.

"I need to make this up to you" his heart pounds through his chest like a jack hammer. "Turn around."

I do as he says. With a facecloth, he massages my back and then his left hand reaches my jewel. His right hand reaches my nipple and he begins to play. "Now that I have a piece of you, Ashby, I want more."

The intoxicating smell of the shower gel and his sensual torment gives me an idea. My throat rumbles.

"God, I love that sound," he murmurs. "I can't wait to hear you moan again, it is so damn sexy."

"Well, I owe you one Garrett." I announced "for taking care of me and being here for me." I spin and face him. I toss the face cloth out of the shower and I take the shower gel and squeeze some of the liquid in my right hand. Then I trail my fingers to his cock. I grab it and rub it fast and furious. Smooth and silky but the veins that run down the length makes me want to run my tongue along them.

His head snaps up as he grunts. Quickly, I drop to my knees. I playfully lick his shaft and the sounds coming out of this man have me dripping already.

"Babe are you trying to kill me?" He places his hands on my head. "You keep this up with that tongue of yours and I'm going to cum in your mouth."

That's all the encouragement I need.

I claim his cock and rub his veins with my tongue while my mouth concentrates on the suction. I glance up to see his eyes roll back and he braces himself with his back against the wall. Two hands hold my hair and Garrett begins to push in and out of my mouth.

"B. A. B. E!!" He calls out to me. "If you don't quit doing that you will be getting more than you bargained for."

I smile but I don't give him a chance to pull out of my mouth. I continue at warp speed. Licking and tasting, enjoying every bit of him. He in returns fucks my mouth.

"AHHHHH, FUCKKKKK!" He moans and cries. He leans back on the shower wall.

The salty and satisfying liquid washes down my throat.

I giggle at him as I lick my lips and slide my way up. At eye level, he caresses my chin and dips his tongue into my mouth—catching me by surprise as he tastes himself.

"Tastes good." He snickers. "Forgive? Fuck Kayla, I could die tonight and be the happiest man in the world. Your mouth could make the president change his mind on a war."

Chapter ELEVEN

Stealing Cinderella….

"You have to learn the rules of the game. And then you have to play better than anyone else."---Albert Einstein

"Garrett, do you know what time Dr. Doyle will be flying into Seattle?" Pacing around my bedroom, I grab my favorite ripped jeans, a pink tank, and a sweater.

"Kay, will you calm down, you're all jittery." He works on his lap top and peers up at me. A carefree laugh comes out of his voice, "How much caffeine have you had?"

"I just need her here." I reach for the pink boxers from my drawer. "I know you probably think I'm crazy, but I'm really not." I throw on my clothes. "She's like a mother to me," I continue, "You'll see when you meet her. She has a way of calming me down."

"I don't think you're crazy. Maybe a little nutty."

"OMFG, I can't believe you really said that." I snag a pillow and toss it at him. "But yes it's your fault, I'm nutty."

"And how so?" he tries to hold in his laughter.

"Well I'm nutty because you make me that way," I reach over my bed and brush his sweet lips. Then I take another pillow and playfully whack is face, "but Dr. Doyle --- is just freaking amazeballs. Are you sure it's OK she stays at your Condo?"

"I'm sure" his cell buzzes. He glances at it and then to me. "Babe, I have to swing by the condo and grab a file for work. I figure we can check on it to make sure it's up to your standards before we get to the airport."

"Okay, thank you." Completely, frazzled from making Patrice's stay welcoming.

"Kay, let's go." He holds out his left hand. "Everything will be fine."

"I just want it to be perfect for her." I shyly shrug my shoulders.

On the way to the airport in Garrett's silver Toyota Tundra, I turn the radio off again and listen to the outdoors. Garrett doesn't say a word, he just smiles as his blue eyes gaze at me through his aviator sunglasses.

His cell rings the tune from one of the James Bond movies. Garrett hits the Bluetooth button on his gray steering wheel.

"Winters," he courtly says.

"It's your fuckin Mary on the way to the airport to meet Kayla's friend," Todd sarcastically whines.

"You're doing a good deed." Garrett holds in his laughter.

"Yeah, yeah." Todd mumbles. "I would feel better if I know I'm picking up a babe."

"Hey, Kay, Todd wants to know if Dr. Doyle is hot." Garrett winks at me and takes my hand.

"She'll chew him up and spit him out." I squeeze his hand. "She does that with a lot of 'little' boys."

"That's my kind of woman." There's a pause and then Todd continues, "She's a Dr. of what exactly?"

"Idiot," Garrett mouths to me then speaks, "but Todd's heart is in the right place. Listen, we'll be there in fifteen."

"Fine," Todd mutters, "are we all set with the merger?"

"We're going ahead," Garrett replies. "As a matter of fact, I'm heading to the condo first to pick up the file."

"Sweet." Todd beeps on his horn as it blows through the speaker then he swears at what's I'm sure is a Sunday driver. "Sorry about that. Anyways, there's a press release that came across your desk you may want to look at."

"What press release?" Garrett asks as his right thumb drums on the wheel.

"I'm not your secretary, Sean is. He did say it has to do with the good ole' Senator Stanton."

"Yeah, I had a feeling that one would come back to bite me in the ass." Garrett squeezes my hand even more "and I'm pretty sure he's pissed because I pulled the funding for his campaign." His veins bulge through his hands. "I was going to back him because of Kayla but now I'm pulling it for my own selfish reasons." His Adams Apple bobs. "I hadn't even discussed this with Kayla."

Shocked and confused, I suck in my right cheek, not saying another word.

"Todd I've got to go," Garrett weakly ends the call. He then takes my hand and rests it on his lap. "Kay, I'm sorry. I pulled it the day I found out." He slows down and pulls into the rest area. He then turns facing   me. He whips off his sunglasses. "I didn't want anything associating me with him."

"It's okay." I fiddle with my fingers. "I didn't even know you had supported him. You didn't know what happened to me." I hide my tears. "But I'm sure he's pissed." I tug my shirt. "Can we talk about this later?"

"Babe are you mad?" He leans in as one hand rests on the steering wheel and his arm rests on the back of the passenger's seat. "I don't know if I could handle it."

I shake my head at him and turn to the window. My phone vibrates. I shiver. "That just scared the shit out of me."

"Hello," I answer. "Hello? What the hell?" I peer down to get the number but it states private. The call ends.

"Who was that?" Garrett's mutters.

"I don't know they didn't say anything." Before I can say anything else my cell rings again.

"It's Vi." I answer it, "Gutterslut, what's up?"

"Superstar," the words whisper through the phone. Instantly, I freeze, and nervously hold on the phone tight. "Please don't hurt her."

"Now, Kayla, You took my warning too lightly," Elijah utters. "I want you back. You have a choice; either your happily ever after or your friend."

"Don't give in Kay," Violet screams in the background.

"Shut up you fuckin' cunt," Edwin swears. A huge thump echoes through the phone; VI cries.

"Kayla, what is it?" Garrett demands. "You're as white as fucking ghost." His eyebrows narrow. "Give me the phone."

"Why?" then only words that slowly comes out of my mouth. Trembling, as I hold the phone, then I grab a hold of my chest. "Vi."

"Put me on speaker, Baby," Elijah orders "and I'll tell Prince Charming what we want."

I hit speaker and Garrett grabs my phone as Violet's piercing screams take hold of my heart. All I can do is wrap my arms around both legs and sob into them uncontrollably.

"What the hell?" Garrett snaps. "Stanton, what is it you want? Money? Fine it's yours, name your price?"

"I want what is ours!" Elijah seductively says, "Kayla at my bedside. I couldn't care less about your fucking money. What

I do care about is the woman in your truck. She is mine, I've told you this already."

"That I cannot do," Garrett abruptly answers tightening his hands around the phone. "Meet me somewhere Stanton and we can discuss this."

"FUCK you Garrett, she has one hour to be at the boat house or I will take great pleasure in fucking this fine piece of ass in front of me," He orders. "Shh, baby." Violet's voice vibrates with hidden cries. "Tell Kayla I won't fuck this blonde beauty gently and the beating will be for every year that superstar has disobeyed us. She knows my anger and she knows that I will enjoy making her bitch of friend bleed."

The line goes dead.

In the dark, musty boat house Edwin Stanton walk towards, Violet Palmer. As the tough blind bitch rests on the couch, her shirt practically ripped off of her and blue eyes swollen. Anger fills Edwin's blood stream. He cracks his jaw and rubs his chin.

"Fuck you Winters." He cracks his neck." You're a dead man when I see you."

"I see you're out of jail Edwin," the seductive voice says from behind. Edwin Stanton's body becomes rigid. Reagan Woodrow.

"Yeah no thanks to my dad who was taking forever to get me out." He walks over to Violet and touches her bruised skin. The blood seeps through the knuckle marks.

"No… I let you sit there," she says as her contacts shine.

"Why the fuck would you do that?" Dumbfounded, he asks, scratching his head.

"You're pathetic," her tone is sharp as a razor.

"Remember our deal. I bring Kayla Ashby to you and you wouldn't hurt Garrett. But her you can hurt. She is nothing but a fucking cunt scab."

"Wow really, you're grown and still harboring feelings of hatred towards her." Edwin chuckles. "I hate to tell you buttercup, Winters is on my shit list. He has been on my list since Kayla took an interest in him. Sorry to tell you but he will get his. Why do you hate Kayla so much? I know why I hate her but what is your beef with her?"

"She's another hoe who ruined everything." Her voice cracks as it whines. "She should have never fucking left Birmingham Alabama."

"Tough shit Darlin'." Edwin blows her off. "If you knew where she was the whole time why didn't you do something then?"

"Because I was waiting for you two asses to make a move." She grunts. "But no, I had to deal with idiots." She trails off. "Well one idiot and one who loves to play cat and mouse."

"Why the fuck didn't you tell me, Reagan?" Edwin's face hardens. "I've looked everywhere for her."

"Unlike you're brother, dumbass, you didn't look too far," The fair hair girl snidely states. "All you had to do was follow the paper trail," she continues. "Your dad may have paid her to leave, but I paid your dad to make her leave."

"The fuck you did." Edwin's fist forms ready to swing. "I don't know what the fuck you're talking about woman. My parents have money. He is the Senator and is running for President."

"Used to sweetie pie; they used to have money, now they are almost on poverty level." She kicks a piece of dirt at Violet. "Dearest Daddy lost his while he was gambling and having fun with any girl that wears short skirts and stilettos. Or should we call the dear ole' Senator. See what he did with his money. Or shall we call your mom?"

"Huh?" Edwin's blood rushes from his head to his feet. His pale face begins to perspire.

"Your daddy gambled away his money years ago Stanton. I gave him the lifestyle, that he was used too," Reagan snidely remarks. "Your mom found out and sealed her own fate when she fucked my dad," it continues. "That ended my parent's marriage so I should thank her."

"You fucking liar," he growls. "The old man may sleep around with anything that has legs, but my mother—hell no." He grits his teeth. "She's too chicken shit to do anything like that."

"Blah, blah…you'd be interested to know your mom has a shit load of skeletons," the bitch continues, "but it's not my place to say that. It is my place to tell you to make that fucking bitch Violet Palmer pay."

"I don't see what she has to do with any of this," Elijah states as he walks by his brother with a damp cloth. "Violet, this will sting but it'll help heal the bruises."

"Again it's not your place to question me, Elijah," she orders. "If you want your daddy and mommy to continue to have their lifestyle, then I suggest you do as I say. Starting with this bitch in front of us."

"Since when the fuck am I one of your pets," Elijah snaps and swings around to her. "I didn't agree to anything."

"Well, then you won't mind if I do this." Electric currents went through his twin's junk. Elijah Stanton holds both hands up surrendering to their own fate.

Chapter TWELVE

Revenge is Such a Sweet Thing....

"The purpose of our lives is to be happy. ---Dalai Lama

"I've got to get her," I rock back and forth in the driver seat then look straight into his eyes. "You need to take me home. Now."

"Kayla, I need you to calm the fuck down." Garrett places his hand on my knee and squeezes it.

"Don't you ever talk to me like that again?" I swipe his hands off of my knees. "You can't expect me to be rational right now. Those bastards have my best friend—who by the way has been there for me since I was a kid." Anger takes over and my body becomes ridged. "I would die for her."

"Kayla," He pushes his hair back and rests it on his head. "We'll get her back. You have to trust me."

"No you don't get it. There is no 'we' in the picture." My body becomes flush. "If I don't go then he'll kill her." Fists begin to form. "Now start this truck, turn it around or I swear I will run back home. I don't care anymore. You can walk away or accept—either way, I'm doing this."

He starts the ignition. "You go, I go. End of discussion." He screeches the wheel like a bat out of hell and flies down the scenic route. He taps on his blue tooth. "Call Officer Jernigan."

"He's not going to be able to help," I snap holding on to the *Oh Shit Handle.* "Officer Jernigan has been taking too damn long to begin with. So I have to take care of this shit on my own."

"The hell you will," he glares at me "Give me a few minutes to see what I can do." Garrett frantically calls in favors left and right. Both thumbs now drum the steering wheel.

I slip my keys into my jeans pocket and loosely slide my hand under the handle to my purse. As we turn into my building's parking lot I jump out of the truck before he stops and haul ass to the beast. I fling open the door and hop in. I throw my purse on the passenger's seat and turn on the ignition then throw the throttle into reverse.

Garrett yells to me. Then my phone rings to the tune of *Pink Give Me A Reason.*

I hit ignore.

I don't care. The only person on my mind is Violet. I burn rubber on the pavement as I high tail it out of there, heading to the one place I know they would lock her up. The one place that still gives me the creeps and the one place that ruined any chance of my happily ever after—The Boat house at the Marina.

I make a phone call with my hands free device.

"Yo! This is Damon."

"Damon this Kayla from Birmingham and I need your hook up." I turn down Dawson Street. "Can you find a way to find -- --- me something in Seattle?"

"For you Birmingham, anything." He states with his urban accent. "I know it's an emergency for you to call me."

"Get me the strongest you can find and it needs to be liquid," I specify. "Remember this should be free of charge because of what happened last time."

"I got it, Birmingham." He says. "Be at Fifth and Main in ten minutes. What's your ride?"

"Black SUV." I flick on the blinker.

"Ok I got you." He says hanging up the phone.

I take a sharp turn. I say a prayer in my head as I drive like a maniac.

"Dear Lord,

I ask today for forgiveness. I know what I'm about to do is a sin. But as you gave up your Son, I'm willing to give up my life for hers. She is my best friend and I will do whatever it is to save her. All I ask is that you don't let her be in pain. Take her pain away right now and be with her. I can handle them.

~Amen~"

My phone is rings.

"Birmingham, pull to the back and roll down the window."

The dark figure in a hoodie and a pair of dark jeans hops off his black bike as it idles. His black   motorcycle boots clunks as he walks.

"Be careful with this one," he drops the bag with two needles of the amber liquid in my lap. "Later."

He's leaves.

I make my way back onto the main street. The memories that pop up in my head are so intense, I pull over to the side and gather my thoughts for only a second. A red BMW passes by.

"Guess one of the gruesome twosome traded in their trucks for a pussy ass car," I murmur.

Within a second, my phone rings. I answer without even looking to see who it is.

"Where are you?????" Garrett speaks with a raspy voice.

"Don't worry about it Garrett," I say, holding my

stomach.

"Kay, you can't expect me not worry. You have no clue what you are getting into," he glowers. "For all we know, they both could have you and Vi at once."

"That's what I'm hoping for," I confidently say and turn into the marina. "I know both of them will be there. I just need the strength to end this."

The phone silences.

"Gar?" I ask.

"Kayla Ashby what in the fuck do you think you're doing?" Officer Jernigan's temper skyrockets.

Shit, Garrett. Only you could think of having a conference call while you're driving.

"I'm saving my best friend." I blow up some of my unruly hair from my eyes. "Look, I know you're recording this so I'll make it sweet and short." The car rumbles as I drive over the pebble stone path. "You aren't stopping me from saving her life.

"Kayla, at least tell me what you're thinking." He gruffly orders.

"Nope, sorry." I hit disconnect.

I throw my truck in park. I grab the two needles and dig into my purse for my lucky matches and place them with the liquid. The serene water crashing the rocks along the beachside as seagulls fly by and family boats wave to the neighbors. A place for paradise. Let's not forget the gorgeous blue country house that sits on the water.

I get out of my car. The salty sea air awakens my senses. This place may looks like heaven made it, but it's a place of hell.

"It's time to play," I whisper.

Harsh screams come from the house. I race to it as my

adrenaline takes over and my legs stretch as I speed to the house.

I slam the door open. In the distance, Violet's hunched over, both of her hands and feet are tied up with cables. Her soft sun kissed skin is exposed with cuts and burn marks. She peers up at me with a swollen right eye and lips--it says it all. Those bastards!!!

I rush to her and slide to where she is. Trembling, I move some of her wet dirty hair. Her breaths are slow and unsteady.

"Vi?" I whisper, seeing her like this, I want to kill both of them. "Did they do more than this? Did they rape you?"

As she lifts her head, her eyes widen and she shakes her head. Tears fall down and it becomes limp. I quickly undo the ties.

"I'm going to get you out of this mess." I touch her cheek.

"You really think, I'm a monster," Elijah's voice travels and hits a nerve.

"Awwwww Superstar, you're finally gracing us with your appearance," Edwin eagerly grabs the ties.

"Shut it Edwin, I'm here now," I snap as I hold my best friend.

I turn my head and there he is; his gray eyes and as he rolls up his white button collar to his fore arm. Edwin, next to him holding a Taser with a devilish smirk.

Elijah doesn't take his eyes off of me. "Edwin, get the ties."

Oh shit Elijah's beyond pissed. I need to think fast.

"You stupid bitch, you know it's never that easy." Edwin takes one foot forward and his fist ready itself in my general direction.

"Enough," Elijah's voice bombs then speaks seductively, "Sweet Kayla, we have waited seven years for you to be back— but it seems like infinity."

"I left because your parents paid me to leave." I say, quickly thinking on my feet. "They didn't want a scandal."

"No, no little girl." He eyes me like a hawk. "You left because you wanted to. Now there's a price to be paid." He sighs. Believe me I will take great joy in making your ass serve the punishment."

"Please, let her go," I plead. "Elijah, I know you quite well." My hands tremor. "You always stand by your word whether it's good or bad. Let her go and I will do anything you want. . She needs help or she'll die. Please, you always had a heart that's been buried down deep." My voice trembles. "Elijah, please."

"Oh God, I love it when you beg." He adjusts the bulge in his pants. "You know it does things to my dick. It's a bigger turn on when I'm fucking you."

I flinch as he slowly moves forward.

"Fuck this cat and mouse game," Edwin snaps the Taser. Violet screams and loses her bodily functions.

"Don't touch her." I nail my heel into Edwin's left foot.

"Owww, you fuckin' cunt." Edwin grabs my hair. "For that you need to suck my cock."

"Edwin," Elijah yanks him off me and throws him across the room. "The same rules apply. You harm her in anyway like you did before I will kill you." His angry face snaps in my direction. His gray eyes grow darker and his lips stern. "Superstar, you know I'm not a patient man." His mouth moistens like venom is coming out of it. "Get her help and meet us here no later than five today." He scowls at his twin. "Edwin what the fuck were you thinking. Keep it up and we will have a dead girl on our hands."

"That bitch had it coming." He rubs his hair.

"I don't understand," I mutter. "What did she do to you?"

"Plain and simple. She told me she would take your place." He rises from the floor. "You're mine, bitch, not VI. You are," He yells, "M.I.N.E."

"You mean both of ours," Elijah interrupts. "Our pet. Not yours."

"You both are sick and need help," I say leaning over my best friend, protecting her.

Violet's bloody hand touches my lower arm. I look at her. Her eyes wander to her purse next to the cloth on the side table and back to me.

The boys keep arguing over who I belong to.

I lean over to the table and gently take the cloth and the pink handle of her gun stands out in her purse. I snag it.

She smiles and nods. Then mouths, "Now."

I release the safety of the gun, just like she taught me. I was always afraid to even hold a gun until a couple of months ago when Violet told me I had no choice. She said that I needed to at least feel it in my hands. She had shown me how to hold and release the safety—just like I just did.

"I belong to no one, you fuckers." I hold the gun steady and fire.

The pistol whizzes through the air and penetrates into Edwin's shoulder. He screams in agony as he drops to his knees in pain. I then aim the gun at Elijah's head. Tears roll down my cheeks as I hear sirens in the back ground.

"Do you really want to do this, Kayla," Elijah says as his

voice travels into my mind. "Remember, I am a part of you," he continues. "I might have abused you, but I also protected you and treated you like a lady as well."

"And that's why I'm so fucked up about love," I close my eyes, then fixate on his. Tears roll down my cheeks as I steady my aim. "I'm sorry Elijah. But you can't control my life anymore."

I shoot him. I miss his head and get the side of his neck. I drop the gun and reach into my pocket—I pull out the needle with the amber liquid as it shines through the light. I pop the cap and charge after him. Elijah tries to block me as he holds his neck. I kiss his cheek and stab him with the needle.

"Parting is always sweet sorrow." I hold him as my emotions take over. He collapses in my arms. Shakily, I get up and walk over to Edwin.

"You fuckin' cunt." Edwin yells. "I'll kill you! Do you hear me? I'll kill you!"

"I told you in the past, I would get my sweet revenge." I sit on his stomach and jab him in the neck with another needle. "Hell's coming for you Edwin and I'm going to enjoy seeing you suffer as it brings you down with fury." I watch as he as squirms underneath me. The liquid flows into his carotid vein.

I watch until there was no more movement.

I walk over to Violet and lift her up with my left shoulder. She smiles at me and whispers, "You made me proud." Then she kisses my cheek. I turn to scan the place and kiss her head.

"It's not over yet," I stated. I take a match from my pocket. "Vi hold on tight."

I scurry over to the boat motor and light the match. Then I toss it in the boat motor. I yank Violet from the house. She's cries and tries to help me, with all my might I tug her along.

Hissing comes from the motor. I look at this nightmare for the last time. Elijah lies on the floor, ironically resting a hand on his heart.

"I really am sorry, Elijah," I continue, a tear drop races down my cheek. "In a weird way, I knew you loved me."

Boom.....

Chapter
THIRTEEN

The Truth....

"If you love life, don't waste time, for time is what life is made up of."-----Bruce Lee

"Wyatt, answer your God damned phone," I yell into the Bluetooth as I'm flying down the road.

"Come on man, I wouldn't call you if it wasn't urgent. So pick up the fucking phone."

I could kill Kayla. For a girl with brains she can be really stupid at times. What does she think? The Stanton twins would hand VI over to her and everything will be as it should? Fuck no.

I hit the number again.

"Someone better be in a coffin," Wyatt grumbles. "It's the butt Crack of dawn."

"Shove it, ass. I don't need your antics," I continue. "They have Vi and Kayla." My right hand slams on the steering wheel.

"What?" The phone moves. "Slow down. What the hell is going on?"

"Get up, I'll be there in three God damned minutes and I'll explain." The wheels of my car squeaks as it hits a corner.

"You must be kidding?" He mutters and yawns.

"Do I sound like I'm fuckin kidding?" I pull at my hair with my right hand. "They got Kayla and Violet. Get your ass up."

"On it. Let me throw on a pair of jeans. Meet me in four." He yawns as he speaks.

"I'll meet you in three and don't forget your gun." The tire squeals again as I pull into his driveway. I run up to the farmer's porch and I try Kayla's phone again; it went to voice mail.

I ring the doorbell.

My twin swings the door open. "One step ahead of you. Putting the vest on along with the holster," he says.

"Let's go," I order.

"Gar, you need to tell me what the fuck is happening," Wyatt stares out the windows. He cracks his shoulder. "Don't rush it. Explain it."

I explained everything from the phone call to Kayla leaving my ass once we got to her house.

"And now Kayla went ballistic, not listening to reason to wait for the police." I stare outside the windshield. "God knows what they're doing to her."

"Personally, I would have driven her to the police station and have her locked up," he states stretching his legs. "But that's me. Have you gone by Mille and Seth's?"

"No. I was frantic and called you," I growl and sped down the street.

"Let's give them a nice house call." Wyatt wickedly smirks. "Before we get into hell, call Officer Jernigan and let him know."

"Fine." A phone call comes through. "Kayla, Baby is that you?"

"No Sweetlips it's your ex." The whore's voice is getting

on my last nerve.

"Reagan. What the hell did you do?" I ask.

"Nothing. I thought you'd like to know I've seen your precious Kayla and she is looking so comfortable with her brothers." she says like she has one up on me.

Which means I'm going to regret asking for her help. "Where is she Reagan? You better not hurt one fucking hair on her head."

"What is it worth Garrett?" She asks.

"What do you want?" The question that will possibly ruin everything in my life.

"What I always wanted," she explains. "You and only you. You give up Kayla and her best friend lives, or misery. Your choice."

"FINE," I grind my teeth. "Help them."

Wyatt mouths, "What the fuck?"

I shrug.

"If you screw with me, I will make your life hell," she replies.

"Whatever, just tell me where she is?" I press on the gas flying down the street.

"None other than the famous boat house," she wickedly laughs and ends the call.

"Yeah, tell me why the hell you just said you would leave Kay for that Bitch," Wyatt is two seconds away from kicking my ass to bloody hell. "If Kay's heart breaks you're going to personally deal with me."

"Look don't give me any fucking shit," I slide up on the manicured grass of the Stanton's yard. "I have no plans on being with Reagan." I stall the car. "I swear on it."

"Good." He opens the door. "Let's get them back."

I don't even turn my truck off. We both fly out the door and run to the red front door of Senator Stanton's enormous house. Since my brother is ten times my strength, he's makes it to the door before me and pounds on it.

"What do you two want?" Millie answers the door. She tightens her silk house coat. "Haven't you caused enough shit?"

"No," I bluntly say. "We need a chit chat with Seth. Where is he?" My hands relax in my jean pockets.

"How the hell should I know?" She's closes the door.

I jam my foot in it and hold it open. "Don't lie to me. Where the fuck is he?"

She grunts. "Follow me."

She escorts us to the pool house. My adrenaline pumps. I could kill anyone at this point—knowing what happened to Kayla inside that place.

Moaning and screaming comes from the pool house.

"Yep, he's in a meeting," she sarcastically says, then opens the door. "Hey, hoe bag, we have company."

She announces our arrival as Seth blows his load in one of his interns.

"What the fuck, Millie?" The Senator says as he zips up his pants and hits his brunette intern on her Ass. "I told you I was in a meeting."

"It seems to be an important one, dear." She glares at the brunette intern. "How old is this one,   sixteen, twelve?" Her arms and palms of her hands wave up. "The older you get, the younger they are."

"What are you talking about?" he grunts.

"Exactly. Get your dick out of her," She says. "The boys want to talk to you." Her demeanor is smug and rich as she crosses her arms. "So when you are done with your play toy, answer their questions."

"I don't have time for this shit," I say. "Seth where the fuck is your boat house?"

"What are you talking about?" He doesn't even look me in the eye, just fiddles with his pants.

"This is getting us nowhere." Wyatt inches his way to Seth and snags his neck. He brings him into a head lock and pounds his face. "Where is the god damned boat house?"

The intern screams and runs out of the house, barely dressed.

"Garrett, stop him from killing Seth," Millie asks. "He maybe a prick but he's my husband."

"Not until he tells us where the boat house is," I demand. "If he doesn't, well you both will have kidnapping on your hands."

"Please, wait," Millie places her hand on Wyatt's arm. "Let him ago."

Wyatt reluctantly let go of his hold. He then cracks his knuckles-- glaring at the Senator.

"Okay." The Senator straightens himself out. "It's the only country looking one by the pier."

"Garrett, please don't kill my boys," says Millie as she tightens her robe. "I know they have made mistakes but they are still my babies. Like you are to your mother."

"What about, Kayla and Violet?" My fingers clench. "The sexual abuse that Kayla endured. And now they kidnapped Violet. Both Millie, are babies." I continue, "Are you planning to write this off like a scandal as well?"

"We had no choice, Garrett," Seth speaks as he clutches his bleeding face. "We were told to send Kayla away."

"What do you mean, you had no choice?" I ask. Wyatt's ready to be set loose.

"By the boy's sister." Millie paces the floor the red tile floor that still looks the same as they did years before. "I might as well tell them Seth, it looks like everything is about to come out soon enough."

"Very well." He flinches at Wyatt's muscles.

"I had an affair years ago." She fingers back her hair in a bun. "It was with someone you know."

"Who the fuck is the boy's sister, Millie?" A pit slams into my stomach. "Who was the man you slept with?"

"It was Reagan Woodrow's father," She mutters. "The boys aren't Seth's."

Chapter  FOURTEEN

Fear....

"When anger rises, think of the consequences."----- *Confucius*

"Reagan?" My voice squeaks. "Their sister?"

"Yeah, Gar, I think that's what they said," Wyatt states in his usual tone to get me back to earth... "You can cuss the bitch out later, but now it's time to get your head back in the game."

"There's more," Millie stutters. "Her parents divorced because of it."

"You sick bitch, all this time I thought those were my kids. Twenty-seven years. Twenty-seven fucking years! All this time you knew they weren't mine." Seth rolls his shoulders. He grew taller as he hollered...

"Yes," She bluntly says with no remorse. "Like the skanks that you knocked up in the past. Who wrote of a large sum in order to keep their mouths shut?"

"You fucking trollup." His gray eyes darken.

"Again, Gar, let's go. They can discuss who fucked who, it's not our business." Wyatt quickly moves and flexes his muscles like he's going to pounce on the dear senator.

Seth blocks his head with his arms and ducks.

Wyatt then laughs.

"Wyatt, please." I look with disgust at the unhappily

wedded couple. "You have a lot of explaining to do after I get Kayla and Violet back." I head out with Wyatt. "And if they do anything to them. I will kill them slowly and painfully."

"Is that a threat son?" The senator asks.

"Don't call me son because I'm not your fucking son. Hell even your sons aren't your sons." I laugh and walk out the door.

We arrive at the pebble stone path. The truck slowly goes over the bumps. "Officer Jernigan, they are at the boat house on the pier; the blue country one."

"Good, don't do anything stupid. Wait for me." He orders.

"Yeah, yeah," I mutter and roll my eyes.

"We will get them Mr. Winters." he states.

"Just hurry the hell up. I want those bastards off the fucking street." I end the call.

"We're almost there." My veins pump as my muscles flex.

"Hold on, killer," Wyatt touches my arm. "You're not going to wait, are you?"

"Fuck no, I'm not." I stop the car in front of the house. "Those are our women in there and I know that you don't want to admit it but you care about VI."

"Never said I didn't." Wyatt opens the door. "Love the girl and care deeply for her. I'm not relationship material."

"Whatever happened to the man who was in love in the first year of college?" I ask. "I mean ever since that year, you look like a Vin Diesel wanna-be."

"She was a wild flower." My brother's eyes drift off and

a tear rolls down his cheeks. "And pushed me away." He shakes his head. "Gar, someday I'll tell you the story of woe."

"I think we both have a lot to learn when it comes to women." I stare at the inviting house. "Let's go."

Once we climb out of the truck, we hear gun shots. Shit.

Our asses move in gear and we run to the house. I smell gas and slow my pace. I yell over to Wyatt. He takes one step onto the dock.

Then the place explodes. My twin body soars and lands by my truck.

"Wyatt!" I rush to his side.

Wyatt lies on the ground bleeding. I tug and punch his shoulder. There's no response.

"The hell you are going to die on me, Bro. You are my constant." I press his chest. "Come on, you can't fucking die on me." I rip open his black wife beater. There is a piece of sheet metal in the corner of his chest right below the tattoo area of his heart. The tattoo of the Celtic knot for lovers and wild flowers. I touch the metal and he jerks. Wyatt's eyes open and shuts. "I think your wild flower just saved your life. Don't worry Wyatt. You always had a heart of a lion." I hold onto his chest, to stop most of the bleeding. I nervously look around for Kayla and Violet.

Nothing but smoke, fire, and gravel. Ashes float all over the place, making it difficult to see. Damn, where are they?

Sirens come. Officer Jernigan is the first on the scene as he jogs to us he yells like a father to his sons. "I thought I told you," He scans Wyatt then calls to the other officers. "We need paramedics now."

"Jernigan, she's still inside please go look for them," I say holding my brother's heart.

The paramedics rush to Wyatt's side. Calling codes and

an oxygen mask rests on his nose. They race him to the ambulance and take off. The noise of chaos strikes.

The fire department arrives, rushing with hoses and ladders.

"I need men," Officer Jernigan calls out. "There might be people still inside that house."

The officer runs as fat as his old body will let him, barking orders to some of the others.

"Jernigan you may want to come see this," one of the officers call out.

"On my way." He rushes to the water.

"Kay!" I hightail it to the scene. Two faces lay in the water facedown. "NO! Violet! Kayla!"

I scream bloody murder as Jernigan grasps my chest. I try to break out of his arms. I drop to my knees. Shedding tears, thinking of the could haves, the would haves and the should haves. Kayla was my girl...my goddess.... my life and I had her where she belongs, right in my arms. It just can't be a short period of time.

Please God, don't let this be the end.

Chapter
FIFTEEN

Where am I....?

"We gain strength, and courage, and confidence by each experience in which we really stop to look   fear in the face... we must do that which we think we cannot."-----Eleanor Roosevelt

I wake up to a bright light shining in my eyes. I flutter my lashes and open them. I have tubes in my arms and a blood pressure cuff that is hooked up to a machine. The annoying beeps don't help with the headache. The white walls and gadget devices built in don't make me feel warm and cozy.

"Where the fuck am I?" I mouth. Roses of every color are throughout the room. An artificial chair is folded out for an overnight guest. I look around and I am in awe at the variety of colors and get well soon balloons. "How did I get myself in here?"

A kind, loving, gentle hand holds mine, smoothing it. I slowly turn my head.

"Welcome back beautiful." Garrett smiles and kisses my head.

"Hi," I respond teary eyed. I smirk then images hit my head like a beating drum. "How? Where's Vi?" I kick my sheets. "Edwin and Elijah? Did they die? What?"

"Slow down girly." Patrice says. I miss that voice. She peeks out at the hall and waves one of the nurses.

A cute redhead comes in. She walks over to me. "Kayla,

I'm Kelly and I will be your nurse today. Now, do you feel any pain?"

"Just my head." I feel the lump on the forehead.

"May I check?" she asks.

I nod.

She walks over to the bed. She checks my heart beat, along the head and the shoulders. I wince.

"I'll ask the doctor if we could get you something a little stronger for the pain." She types the info in my chart.

"No narcotics," I bluntly say.

"Miss I understand, but you have more than a mild bump," she explains. "It'll be a mild pain killer. But it will help with the migraines."

My eyebrows knit and I can't explain why.

"Kelly, dear can you get the doctor. I'll explain to him why she doesn't want anything stronger than Tylenol or Advil," Patrice says with her Texan smile.

"Okay," She sighs. "If you need anything, just press the call button."

"Will do," I say.

The nurse heads out the door to call the on call doctor.

Patrice sits on the side of the bed. "Darlin' what do you remember?"

"Not much. I remember seeing Violet getting tazed. I remember me seeing red and trying to help her." My head hurts as memories come to. "Is she okay?"

"She's fine love, only had a few bumps and bruises." Patrice taps me on the knee. "She was released a few days ago."

"A few days?" I ask. "How long have I been here?"

"It's been two weeks," Garrett chokes. "The doctors put you in a medically induced coma because of the swelling when you hit your head." He brings my hand up to his face and lays on it. "You've been off the machine for a few hours and you just came to."

Dr. Doyle looks at me and smiles. "Wyatt made it out of surgery and he's fine, he was touch and go for a few days."

"Wyatt?" I move up. "How?" Tears protrude and fall. I shake my head rapidly. "No. No. I didn't tell him. He should have been at a safe distance."

"Babe, Wyatt came with me." Garrett closes his eyes. "He made it to the front porch and then the   explosion happened." He caresses my right hand with his face. "The bastard scared the shit out of me."

"No," I rest my left hand over my face. "I was trying to protect everyone from Edwin and Elijah." I sob. "Now look at the mess I brought everyone into." I crack and breakdown. "Violet's now marked, Wyatt almost dies and you….You must have sacrificed something."

"Baby listen to me. You didn't bring havoc to anyone." He states.

"But I…" Before I could finish, Garrett leans in and kisses me hard on the lips—showing his love with every emotion he could give me with this one kiss. He then leans on my forehead. "They're fine. Violet keeps coming by to check on you. Anytime I mention your name to Wyatt, he wants to remind me that if I hurt you in anyway—injured or not, he'll kick my ass to no end."

"Damn straight bro, and don't you forget it." At that moment Wyatt walks in, and he comes and kisses my cheek. "Ashby, you have scared the shit out of me, I thought you were dead. Don't you ever go and do something that stupid ever again."

"Yes, dad," I say joking. "So how are you feeling? I am so sorry you were injured."

"Buttercup, I am fine, I had the best doctors take care of me. It was strange because she reminded me so much of Ariel Jamieson." he smirks.

"Who is she, Wyatt?" I ask. "I have never heard you speak of her before."

"She is the one who got away. She pretty much changed my life for the good and also for bad," he says and looks up at Garrett. "I'm now ready to share my story of my wildflower. If you don't mind me telling you now?"

"No, I don't mind at all, I would love to hear about her," I say as I rest my head near Garrett's side.

"Okay, here we go." Wyatt grabs a black chair and flips it to the back. He then saddles it. "I remember thinking of her when I heard the blast. She was the last thing I was thinking about. I have never been one to admit that I have a heart because Ariel broke it so many years ago. But this is what I remember hearing from the blast...

"We're going to lose him... Jacey I need..... Hit him....do it again.... We got a rhythm folks. We need to leave part of the metal in...."

The only voices that circles around my ears are doctors, I can't open my eyes, I just see the color of white that turns into black; black turning into a memory that I locked up for years. The picture of the woman who I never thought I would have an image of again.

Her face, her smile and laughter. It brings me to the first day I saw her, and the first day she captivates my heart. Though women have come and gone from my bed, there is only one who became more than a friend and woman who also crushed my heart—Ariel Jamieson. Like all things in my life that has gone sour.

I never had an easy life. Our father used us as punching bags, especially when he was on the bottle. Since I was younger, I was the easier target. Even though, my twin took the heat most of the time. I was the one that protected my mother from the beast when Garrett wasn't around. What the old man didn't know--the more he used me as his own target, the more I worked out with weights and barbells plus, being in sports was my advantage too—waiting for the day I would truly protect my mother from him. I grew up and at 6' 4 I tower over most men, including the old man.

The day he slammed my mother against the stove and tried to burn her hair-was the day anger controlled me. I rammed into dad and we both fell on the floor. I whaled on his face.

Blooded gushed out of his nose. The hatred that I had toward him became my ally. I spoke in a different language as I continued my torment on him.

Panic stricken, my mother called for Garrett. Garrett pulled me off of the beast before I smashed his face in even more. Hateful words like, whore, bastard children came out of the old man's mouth. Wobbly from the booze and my pounding, he grabbed a knife. Garrett stopped him in his tracks. He held my father until he calmed himself down. After, Garrett told my dad to leave that he would take care of us.

Four years later, I'm a freshman at The University of Oregon. Four hour drive home --counting rush hour traffic—just in case my mother needs me. I remember this year like it was yesterday. The big campus in the center of Eugene is like a town in itself—with the courtyard well kept, the ray of flowers spread all over the place, and the old antique buildings shine like they're fucking new. My favorite place is Lillis Business Center—best cup of Joe and food for a college kid's budget. The best part of Oregon, I get the best of two worlds—beaches and mountains.

A couple of weeks into college time is not a good way to start off the school year. I look like I just rolled out of bed with a scruff on my face and just fucked hair. I wander through the campus with a coffee in my hand stepping on the rusted leaves as they crunch. My brown barn coat flaps in the wind and the long plaid scarf that Violet gave me for a going away present droops along my neck. This incredible laugh catches me off guard.

"That is the sexiest laugh I have ever heard," I whisper. I search around the courtyard and track it down. Up the steps and to Lillis, I search. "Am I not getting enough sleep that I keep thinking with my junk and not my mind? I'm losing it." I hear the laugh again. This time I jog to where it could be. At the front of the university theater, she stands with a group of dancers. This prima ballerina with legs for days, her pink lips shine as she talks.

Long flowing red hair that my hands could get tangled in and soft green eyes that are inviting. In other words her body says' fuck me hard all over'. She even has fullness in her breasts, which means a man can get lost in those.

I have to get to know her. I make my way up to her and put on the best move yet. "Hey, how ya' doing?" I smirk and furrow my eyebrows. "Name's Wyatt Winters." The group of dancers giggle at me...

"Wyatt," she tries not to laugh, but the half crescent moon says other ways. "I'm Ariel and what brings you to the performing art center?"

I playfully flip out the map. "I'm lost. I'm looking for Mr. Watson's music class."

"You are one of the cute ones," she says and plays with my hair like I'm a pup. Then she laughs. "Well, you are way off. I'm heading there, so I can show you where it is."

"Later, girls," she waves to them. "Remember, Mac's tonight, support my guy."

They roll their eyes. The short blond one mutters, "This fundraiser better be worth it."

"Have I ever disappointed you?" She asks. A lot of confidence for a petite woman. "Later loves."

She scoops her arm and locks it with mine as we mosey along to my next class. Her ballerina vibrant pink skirt flaps in the wind showing her black leggings as she bundles her jacket leaning closer to me. She asks me questions about where I was from and why did I choose Oregon.

"I needed a break from the Seattle," I say. I smirk and ask, "What's a ballerina doing at Oregon and not Julliard?"

"If you must know, family," she states. Her smile is a piece of heaven and it's also contagious. "They're all I have."

As soon as she brought it up, I thought about my past as she mentions family.

"What?" She nudges me.

"You said family," I answer. "It's usually something I would say."

We stop at the center of the music hall. She takes hold my two hands and gazes into my eyes. "So, here we are Wyatt, I take it you're a music major although I don't see any instrument," she. Smiles.

"Are you planning to be a rock star like the rest of the naïve freshman boys?"

"Yeah, no," I tighten my grip. "I play a variety of instruments." Her soft buttermilk skin really needs a man's tongue. I can deal without her sarcastic remarks. I simply reply, "My major is both Music and Business."

"Are you planning to be a manager," her voice has the

sweetest most enticing voice I've ever heard.

"Not exactly, I want to own a club," I say, "And not just any club, a club that fits all kinds of people, you know with live music, a DJ that rocks, and a private lounge."

"A club." She smirks then folds her lip on the right side, checking me out. She gazes back up to me with those innocent green eyes. "Do you know what I do?"

"Ah, ballet?" I stupidly answer.

"I have to give you some credit." She flops my hair again. "You are a cute one," she continues. "Tell you what, instead of saying what I do, why don't you come to Mac's tonight."

"Yeah," I say, jumping at the bit.

"Wyatt, it's not a date." She scans my whole body over, again. "You should be a perfect replacement,"

She utters then bobs her head. "The music room is up the stairs to the right. See ya' tonight."

She carries herself with grace as she skips down the pebble stone path.

"Where is Mac's," I yell.

"Just ask around," she skips backwards, calling back.

Mac's, the club of all clubs. Or at least that's what the entire campus says. The club looks like a tower in the corner of the city with a cool sign that has a Celtic knot on it and thin green neon lights that has the clubs name.

Waiting in the line the never seems to end, I check myself out. "Okay, jeans no holes, shirt decent." I smack my forehead. "What the hell is wrong with me?"

"Wyatt," Standing with someone who looks like an ex-marine that could be commando, Ariel waves to me. She looks like a vixen with her tight ass blue jeans and black shirt. Her red hair is pulled to the side, showing her delicate neck and shoulder.

I pointed to myself. She shakes her head and whispers in the commando's ear. I shy away and my head drops. She's obviously not interested.

Then I hear the sweetest voice coming out of those lips. I snap my head up.

"Shorty, wanna get down..." Ariel sings Diggity through the mike as she reaches into the audience. A Capella group chimes in. "I can't get it out of my mind.... I like the way you work it...."

After, the whole crowd chimes in acting as background singers.

This woman is freaking amazing.

Then music pours out of the club to the line. She tosses the mike to commando and dances her way towards me, stopping along the way getting others to dance. An uncontrollable smile hits me like a baseball bat as she puts me in a trance with her moves. Once she reaches me, she clasps onto my right hand.

"It's time to show me what you got, Winters." she winks.

"I don't dance," The words just fall out of me.

"Of course you can," she says.

"No, serious," I stutter. "I can't."

"Well we have to fix that," She holds my right hand in the air as she twists and dances. She then relaxes her back close to mine and places my hands on her hips. "Now, just move with my hips." Her head rests on the crock of my neck. I quickly whiff her fragrant perfume... Sweet baby powder pours into my core and my cock hardens and all I want is to have her for breakfast, lunch and dinner.

I move my hips slowly with hers, she softly moans. I reach to kiss her, but she spins away from me and holds my right hand in the air as we dance our way in front heading towards the front of the club. "Micah, he's with me."

The bouncer could make guys change their mind about their sexual preference. His sea eyes check out my semi-date. My fist closes ready to swing.

"Micah, when are you going to learn to keep your eyes on the patron's face and not their body," Ariel flips her hair. "You have been manhandling women left and right—which loses the house money." She stumps her foot. "You need to start charging the girls cover or Mac will hear about it."

"Easy wildflower." Micah's southern accent didn't faze her.

"I mean it." Ariel's green eyes glowered at him. "Come on Wyatt, let me show you what you want."

My eyebrows furrow. I relax my hands in the pocket jeans.

Micah hardly laughs.

"What?" I snarly ask.

"Dude, even I know sex is never on this woman's mind," he says and nods to Ariel. "I hope he's up to the challenge when you leave."

"If I can deal with all of you," She grabs my hand and smirks. "Mark my words he will be better."

We stroll through the oak stained doors into the booming noise of the club. A girls' band wearing nothing but lingerie is playing the guitar hard as the crowd rocks. Young girls in tight ass jeans dance their way on the bar. Other woman entertain the customers with flipping bottles as they pour.

Ariel checks the time on her watch then brings me to the stage. We listen to the club's band for an hour, then head upstairs to the VIP lounge.

"The band was hot but they need to tone down on the bass," I naturally say. "It echoes through the club and vibrates the floor. "So, you end up getting more noise than actual base music."

"Well, bass guitar or not, it's the hottest college band around. I was lucky enough to grab them." She replies, pursing her lips.

"I didn't mean to…" I smooth my blond hair. "I'm sorry. My words got away with me."

"No need to, and don't." She messes with my hair again. "I like it like that."

"Messy?" I ask.

"Messy," she replies. "Come on, Mac wants to see you."

We walk over to a man. His hands lean on the brass rail. She taps on his shoulder. He's a man who towers over me, full of tats and long black hair pulled back. What's worse…his hands could crush you, never mind his arms. This guy is someone not to mess with.

"How did the Swim Club do?" she asks.

"Show was a sell out tonight, Jamieson." His relaxes his arms on his chest. "The swim club made over 10K." He peers down at her. "The band's not bad either."

"What can I say," She gleams. "Sex sells, Mac, Sex Sells." She tugs me forward. "Mac this is Wyatt Winters. I think he would be a great replacement."

"Let's, hope so, Jamieson," Mac's muscles naturally flexes as they hang to his sides. "I don't need someone who wants girls left and right."

"He would be nothing like you." She smirks. "You have to trust me."

"Um, I'm replacing you, Ariel for exactly what?" I ask. I then stare up at the giant man before me.

He chuckles. "Nice, Jamieson. You found a replacement that wants more out of you." He punches my shoulder. "Good luck, Wyatt with this one." He then looks at Ariel. "Have him swing by the club tomorrow after the shock factor wears off. I'll go over the commission and what I expect. Later."

The bear of the man heads down stairs.

"So, what do you think?" She gazes into my eyes.

"You created this?" I ask as I admire the view in front of me. God, Girl with brains and hotness. I don't know how much longer I can control the animal within.

"Yep," she answers and looks at the crowd. "Everyone's into Coyote Ugly and men always love woman in lingerie, so I combined the two. Welcome to Seven Shades of Friday Night."

"Sounds just about right." I chuckle. "What did the Swim Club need that was dire urgent? New speedos?"

"Wyatt, it's for a little boy who needs a bone marrow transplant." Her green eyes soften. "It was one of the swimmer's sons."

"Oh," I rub the back of my neck. "Sorry."

"You didn't know," she says and her hands lean on the banister. "If you look at people from a distance, you won't be able to get to know them as a person. You see that heavy set girl over there." She points to a girl that's particularly large as she dances. "She maybe heavy, but she's beautiful. Just by looking at the smile on her face. Genuine and sincere." She peers up at me than back to the crowd. "Every person down there is cool in their own right. You just have to get to know them."

"You sound like an angel," I blurt. Then I stumble over

the rest of my words. "That is, if you...ah..." I clear my throat. "What is that you want out of me?"

"Slow down. I just want to help you." She taps my hand. "You can be so cute. And your eyes are so blue that any girl could fall for you with them." She coughs and continues, "Wyatt, my job here is to set up fundraisers or parties to make the bar money. Plus, help manage."

"I don't understand," I utter and look at the dancing crowd having a good time. "If you have a decent job, why are you leaving it and still in college for that matter?"

"I'm in college to better my life and my family's," she brags. The dream of success fills her eyes. "After graduation, I'm off to London to open up clubs." She sighs. "Look, the money is really good, I'm able to pay for college and keep an apartment."

"London?" My Adam's apple rises and falls. "So you really want to leave all this; friends and family, for group of strangers in London."

"Wyatt, slow down again." She slowly waves her hands down. "I want to do this for my family. I can also help you learn about the night life."

Every Friday night for the first semester, I would meet Ariel at the campus and we would listen to live music, she would then teach me tricks on how to make a pub or club successful. She even helped me with the worst and boring subject in the world—Business Law. The more we hung out, the more my heart grows fonder of her. I needed to tell her how much she meant to me before she left, well after I study and pass finals.

The rain never ceases to end today as I stare out the window. The drops tap on the pane like a drum outside Lillis. I wonder when we are going to take the next step in our relationship.

"Wyatt, are you with me?" Ariel's milky white soft hand gently touches my right.

"What?" I slowly turn my head towards her.

"Exactly." Her glasses reaches her nose as her soft green eyes gaze into my mine. "How are you going to focus on your studies when I'm not around?"

"Don't go to London," I abruptly say. "Then you could be my conscious and I won't do stupid things." I place my right hand on hers and give her the Winters's stare that I perfected in high school.

"Wyatt, we talked about this and those baby blue eyes are not going to charm me to stay." She drops her head to my hand. "I'm told you before and I'll say it again, I'm not the relationship type and you have..."

"We're only we're only nine years apart... It's not like we're in the double digits." My face softens as I try to have her look at me. "I haven't felt this way with anybody but you."

"If that were only the case," she utters as the green in her irises glisten. She watches the rain outside. "But we can spend as much time together before I leave."

She snags her umbrella and rises up quickly from her chair. She brings me up close to her heart and looks up at me. Her eyes dance as she gazes into mine. "Since you're done with finals, let's have fun. Race you to your dorm."

"What?" I ask as my eyebrows rise. "Now. In the rain?"

"You have to trust me." She takes my hand and leads me out of Lillis into the pouring rain.

She opens her umbrella and jumps into the puddle on the pavement then reaches for my hand. "Come on," she excitedly says.

"Uh, no." I scratch the back of my head.

"Just trust me," she says, giggling like a kid. "How are you going to open a club when you can't let the kid inside you come out and play?"

"I never was a kid," I explain, "even when I was young."

"Well that explains it." Mischief is written all over her face. She then kicks the dirty water from the puddle onto my jeans.

"Hey!" I complain as I look at the mess on my leg.

"The only way to get back at me Wyatt, is to join me." She keeps skipping into the puddles.

I reach one and jump in it. Laughing, I did the second one. Like a kid I could have been, I chase after her hopping and jumping in the puddles. Once we reach the hall to my dorm I scoop her into my arms as we laugh uncontrollably. Her umbrella twirls low to the ground. Wet pieces of her red hair stick to her face.

We both catch our breath. Holding her closer I push some hair out of her face and draw my lips to hers. After what seems like forever, I watch her expression. She blinks but doesn't do anything.

"Ariel, are you going to say something or did I just do the biggest mistake of my life?" Moisture forms at the corner of my eyes.

"I told you not to settle down with me." With her soft hands, Ariel leans back and claims my lips. Passionately and effortlessly, she deepens her kiss. Our tongues thrust together while my hands trail down to her ass. I squeeze it and pick her up.

Her legs wrap around my waist. Moving one step at a time I lead her in my arms up the stairs groaning and claiming every bit of this girl with this one kiss. I keep climbing to my dorm. Thank God my roommate isn't here. I push open the door and lay her down on my bed.

My mouth takes control as I tug on her ear with my teeth. She moans and whispers, "Oh, Wyatt."

I peel her out of her wet clothes and begin my exotic torture. I nibble my way to her soft succulent breasts. Sucking and pulling on the right nipple, I reach over to the left one and smooth it. Her body bucks.

Then I lick and press my mouth down making a pathway to her cleft. I push my finger in and out, then massage her folds. The wetness of her cleft glistens as cum drizzles down. The intoxicating aroma draws me in to it.

"Hmm," she moans and loosens her legs and body even more. With one lick I taste her sweet saltiness and her juices flow into my mouth while I take her as my own. I dive into her heavenly bliss nibbling her treasure spot. Ariel's feet rests on my shoulders. God I love her feet, as they massage my neckline. Which pushes me over the edge and I grunt inside her and my tongue dips deeper inside. Her cleft pulsates as she takes in her pleasure.

"Wyatt!" She moans and screams. She then squirts into my mouth.

Letting her legs drop to the side, I lick my lips as a devilish smile spreads across my face. Realizing she is mine for the tasking, I rise up and kiss her mouth, my tongue dips in and taunts her. While my penis plunges into her center core. Her body arches and those ballerina legs wrap around my waist as I thrust into her. She tightens her grip, the more I thrust. I moan as we cum at the same time. "El, I love you," I grunt and fall on top of her. The three words I shouldn't have said.

She kisses me while tears fall from her cheeks. Then whispers in my ear, "Wyatt, remember I will always love you, but I'm can't commit."

"I can always make you change my mind," I utter and kiss her forehead. I then rest my head on her chest and fall fast asleep.

After the dancing and the amount of drinks that passes through the bar, my head spins as the night life slows down and the club empties out.

"Wyatt, you need to slow down," Mac clasps his hand on the shot glass. "El's on her way to get you."

"Why did you call that bitch," I snap and continue to slur my words. "Did you know I gave her my heart and she crushed it?" I burp. "She's this angel who's also some kind of devil."

"Yeah, my friend, you need to sober up," Mac switches the shot glass with coffee. "Come by here tomorrow and I'll tell you why El is the way she is."

"Mac, I got it from here." With a heavy sigh, Ariel taps her feet. "I leave you alone for a week and you're a mess."

"You didn't," I stand and tumble. "You just left me alone in my bed. Not even calling me or..."

I burp again.

"You sound like a whiney woman." She grabs my coat. "Come on, Wyatt, Let me take you home."

"To what, my dorm?" I lean and touch her hair. "Or your apartment so we can finish what we started. I think I need to teach you a lesson."

"Wyatt, I'm warning you, don't," She softly says as a moan sneaks out.

"What you had no problem a week ago," I skim her breast that hides behind her mauve shirt. "Before you told me you loved me and ripped out my heart."

"I warned you," She snags my pinky and twists it.

"Owww, Owww," I mutter as I fall to her knees. "God damn it, El, I'm sorry."

"Good." She throws the navel jacket at me. "Pull yourself together Winters and meet me outside."

I meet Ariel outside. Mac and Micah had to carry me to her. They release their hold and my body sways back and forth.

"Mac and Micah, catch him," Ariel shouts.

I then black out.

I wake up to my eyelid being lifted up as a pair of big crystal blue eyes examining me.

"Pulses are normal, skin color okay, and his eyes are creepy blood shot blue but no other disease in it." My eyelid snaps back in my face.

"Ow, you mother--" I flip off the couch. I scratch the back of my head and see a fourteen year old girl who has brownish red ringlets gently drop on the sides of her face and a faded pair of blue jeans and white flowered tunic. Freckles, cover her nose. She is cute as a button. Scary thing is she is the identical mini me version of Ariel except for her eyes.

"Easy killer, I'm sorry," she panics. "My mom doesn't bring a guy or anybody home. I thought you were sick or dying."

"Sick or dying?" I ask and slowly sit up on her beige couch.

"Well, you're pale and I heard you hacking last night," she stutters. "I thought for sure you had some kind of illness or disease," she mumbles the rest.

"Yeah, it's an illness alright," I rub the back of my head

with my two hands as I duck forward. "It's called a hangover."

"Hangover?" She checks the back of my head. "You also have a bump which could have given you a contusion."

"Contusion?" I must have hit my head hard. "How old are you?"

"Fourteen," she answers. "You must be hungry and I have to start cooking," She glances over to her bedroom then back to me. "I need some help."

"I don't cook kid," I mumble. "I usually call for take out."

"You don't cook." She shows her teeth with her smile. "Why did my mother bring you home?" She shakes her head. "She told me in the past, that the one she brings home would be the one she keeps. And you don't cook. I think my mother made a major mistake." With disappointment in her eyes, "I guess I can try to make something easy, like French toast."

She wanders to the kitchen area.

I rise up and rotate my shoulders. I look around the place; the open floor plan brings out the antique fireplace and living room with black and white photos of family and friends all over the walls. I follow her to the kitchen area and sit on the stool.

She grabs eggs and milk as she balances them to the counter. She then takes a bowl and drops it on the counter as the hollow noise goes around the apartment.

"Oh, shit." She steps around the corner and as her blue eyes search out of the kitchen area. "Phew." She comes back and starts mixing the ingredients. "She's been working way too hard lately." She keeps stirring what looks like glue. "Hmm." She picks up the spoon from the mixing bowel as slop drips from it.

"I think I missed a step."

"I'll say," I lean over the bowl. "I don't think it's

supposed to look like that."

She peers up at me. "You shouldn't judge someone's cooking when you only get take out."

"Did anyone tell you it's impolite to talk to a grown up like that?" I lecture.

"No offence, guy." She checks me out like a mother. "If you show me a grownup, I'll give him my utmost respect." She opens the microwave and pulls out a loaf of bread. "I mean you're what five years older than me." She's about to turn on the stove.

"Hey, wait," I stop the girl in her tracks. "Let me at least turn on the stove."

"I may not cook but I have watched my mom quite a bit when she cooks." I drop down from the stool and go around the counter. "Medium heat should do it. We don't want to overcook things."

"You burn French toast not overcook them," she gives a half smile. "There's hope for you yet."

"Addyson Grace Harrison, what are you getting yourself into?" Ariel's motherly voice sends a smile to my face.

"Nothing, mother," she calls out.

"I bet," Ariel strolls into the kitchen area "other than you two making mess."

I felt like a kid getting caught with my hand in the cookie jar. I rise hands up in surrender and bring on the charm.

She winks and steps behind Addyson. Ariel has a kid????

"Why don't I make something special today," She says and taps Addyson's shoulder. "Addy, you've been working just as hard as me." Ariel peers up in my direction. "Wyatt can you go into the fridge and grab the cooked sausage and peppers?"

"I'm very proud of you," Ariel utters to her teen and kisses the top of her head.

"Mom, don't embarrass me like you usually do." Addyson just naturally smiles. "But since you want to cook and I'm far ahead in school…" She cups her fingers together and begs, "Can I please go online?"

"Yes." Her mother said. "No chat rooms or places like My Space."

"Mom, My Space is so passé." She then runs into the other room.

"She is too much like her father," She cleans up the glue and giggles. "Always acts older then her age. Could you break six eggs and put it into the bowl." She gives me the bowl, "while I cook the peppers."

'Um," I rub the back of my head. "Breaking eggs?"

"Wyatt, have you ever cooked?" she asks.

"No," I answer and smile while I examine the egg and put it gently back down in the carton. "I had a mother who did everything."

"That explains it." She grasps the egg from the carton and places it in my hand. She gently holds my hands from behind. "Okay, now we are going to break it."

She gently uses my hands as she breaks the egg.

"There," her voice becomes raspy.

"Yeah," I utter, about to kiss her.

Ariel moves quickly. "After that I'll teach you how to cut peppers."

Clumsily, I broke the eggs. I think I got more on the counter than in the bowl. "Ah, ready as they'll ever be."

She tosses the wet rag at me. I chuckle and wipe the mess.

"Come here." She grasps my hands and hand takes the paring knife and gently rests it in my hand. Then she shows me slowly, seductively, how to chop the peppers. "Just slow and steady."

I reach in and kiss her.

"Wyatt, are you sure?" She folds the corner of her lip and then says, "You'll only have us for three months and then I'm gone."

"It'll give me three months to convince you to stay," I snicker.

"I'm telling you Mac, the sensor should tell us how many pours each bartender did." Ariel walks behind the bar and taps on the IPad that rests on the counter. "Hmm." She flips the IPAD over and points to the blue bar. "You lost sales because of the over pouring."

"Ariel, I have the best bartenders around," Mac grunts and cleans the gutters of the bar. "How do you suppose I cut back on the drinks?"

"I don't know," she says, her mind starts to ponder. God I love that brain of hers.

"Why not a five drink rule, Mac?" I suggest.

"Interesting young grasshopper." Mac scratches his chin. "How will that cut down on the over pouring?"

"It might not," I ramble. "If you do five good drinks, raise the price, you make your money back and not have to deal with the angry drunks. Chances are people will only buy one or two, but since you have cover charges and other fundraising ideas, it might work."

"What do you think, Wildflower?" He asks Ariel as she taps the IPad.

"What do we have to lose," she states. "It might work."

I look at Addyson—her child's breathing was quick and she begins to shake.

I rush over to the girl.

"Addy look at me, honey?" My eyes widen with fear. "Baby, can you tell me what's wrong?"

She shakes her head no. Then squeezes her fists.

"Addy?" Ariel calmly strolls around the counter. "Addy look at my face."

"Look at what he wrote." She points to the laptop she was on.

Ariel reads it and scowls. She then shows Mac.

"This is uncalled for, that boy needs to be shot." Anger stirs in Ariel's voice.

"No, Mama, don't," Addison whimpers. "I didn't, I didn't..."

"I got you baby, let it all out." Ariel embraces Addison until she calms. She then lifts her face up towards her. "Better."

"Yeah." The fourteen year old nods.

"I think being with Grams and Pops this weekend will be a good break for you." She wipes Addison's ongoing tears. "Come on, let's get you into the bathroom and cleaned up."

"Hey? She is going to be alright?" I ask. Seeing Addison come apart like the way she just did took a toll on me. After all, the girl's like a daughter.

"She's fine, she had a panic attack." Ariel takes a hold of the child's hand. Ariel then wraps her right arm around Addison's shoulders as they walk to the bathroom.

I can't believe how lucky I truly am. Having these two girls in my life is a blessing in disguise. But I'm worried about

Addison having these attacks at such a young age.

"Mac, why would Addy get attacks like this?" My throat dries.

"Because of an ass of a fifteen year old who played with her emotions and slept with her," he angrily answers. "Because she didn't want to do it anymore he began to call her rude words and broke her heart."

He shows me the laptop. Addison Jamieson the cunt was plastered all over the chatroom page. "Ariel has been fighting with the school, parents and the state about verbal abuse like this."

"Well what does the kid look like and what's his name?" I curiously ask.

"You know, Ariel will kill you if she finds out the boy was beat upon, even if she does love you. Speaking of" Mac puts the bar back together. "You got to let the both of them go," Mac voice creeps behind me. "Before both of your hearts are shattered."

"Mac, come on," I say. "I know she's leaving and I know that in a few years, when I finish college I can get her back." I play with my thumbs.

"You think it's that easy young grasshopper," he states. "You are more naïve than I thought you were."

He stops the wiping. "It's time to tell you about our girl and maybe it'll sink into your head. As you know Ariel lived in the projects with me and Micah," he sets up a hard drink for himself. "And Joe Harrison. We were all close to each other and Ariel loved him." He raises his shot glass to the ceiling like he's saying cheers to heaven and downs the shot. "It was mine and Joe's senior year when he proposed to her. Of course Ariel at the time was fifteen but she was faithful. They had it planned out. He was going to do his time in the Air Force and she was to finish up high school and head to Julliard.

"But life had an unexpected twist for our little girl. She got knocked up and Joe was killed in a plane crash heading over unchartered territory. Imagine, no place that was really home; only alcoholism, no fiancé, no cash, or Julliard, but a baby."

My heart shrivels up in my chest (don't want to make him look wimpy) as he explains the rest. I can't imagine what she went through all l this at an early age. I thought I had to grow up because of the ole'man, but Ariel? She had no choice but to grow up.

"Despite the rocky road she had, Ariel pulled her shit together, raised Addy and got into Oregon. I took her in and had her help me with the bar. She was able to get an apartment and pay for tuition while my business paid for health insurance and school for Addy."

"What about Ariel's mother?" I ask. "I just don't understand how she can go through raising a child by herself."

"Lois?" He laughs hardly. "She's a major alcoholic. Ariel spent more money on rehab and taking care of her four brothers. If I didn't intervene, she would be stuck in that hell."

"Then who's Grams and Pops?" I ask.

"Joe's parents," he bluntly says... "Wyatt, there's a reason why she's called wildflower. It's not of the partying or the alcohol beverage she can whip up in her mind. It's because of her spirit. She has a free spirit that can't be tamed. And with that spirit can cause heartbreak. If she loses the chance to go to London, her spirit will get crushed and it'll be like losing Joe all over again. I love you like my family, Wyatt, but Ariel's is a little sister to me and I'll be damned if her heart gets shattered again."

The football players of St. Pies School fool around at the football field, calling out the stats on how many girls they slept with. One blond boy with dangerous brown eyes calls out the most. The smug look on his face and his arrogance towards teenage girls make me sick. That must be Mark Peterson that Mac told me about. Mac said to stay away from the battle, but not the kid who started all of this drama to Addyson. I wander over. The guys blinks their eyes. Scared to death just glancing at me, they moved to the side.

"Looking for Mark Peterson," I announce.

Blondie flips his bangs and answers, "Yeah that's me, what's it to ya?"

The whistle blows and the rest of the team high tails it to their coach.

"Before you run like a lady to your coach, Peterson." I snicker then snag his wrist and flip it around to his back, making him scream uncle. "Addyson Jamieson is what it is to me, you little punk." I squeeze harder so he can feel the agony. "You ever post shit on any site or mouth off to her, even breathe in the same FUCKING AIR as her, I will be back and you won't have a leg to stand on. UNDERSTAND?"

The dork nods.

"Good." I release his hold. "Run along now Mary."

He jogs to the practice and I walk back to my car.

Despite, Ariel's rage towards me because of the Mark Peterson incident, she let it slide, due to the fact, that the kid stopped his bullshit and stayed his distance from Addyson.

And now, my nineteenth birthday pops up and it's Ariel's last day. The girl has been on the phone nonstop making arrangements for tonight. Passing back and forth in her living room, she plays with her hair waiting for a band manager.

I reach over and snag it then press the end button.

"Wyatt..." she reaches for the phone. "I was on an important call. It's about tonight."

"And you need a rest and I think I know how." I brush my lips against hers.

She reaches over and snatches the phone. Pulling away, she walks backwards.

"Oh, are we going to play," I utter with a devilish grin. "Can we role play? How about baker and the gingerbread girl, I'll be the baker." I playfully stalk toward her.

"Don't go there," she snickers as she wanders backwards. She then races to her room laughing as I chase after her.

Blindfolded until we get to our destination spot, the music, pounds as the band *Limp Bizkit* play. Whispers circle around me. The band abruptly stops.

"Ready, on the count of three. One, two, three," she whips off the blindfold.

"Happy Birthday, Wyatt!" The whole bar shouts. The girl crammed the place with friends from the past and college. Even Violet Palmer my cute blonde best friend that has a hold on my heart holds an oversized sheet cake, with my old baseball team photo on it.

Ariel even managed to get Garrett. Unfortunately, his tagalong, Reagan, was here as well.

"Are you surprised," she whispers. "I found your friend Kayla, but she couldn't come so she sent a card."

"Wildflower, this is the best birthday I ever had," I utter and brush her sweet soft pink lips with mine. "You managed to get almost everyone I care about under the same roof and on top it off, you managed to find one of my best friends."

The band jams and the place rocks.

"How did you manage to get *Limp Bizkit,* here?" Holding her tight, I peck her lips again.

"I have connections," she shyly utters.

I lift her chin and kiss her passionately one last time.

The party hits off with a bang, I dance with Violet as Garrett tries to smooth talk Reagan.

The boy really needed to look around for Kayla, instead of trying to get into Reagan's pants.

I search the whole dance floor, no Ariel.

"Hey VI, can you give me a sec?" I ask.

"Um, sure," she hesitantly smiles as she walks up to the crew.

"Okay their faces are priceless," I mutter as I search for my love. From the VIP area to the office, no sign of her. "Ariel, please don't do this."

I stroll outside and saw Micah manhandling two idiots that, as Ariel would say, trash that don't belong in the club.

"Micah, where's Ariel?" I ask. I hold onto my chest as pressure of my heart pounds on it.

"Yeah, about that grasshopper," Micah scratches his head. "Mac wants to talk to you."

Mac comes around the corner with a note. Water fills the bottom of his eyes. I knew in a heartbeat.

Ariel left and had not said her good byes. I collapse on the curb as I come unglued. Mac sits down next to me.

"She saw you with your friend Violet," he explains as tears build up in his eyes. "Wyatt, she gingerly smiled at the site of you two and said, she'll make him happy and it's as it should be. She even gave me the note and hug saying how much she'll miss all of us," he calmly says. "The gracious woman took one more look at you with a tear in her eye then she gracefully strolled out of the club." He hands me the envelope. "She did want me to give this to you."

"I'll give you some time to digest the info." Mac grabs hold of me and taps my shoulder. "Micah, give him a minute."

I shakily open the envelope and breathe in her sweet melon scent one last time.

My Dearest Wyatt,

This is the only way I could tell you goodbye.

Goodbye…

Saying goodbye is never enough and always a loss.

When both hearts shatter because one has to leave.

No words can explain the depth of my love.

For, I love you with my heart and soul.

And my heart stopped when it was time for me to go.

From the first time I met you I fell for your charm and

Melted by the way you smiled at me.

The day I died was the day I said my good byes.

I will always love you.

Your Ariel.

The note drops out of my hands a floats to a pair of hands.

"Wyatt?" Violet's southern voice is what I need.

"Yeah," I rub my eyes.

She plops down next to me and doesn't say a word. Just grabs me like a mother and holds me.

I cry on her shoulder...

Colors begin to blur and a light peers into my eyes. A glance at the crystal blue eyes again "Pulse is normal, skin looks good and heartbeat's regular. Congrats, Ladies and gentlemen, we saved another life.

Let's get him into recovery."

"Jamieson, you may be in diapers, but you sure know how to save a life." A joke was at the expense of this young doctor.

Her musical laughs brought joy into my heart, reminding me of the same laughter that captured my heart years ago.

I look over to my very manly best friend Wyatt as he wipes the tears from his face, matter of fact I look around and I don't see a dry eye in the place, Garrett is rubbing my hand and says, "I can't compare to his story but I can say this...I would do anything for you Kayla Ashby. I love you, always have and always will."

"So Wyatt, have you ever spoken to her or..." I gulped as I use the sheet for a tissue.

"I keep in touch, Kay." He leans in and hisses my forehead. "From time to time. The problem was I competed with a ghost. I would never be Joe. And she never wanted to replace him for me."

He slowly rises and heads out the door.

"I never want to lose you, like I thought I did back there." Garrett kisses me again.

At that moment Millie and Seth walk into my room. Garrett narrows his eyes and I glare at them grinding my teeth.

"What the fuck do you want? Why are you here?" I

snap. "Why now?"

"Kayla, we're sorry for everything," Seth, sincerely apologizes. The man's hair looks like a skunks and the bags under his eyes are more prominent. Wow, did he take a beating.

"You say you're sorry, but what about the past? What about the years your boys abused me and then you treated me like shit?" I suck in my lip then continue. "The fact that they raped me and you never did anything. Then when I get the nerve to tell you, you tell me to leave." I whack the mattress of the bed with my right hand. "What kind of monsters are you?"

"They came here to answer that question. It's time to open your ears and heart and shut down your mind." Patrice taps my hands.

I jerk my hand out hers and scream, "You're on their side." She takes it again like a mother. "Kayla, I'm not on their side, I'm always on yours, but you need to hear some of the things that they have to say." Patrice sternly stares at Millie. "You may continue."

"I was never a good mom. I didn't know how to be a mom. I never had someone to help me." She wipes a tear from her face and continues on about her life in a trailer, her starvation and poverty, finally, the day she met Seth and he was willing to take care of her. So she jumped at the chance. "Little did he know, I was pregnant by Jason Woodrow." My mouth must have dropped. As she continues, "Kayla, close your mouth, one thing I did right was teaching you to be a lady. So I married Seth even though I knew he was a womanizer, and let him believe that Edwin and Elijah were his kids." I look over to Seth. I see a man that has aged for the first time of his life, but Millie's still looks like a freaking model. Does this woman ever show any signs of remorse?

Officer Jernigan strolls in. "Kayla."

"What is going on?" I nervously scratched the top of my hand.

"I've come to tell you that Edwin and Elijah are......."

Damaged Love

&

Forever Bound

Book Two in the Bound
Series

by

Layla Stevens

Damaged Love and Forever Bound

Copyright © 2015 Layla Stevens

Published by: Scilicet Group LLC

Cover Design by: Rachel A Olsen

CHAPTER ONE

Who Lives and Who Dies

"My family is my strength and my weakness."

~Aishwarya Rai Bachchan

Officer Jernigan strolls in. "Kayla."

"What's going on?" I nervously scratched the top of my hand.

"I've come to tell you that Edwin and Elijah are..."

"Well spit it out. Officer Jernigan, they are what?"

"Well I hate to say this, we lost Edwin. The doctors did all they could, but he was too damaged. His heart could not take the drugs that were in his system. There was no way to save him. They tried everything they could, but there was nothing else they could do."

I hear Millie scream and start sobbing.

"Elijah is still touch and go. Right now he's in a medically induced coma. It's safer for him."

The shrieking and screams from Millie tear me apart.

I stutter, "I'm so sorry Millie, but he was going to kill me and Violet. I know my words will never bring him back."

"Kayla, you killed my son," bitterness and anger color Millie's voice, "I will never forgive you for this. You are dead to me, Kayla. You should have stayed gone and never come back. We were all better off without your stupid ass."

"Now, Millie don't be so dramatic," Seth states. "She was protecting herself from your sons. What did you expect her to do? Let them rape her all over again? We should have done something years ago. Maybe then they wouldn't have turned out the way they did. They didn't have the best childhood either. They had us, but we were never really parents. We were always too self-involved. I was always chasing a skirt, and well, you were doing whatever it is that you do. Frankly, I have no idea what it is you do all day long."

"I don't give a rat's ass what she was doing. My son is dead. How the hell are you so God damned calm and collected Seth? Our son is dead. D. E. A. D. What part of that don't you get? He is not waking up. And as far as me doing stuff all day long, I take care of our house and make sure that your whores are paid for."

"I get it Millie, but as you just said, the boys were not and are not mine. So excuse me for a minute if I am not kissing your ass."

"Officer Jernigan, thank you for telling us, what happens now?" I ask.

"There will be an official investigation, Kayla, so don't leave Seattle. And don't make me come looking for you."

"Am I under arrest?" I ask and wipe away a single tear

that rolls down my cheek.

"No, not yet, but I will be questioning you and Violet. As soon as Elijah wakes up, we will question him. For now, make sure that you check in with me."

"Yes, I swear to everything holy I'm not going anywhere. Hell, I don't even know when I'm getting sprung out of here. I just woke up. All I know is that it's mid-afternoon."

"Millie, come on," Seth says, tugging on Millie's arm. "She listened to what you had to say, and now we have a funeral to plan. We need to go get an update on Elijah. He needs his parents. Even though I'm not his biological father, I will never turn my back on him. I've raised him since he was born. He may not be mine by blood, but God damn it, he's still my son. And not even you can take that from me."

"Kayla, I'm warning you. Stay away from my family!" Millie shouts.

"Is that a threat, Millie? I don't think Officer Jernigan heard you."

"No dear, it is not a threat," she says, her voice eerily calm, "I was simply telling you to stay away from my son. You've already killed one of them. I don't want to bury the other."

"Millie, I am not even going to try and tell you that it was an accident because you'll believe what you want. Know that I did what I had to do to in order to protect myself and Violet, but I will say he got what he deserved."

"Kayla, you will regret the day you came to live with

us!" she was screaming as Seth was pushing her out the door.

"I have always regretted living with you Millie. I wish I had my birth mother, and I never fucking knew you and your stupid ass family."

"Kayla, dear, why don't you rest? I'm going to head to Garret's, and I will check on you later." Patrice leans down and kisses my forehead.

"Dr. Doyle, give me a few minutes, and I'll take you home. Let me give Kayla a kiss and tell her I love her," Garret says, standing up.

"First, Garrett, we're all friends. Please call me Patrice. You stay here with Kayla. She may need you through the night."

"Well, at least let me have Wyatt take you. There is no reason for you to rent a car."

"No Garrett, I'm fine. I'll call a cab and will be back in the morning."

"Patrice, I'd be happy to take you to Garrett's if you want. It is on my way home," Officer Jernigan offers.

"Officer Jernigan, are you flirting with me?"

"Ma'am, I'd be honored if you would allow me to take you home. I know this city like the back of my hand, and I'd hate for you to get lost."

"Officer Jernigan," Patrice begins.

"Please call me Rodney," he interrupts. "I am only Officer Jernigan when I'm at work, and I won't worry about work until tomorrow when I have to write up the reports."

"Okay, Rodney," Patrice says. "If you insist on taking me, then you must know I'm starving. I need to eat, and I'm not one of those salad eating women like you're used to. I like to eat. I'm from Texas, and we eat steak. If you can handle that, then we have a deal. No funny business, you hear me?" She gathers her belongings and tells Rodney she is ready to go.

"After you, Patrice," Rodney says, gesturing to the door.

"You two behave, and don't do anything I wouldn't do, Patrice," I call out.

"Kayla please, if I wanted to get busy honey, I would." Patrice replies

"Well, alright then. You have fun, and if you need anything, Patrice, just let me know. The house is stocked though, so you should have everything you need," Garret says.

"Okay Garrett. Thank you so much for everything, and above all, for taking care of Kayla."

"Please, it's my job. I would do anything for her," Garret bends down and kisses me on my temple. "I would move mountains for her Patrice, and one day I will make it official and make her my wife."

"Oh wow," I say. "Garrett, honey, please tell me that is not my proposal because if it is, you suck at being romantic."

"No babe, I promise when it's time to make you mine, I will do it the correct way. It will blow your mind, so don't fret," I whisper in her ear.

"Yeah, I am not even on the page of talking marriage babe."

"Yes Kayla, I know you're not ready for marriage but I hope one day I can change your mind."

"One day, but give me time. "

"Kayla, I will give you as much time as you need. Don't you know I love you, and I'm not ever letting you go again? Now that I have you, it's forever."

Just then the door swings open and a tearful Violet comes running to my bed side.

"You bitch, you scared the shit out of me! First, you save my life and then you don't wake up. I'm so proud of you and how you took both those assholes down. Kay, you are the strongest woman I know." VI says all at once.

I look into her eyes and see she is still healing from the beating she took from the fucking Stanton twins.

"VI, I'm so sorry they involved you just to get to me. I'm sorry for everything they did to you." I turn to both VI and Garrett, "This is why I left so none of this would happen. I come home, and what happens? My two best friends are hurt and the only man I ever loved is a wreck because of me," I say and tears start to fall down my face.

Before they can say anything I go on, "Elijah is going to be out for blood since I killed his twin and tried to kill him."

I can't stop the tears now. VI takes one hand and Garrett comes to sit by me on the bed, wrapping me in his arms.

"That scumbag will not hurt you again baby," Garrett says

VI adds, "I'll kill him if he ever comes near you again."

I know they believe what they are saying, but they do not know the real evil he is.

The rest of the night I am restless. I lay in Garrett arms and have nightmares throughout the night.

The next morning Patrice comes in with Officer Jernigan, who asks if he can take my statement of the events and what led up to it.

"I have nothing to hide anymore Officer Jernigan."

"Okay, let's begin," he opens his little notepad and clicks his pen.

"I know these were your adopted brothers, so do you want to tell me why you suspect they were targeting you at Club Fuchsia and then going as far as kidnapping your best friend to draw you out?"

"It started when I was a kid. I was physically, emotionally, and mentally abused. I was raped by both of them over and over throughout several years. And then they threatened to get rid of all of those I love. They even said they'd find my birth mother and kill her too. They took VI knowing I would do whatever they wanted to get her back safe and sound. Little did they expect I was ready to fight back for the first time in my life and not submit to their demands."

He motions with his hand for me to go on, so I tell him,

"I worked on distracting them long enough to get the gun, and I turned and shot both of them. But I was afraid VI was going to die from the beating and tazing she took."

His questions seemed to go on for hours when in actuality they lasted 45 minutes. By the end I was in tears and told him, "I fear for my life and the lives of those that I love. And once Elijah wakes up, he will be out for blood and will seek revenge for his brother's death. He will think that his brother's death was on my hands. Which I guess it was, but if you want me to say I am sorry Officer Jernigan, I won't say it. "

Officer Jernigan stands from his chair and tells me, "As far as I'm concerned, this was a case of self-defense and no charges will be filed." he turns to Patrice, "I will pick you up after my shift for dinner." He kisses her forehead and turns to walk out of the room, but before he gets out the door he turns to me and says, "Kayla, I will have one of my best men stand guard outside this door until you are released. Then I'll put your home on the patrol unit's route to be passed by every few hours, as well as your friends homes."

The next two days in the hospital drag by before I am finally released to go home. I am getting tired of being poked with freaking needles.

"I told the nurse if she came at me one more time for blood I was going to stab her in the eye with her own damn needle." Of course that got a round of laughter from all who were in here. But I am done, I am ready to go.

"Garrett, please go ask the doctor when I can leave. I am going crazy in here."

"Okay love, I will go ask but you can't be threatening everyone. They are doing their job."

"Shut it Winters. I don't want to hear it. I am ready to go. If it were you here, you would be saying the same thing."

"Possibly love, but just let them do their job without giving them too much grief."

"I can't promise that. I'm sorry I'm being irritable but I know he is here in this hospital and there are only a few floors that are separating me from him. As much as I want to have faith in the Seattle Police Department, they have not always done their jobs before.

"Yes that may be true, but you need to heal and remember Elijah is still in a coma."

"I understand that, but I want to go home and soak in my tub. I want a glass of red wine and I want to just relax. You can't relax in here. There is always something beeping and people constantly checking on you."

"You will be home soon babe and then you and I can soak in the tub together."

"Hey, I never said I wanted you in there with me."

He grabs his heart like I hurt him, and says "Babe, I am sorry but you will no longer be out of site, so suck it buttercup, you are stuck like chuck."

"Ugh, you asshole! You and your brother know I hate being called that!" While rubbing his arm where I gave him a love tap he says "I thought this place was supposed to be a sterile environment? And yes, we know you hate being called that, but seeing how you are basically on bed rest there is nothing you can do about it."

"Oh you just wait, I know how to shut you up...I can just say no."

"Say no to what?" He looks over at me

I smirk, and say, "You are not getting laid for a month of Sundays!"

"Oh Shit, I will be good, I swear."

"Yeah, yeah. Blow it out your ass."

I look at the door, and my nurse is smiling and holding papers in her hand.

"Kayla, I have your discharge papers."

I squeal, and almost jump out of the bed.

"Easy there killer, there are some rules you need to know about."

Damn rules, "Okay, lay them on me."

"First, you are getting out of here because we were told you have someone to take care of you around the clock. Is this true?"

"Yes" I hear in unison from the rat pack—Patrice, Wyatt, Garrett. Rodney shakes his head.

"Well I guess they have spoken for me, so that rule is taken care of. What is next?"

"Second, you are basically on bed rest. No work, no walking around, and no stress."

"Bed rest, really? I feel fine. Why do I need to be on bed rest?"

"Well, I can throw these papers away missy, and you can stay here for the next couple of weeks."

"No, no, no! Bed rest it is," I practically scream at her.

"That's what I thought. Next, if you have any headaches at all, you are to call your doctor. Is that understood?"

"Yes ma'am," I give her a salute.

"I can't stress this enough. No stress Kayla. If you stress, it could cause all kinds of problems for your health. So I just need a signature from you, and then I will take out your IV, and you can be on your way."

"Okay, I will do what you say, I swear, I have been in here long enough and no offense you all are a kick ass staff, but I want my kind sized bed and my seven head shower."

"No offense taken dear. We understand and want you to be able to stay home. That is why the rules of discharge are so important for you to follow."

"We all will make sure she does what she is supposed to do," says Patrice.

"So Kayla, now that I have gone over everything, do you have any questions for me?" the nurse asks.

"No, not that I can think of. I am sure my family here

can answer everything for me since they were the ones who were awake when the doctors were talking to me in the beginning. I take that back, I do have one little question?"

"Sure doll, what is it?"

"I'm freaking starving! Can I eat normal food?"

"Ha ha, yes just take it easy. Your throat will be sore for a while because of all the tubes and stuff we had down your throat, but it should be okay within a few days."

"Oh thank god, because I am craving Ivar's."

"That is a good place; just take it easy and you should be fine."

"Thank you so much. I am sorry, but I never even asked your name."

"My name is Kerrigan."

"Oh wow! What a beautiful name. Well I would say that it has been nice knowing you, but to be honest I hope I never see you again. And I mean that with no disrespect."

"Yeah, I know what you mean. None taken. Again, please take care of yourself."

"I will, I promise. Patrice, will you please help me get dressed? And the rest of you, can you wait outside please?"

"Yes Kayla I will," she says, ushering the rest of my dysfunctional family out of the room.

"Thank you for staying Dr. Doyle. I am sure you have

other patients."

"Kayla dear, I told you from day one that I would always be here for you. And I have a staff of people who can work for me at any time."

"I just want you to know that it means the world that you are here. You know that I have longed for my birth mother, and well, you are the closest thing I have to a mother."

"Oh Kayla honey, you just made my day because I think of you like a daughter as well."

I get up and hug her neck and I see a tear roll down her cheek.

"Hey Patrice, can I ask you something?"

"Sure, you know you can ask me anything."

"The other day when Millie was in here, she said we all have secretes. What did she mean when she said that?

"Oh, it was nothing worth talking about. One day I will tell you all about me, but let's get you better first?"

"Okay, but you know I will not forget about this."

"Yes Kayla, I know this all too well. I promise one day, when I know there will be no interruptions, I will tell you but not right now. Let's get you dressed so that you can go home and relax. You may as well accept it because that's all you will be doing."

"Yeah, please don't remind me. Before I get too relaxed, I need to call and check in with my job. Hell, I don't even know if I still have a job. I hope so because my medical bills are going to be off the charts."

"Your work will be there in a couple of weeks dear. You are going to do what the doctor said. You are going to relax and nothing else, do you understand me?"

"Geez, I got it drill sergeant," I smile at her, grab my bags of stuff, and open the door. When I look down, I see my chariot—the wheelchair they make you ride in when being discharged.

I look over at Garrett, and he smiles at me before saying, "Get in my lady, and I will be your escort for the ride down."

Something about that man gives me goose bumps in my lady parts. Damn I can't wait to get home so I can do some naughty things to him.

CHAPTER TWO

Finally Home

"Don't be pushed by your problems. Be led by your dreams."

~Ralph Waldo Emerson

I'm finally going home. Garrett is driving me, and I am gazing out the window wondering what Elijah is going to try to do next. I'm startled when I feel a hand squeeze mine as a tear falls from my eye.

"Kayla? Baby, please don't cry. I can handle anyone else crying, but you I can't. Let's wipe those tears and get you safely inside your house." Garrett says, kissing the back of my hand as he pulls into my driveway.

"If only you knew the fear I keep bottled within. I keep it from you and the others in order to protect you. Babe, if you only knew the pure hell they put me through. You know everything I went through because I have shared everything with you, but you can't experience the feelings. Knowing is not the same as reliving every minute of every day of torture. If you could experience those feelings—my feelings, then you might understand how afraid I am."

I'm scared shitless for me and for my little family. No, we aren't a blood family, but these misfits are the only family I have, and I'll be damned if I let some trifling, Twatwaffle destroy what little bit of happiness I have.

A few seconds later, he is coming around the truck and lifting me out. Instead of placing me on the ground, he carries me into my home and manages to disarm both security systems I have in place. At last, he sets me down on the sofa and asks me what I would like for dinner.

I tell him Chinese, and he has it delivered, but while we are waiting the 50 minutes for delivery, he runs a hot bath for me to soak in and wash away the grime from the hospital stay and the events that led up to it. While I'm soaking, I have music playing softly in the background, and I'm trying my best to keep my mind off of anything to do with Elijah and what he might do if he gets his hands on me again. The worst thing I'm trying to avoid is what I am going to have to do to keep my loved ones safe. When I come out of the bathroom wrapped in a pink towel and my hair pulled up and wrapped in another pink towel. I dry off and soon I'm in my comfortable clothes; an over-sized shirt, some boxer briefs, and yoga pants.

I go downstairs to find Garrett has the table set. The food is served and there are even candles lit in the center of the table. His chair is next to mine so we can have a romantic dinner, and the sweetest song is playing in the background. I could not even tell you what song it was because it was just an instrumental version.

Garrett walks over and takes my hand, kissing my cheek and then my lips. He tells me I look beautiful. I watch as he walks to the table, pulling me behind him. He pulls out my chair and allows me to sit before taking a seat himself. A true gentleman. How lucky am I?

We make small talk as we eat, and every once in a while he'll feed me a bite of his food.

"Babe, why are you not eating?" he asks as he moves closer to me and kisses me on the cheek.

"I'm sorry. It's hard to eat when I know either Millie or Elijah will try and do something. I know you think I'm crazy, but the look in her eyes when she found out that Edwin died was pure hatred. I always knew she was not my biggest supporter, and I think her telling me all the shit she did that day was just to make her look good. I know there will be major problems. She is not going to let this go. According to her, I killed her son. Yes, I guess you could say that I did, but I was tired of him hurting me and the people close to me. I will never forgive myself for them hurting VI, and I could kick her ass for going there in the first place. Is she fucking insane?"

"Okay, let's deal with one thing at a time. First of all, you are safe. You are here at home, and there is safety in numbers. Second, VI is a grown woman, and you know as well as I do that there is no stopping her once she has her mind made up. And third, I would have done the same thing as her. She beat me to it. So if she is insane, I will be right there rocking in my straight jacket beside her. Come on babe...that was supposed to be a joke. You know, ha-ha, funny."

"I just don't see the humor in all of this. Wyatt was hurt, VI was almost raped, and you are over here cracking fucking jokes. It is not comedy hour at the Apollo Garrett. This is real fucking life. They are not sitting back and laying low. I will swear on my life that Millie is planning something. I can feel it."

"Okay, so say you're right babe. What are you going to do about it?"

"I won't tell you my plans Garrett because I don't want Officer Jernigan to get you with accessory to any of my possible crimes.

"I will not let you go half-cocked to deal with the crazies on your own. So I expect you to be honest with me. Kayla, I love you and I want to protect you, but I can't do that if you won't let me in on your plans. I am not some weak man, so please don't treat me as one. I know you are thinking, I can see the wheels turning in your beautiful head, but I know I am not going to get any answers right now but I am telling you I will not drop this."

"Okay. Garrett let's clean up and then watch a movie."

After we cleared our plates, we laid on the sofa together. I lay in his arms and finally feel myself begin to relax. I lift my head off of Garrett's chest and kiss him softly, slowly, and seductively.

Garrett kisses me back with the same passion I am giving him, and he brings his arms around my body a little tighter. I lean up and grasp his face, and as I deepen the kiss, I am wanting more.

I want to feel him inside of me. No, I need to feel him inside of me. I whisper, "Make love to me."

He smiles and says "Baby, you don't know how long I've waited for you to say those words to me. I thought I lost you, and when I got you back in the hospital, the only thing I wanted was for you to wake up so I can make sweet, passionate love to the only woman I have ever loved and will ever love."

I am now sitting up and I am undressing him when he tells me to take it slow.

I roll us over, and he nudges my legs open and lays between them. He kisses my lips and moves to nibble along my jaw. Following the contours, he finds my earlobe and sucks gently. Never remaining in one place too long, he trails kisses down my neck and across my throat until he reaches my T-shirt.

He rips the shirt over my head and finds I'm not wearing a bra. His lips roam across my collarbone and then to my taut nipple. He plays with it a split second before taking it into his mouth. He sucks and flicks it with his tongue.

Garrett tortures me with his mouth while his thumb and forefinger are on the other nipple.

I am craving more and I have a tingling in my core. Garrett's hands glide down my body, pulls off my yoga pants and boxers as his lips trail down my body, stopping to kiss in between my hipbones.

All of a sudden his head dips between my legs and he starts licking and sucking on my swollen clit. I feel one, then two fingers slowly slip inside of me massaging the front wall of my pussy. It drives me insane. I grab his hair and pull him in even more, wrapping my legs around his shoulders. As I begin to climax I call out his names, and he doesn't stop until I cum.

I glance down at him and he's looking up at me, licking his lips, "You're the best dessert I could ever fucking have."

He then crawls back up my body and plunges his tongue into my mouth. I can taste my juices on his tongue and it excites me. I feel the head of his cock at the entrance of my core, and then he enters me slowly. I moan loudly, making him stop for a second. I want to enjoy this moment, I pull him closer so that he is now all the way inside me. We have a rhythm all our own, and I see fireworks in my head. This man knows how to make my body scream and quiver. We slow dance with each other, a dance only unique to us.

"God I have missed this," I whisper.

He says "You have no idea. Your body was made for me. We fit perfectly together."

We take it slow and make love to each other before we both collapse. Slow kisses from him send chills all over my body.

Garrett is on the side of me and pulls me into his arms, kissing my neck. Then he turns my head so my ear is right next to his mouth and he whispers "You're safe with me."

I turn my head with sleepy eyes, give him a kiss, and all I can say is I love you. I hear him say I love you too, and then I must drift to sleep—the first restful sleep I've gotten since I've woken up. He is like a security blanket that I can wrap my soul in.

The next day I wake up in my bed, wrapped in Garrett's arms. He must've carried me up to bed at some point during the night. I don't even remember falling asleep. But after a night of love making, and just getting out of the hospital I was exhausted.

I know today is Edwin's funeral, and if I'm not there to

see the evil monster go into the ground, never to come out of it again, then I will never truly have closure. I have to see it to believe it.

I know that I am not welcome, but I have to start to come up with a plan. When I try getting out of the bed Garrett wraps his arms tight around me and asks, "Where are you going baby?"

I give him a quick kiss and tell him I need to take a quick shower but today is the funeral and I have to be there.

Garrett jumps to his feet and screams "Are you fucking kidding me? You are not going to that funeral."

I look him dead in the eyes and tell him if I don't go I will never have closure.

"Babe, you know you are not welcome there."

I give him a small smile and tell him I have a plan and that I need him to be there by my side.

He walks over to me, kisses me quickly and says "I'm not leaving your side, no matter what your crazy ass wants to do. I will be right there with you." He takes my hand as we go into the shower and emerge quickly, dressing in black. I am wearing a pair of black skinny jeans, a charcoal sweater, and thigh-high boots. I grab a black jacket and get dressed to look the part of a person in mourning—not that I'm in mourning, but I don't want to stand out. I look the part of a grieving family member. I throw some water-proof mascara on my eyes and some simple pink gloss on my lips.

Before long we head to Lakeview Memorial Cemetery in

Seattle. Garrett and I are keeping a safe distance and bringing flowers to an unknown grave. We act as though we are just there to pay our respects to that person. I look at the graves of so many people along the way. There are some celebrities buried here such as Martial-arts film star Bruce Lee and his son, Brandon Lee.

So not to draw attention to ourselves, we watch the services and I am shocked to see Jason Woodrow there. I'm even more shocked to witness a confrontation and words are exchanged between him and Seth. I whisper to Garrett, "Look, Raegan's dad is here." I can tell this is going to be good.

I can hear Jason's raised voice saying, "If I would've raised those boys, my son would still be alive, but no, you had to raise them and let one get killed and the other be put in a medically induced coma. It's because you can't control them and their actions," then goes on to say "Millie never told me I was a father. I would have taken care of them had I known."

Seth voice raises and tells him "Those are my sons! Get the fuck off of my son's grave, or I will have you forcibly removed. I have raised him since birth." That's when Jason swings a right hook at Seth, who takes a step back and jabs Jason in the nose with an uppercut, knocking him to the ground.

After getting on top of Jason, Seth starts to pound him. There is blood on both of them, torn shirts and bruised egos.

Jason is able to roll them over and take control of the fight, beating Seth. Jason punches him in the ribs and then goes to Seth's face which is bloody. Both men are winded.

Both men are saying that was my son. Eventually, some

of the onlookers break up the fight that is sure to be on the ten o'clock news. With all the media surrounding this funeral, I'm sure they captured everything on camera. Millie is screaming at both of them, causing more of a problem.

Soon though, everyone leaves the cemetery and it is quiet. I am in tears. I am so angry and upset that I drag Garrett to the grave. I fall to my knees and start pounding my fist into the fresh dirt. I am taking all my anger out on the ground. Dirt is flying everywhere. I spit on the dirt, only to hit it again with my fist. I start cussing out Edwin for everything he's done to me, calling him a fucking bastard and I'm screaming how much I hated him. "You fucking prick, I hate you! I am glad you are dead! I hope you are enjoying Hell!"

I then feel Garrett's arms wrap around me and he tells me, "Baby let's go!"

I say hell no, and I stand up, grab him, and kiss him with everything I have. I tell him I need him—here and now, hard and rough.

He looks at me dumbfounded, but he grabs and kisses me and says, "If you need me baby, you got me."

I try to unbutton his jeans. But he stops my hands.

"No, not here. We are not going to have sex on this grave Kayla. I know that you are hurt and you have every right to be, but you are not going to sink to his level."

"Garrett, please take away all the pain." I slap my fist onto his chest.

"Kayla you can hit me all you want if that will make you

fill better. I will be your punching bag."

I try again to get into his pants. He throws me over his shoulder. I'm kicking and screaming at him to put me down.

"I will not put you down, I am going to take you home, where you can calm down."

"Why are you such an asshole?" I scream.

We get to the truck and he literally throws me in the truck and slams the door. I am stunned because I have never seen him like this.

"Kayla, normally I don't say much, I accept that you have issues with them, but to try to have sex on a dead man's grave? You need to get yourself together!"

"Don't you dare tell me I need to get myself together, you have no fucking clue how he hurt me!"

"Kayla, you are acting like a child. Yes he hurt you, but the man is dead. You watched him get put into the damn ground. Do you really think it's okay to have sex there?"

"I just wanted him to know that he has no power over me any longer." "Do you know how to take your power back Kayla?" "No, I don't Garrett." I say crying. "You have faith in yourself. You hold the power, not them. Take your power back. Show the world that you are better because of your past. Don't be a statistic."

I never thought Edwin's death would make me feel like this. I am so pissed at him. I have wanted him dead for years, but I am also torn. He was always the lesser of the two evils.

When his brother was harsh and cold, he was caring and warm. I know it sounds crazy to think like that of someone who hurt you, but I always thought Elijah was the leader and Edwin just followed. He did what he was told to do.

Though I am still in tears, I can't believe I was so enraged at the gravesite that I did that to Garrett, but the entire way home he tells me not to worry about it. He's there for whatever I need, whenever I need it.

Today, I needed him more than I need anything else. He took every hit I gave him today.

CHAPTER THREE

A Night Out

"If things seem under control, you are just not going fast
enough."

~Mario Andretti

While we are driving, I decide I do not want to go home
so I tell Garrett to take me to the club. I am tired of sitting at
home and it has been less than twenty four hours since I was
released from the hospital. After telling Garrett, I call VI and tell
her and Wyatt need to meet us there.

VI says "Great! They have an awesome band playing
called Jaded. Besides, we can all use the night out and a good
time after everything that's happened"

I hang up with VI, and Garrett turns the beast in the
direction of the club. He grabs my hand and says, "Babe, are you
sure you want to go back to the club?"

"Yes, I'm sure. I know what happened last time we were
there, but I need to get out of the house before I lose my damn
mind."

"Okay babe, I was just making sure. I know you hate
sitting around and not doing anything but you need to rest."

"Yeah, yeah. I know I do but give me tonight please. Let me just enjoy a night out, and I swear on my pink Coach purse I will lay low tomorrow."

"Wow! Swearing on a pink Coach purse. You must mean business because that's like a Bible for you."

"Why yes dear it is. That is why I swore on it instead of the Bible. If I swear on a Bible, I might go to hell, but if I swear on my purse, you know I mean business."

"Touche' babe, touché."

It doesn't take us long to get to the club. When we pull in, I see Wyatt's crotch rocket parked right up front and VI's car around the side. That lets me know they are here already. Before Garrett can even shut off my SUV, I am out and headed for the door.

Once outside the door, we find VI and Wyatt waiting for us at the V.I.P. entrance.

We make our way inside and I'm surprised. The band is kick ass.

Garrett and I are on the dance floor bumping and grinding to the music. He's covering me in kisses, not giving a fuck who sees. Quite frankly, I don't either. I look around and suddenly see the bitch Reagan walk up. Garrett must see it too because he takes my hand and leads me back to the table where VI and Wyatt are waiting with our drinks. Unfortunately, she follows us.

I sit on Garrett's lap, and Reagan becomes enraged. She is ranting that I stole her man, and she has come to claim what is hers.

I get up in her face and tell her if she doesn't get out of my face I'm going to knock her for a fucking loop. I'm so not in the mood to play her games. I watch her turn around, thinking she was leaving, however the bitch grabs a drink from the table and has the balls to throw it into my face. Before I can react, VI snaps and spins out of control.

She screams, "I whooped your skanky ass in school, and I will do it again. Reagan didn't you get the memo, you are old news. He doesn't want you. He has moved on to greener pastures. So bye Felicia!"

She grabs Reagan by the hair and slams her head onto the table. She then pushes her onto the ground, straddles her waist, and pounds on her face. Reagan tries to block the blows, and VI moves to her ribs. VI hits her over and over. Finally VI gets up, grabs Reagan by the hair, and pulls her to her feet, dragging her out of the club. There is a crowd gathering and VI doesn't want witnesses.

I follow to make sure she doesn't completely lose all self-control. When I walk into the night air, I see her throw Reagan into her car. Yes, the little red car I saw that I thought was one of the bastards had traded their truck for. The one I saw when I was headed to the boat house to save VI.

Of course this enrages me even more, but I hear VI say, "If you ever come near Kayla or Garrett again, I swear to God I will make your life a living hell. After what you allowed to be done to me, you're lucky I don't shoot you here and now on the spot!"

"Garrett, will be my man again, you wait. He will grow tired of the used up wanna-be."

VI reaches into her purse and pulls out a Taser. Hell, I didn't know she even had one. Before I can react, VI is touching Reagan with it. She starts burning the bitch's chest screaming, "How the fuck do you like it you cunt? You stood there and watched them do this to me now it's your turn to live with scars. How does it feel bitch?" I have never seen VI like this.

VI then turns and walks away. She spots me at the corner of the building and makes her way toward me. She breaks down and cries, "That bitch saw what they did to me and did nothing to stop them."

"Kayla, all she was after was getting Garrett away from you. She didn't care what they did to me or you."

"She's lucky I don't shoot her here on the spot."

I hold her in my arms and tell her, "She will get hers when the time is right, but right now is not the time. We need to pull ourselves together."

I give her a moment to compose herself. I see the fucking trick and I walk over to the car. I spit in the bitch's face and pull her by the hair to look at me. When I see her face, I punch her five times and tell her if she ever lays a finger on my best friend again or let anything happen to her or even attempt to come near my man, she hasn't seen who the real threat is yet.

"I'm the bitch not to be fucked with!" I slam her head on the steering wheel, knocking her out. I turn around and walk back to VI.

I am thankful that no one is in the parking lot to see what has happened. I know where the cameras are and I hope that none of them are situated to spot that bitch's car or record what has been done, but if so, we will deal with it when the time comes.

"Come on gutterslut, let's go get our men and work off some steam on the dance floor. I need a damn drink."

She looks down at her hands and sees the blood, and I pull her into the club and make a beeline to the employee lounge and immediately lock the door.

"Come on babe, let's get you cleaned up."

She looks up at me and wipes her face, and for the first time I actually see her tear soaked face. Her mascara is running down her face. And I see what looks like a fat lip. I grab the first aid kit and start to clean her up. She is trembling, and crying.

"Kay, I am so sorry. It's always drama with her and I was fed up. I could not take it anymore."

"Shhhhh, you have nothing to be sorry for. She had it coming. And when did you get a damn Taser? I knew about your gun because, well hell, I have shot that, but a Taser too?"

"Kayla, I bought it after my last run in with her. I knew that I'd see her ass again and I wanted to make sure she would feel the same pain I felt. I am not playing anymore. She better hope and pray that I don't see her in a dark place around town, because I swear to everything holy, I will kill her."

"Geez, Vi, tell me how you really feel."

"Anyway, enough about her, I don't want to hear her name for the remainder of the night. Let's go find those Winter men. I'm sure they are freaking the fuck out."

"We have been gone for a while now. So, speaking of the Winter men, are you and Wyatt like together, you know, have you guys made it Facebook official yet? Because you know unless it's online you are not official."

"No gutterslut, we have not given it a label or title. We're having fun, and he is sooooo much fun!"

"Okay, no labels, I got you. Does he know you're in love with him?"

"Wait! Who said anything about love?" VI asks.

"You didn't have to say it VI. I know you. You're my sister from another mister. You can try hiding it from Wyatt, but you can't hide it from me no matter how hard you try.

"Kay, yes, I love him, but I am not going to be the first to say those words. I don't have to worry about him saying that because Ariel broke his heart, and he has made it clear that there will never be anything serious."

"I don't know about that. I see the way he looks at you. I saw the look on his face when you were in trouble. He loves you too. Wyatt may not be ready to admit it, but he loves your ass despite your reluctance to admit it to the world. Okay, I see the look you are giving me. Enough with the heavy talk. Let's go dance and have fun, but know a good man like him won't remain single forever."

"Kayla, I love you to the moon and back, but if you open

your big mouth to Wyatt, I swear I will sneak in your house and destroy all your shoes, and then pour bleach on everything you own that is pink."

VI is laughing so hard, I think she may fall down. I hold my hands up to surrender. When my shoes and signature color are threatened, I know when to surrender despite VI's joking.

"That is what I thought you ass. I mean it—keep your trap shut."

I raise my hands and do the scouts honor, and she hits my shoulder and we both start laughing.

"Damn. Did you guys fall in the bathroom or something? Is everything okay? After Reagan showing up here, I want to make sure you are fine." A strong, familiar voice whispers in my ear. I turn around and see Garrett's sexy face.

"I am fine. She does not worry me. It was only girl talk, and then someone in there needed a tampon, so I went out to the beast and got her one.

I see VI look at me and I know she will have my back. Though I am not worried, I don't think he would care that his ex is sitting in the parking lot with a broken nose and now has some wicked scars.

After we get back in the club, VI takes Wyatt by the hand and drags him into the VIP lounge. The next thing we hear are her screams. Flashbacks of the first night I was here came into mind, how I had watched Wyatt and VI. Suddenly, I was turned on. I grabbed Garrett and lead him into Wyatt's office.

"Babe, where are we going? I thought we were going to

the dance floor."

"No. I have other plans for us at this moment." I rub his cock through his jeans as I drag him into the office. Slamming the door behind us, I push him against it and lock the knob.

"Babe, normally I would not complain, but we are in a public place."

"Shut it Winters, a girl has needs. And right now I need you. I have his pants undone and I am on my knees, within a second I have his dick in my mouth. I take long slow licks and then I suck on the mushroomed head. I cup his balls and use my other hand while using my mouth on his dick. My assault on him makes him weak in the knees, and I can feel his knees shaking. I peer up at him through my lashes and notice that his eyes are rolling in the back of his head. I go for the gusto and I take him all the way into the back of my throat and it doesn't take long. I can feel that he is close. I sneak my finger into his ass and that is all it takes. I now taste his thick cum. His balls tighten, and I am milking him. I take every last drop and then swallow it all. I clean him up with my tongue and kiss the head.

I start to stand up and the next thing I know I am turned around and my face is pushed up against the wall. My jeans are being pushed down around my ankles. He is reaching his hand under my shirt and has my nipple in his hands. Within seconds he is inside me, thrusting and making me scream out his name. We have never had sex like this and I fucking love it. I tell him to fuck me harder and I feel a slap on my ass before his hands wrap around my throat. He whispers, "Your pussy is like a fucking drug. One taste and you're fucking addicted."

I push my ass into him and he takes his other hand and

has found my clit. He is fucking me from behind and has a hold of my clit with his thumb and I am seeing stars.

"Babe, tell me whose pussy this is."

"It's yours!" I scream.

"Are you sure? I don't know, maybe I should stop."

"Don't you fucking dare" I scream "This is your pussy, baby. Now fuck me harder!"

He pumps a couple more times and we come together. We are both breathing heavy but he pulls my face towards him and gives me the most passionate kiss I have ever had.

"Kayla honey, what are you doing to me? I am not someone who has sex in public places, but today we almost had sex on the grave of a dead man and now my brother's office. I swear I am not complaining so don't take it that way, but are you sure you are okay?"

I stand there for a minute just looking at him, I shake my head and tell him I am fine. "Don't worry about me babe. I promise if something is bothering me I will let you know."

"But I do worry. I know that you still have your demons you are working through, but I am here. Please don't leave me out of the loop. I will listen and I won't judge."

"I know that babe, but I am fine. Now let's go get a drink because I am suddenly thirsty. You wouldn't happen to know why, would you?" I ask, laughing and pull my jeans up and adjust my bra so that I am fully covered.

The steady beat of the music is hypnotic and I catch

myself swaying to the beat. Garrett grabs my hand and leads me on the dance floor. He is holding me close and we are slow dancing to Ed Sheeran's Thinking Out Loud. Garrett is singing the words to me and it melts my heart. I whisper, "I love you Garrett."

He places my hand on his heart and says "Babe, you have my heart and I love you too. "

I kiss him softly on the dance floor while we are swaying back and forth. There is a room full of people around us, but I don't see anyone, just him. It is like time stands still during this song.

The next thing I know the song is over and I am being led over to the bar.

"Hey Buttercup, that was some hot moves out there on the dance floor." Wyatt says playfully.

"Hey don't be jealous Wyatt. I know how to make my man happy."

"Oh believe me. Vi makes me very happy." Wyatt says.

"Yeah the whole club knows how happy she makes you." I look over to VI and I could see she doesn't care that the whole club heard her have sex.

She looks over at me and says, "Sorry about that, but I was horny and wanted to get laid. It is not my fault that I am a vocal person."

"Let's go. I'm beat. It has been a long day and I am ready for my bed."

"Vi, are you coming home with me or you going to Kayla's?" Wyatt asks.

"Everyone can stay at my house. I have plenty of room."

CHAPTER FOUR

The Past Always Comes Back

"My life is perfect, even when it is not."

~Ellen Degeneres

Kayla and VI are both passed out in the beast and my baby looks like an angel. I see her smile in her sleep and I hope that she is finally having good dreams.

Once we were back at Kayla's, Wyatt and I carry the girls inside and put them to bed. I take a quick shower and brush my teeth then I go down to the kitchen for a snack while Kayla sleeps. I am walking down the hallway when angry voices greet me and fill every room of the house. Who the fuck is here? I peer around the corner, and I see Patrice talking to Seth.

"Patrice, I know damn well you remember our night in college," Seth states.

"You mean the night you raped me? I was a virgin you motherfucker. I know you slipped something in my drink because I only had one drink and there was no way I was willing."

"Our night together was magical. I didn't have to rape you, you were more than willing. Besides, you know as well as I do that Kayla is your daughter as much as she is mine." He states.

"If you knew she was your daughter, how could you let what happened to her happen, and then treat her like nothing?" Patrice says crying.

"I didn't know then, but I know now. I knew the moment I saw you standing by her bedside in the hospital. I knew you looked familiar. I would remember you anywhere."

"That doesn't mean she's my daughter, but I do care for her. I don't know what happened to my daughter. I gave her up at the hospital. I never even held her. The only thing I remember from giving birth is how perfect her little cry was. They rushed her out of the room, and I cried myself to sleep that night. I could hear her crying all night long. So I left the next morning before staff change."

"You are in fucking denial woman. That girl is ours."

"Seth, I want you to keep your god damned mouth shut. Your family has hurt her enough, and she does not need any more fucking stress. If you so much as look in her fucking direction, I swear on everything I hold dear, I will kill you. And you can take that to the damn bank" Patrice screams.

I can't believe what I am hearing, and I know it will kill Kayla to hear this. I don't know what to do. I can't tell her, and it takes everything I have not to go into that room and beat the fuck out of Seth for what he did to Patrice, and most of all, what he let be done to Kayla. At one point I really respected Seth. He had promise as a kick ass senator, and most likely would have made for a damn good president. But now that I know him, I am glad that he has taken a back seat in politics.

I quietly head back to our bedroom, crawl into bed, and hold Kayla close. I can't help but wonder how in the hell she'll survive this. She will be crushed to know Seth is her father, though I know she will be happy to hear she has a mother. But she can't know this. With a heavy heart I sigh and try to sleep. I toss and turn and listen for Kayla's steady breathing. That is somewhat calming but I know her life is about to change, I just have to figure out how to tell her.

I fell in love with her back in St. James church when she was teaching me how to read. Even when I was going to be married to the gold digging whore, I was picturing Kayla walking down the aisle. That was the last thing I thought of before falling into a restless sleep.

The next morning we wake to the smells of coffee and pancakes. When we get downstairs, we find the news declaring Seth has officially pulled out of the presidential race. The rumor is he pulled out because of the scandal regarding his family.

"About damn time," Wyatt declares as he walks around and kisses the top of Kayla's head. He walks to VI and wraps his arm around her waist and pulls her to his side.

"I would kiss you, but I have a major case of morning breath." VI tells Wyatt.

"Awe, babe you know I don't mind your breath anytime."

"No! That's gross! Don't come near me." VI mumbles as she is covering her mouth with her hand. "Sorry you are just S.O.L. There will be no kissing until I have coffee and get the funk out of my mouth. So just calm your jets there big boy."

"Damn! No love this morning. You suck babe."

"We all know I suck, and that I swallow too, but until I have coffee and brush my teeth, there will be no kissing, so suck it up buttercup."

"Awe, aren't you guys so freaking cute. Wyatt dear, when are you going to make an honest woman of VI?

"Kayla geez, you made me spit out my coffee. You ass," VI says.

"I thought you said you swallow? I guess you spit as well," I go over and give her a big hug, "it's okay if you spit." I hit her on her arm and tell her I love her fucking face.

Patrice comes out of the guest room looking like she saw a ghost. She won't look at me—in fact, she says her goodbye using the excuse she's going back to Garrett's place to get ready for a date with Rodney.

I tell her bye and ask her if everything is okay.

"Yeah, everything is fine. Don't worry," she says rushing to the door.

When she opens the door, Rodney is standing there, fist raised to knock on the door. He doesn't waste any time and asks Garrett to go to the station to answer a few questions about Seth's attack.

"Babe, do you want me to go with you?"

"No. Stay here and rest. I am sure it won't take long." He says and kisses me on the forehead.

"Okay, I love you."

"I love you too babe," he kisses me again—this time, softly on the lips.

I watch him walk out the door. I turn and run into Patrice.

"I am so sorry, Patrice. I did not mean to run into you."

"Kayla, it is okay, but I really have to go."

Next thing I know, the door is being slammed behind her.

"VI, do you know what is going on with Patrice?"

"No, I was just about to ask you the same thing."

"Has something happened back in Texas with her practice or something? I swear she was fine yesterday. I will get to the bottom of this, but first, I am going to go and get dressed and then go to the police station. I want to be there with Garrett because this is my fault after-all."

"Kayla, it isn't your fault. Garrett is a grown man who was trying to find his woman." Wyatt says.

"You were there too, weren't you Wyatt?"

"Yes buttercup, I was there. I was the one who gave him the black eye."

"So there is no way he can get into trouble over this, right?"

"Well, I can't answer that because we did go over to his

house. We did kind of interrupt Seth's sexual encounter, and then he proceeded to get a beating that he had coming."

"You mean you guys walked in while he was having sex with Millie?"

"Oh no, Millie walked us back to the pool house, and he had some young intern bent over the pool table." Wyatt said.

"Oh my god, are you freaking serious? Millie was there when he was having sex with someone else? That family is dysfunctional."

"Well, they surely put the FUN in dysfunctional." VI piped in.

"You are so right VI. Now I have to go and get dressed so I can go check on Garrett."

"Okay. Love your face."

"Love yours too, gutterslut." I yell from the hallway.

I walk into my big, over-stuffed closet and pick out a pair of black leggings and a hot pink long sweater. Before walking out, I grab a grey and pink scarf and my black faux suede and thigh high boots. I don't even bother taking a shower. I spray on some Wings perfume and get dressed.

I throw my hair up in a loose bun and grab my purse and head out to the beast. Jumping inside, I pull out and make my way to the police station. In the parking lot, I throw the beast into park and head into the building through the double glass doors. I walk in like I've been there a million times before.

CHAPTER FIVE

Dealing with the Truth

"When you reach the end of your rope, tie a knot and hang on."

~Franklin D. Roosevelt

When I get down to the station, Rodney takes me into an interrogation room and starts asking me questions.

"Garrett, how long have you had a grudge against Seth?"

"I would not say it was a grudge. I just don't like the man." I tell him.

"Have you ever passed by his house with the intent to hurt him?"

"Hell no. I run a successful publishing company. I don't have time for plotting to hurt some low life. And yes I know that comment makes me look guilty but to be honest, it was about time he felt some of the pain Kayla has felt for years."

"Son, I won't say he didn't, but you and your brother really put a beating on him."

"Yes, I know this, and if we have to, we will do what it

takes to make it right, but I had to find my love. I have seen the way you are toward Patrice. Can you tell me that you would not have done the same thing if you knew she was hurt?"

"Off the record, you are right but I still have to ask these questions."

"I know what is next. I have nothing to hide Officer Jernigan."

"I have just one last question Garrett, and this one is the most important of all questions. How long have you known Kayla was his daughter and Patrice was her mother?"

When that question was asked, we heard glass shattering and ran to see what was going on out there.

I see Kayla, and she has tears running down her beautiful face. She has a cut on her hand and it is bleeding badly.

One cop is cleaning up the broken glass and another is bandaging her hand.

All she says to me is, "How could you? You are supposed to love me."

She starts beating on my chest and screaming profanities. Kayla is crying and she never cries.

It takes two cops to pull her off me. Then one tells me to head home—the interview is over.

I tell the officer that the only home I am going to is Kayla's because I have to fix things.

I will not lose her over some half ass conversation I

overheard. There is no fucking way in hell I will allow this to break us.

We have been through way too much for something like this to damage our relationship, so I go and wait by the beast for her to come out.

***

I sit in one of the interrogation rooms while a cop, who moonlights as an EMT, bandages up my hand. For one split second I wondered what it would have been like just to end it right then and there. I could have with the shattered glass. I could have bent down and picked up a piece and ended it all. But that is the coward's way out and I am not a fucking coward.

After they are done bandaging me up, I grab my purse and walk out the doors. I look out to my beast, and I see him standing there. I hold out my hand telling him to shut his mouth but I know I have unfinished business. If he kept something like this from me, then what future do we have?

"Garrett, I am mad at you. Why in the hell did you think it was okay to keep something like this from me?"

"Babe, please let me explain, I swear I only learned about this last night when we came home from the club. You had fallen asleep, and I carried you up too bed. I grabbed a quick shower, headed down stairs, and I overheard Patrice and Seth screaming at each other."

"Why didn't you wake me up? Or better yet you could have told me this morning. But oh no, you kept this from me. How can I ever trust you?"

"Honey please, I wanted to make sure before I said anything. I know how you wanted to find your birth mother. And I would have never wanted to give you false hope. If I would have said anything I would not have had any proof."

"Garrett, you kept something huge from me."

"But you've kept things from me. Such as your rape?"

"That is different. You all know why I did that. I was trying to protect you all."

"Yes dear, I get that, but you did keep that from me. I know it's not the same, but I wanted to make sure of the facts, and not come at you with half ass answers."

"I guess I see where you would want to wait, but how can I trust you? How can we have a future if you are going to keep things from me?"

"Kayla baby, I love you more than life itself. I would never intentionally keep things from you. If it makes you feel any better, I wanted to go downstairs and beat the shit out of Seth. Babe, all I am going to say is listen to Patrice, hear her side before you just write her off. Please listen to her."

"What are you not telling me?"

"Kayla, let's go home and you talk to her. She will tell you what you need to know. All I ask is that you fully listen, not just with your ears but listen with your heart. It has never guided you in the wrong direction."

"Okay, get in and let's go, but I am still pissed at you and you have some major ass kissing to do."

"Honey, if you forgive me I would gladly kiss your ass every minute of every day. Look baby I know you are mad at me, and I know you feel I betrayed you, but I love you and I know we can get past this if we try."

"Just get in the beast Garrett."

Before he can talk or say a word, I hold up my hand and say, "Look, I love you, and I don't want to lose you, but I am not ready to talk right now."

When we pull up at my house, Patrice's car is there along with Wyatt and VI's.

Garrett and I walk in the house, and they see the look on my face. I can tell they know something happened.

"Patrice and Kayla need to go talk alone, and I stress the alone part."

Patrice, looks over at me, and I can see she knows that I know.

"Kayla come on. I know that you have questions, and I will do what I can to answer them for you."

CHAPTER SIX

Old Skeletons

"Forgiveness means letting go of the past."

~Gerald Jampolsky

"Patrice, when were you going to tell me?" I demand to know as soon as we got into my office. I did not even give Patrice a chance to close the door.

"Kayla sweetie, calm down. This is not something we know for sure. We have to do a DNA test."

"And don't Kayla sweetie me. Fuck! A DNA test? Did you know this whole time? All this time Patrice? You have been my confidant. I trusted you. I am so angry I don't even have the words at how upset I am. Did you suspect it all this time? What about all the times I asked about my birth mother? How many times have I told you I wanted to find her and yet you said nothing? You said not one fucking word. Why now?"

"Kayla calm down so we can talk about this as adults."

"Fuck that! Where were you when I was being raped and tortured? How can you even stand here and be so damned calm? This not only affects my life but yours as well. Why not come find me? How can you say you love me, when you lied to my face every day for years?"

"Kayla I am not going to say it again. Calm down and allow me to explain things to you."

"Don't pull that mother tone with me. You have no right to tell me to calm down. I won't calm down until there is a fucking DNA test and I know if you betrayed me or not."

"Kayla, damn it, listen to me! I never betrayed you. I never had proof. If you want a DNA test, I'll have Rodney have one ran. Yes, you have the right to be mad and upset with me but please do not speak to me like I don't care about you."

"I will talk to you any damn way I want right now." Suddenly I collapse into my desk chair in tears and I can't pull myself together. Patrice runs to my side but I yell at her, "Don't you dare touch me. I need to be alone to think. Please get out."

"Okay Kayla, I will leave right now, but I am not leaving the house. We will continue this conversation later, after we both have time to think. I am truly sorry. And I hope that you can forgive me."

"I have one question for you Patrice."

"Okay, I will answer anything you ask." Patrice says as she is wiping a tear from her face.

"Did you love him?"

"Kayla, I was in college, and I went to a party. I had one drink, just one. I set my drink down for literally two minutes, and when I came back into the room, I drank my drink and it was not long before I felt light headed. So I walked outside to get some air. There were a few people outside talking and smoking. So I walked over to the back of the property because there was a lake back there. I sat down on the ground, and I guess I fell asleep. But I felt someone touch me. I tried to scream, but there was a big hand over my mouth so I bit him. All of a sudden I felt something inside me. He was raping me. I went numb. I was a virgin. I was saving myself for marriage. It wasn't long, and he was done. I looked over at him and he looked familiar but I didn't know his name. I went home and took a shower, and never thought about it again. I was scared and embarrassed. I did not think anyone would believe me so I never said anything.

I did not even know I was pregnant until I went into labor. I know it sounds crazy but I honestly did not know I was carrying you. When I went to the hospital I thought I was having just bad cramps. Well come to find out I was in labor. I had you, and the doctor asked me, if I wanted to hold you, and I told her no, because I knew you were a product of rape. I turned over and tried to sleep, but I heard you crying all night. I got up and left, I could not handle hearing you cry. I did walk past the nursery and you were the only baby in there and you were so beautiful. I looked down and you were crying and you happened to look my way and for one brief second you stopped crying. I walked out of the hospital because I was not able to take care of myself. I knew the hospital would place you. But If I would have known that they placed you with Seth and Millie I would have kept you. Honestly Kayla, I thought I was doing what was best for you."

"Patrice, I am sorry that you were raped but I need time to think" I say as I am walking to the door.

"Kayla, I will be right here when you are ready to talk. I love you Kayla and I hope that one day you will forgive me."

"I am sure I will, but right now I have to gather my

thoughts. I do love you too."

I go to my room and lay on my bed and cry. I should have known that she had a horrible story. She is just like me. All these years I have wondered who my mother was. In a way if this was true and she is my mom it would be a dream come true. She has been the mother figure I never had and I did have an instant bond with her and felt more than a client relationship with her.

But where was she all those years? I get she was raped, but why not come take me away from Seth? Why not tell me that she was raped too? I thought we were more than patient and client. I thought we were friends.

I am so torn up, I don't know what to do with this. My heart is being pulled in several directions, and I can see why Garrett didn't want to tell me.

I am about to have a fucking nervous break-down when VI taps on the door and walks in.

"Girl, I saw Patrice and I overheard her call Rodney to arrange a DNA test. What the hell is going on? You look like you've seen a ghost."

I look up at her with tears running down my face and answer my best friend, "I just found out today that Patrice was raped by Seth and that I may be the child of rape. In fact they both are certain of it. The fucking bastard, who let me get raped for years and then threw me out with a check like some common whore could very well be my father. The woman I trusted for two years with everything is or could be my mother. So tell me what to do? VI, I have no fucking clue who I am. If it is true, I am a product of rape. My mother walked away from me because she was abused. The two people who were supposed to protect me didn't. So excuse me while I throw a pity party."

She runs over to me and wraps me in her arms.

"Oh fuck honey, no wonder you look like shit. What can I do? Do you want to talk or cry? Whatever you need I am here for you."

"No VI, I am done crying. I need to pull my shit together and go to talk to Garrett. And I need to apologize and make sure we are okay. I hope and pray that he can forgive me."

Just then he walks in the room.

"I am ok and we are more than ok baby. I am more worried about you and how you are holding up."

I run into his arms and just ask him to hold me because in his arms is the only place I feel safe and loved.

He picks me up carries me to bed and I lay in his arms

He tells me "If you are going to cry, let me be the one holding you while you do."

And the flood gates open again. I don't know how long we lay there but when I'm all cried out we go and take a hot bath.

"Babe, come here and let me just hold you." He says while we are in the bath tub.

"I'm so sorry."

"Babe, it's okay. I knew you were hurting and you lashed out. I should not have kept that from you. I swear I will never keep anything from you again."

"I know you didn't. I was just mad and upset."

"So did you and Patrice talk?"

"Well sort of. She told me that she was raped by Seth and I listened. When she was done, I walked out, but I did tell her I loved her."

"Honey, you learned some hard truths today and I know that you will have your faith to get you through this."

"Garrett, I know you are not a spiritual person, but will you pray with me?"

"Kayla, I'd move mountains if you asked."

So we say the only prayer that he knows.

Our Father in heaven, hallowed be your name.

Your Kingdom come, your will be done, on earth as in heaven

Give us today our daily bread.

Forgive us our sins, as we forgive those who sin against us.

Lead us not into temptation, but deliver us from evil.

For the kingdom, the power and the glory are yours.

Now and forever.

Amen.

"Thank you Garrett, I know that your spiritual side is not something you talk about a lot. But I want to thank you for praying with me."

"Honey I believe, but I was never taught how to pray. So please be patient with me and I will learn."

He bends down and slowly kisses me. I let out a soft moan.

"Kayla, if you keep making noises like those I will take you here and now."

"It wouldn't be the first time we have had sex in this tub babe." I reach down and stroke his already hard cock. I turn around and sit on his lap.

He kisses me on my collar bone and I let out a hiss as his teeth graze my skin. He bends his head down and grabs a nipple. He tugs on it with his teeth. I reach down and place him at my entrance, and with one swift thrust he is inside me. I close my eyes and slowly ride him.

"Babe, open your eyes!"

My eyes snap open, and I see the look on his face. I see the love that he has for me. I see the compassion.

I swivel my hips and bite his ear and that is all it takes. He grabs my shoulders and thrusts into me a few more times. I feel him tighten inside me and I know that he just released himself deep inside me.

He kisses the scars that line my body and whispers "You

are so beautiful Kayla, and I love you so much."

I lay my head on his shoulder just enjoying his scent. I inhale and tell him, "I love you too."

We get out of the tub, and he towels me off. I grab my old, worn out jeans out of the closet with a coral shirt and matching flip-flops. After, I apply a touch of mascara and do a quick fishbone with my hair. Garrett laughs at me because I have on boxer briefs.

"Babe, do you own any girlie panties?"

"Yes I do but these are comfy, and I'm just at home. But if you want me to start wearing what you call girlie panties, then you need to buy me some."

"How about I give you my credit card, and you can pick them out?"

"Umm no, if you want me in sexy panties or lingerie, then you need to go and pick them out. And you can't take VI with you." I laugh.

"Not cool Kay, not cool at all. But since Christmas is right around the corner I will have to be thinking about your gifts."

"Oh hell, that is right. The holidays are right around the corner. The last few months have passed so fast, and I have had my head up my ass."

"Not true, you have had a trying time. Come on, let's go downstairs and see what everyone is doing. I am sure they are wondering what we are doing."

"Let them wonder. I am grown and this is my house." I lean over and kiss on his lips.

We go down stairs to find Wyatt cooking lunch.

VI and Patrice are talking.

VI is in her mother hen mode, and Wyatt is listing to them, asking a question here and there in his big brother mode.

"Patrice, all I want to know is if there is anything else that we need to know."

"No, I don't think so. I have told Kayla everything that I can remember."

"Okay you guys, I appreciate you all worrying about me. But I am grown and I can handle this. All my life I have wanted to know who my mother is, I now have a possible person. If Patrice is my mom, I will have some things to work through, but I will get through it. I do want to do the DNA test just for my sanity. No offense Patrice, but I don't want to take Seth's word."

"No dear, I didn't think you would. That is why I called Rodney and told him to run your blood against mine. I gave him a sample already so we will know soon."

"All I ask is that you all give me time. I am not asking for much. Just give me space."

They all shake their heads in agreement.

CHAPTER SEVEN

Chasing Dragons

"There comes a time when you have to choose between turning the page and closing the book."

~Unknown

I have started to go crazy waiting on the results. My dysfunctional family has gotten on my nerves. I love them dearly, but if they don't let me out of the house soon I may have to smother them in their sleep. Of course I won't, but they are pushing my buttons.

I have been counting down the days until I get the call. It has been four whole weeks since we sent off for the DNA results. I am pacing around the living room when my phone rings, it is an unknown number so I let it go to voicemail. I keep staring at my phone waiting on the notice that I have a voicemail. Within a few seconds I feel it vibrate. With shaking hands I hit the voicemail button, type in my code, and I hear the message. I know my life will change as soon as I hear the first words.

"This message is for Kayla Ashby, your results are in and we are 99.999997% that you are indeed the child of the alleged mother and alleged father."

I drop my phone and start crying. No one is in the room

at that particular moment so I can cry in peace. But my peace does not last long because soon everyone is running toward me.

"Kayla honey, what is it." VI asks.

I glare up at her and she knows exactly what is wrong with me.

"I am not mad that she is my mom, at least I don't think I am. I am hurt, but I am not mad any longer. I wanted a mom for so long and now I finally have one. But the fact that Seth is my father that is what is bothering me. He raped my mother, and here I am. I have no clue how I feel about that. I am thankful that my mother did not go the route of abortion, but how could she when she didn't even know she was pregnant. Seth on the other hand has always been a prick, and to thank I was raised by my real father all this time." I think to myself what will Millie think? She already hates me, maybe she has known this whole time, but why wouldn't she ever tell me, or tell Seth for that matter. I guess anyone can keep the paternity of her biological kids from their birth father, why wouldn't she do the same for me? She had to have known.

I go lay on my bed and pull out my journal from the bed side table. I will write out my thoughts because right now I really want to find a dealer.

Screw this. I slam the journal closed and gather my purse, my keys, and slip on my boots. I open my window and climb onto the fire-escape to the garage. I quietly unarm the beast and get in, fasten the seat beat and head out of the garage.

I hit the automatic dial feature on my console and ask to be connected to Damon. Within a few seconds I hear

""Yo! This is Damon."

"Damon, this is Kayla from Birmingham, and I need your hook up again."

"Birmingham, how have you been? I have not heard from you in a few months. Are you still in Seattle?"

"Yes Damon, I am. Can you please have someone meet me at the same place as before?"

"Birmingham, are you in some kind of trouble? You know people talk and there are rumors going around that you have some people that need to be taught a lesson."

"No Damon I am not okay, but I don't want anyone teaching any lessons, at least not right now. But thank you."

"No problem, you know I'd do anything for you Birmingham. So what are you looking for?"

"I'm looking for something to chase the dragon."

"Wow Birmingham, going for the hard stuff huh?"

"Yes, I am. I need a gram, and I want it pure. I have the cash. All I need to know is if you can get it to me? And how long will it take your guy to meet me."

"Birmingham, give me about ten minutes, and I will have someone meet you."

"Thank you Damon."

"You are welcome Birmingham, and I will call you right back and let you know if it will be the same guy on the motorcycle or not."

Okay, I'll be waiting. I'm coming off Pike Street, so let me know where."

"For sure."

I hit the end call button and it was silence once again in my beast.

I pull over off Everett and hit Hwy 99, which is the center for drugs and prostitution. I see hookers, drunks, and drug addicts everywhere. The buildings along the way are so run down and look like they could be crack houses. There are several pay by the hour motels that litter the street as well. There are pawn shops, and adult entertainment stores on every corner.

The bikini clad women are standing in the nasty, little espresso stands and prostitutes are on the street dressed provocatively and looking cheap and whorish. They all look like they have been rode hard and hung out wet.

My thoughts are disturbed by the sound of my phone ringing and I hit the answer button on my steering column.

"Birmingham, where are you?" Damon is asking.

"I am off Hwy 99 near the Boulevard Motel." I tell him as I am looking in the rearview mirror.

"Okay, pull into the back of the parking lot and Chase will meet you. He is the same guy as last time. He drives a black motorcycle. It will be one hundred and twenty bucks. I had him get some rigs as well because I was not sure if you had them."

"No I did not, thank you. I was not thinking when I

made the call to you Damon."

"Well Chase will be there in just a few. Let me know if you need anything else."

"Damon, I know this sounds crazy but thank you."

"Birmingham, are you sure this is what you want to do? You know it has been seven years since you used. And I know how hard you worked on your sobriety."

"Damon, it is none of your business, no offense, but I am a grown ass woman and if I want to fuck up my life, then it is all on me. So thank you very much for getting me some Brown Sugar, but I really don't give a rat's ass on your opinion."

"Wow Birmingham, you must be dealing with some harsh shit because of all the years that we have known each other, you have never talked to me like that."

"I'm sorry Damon. Really I am, but I have had a really shitty day, and all I want is to forget."

"Okay, I get that, and I am so sorry. But he will be there in just a few minutes."

"Thank you, Damon."

"No problem, listen if you change your mind on that lesson please let me know. I will make a trip to Seattle if I need to."

"No, that is not necessary at the moment. And I will, I promise." I hit the end call button.

It doesn't take long and Chase is right beside me on his

crotch rocket. Again, he is in all black. I see him casually get off his bike and stroll toward me. For a second I want to haul ass out of here, but instead I roll down my window.

"Birmingham?"

"Yep, that's me. Do you have what I am looking for? Pure uncut Mexican Mud."

"Yes, here is your Black Pearl and that will be one hundred and twenty bucks."

I hand him two hundred bucks and tell him to forget that he's ever seen me.

"No problem doll. If you ever need anything else, I can be reached at {206}-555-5577 and my name is Chase."

"First off, I am not your doll, and if I ever need anything again, I will go through Damon like I just did. Now if you will excuse me, I have something to do."

I roll up my window and decide that I am going to get a room for a little bit. I drive to the front of this flea bag motel and get out. I walk up to the window and see a sign that says free condoms. Wow! Really?

I ring the bell for service and it doesn't take long before an older Asian woman is walking over to the window.

"How long"

"Excuse me?" I ask.

"How long do you need the room?"

"Oh okay, for the night," I tell her. Her face lights up.

"That will be seventy five dollars."

I hand her eighty dollars and tell her to keep it.

She smiles and says "Room fourteen."

I don't even bother to say thank you. I simply walk out the door and go straight to room fourteen. I put the key in the door and open it. The room is small, but it is clean. Or at least it smells clean. I turn the television on for back ground noise.

I pull the drugs out of my purse and I am looking at them when my phone rings. I look at the caller ID and its Patrice's number that flashes across the screen.

I look down and see that I have missed eleven text messages. A few from Garrett, a few from VI, and even one from Rodney. I am sure by now they have discovered my Houdini act. I don't answer the phone and don't hit ignore. I know it won't take long for Rodney to find me.

My phone rings again and it's Damon, I immediately answer it thinking something is wrong with the goods that was just delivered to me.

CHAPTER EIGHT

The Longest Ride

"Whoever is happy will make others happy too."

~Anne Frank

"Drop the needle Kayla," Rodney and Garrett are screaming at me.

"Get out of my fucking room, and who are you to tell me what the hell to do? You are not my daddy. My dad is a man who raped my mother, and the last I checked Rodney, you are not Seth Stanton."

"Kayla honey, please drop the needle. I love you baby. Please look at me. We can get through this."

I glare at Garrett and tell him to leave me alone, that he has nothing to do with this.

"Baby, please put down the dope and let me have it. You can take your anger out on me. Please don't lose your sobriety."

"What does it matter to you? You are not the one who it will affect."

In the blink of an eye I am being tackled and the dope knocked out of my hand.

"Get off me you ape! I can't breathe."

"It was the only choice I had. You can be pissed at me all you want, but I will not apologize. I told you I would protect you. Kayla, god damn it, why are you so hard headed? You have a family. Let us help you, but we can't do that unless you talk to us. We are not mind readers. Now I will get off you, but you are going to get your ass in the damn truck and we'll talk about this when we are all home. Call it an intervention or whatever you want, but I will not stand by and let you fuck up your life."

"I am not four Garrett. You can't make me get in the vehicle. Last time I checked, I was an adult. I am very capable of making up my own mind."

"Woman, I will not tell you again to get up and go get in the truck. If you don't I will go caveman and throw you over my shoulder and toss your ass in the truck. Now if you think I am playing, try me."

"You wouldn't dare."

"Okay, your choice." Garrett said

And before I can stop him he has me up and over his shoulder. My ass is in the air. I am beating him on his lower back, screaming for him to put me down.

Next thing I know I feel a slap on my ass and I scream. Not because it hurts but because I was shocked he did it.

"If you want to act like a child, I will treat you like a child. Children get their asses spanked when they are not listening so you have two choices, you can stop hitting me and act like the grown woman that you claim to be, or you can continue to act like a child. If you choose option two, then I will stop what I am doing and bend you over my knee and spank your ass."

As mad as I am at him I can't help but laugh at him.

"Put me down, please Garrett. I will be a good girl for now, but just know I am not happy with you."

"I know this and I can respect that, but you left me no choice."

"There is no need to be a smart ass Garrett. I said I would do as I am told for now. Don't think I will always be this obedient because it will be a cold day in hell. But for now I will do as you ask."

I get in his face, and point at him, "I will tell you this Garrett, I love you but I have issues, I am not perfect, and occasionally I will fuck up. So if you want to be with me you will need to know that I will slip. I have relapsed several times, and if you can't handle that, then we can call it quits now before either one of us hurts the other."

"Babe, I know you are not perfect. Hell we all have flaws, but we need to lean on each other when times are rocky. I am here, let me help you. I promise I am strong enough to help."

I glance around the room, and I see Rodney bagging up the dope and rigs and shaking his head.

"Kayla, do you know how worried your mom is about you?" Rodney asks.

I glare at him because I don't know if I will ever call her

Mom. Me being a smart ass, I say "Patrice. It's Patrice. I can't call her mom."

"Just give her a chance. You know this is not just hard on you Kayla. She did what she thought was the best at the time. I know that she has been haunted as well. So when you are in your self-destruction phase, remember that you do have a mom that loves you. She may not have raised you, but I am sure giving you up was the hardest choice she ever made. So walk a mile in her shoes, and quit giving her shit."

"Rodney, you have no idea the hell I have lived. I was tortured and raped for years, and my biological father knew about it."

"Yes Kayla, I do have an idea. You need to remember I am a cop. I have seen some really bad shit over the years. And each time there is a victim, my heart breaks a little bit more. I am sorry for that but your mom, yes I said your mom, is hurting too. She just relived her rape and now she has a constant reminder. Guess who is her reminder? You are her reminder. So grab your big girl panties and stop being a brat because the pity train has derailed at the corner of it's time to Suck it up Street and Move on Avenue, and then crashed head into We all have problems Place and Time to get the hell over it Boulevard. Hell Kayla I have an aunt, her name is Sheila, and guess what? She is blind and paralyzed and she doesn't have a pity party. She lives in the dark every damn day and she is scared of the dark. And what are you doing? You're sitting here crying because you don't like your birth parents. Well wake up sweetheart. You don't get to choose your damn parents. No one likes their damn parents. Hell I am sure Garrett didn't like his either, but you don't hear him crying. So I am going to say this one-time and one-time only, you want me to treat you like you're an adult, then you damn sure better act your age and not you're fucking shoe size"

I look at both men in this room and I know that they are speaking the truth. Hell Rodney doesn't even know me and he is speaking the truth. So I walk over and grab my purse and walk out the door.

A few seconds later I hear the footsteps of them behind me.

"Garrett, you take Kayla's truck back and she can ride with me.

"No I can drive myself. I am not a child."

"Kayla, I am not asking. I can be an ass and take you to jail. So ride with me voluntarily or you ride in the back with cuffs on."

I look at him stunned. "Are you serious Rodney? You would arrest me?"

"I am very serious Kayla. You could be charged with a controlled substance and drug paraphernalia, which can result in one year in prison and up to a five thousand dollar fine. Do you really want to take that chance and see if I will arrest you? Because I promise I will have no problems arresting you."

"First off Rodney, you guys kicked in my door. Did you have probable cause? A warrant? No, I never saw a warrant. You can't use the drugs as evidence because guess what, you have violated my 4th amendment rights."

The look of shock is written all over his face.

"Oh didn't you know? I was pre law before I changed majors and became an architect. So if you are going to spit the law at me, I guess your ass better make sure that you are on the right side of it. I do believe what you guys did was an unlawful entry and guess what, you can't do jack shit, but just for shits and giggles I will go with you, not because you are making me, but because I am not in the mood to argue with you any longer."

"Babe, I will see you at the house."

"Okay, see you there. I love you."

"I love you too babe, and please listen to him. He's only trying to help you. He loves your mom, or Patrice as you are calling her. Think about her during all this. I am sure it's twice as hard on her."

He leans down and kisses me on the forehead.

"Come on Kayla, we need to talk." Rodney states.

"Okay, so what do you want to talk about Rodney?"

"Well first off, I think you owe Patrice an apology. She was scared shitless. She had went into your room and you were gone. She was coming down the stairs panicking when Garrett got the call from your friend Damon."

"He's not my friend. More like a frenemy."

"Anyway, whatever he is, his phone call most likely saved Seth's ass because she was sure that someone had taken you."

"Rodney, I know you are only looking out for Patrice, but I really don't owe anyone anything." I cross my hands over chest and let out a loud breath.

"I'm sorry that you feel that way. Because regardless what you think, Patrice loves you and she is hurting just as much if not more than you are."

"How in the hell do you figure that Ace?"

"She has felt guilty for over twenty-five years. When she walked out of that hospital, she had the best of intentions. She wanted what was best for you. Do you think she would have packed up and flew across the damn country for just anyone? No, she has a bond with you. There was something inside her telling her that she could help you. And why you do you think that is?"

I shrug my shoulders and gaze out the window and watch Seattle pass us by.

"Kayla, you are not dumb. I know that you feel the same bond she does. She loves you and I know deep down you love her too. Yes, you have a right to be upset, but have a little compassion for her. She is hurting just like you. So if you can't find in your heart to show her you care enough to simply apologize for acting like a spoiled brat who didn't get a pony for her birthday, then you need to tell her to go home. She deserves a chance Kayla."

"Rodney, I will think about it, okay? That is the best answer I can give you right now. I will be civil and respectful of Patrice. I can't offer anything else right now. I am sorry. "

"All I ask is that you try. Walk in her shoes for just a minute. Imagine giving up a child then finding out that the child you gave up was raised by monsters. Don't you think she has enough guilt?"

With that, I get out of the police car and I see the beast parked in her spot so I know Garrett is home.

"I will be up in a minute, Rodney."

"Kayla no offense but can I have your purse? "

"You know, I'm too tired to even argue with you. I only want to gather my thoughts before I walk into my house, but if it'll make you feel better, take my damn purse. You won't find anything else. Hell, you already have all the damn dope.

"Kayla, believe me when I say I don't want to be the hard ass. I have really grown to like you. You remind me of myself when I was younger—stubborn and very hard headed but in the end you will do what is best."

"I'll be up in a few. Please allow me to stand here and look at the Seattle skyline."

He nods his head and hits the elevator button. I hear it ding and then going up.

I walk over to the edge of the parking garage and see the city of Seattle. It is around eleven at night so there is a brisk breeze blowing in the air. This city is so impressive at night.

In the distance I can hear the soft music coming from one of the many organs at St. James Cathedral. I catch myself walking in that direction. The soft music is soothing. It doesn't take long before I am standing outside the massive doors. I walk up the steps and pull open the big wooden slabs. It feels like a higher power is gliding me across the black and white checkered floor. I see all the candles that have been lit for those who are needing prayers. I stop and light one not really knowing who I am praying for, but it just feels right.

I dip my hand in holy water and place a cross across my body.

I make my way to the front of the church. I look up and see all the beautiful stained glass. Each one cascades a different light.

The lights are dim and it's creating a soft glow around the cross.

We are in the season of Advent so the reds and gold's are perfect shades.

Up in the choir loft I hear the sweet sound of Christmas music, and I know immediately that it is the children's chorus. They are singing Oh Holy Night, which is my all-time favorite Christmas Carol.

I make my way to the third row which is the one I always sit at. I pull down the small bench under the pews for prayers.

It is not long and I feel at peace. I get back up in the pew and just think about my life and where it is going. Can I actually have a relationship with her? Could I do what she did? Have a baby and just walk away? I know she had her reasons, but why not tell me as soon as she suspected? Was there ever a clue? I have asked myself who am I?

I close my eyes and I pray. I say a prayer that I used to say when I was trying to kick my old habits.

Lord,

I commit my failures, as well as my successes into your hands, and I bring for your healing the people and the situations, the wrongs and the hurts of the past. Give me courage, strength, and generosity to let go and move on—leaving the past behind me, and living the present to the full. Lead me always to be positive as I entrust the past to your mercy, the present to your love, and the future to your providence.

In your name I pray,

Amen

I guess I nod off because the next thing I know, I wake up and Patrice is right beside me. She has tears in her eyes.

"Kayla, I understand if you don't want to talk to me, but if you will listen to what I have to say, then I will leave you alone. Will you at least listen to me?"

"Yes, I will." I wipe a tear off my face and she grabs my hand, and I don't pull away.

"Kayla, can I tell you about my past and then you can make your choice?"

I nod my head yes.

"I was raised dirt poor. My dad was lower class and did not have a pot to piss in. He was a good man when he was not in a chemically induced state. He was much like you when I first met you, I swore that you looked just like him. My father had a lot of problems. I was told that he was a manic depressant and was bipolar. But he also had a drug problem. His drug of choice was Meth or some street terms that you would know are crank, chalk or speed. When he was high, he was meaner than a rattlesnake. He would say hateful things. I remember one night he was so messed up that he made me undress and stand in the kitchen on a bed of rice, because he thought I had lied about where my mom was."

"You see my mom passed away shortly after I was born. Everyone says that she died from complications of child birth. I have no memories of her at all. I stayed with my grandmother the majority of the time. She did her best but she was aging and when she passed I had no choice but to live with him. When I was a teenager and had my fill of the verbal abuse, I left. I did not have two wooden nickels to rub together, so I knew I would not get far without an education and money. So what kind of job can a woman find with no experience? I took the first job I could get. I am not proud of it. I was a stripper. My stage name was Phoenix. I made good money and before long I had an apartment. For the first time in my life I was truly living. I was enrolled in college and I was doing really well in school. I was one semester away from getting my degree in Psychology."

"I went into work one Friday evening and a friend of mine named, Rayna, said that there was a party and we needed to go. They were paying top dollar for a couple of girls to dance for some frat guys. So I agreed and went to the frat house. It was loud and the guys were already drinking heavily. Of course I didn't care that they were drinking, I was there to make money and leave. After our dance was over, I went up to the bar area and asked for a Sprite. There was no alcohol in the drink at all. Or at least there was not supposed to be. But now that I think about it, there was most likely vodka in the cup. It's clear and has no smell. So I drank half of it and had to go the restroom. I was only there for maybe a minute and I had asked Rayna to watch my drink. When I came back she was talking to Seth, I had seen him around campus before, but I never talked to him, so we all talked for a few minutes and everything was going good. He seemed so nice. He was good looking. I had noticed he had a white ring around his ring finger. I even asked him if his Wifey had let him off the ball and chain tonight. He of course laughed and said something like that."

"I excused myself because I needed some air as the room was starting to spin. I thought it was just because there was so many people and the music was really loud. So I walked outside with no direction in mind. I was just wandering and I spotted the water at the back. I have always been mesmerized by water at night. I started feeling really tired, so I took off my jacket and sat down on it not thinking I would fall asleep. But I did. I remember hearing voices, I knew there were several people around. I kept trying to open my eyes but it was like they were glued shut. But all of a sudden there was someone on top of me. His voice was so familiar. I had just heard it. I remember him saying you are not the one I was planning on but you will work."

"He held me down and had his hand over my mouth. I remember biting his hand. That did not even phase him. He kept telling me what a lucky woman I was because he could have any woman he wanted. When he finally finished, he got up and walked away. I laid there for a few minutes because I was embarrassed. When I did leave, I went back to my apartment, took a scalding hot shower, and then packed up all my stuff and left. I got in my car and headed to Texas, and I've lived there ever since. I had all my schooling transferred to Baylor College and finished there. I got my degree in Psychology. I also have a practice in Birmingham and that is where I met you."

"When you were born I did not even name you so you were given a name by a nurse. I do have your hospital bracelet that I had on and it said baby girl as your name. I am so sorry that you had a hard and rough life. Believe me if I could have traded places with you, I would in a minute. I hope you can forgive me one day."

Patrice begins to get up, but I stop her.

"I'm sorry I scared you. Can you ever forgive me Mom?"

"Oh honey, there is nothing to forgive."

We are both crying. And she whispers I love you.

"I love you too, mom. Now can we please go home? I am sure Garrett is going out of his mind. Oh, how did you know where I was?"

"I followed you. I knew you would not come right up, and I was right. What made you come to this church?"

"I don't know. I heard the soothing music, and I just love it here."

"Me too dear. Me too."

CHAPTER NINE

Dealing with Life

"Forget what hurt you, but never forget what it taught you."

~Unknown

It has been two long weeks since we got the DNA test back. Patrice is my mother, and we are working on our relationship. It is weird, but we are both trying.

Seth tried calling my cell when he got his copy of the DNA test. I didn't even bother answering it. I don't want to hear a word that prick has to say. As far as I am concerned, he can go to the seventh circle of hell and burn to death, for all I care.

Garrett and I were in bed later that night and he was holding me after a hot session of love making. We were talking while I am laying on his chest, and he rubs my back

"So how do you feel now that everything is now out in the open?"

"I am glad Patrice is my mom, but it still sucks ass that the prick is my dad. But I don't want to think about him after the mind blowing sex. I just know as long as I have you I will make it through anything."

"You will never lose me. I will be here forever."

"I love you Garrett."

"I love you too Kayla."

We fall asleep in each other's arms, but sometime later I wake up screaming.

"Kay honey, are you okay?"

"Don't touch me. Get away."

"Kayla, it's me Garrett."

"Please don't hurt me. I am begging you."

"Please don't push me away. I will not hurt you Kayla. Come talk to me. What is going on? Was it a nightmare?"

I look up and notice I am at home and not back at the pool house. I am crying and shaking. I get up and run to the bathroom and slam the door shut and lock it. Seconds later I hear Garrett.

"Kay, please talk to me. What is going on?"

I ignore him and turn on the hot shower and I strip.

I stand in the shower and I cry. I have not had a nightmare in a long time, but this one was bad. I scrub my body trying my best to get their scent off me. I know in my head it was only a harsh nightmare but my body is telling me it was real. I hate them.

I sit on the bench and cry until the water turns cold, and even then I still sit and cry.

I finally turn off the water and look at myself in the mirror. I look at the bright red scars. I run my fingers along the jagged edges. The scars are a constant reminder of my past. I grab the fluffy robe and head to the door. I open it and see the whole family in my room.

I don't even get out of the room, and I am being bombarded with questions.

I shake my head at VI, and she knows to get everyone out.

It's not long before it's just VI and I. She sits there waiting on me to say something first.

"This one was really bad," I whisper.

"Do you want to tell me about it?"

"Not really. I just want to sit here. Will you brush my hair like you used to when we were younger? It was always so calming."

"Absolutely, give me the brush and go sit at the vanity."

"Will you tell me about you and Wyatt? Tell me something to get my mind off the nightmare."

"Hmmm, what to tell. He is this super romantic guy. He holds me at night like he is afraid I will not be there in the morning. But sometimes he will say her name."

"Whose name?"

"Ariel. You know, his wildflower."

"What does he say?"

"Nothing really, but I can tell he really loved her. She did a number on him. She left and never looked back. I met her once back in college. She was nice and she was gorgeous. He has a picture of her in his wallet. It's old and bent, but it's still there. Before you go all saintly on me, he showed me her one night. He was wasted. I had to go to the club and pick him up. Girl he was shit faced."

"When was this? And why didn't I know about it?"

"Well it was as soon as he was released from the hospital. You were still in the coma, and he went to the club and got drunk. When I walked in the door, the place was destroyed. He had taken a baseball bat and destroyed his office. He was so upset."

"Why? It was not his fault. It was mine."

"Kay, don't you know those men love you. Both Garrett and Wyatt love you more than all the words in all the books in the world."

"Wow that's a lot of love. I think I hurt Garrett's feelings tonight though. I screamed for him not to touch me. And then I got up and ran to the bathroom and locked him out."

"Oh Kay, he understands."

"He has understood a lot here lately and I can't keep asking him to understand. You should have seen his face when I had the needle in my hand and he tackled me. VI, he was scared shitless."

"Speaking of that night, what the fuck were you thinking?"

"I wasn't. Plain and simple. I was not thinking about anything or anyone. I heard that message and my heart stopped and I just wanted to numb the pain. That was the only way I knew how to do it."

"So this Damon fellow, have you talked to him?"

"No, I have not. I did send him a message telling him that I was okay. He has messaged me several times checking on me but I have not responded to any of them. I am thankful that he called but I am mad as hell at him. He had no right."

"No Kay, he did not, but your family is glad he did. You should have seen Garrett when he got the call. He was scared that Rodney wouldn't make it in time. He didn't give a Rodney a chance to tell him that he could not go. He was out the door and getting in Rodney's car."

"That night was a nightmare and I owe you an apology."

"Me? Why do you owe me an apology? Kay, you are grown. No-one can make decisions for you. Do I approve? Hell no, but do I think you owe me an apology? No ma'am I don't. I know things have been difficult for you."

"That is an understatement."

"Come on lets go tell the family that you are okay, so they can quit pacing. I can hear them from here."

"Do I have to go down there? I really made an ass of

myself."

"Yes, you have to, but luckily for you, we all love your ass, so you will be fine. So get dressed and let's go have some coffee, since the whole house is wide awake at freakin four am. Maybe we can get lucky and there is breakfast made."

"I will be down in a few. Let me get dressed."

"Okay gutterslut, love your face."

"Love your face more."

"I doubt that, but I will let you think you won."

Soon I am alone with my thoughts. I walk over to my double French doors that lead to my custom patio. I open the doors and there is a subtle breeze. I walk out and look over the city. The Seattle skyline never looked better. To the left of me is the ever impressive Seattle Space Needle. In the distance I can see the snow-capped mountains of Mt. Rainier. I am close enough to the water that I can watch the ferries pass. Down below me is Pike Place market, where crowds gather to watch the fisherman throw salmon.

Seattle is a posh mosh of head-spinning whirlwind of just everything you can ever want. To the right of me, I see the twinkling lights of downtown. I can see the big Ferris wheel. I look over my patio and I see the large red oak chairs and the massive table tucked in the corner I have my own piece of heaven, I have my atrium. I have everything from my favorite white roses that have pink edges to my butterfly plants that bring in butterflies. I have a Peperomia which adds a splash of color. I have a Chinese Ever-green that has shades of silver and gray and several varieties of Ivy. I have a Dracaena which looks like a cornstalk. I have several snake plants, spider plants, a Boston fern that is virtually indestructible. I even have a Crown of Thorns plant, and in the center I have a stone water feature. I had it custom built. It is in the shape of a cross and the water flows up the cross instead of down. I have a stone pathway leading back to the French Double doors. I look over and I see Garrett staring at me.

"Are you okay?"

"Yes I am fine. I'm sorry. I thought you were Elijah. I was having a very bad nightmare."

"Do you want to talk about it?"

"No I don't. Garrett, are you sure you want to be with me? I'm toxic. I don't want to hold you back from someone who could be better than me."

"There is no one who could ever be better than you. I mean it when I say you are the one I want."

I run to him and start crying in his shoulder. "I just don't want you to have to settle."

"There is no settling. I promise. I wouldn't have been settling with anyone else."

"I'm tired. Can you please lay with me until I fall asleep?"

"Of course. "

We get back into the bed and it doesn't take long for us to fall asleep.

***

"Seth you have been pacing this house for two weeks. What in the hell is going on?"

"What did you ask Millie? I am sorry, my mind is elsewhere right now."

"Yeah, no shit. You have not even said five words to me since the funeral. And thank you for causing a scene at Edwin's funeral. How did Jason even find out? Now he is threatening me with lawsuits because I kept the boys from him."

"Millie, I don't know how he found out, but you did tell a room full of people your sad story at the hospital."

"I bet it was the little gold digging bitch Kayla."

"Don't you dare call her that? You have caused her enough shit. Leave her alone."

"Wow Seth, when did you start caring for the little trollop?"

I walk over to Millie, and got in her face and tell her to back the fuck off. "Leave her alone. She is none of your concern."

"Oh bull shit Seth, she killed my son. Don't tell me that she is not my concern. All this time you have raised Edwin and Elijah as your kids, and you are taking her side. Have you lost your mind?"

"Millie I am not going to have this conversation with you. I am warning you, if you don't back off, you will regret it."

"Is that a threat Seth? As I told that whore in the hospital, I don't deal well with threats."

I reach over and slap her across the face, "I told you to shut the fuck up. Drop your hatred for Kayla now. I will not have this conversation again."

She grabs her cheek and gets to the door. "Seth I have covered your ass for years and you can't even do one thing for me. That is okay. I got you."

She slams the door and the windows rattle.

I try to call Kayla several times. I need to talk to her. I need her to know how sorry I am. Of course, no answer.

I leave her a message. Telling her it's urgent. I try Patrice.

"This is Dr. Doyle, how can I help you?"

"Patrice, this is Seth, Please don't hang up. I need to talk to Kayla."

"Good luck with that Seth. She wants nothing to do with you. You raised her all these years, and you let those monsters rape her. They may not be yours by blood, but they are just like you."

All of a sudden the line goes dead.

CHAPTER TEN

The Holiday Brings Stress

"Only you can control your future."

~Dr. Seuss

"I can't believe it is already Thanksgiving. I have never had a real family dinner. So this year I am going to cook. Lord help me. Mom, can you make me a list of things I need from the store?"

"You're serious? You want to cook?"

"Yes. Why are you guys laughing?"

"None of us have seen you in the kitchen other than to grab some wine or to eat the food someone else prepared."

"You guys can joke all you want."

"Do you have any idea how to cook? Do you think you can prepare something like Thanksgiving dinner?"

"Well, I have Googled it and watched You Tube. How hard can it be?"

"Kayla sweetheart, I can cook the meal. Well, we can order a fried turkey, and then I can make the rest."

"You guys, will you please trust me? This is something I want to do so please shush and make me a list. We only have a few days before Thanksgiving, so I need to get my turkey now. Please write down everything I'll need. I need to get to the store."

"Well, can you tell me what you want to make?"

"Hello, I just told you guys I have never had a real Thanksgiving dinner."

"Wait, Seth and Millie never fixed holiday meals?" VI asks.

"Nope, never. They were always out of town for the holidays. The help always made seafood for the holidays. That's why I'm asking for a list. I have no clue what I need to buy."

"Come on buttercup. There's no need for a list. You and I will go shopping." Wyatt said.

"I'll let the name slide you ass, but only because you are taking me shopping. Let me grab my purse and then we can be on our way."

"Who all is going?" Wyatt asks.

"Just you and me stud. Come on."

"Hey now! You have a man. Don't be flirting with mine." VI says, laughing.

"Oh VI, your man couldn't handle this." I run my hands down my side laughing.

"Kayla babe, you would be ruined for any other man."

Wyatt joked.

"Brother, if you were anyone else I'd knock you out, but seeing how we are blood, I'll let you live." Garrett laughs.

"Come on Wyatt. I want to go before all the fat turkeys are gone."

"Oh hell, I better go."

"Let's drive the beast, but you can't touch my radio stations Wyatt, and I mean it."

"There better not be country blaring in my ears."

"Just for that smart ass, I will make sure of it."

I grab him and pull him to the door. I grab my keys, my pink Coach purse, and put my Gucci sunglasses on before heading out the door.

We get to the beast and I hit the alarm to unlock the doors. I get inside and push the button to start the car. I fasten my seatbelt and turn the radio on. I'm greeted by Meghan Trainor's Lips are Moving.

"Aw Buttercup, this is not the good music, but this is an improvement. You're may finally be moving up in the music world."

Ignoring his comment, I ask, "Okay so what store are we buying out?"

"The only one I shop at—PCC Natural Markets."

"Okay, let's go do some damage."

We are only a few minutes away so we make small talk until we arrive at the store. I have never shopped with Wyatt and he will soon find out that shopping is an excursion with me because I go down every single isle.

A while later, Wyatt says, "Kayla, are you serious? We have everything already."

"Oh hush cry baby. We have only been here for over an hour. But you're right, I think we have everything on our list." I grabbed the biggest turkey I could find. It's a beast at 23 pounds.

We get up to the register, and she rings everything up and gives me the grand total of three hundred twenty seven dollars.

"Kayla, have you lost your damn mind? Its only one dinner!"

"Yes but it's my first family dinner. So like you tell me, suck it up buttercup. Now load those groceries so we can head back to the house because I am excited to start baking."

"Oh God! I just know you're going to burn your house down." Wyatt groans.

"Well if I burn the house down, I can design a new one."

"Ooh, well played Buttercup!"

***

Over the next few days, I search every cooking website I can think of because I want to show them that I can do this.

I have made several pies—Dutch apple, spicy pumpkin, and a southern pecan pie. I am standing in my kitchen, and I have flour everywhere when Garrett walks in and starts laughing at me.

"I should so record this because you may never cook another meal again."

"Ha-Ha, very funny. I am trying here."

"It smells good in here—smells like a bakery."

"All I can say is I am trying and if it doesn't turn out, there's always Chinese."

"I am really proud of you. I have never seen you in the kitchen, and I find it really sexy."

He comes over and wipes some flour off my nose and gently kisses my forehead. "I will let you butter my buns later."

"Is that a promise?"

"Yes it is."

"What is your favorite thing about Thanksgiving?"

"Oh wow, as a man I know I am supposed to say football but I love the food. So don't mess up my favorite part."

"It's not like I didn't have enough pressure. Thanks for adding to it, Asshat! Anyways how is work? Sign any one new lately?"

"I am working on signing this new and up-coming author, but I can't discuss anything. She is pretty kick ass, though. I am excited."

"Yay! I hope you sign her! How is your mom?"

"She is good. I think they are in Europe right now. Wyatt invited her for Thanksgiving, but she said they were not going to be here. I know what the answer to this will be, but I'm going to ask anyway. Have you talked to Seth?"

"No I have not. He has called me several times and sent me lots of texts messages, but as far as me actually listening to him, the answer is no. As far as I am concerned, he can go fuck himself."

"Kay, isn't that a little harsh? He is your father. Don't you think you should hear him out?"

"Garrett, you are walking on very thin ice. I have nothing to say to him. One day maybe I will forgive him, but that day is not going to be today."

"Okay, I won't bring it up again. I was just asking love."

"Yes I know and thank you, but right now he's a sore subject for me."

"I get it. I don't agree with you, but I get it."

"Garrett, you hated your father. He beat you, your brother, and mom. So you mean to tell me if he was alive that you would have something to do with him?"

"You talk about your faith all the time Kay. How is it you can have faith in some things but not others? I am an adult now, so yes I would try to have a relationship with my father. Remember babe, tomorrow is not promised to anyone."

"I am done with this conversation. I have food to prepare so if you are going to keep giving me shit, please leave the kitchen."

I watch him get up and leave. I turn and face the window by the sink, and I can't help but break down.

I take off my apron and throw it on the granite counter. I grab my keys and walk out the door. I have no destination in mind, but I know I have to get out of the house. I get in the beast and just start driving. I drive for a few minutes, and I end up at Seattle's Great Wheel.

I have never been here, but it looks like a great place to just sit and think. There is a park bench right out front, and I walk over and take a seat. I watch the kids—their little faces light up when seeing the great wheel for the first time. I watch the lovers strolling along, hand-in-hand and an older couple who look like they have weathered many storms together. They are sitting so close that they look like one. She lovingly looks up at her partner, and he gently kisses her cheek. I watch as they get up and dance. There is no music around, but they are in perfect harmony. I notice that he never lets her hand go. He holds her like she is his reason for breathing. You can tell that he loves her unconditionally.

I sit there for a few more minutes and I see a man and a little girl. She can't be more than five or six. She has on a white flowered dress and has her hair in braids. He has on slacks and nice dress shirt. She is crying and it looks like she hurt her knee. He has bent down and picked her up. He walks over to a table and sits her down. He gets down on one knee and examines her knee. He gives it a kiss, and she stops crying. Just like that...one little kiss and she was over her pain. Is it really that simple? Can a father's love really be like that?

I know what I have to do. I have to forgive him—Garrett was right. My faith needs to be overall, not just one sided.

I get back in the beast and head home. I look at the clock, and I have been gone for a few hours. I left without my phone, so I am sure there will be an APB out for me.

I get home and there is no one there. So I go straight to bed. It has been a long day and I am exhausted.

***

Thanksgiving Day is finally here, and I find myself up before everyone else. I had the turkey in the oven before five that morning, and I have all the sides made and the table set. The only thing I'm waiting on is the turkey to be finished. Everyone else is in the living room watching football, and I can hear them yelling about a play.

I love hearing them laugh.

I look over and Rodney is walking into the kitchen for another beer.

"Hey Kayla, how are you today?"

"I am good and you?"

"I am starving. That bird needs to hurry up. I think my stomach is touching my back."

I look at him and laugh because he doesn't look like he has ever missed a meal.

"Kayla, don't let this belly fool you. It's hard work keeping this shape."

"You're such a mess, but I see why my mom is crushing on you. You're one of the good guys."

"Can I tell you a secret?"

"Well sure Rodney."

"I'm kind of crushing on her as well."

"I knew it. I can see the way you look at her."

We are interrupted when the oven timer goes off. The turkey is done!

Rodney's eyes light up, "Let me get that out of the oven for you."

"Fingers crossed it is done because if it is not, we will be eating Chinese."

"Oh God I hope not. My mouth is watering just from smelling this bird in the oven."

Rodney takes the turkey out of the oven, and I put it on the platter.

"Rodney will you do the honors of cutting the turkey?"

"I'd be honored. Of course that means I get to taste it first, right?"

"Sure, that way if it's not good, you can tell me."

"It will be fine. Look at this Kayla, this is a beautiful bird."

I yell for everyone to come and eat.

We gather around the table and I say a prayer.

O Gracious God, we give you thanks for your overflowing generosity to us. Thank you for the blessings of the food we eat and especially for this feast today. Thank you for our home and family and friends, especially for the presence of those gathered here. Thank you for our health, our work and our play. Please send help to those who are hungry, alone, sick and suffering war and violence. Open our hearts to your love. We ask your blessing through Christ your son. Amen.

Dinner was a hit. Everyone has a belly full of food and we are sitting around enjoying each other's company when Rodney's phone rings.

"Excuse me, it's the station."

We make small talk for a few minutes and when Rodney walks back in, I can see something is wrong.

Patrice walks up to him and grabs his hand, "Honey, what is wrong?"

"It's Elijah. He was released from the hospital."

CHAPTER ELEVEN

The Plan

"There's a terrible price to pay for stress in your life - it really takes a hit on your heart."

~Leeza Gibbons

My world stops when I hear Elijah has been released. I go into complete panic mode.

"Kayla, I will make sure there are extra cops patrolling this area."

"It won't make a difference. He will make me pay. He is going to be worse now after his brother dying. Edwin was actually less evil than Elijah. At least Edwin had half a heart. Elijah is outright cold and he doesn't care about going to jail. Can't you see it doesn't scare him?

"I promise, you will be safe."

"Rodney, no offense, but you can't promise that, so please don't make promises you can't keep."

"Well, I can do my best, but for now, no more outings on your own."

"I'm sorry, but there is no way in hell I'm going to stay

locked inside. It doesn't matter where I am or if I'm alone or in a crowd. He wants me and he'll make it happen. He is a snake and will strike when and where he wants.

"Is there anything we can do, Rodney?" Patrice asks.

"All I can offer is make sure you watch your surroundings. Patrice, I don't think he knows anything about you, but please keep your eyes open. VI, Wyatt, and Garrett, you know he already has it out for y'all. So my advice is to stay home. Don't go out shopping for Black Friday."

"I'm sorry Rodney, but I will not miss shopping because of him. I have plans tomorrow, and he can kiss my ass."

"Kayla, what plans do you have?" Garrett asks.

"I'm buying all your Christmas gifts, and none of you are coming with me. I will take VI's Taser."

"Kayla, did you not just hear what Rodney said?"

"Yeah I heard Mom, but I have plans. I will check in every hour. Don't worry. I will be fine. I am tired of living in fear. I looked over my shoulder for seven long years, and I refuse to do it any longer. This is not open for discussion."

I walk out of the dining room because I am done. I head down the hallway and go to my room. I walk across the floor to the double doors and out to my patio taking a seat on the dark chocolate chaise lounge. This is my thinking spot. I have to come up with a plan to deal with Elijah because if he isn't dealt with, this nightmare will keep repeating—kind of like the movie Groundhog's Day.

My thoughts are interrupted by VI.

"Kay, I see the wheels in your head turning. You are practically smoking out of your ears. So tell me your plan because I know you are forming one. If I need to be an alibi I will."

"VI, you know me too well, but I will not let you or anyone be an accessory to my crime or crimes."

"Kayla, I am not asking. You either tell me, or you don't get to leave without me. I am not playing. You remember what happened last time you didn't let me in on your plan."

"Well, last time there was no plan. You ma'am went in there half-cocked. I just refused to wait on back up."

"Do you want me to go and get Wyatt and Garrett, or Rodney for that matter? Because I will."

I pull her arm back and tell her, "No, I don't want that, but I seriously don't have a plan—just an idea."

"Okay, so spill it sis. I am not playing."

"Okay, so I am going to make a call to Damon. He has told me he can come and teach someone a lesson."

"Okay so make the call now. I want to hear what your plan is."

"Dang you are pushy."

"No, I am being protective."

I grab my phone from my bra, and I dial his number

"Yo, this is Damon."

"Damon, this is Birmingham."

"Birmingham, are you okay?"

"Yeah, I'm fine, but this is not a social call. I need your help."

"Okay, but I'm telling you I'm not selling you anything ever again."

"No, this has nothing to do with that."

"Okay, so tell me what it is you need."

"The last time we talked, you said you would come and teach someone a lesson for me. I need to call in that favor now."

"Okay, when do you need this done?"

"I need it done like now. I'll pay for your flight out here and pay you whatever you ask for when it's done."

"Okay, when you say done, do you mean like done-done?"

"No. Here's my plan. I need your goons to beat up someone and torture him for six hours."

"Okay, I can do that. Give me an hour to get to the airport. I will be traveling with two men."

"Okay, three first class flights are being booked right now."

VI nods her head and get on the computer.

"Will you need transportation and lodging while you're here?"

"No Birmingham, I can handle all that."

"Okay deal, but I have one more favor and I know you said no, but can you get a rig when you get here?"

"Do I want to know what for?"

"No, you don't. The less I tell you, the better off you are."

"Okay, I'll let you know when I land."

"Thank you Damon, for everything. Oh, and I'm sorry about the other day."

"No worries. I just hope I got them there in time."

"Yes, you did, but barely."

The phone disconnects, and I know our conversation is over.

"Are you sure about this, Kay?"

"Yes, I am ready for this shit to be over, but I do need your help with one more thing."

"Okay, name it and I'll do what I can."

I need you to go shopping for me because I can't come back with no presents. I want you to take my card and buy for everyone. We also need a Christmas tree and decorations. I want you to meet me at Northgate Mall in the food court at four pm."

"Is there something you're not telling me, Kay?"

I smile at her, and she knows I am hiding something.

"I told you I won't tell you everything because I don't want you to know how evil I really am. Now go get some sleep and be ready to leave at five am."

"Holy hell! Are you out of your fucking mind? That's before the chickens even get up."

"Well, I can leave you here."

"No, no that isn't necessary. I'll be ready. We will need to stop by Starbucks first thing."

"I can handle that."

My phone rings, and I see its Damon.

"Hello Damon."

"Hey Birmingham. We are headed to the airport."

"Okay, your tickets are there. Talk to you soon."

"For sure."

The call ends again.

"Go to bed VI. I love your face."

"I love yours too."

She gets up and leaves the patio. I follow and walk over to my closet and pick out my clothes. I choose a pair of old jeans, a tank top, and an old sweater. I grab my tennis shoes, jacket, and my black knock off purse. I lay them on the chair by the vanity.

Garrett walks in and sees that I have clothes laid out.

"You're serious? You're really going shopping?"

"Yes Garrett, I am. VI is going with me, so calm down. We're leaving at five in the morning."

"I can't believe that you are going to do this. He has already hurt both of you once."

"Garrett, I can't live my life in fear any longer. I've lived that life and I am over it."

"Kayla, you're insane. Why go out looking for trouble?"

"Would it be better that he come here and hurt me in my own house? I don't think so, Garrett. I am over my fear of him. He can't hurt me anymore."

"How do you figure? He can kill you, and you know as well as I do, he will do it if he has the chance."

"I'm not going to stay cooped up. I'm sorry, but this is not open for discussion."

"You're hiding something. You're too calm."

"I am hiding nothing, Garrett. I am going shopping. I have a home to decorate for Christmas. Tomorrow is the biggest shopping day of the year. I have not missed a Black Friday sale since I was sixteen, and I will not miss this one."

"I don't understand you. I don't see your logic."

"I'm asking you to have faith in me. It will all work out."

"I can see that I'm not going to win this battle."

I tap him on the shoulder and tell him, "No babe, you're not. Let's go to bed. I'm tired, and I have to get up in a few hours because I have a dent to put in my credit card."

"Okay, let's go to bed."

We get into bed, and I lay on my side with Garrett behind me. I can feel his erection forming, so I stick my ass out further and hear him hiss.

"Babe, you are making things rise up down there."

"Who? Me? Never. I'm an angel."

"A naughty angel in the nicest way possible."

"Babe, fuck me, please?"

Without hesitation, he was inside me.

I roll us over and am on top of him. He is holding my hips and grabs my breast.

"You're so sexy."

I glance down at him and his eyes are rolling back in his head. I know it won't be long now before his release so I do a hoola-hoop motion a couple of times and that's all it takes. He is saying my name as he climaxes. It isn't long before I find my release.

I collapse on his chest and listen to his heavy breathing while he runs his hands down my spine, sending chills down my body.

He whispers, "I know you're hiding something babe, but I am going to trust you."

I act like I don't hear him and calm my breathing. It doesn't take long before I'm asleep.

CHAPTER TWELVE

Time for a Lesson

"The best road to progress is freedom's road."

~John F. Kennedy

I can't say I ever really fell asleep. It was more like I dozed on and off throughout the night. Garrett on the other hand was sleeping—his snoring was his giveaway but I can't say I mind because he looks so peaceful when he sleeps.

I get up at four-thirty and get dressed. I walk over to the patio doors and check the weather. I open it, and can feel the cool rush past my legs and the rain pelts off the patio. This is perfect. The weather will wash away all evidence. I glance around and see a black vehicle parked down the street from my house. I know who it is, but I'm going to act like I don't see him. In order for this plan to work, I need to act normal.

I quietly leave the room and go wake up VI. Just as I raise my fist to knock on the door, it opens. I stifle a scream and put my hand over my mouth and on my heart.

"You bitch! You scared the shit out of me."

"Sorry Kay, I didn't mean to."

I whisper in her ear that Elijah is parked in a black

vehicle down the road. She taps her purse, and I shake my head.

"Come on, let's go get Starbucks."

We gather our stuff, and I see a light on in the living room. We walk over and see Rodney there.

"You girls really are going, I see."

"Yes," we say in unison.

"Well, since I can't stop you, I want you to take this can of mace."

"Thanks Rodney." I grab it and stuff it inside my purse. "Take care of the house for me while I'm gone. I have tons of presents to buy. Oh, be ready to unload my truck when we get back."

"Oh great! Really? I get the joys of being the muscle?"

"You're the one playing house with my mom, so yes sir, you do."

That gets a laugh out of him, and we walk to the door.

When we walk out to the beast, I quickly unarm it and we jump inside. I turn the heat on, and VI turns the seat warmers on. It doesn't take long before the truck is a perfect temperature, so I throw it into reverse and back out.

We get out on the road, and I get a text stating Damon is in Seattle.

I hit the automatic dial on the wheel, and Damon answers.

"Birmingham, where are you?"

"I am just now leaving the house, but we have company following us."

"Oh damn! He's a quick one, isn't he?"

"You have no idea."

"Okay, so I did my homework on him. He has a temper, correct?"

"Oh yes, very much so, and his temper is going to be off the charts today. His brother is dead, and it's my fault."

"Okay, so what is the plan?"

"I was going to drop VI off at the mall, but seeing how I have company, she's going to have to ride along. I didn't want her to be part of this, but it looks like I can't prevent that."

"I know where there's an abandoned warehouse." VI says. "It's actually condemned and due for demolition this week."

"Okay, can you give me the address? That's where we'll make the magic happen."

"Perfect, we're only about a block from there." Damon says.

"Us too. I'm going to pull in and get out of the car. That is when I want your guys to grab him. Then VI and I will leave, and you can do whatever you're going to do. Remember, I want him alive. I want the last face he sees to be mine."

"Done. Not a problem."

"We're pulling in now."

"We're here but hidden, so come on in."

I look over to VI and tell her I love her.

"I love you too, Kay. Now let's get this fucking bastard."

We step out of the beast at the same time. I walk to the back and see the black car pull in right behind me. A chill runs down my spine.

He opens the door and says, "Superstar, you've been a naughty girl, and you need to be punished."

"Why are you following me? I know the police told you to stay away from me."

He moves closer to me and grabs my face.

"You fucking bitch! You killed my brother. Did you actually think I'd stay away? Oh, look! You've brought me a play toy."

"Leave her alone you bastard!"

I feel a sting across my cheek and taste the metallic taste of blood.

"You fucking dick! I can't believe you hit her. Have you lost your fucking mind? Didn't your daddy teach you to keep your hands to yourself? Oh that's right, you don't know your real dad, do you?"

That got her face slapped and before I know what is

happening men come out of hiding and grab Elijah. They have a black sack over his head.

I hear him scream, "You set me up, you fucking whore, and I swear you will pay for this."

I look over at Damon who is smiling. I know he is going to have a good time because he can't stand rapists. His sister was raped.

I hold up six fingers, letting him know I will be back in six hours.

He shakes his head, and then Elijah is taken inside the warehouse.

VI is pulling me into the beast. She has the keys and throws me inside before placing the truck into drive and peeling out of the parking lot.

"Let's get the hell out of here."

"I agree VI. Let's go shopping."

"Wow! Really? We aren't even going to talk about him?"

"No we aren't. I want to go shopping. I have things to buy."

"Okay, where are we going first?"

"Well, let's start off at the mall because I might be able to get everything there instead of going to several places."

"Okay."

"VI?"

"Yeah?"

"Thank you."

"Girl, you know I got you. I wasn't going to let you do this on your own."

"I know and I'm thankful for that. I was scared shitless back there. He is just so unpredictable, but enough of the heavy. Let's go spend some money."

"Done."

We get to the mall in a few minutes and it's starting to rain hard outside.

"Hey VI, look! There is a parking spot right up front."

"Hell yes!"

She whips the beast into the parking spot. I take my purse and throw it over my chest sideways. She hits the alarm on the beast and we are walking arm and arm into the mall.

"So what all is on your list?"

"Well, I have to get something for everyone, but I know what I'm getting Garrett. I guess we can start there."

"Oh, what are you getting him?"

"I'm buying him a cross necklace. He has been trying with his faith lately and I want to get him something that could help."

"That's a great gift. He'll love it."

We end up getting everyone something at the jewelry store. I bought Patrice a beautiful ring that says mom on it. I got Rodney an engraved money clip. Wyatt got a sterling silver flask that says Suck it, Buttercup. And while VI was busy getting her gift to Wyatt, I got her a gold ring with two dolphins. She has mad love for them. I also ordered her a dolphin cruise on a glass bottom boat. She will get a day of pampering from head to toe.

"Kayla, there is a Christmas store right there. Let's go in."

"Okay, I want to do white lights with silver decorations and a splash of hot pink."

"I knew you were going to say that."

We walk into this store, and it's so beautiful. Everywhere you look there are Christmas ideas. Since I've never done the whole Christmas thing, I know my credit card is getting ready to have a major workout. I need everything.

I look around the store and see do it yourself gingerbread house, lights in every color, lights that play music, and there are candy canes, bells, and garland. I grab a few of the apple cinnamon broom sticks, stockings, and decorations.

I get candles and towels, and I look over and see an angel tree topper. It is gorgeous. She has blonde hair, green eyes, and a beautiful black and silver velvet dress. She also has silver wings and a halo. She is speaking to me and I know I have to have her. Looking around, I see a sales lady and I go ask for help, leaving VI to shop.

"How can I help you today?"

"I saw a tree topper that I am hoping is for sale."

"Well honey, you're in luck. Everything here is for sale. Can you tell me where it is?"

"Oh sure, it's right back here." We walk toward front of the store, and I stop where I thought the angel was. When I look up, it was gone.

"Honey, there is nothing there. Are you sure there was an angel on top?"

"Yes, but I guess someone else bought it."

I go back to the back where the registers are, and I tell them I'm ready.

"What's wrong, Kay?"

"I found the prettiest angel, and I went to get a lady to help me but when I came back, the angel was gone."

"Aww babe, I'm sorry. We can find another one."

"No, it's okay. I'll just make a tree topper out of ribbons."

I am waiting on the cashier to finish ringing up my load of decorations and I look down and see I have a text message from Damon.

It read, "Hey Birmingham, all is ready."

I reply "okay."

When the lady finally finishes, I see the smile on her face when she looks over at the total. It's seven hundred, sixty-four dollars.

"Holy shite Kayla! What did you buy?"

"Everything. I had nothing."

We gather all the bags and walk out the door as I tell VI it's time.

She nods her head, and we walk out to the beast, load our stuff, and get in.

"Kayla, what is the plan for Elijah? You mentioned a rig. I think I know what it is."

"Well, what is your guess?"

"Is a rig a needle? You use to shoot up, right?"

"Yes VI, that's correct."

"So what exactly are you going to do with a needle?"

"I've already told you I'm not telling you everything. If we get in trouble, I don't want you to go down for my stupidity."

"Kay, you're my ride or die. I'd do anything for you. I just need to know what's going on."

***

The guys grab Elijah and cover his face with a blacked

out hooded cover. We have all worked together before so no words are needed. I give the motion for them to take him inside, where I have everything all ready.

***

I want to make Kayla proud, I have much love for her. I push this sorry bastard into a chair, and quickly my men have him tied down.

"Let me go you bastard, this has nothing to do with you."

"Oh but it does, you hurt my friend and now I am going to hurt you."

"Kayla is a whore, why in the fuck would you want to protect her. That stupid ass bitch got what she deserved."

"Oh really, you think I should force you to have sex? Tie you up and rape you? Take your ass and make it mine?"

I get the battery charger and touch the ends together. The sound of electricity makes Elijah jump.

"What was that?"

"Oh that is no concern of yours. I will show you what it is later."

"Why are you doing this? I have money, I will pay you whatever you want."

"Oh, you think I am doing this for the money?"

"Well, what other reason would you be doing this for?"

I rip the hooded cover off his eyes. It takes him a minute to adjust to the light.

"I am doing this because for years you and your stupid ass brother hurt my friend. I can't do anything with your brother because well, let's face it he is now worm dirt."

"You sorry mother fucker, I will kill you for talking about my brother like that."

"Oh you will kill me huh? I'd like to see you do that." I grab the clamps off the battery cables and I attach one to his left nipple.

I watch as his eyes get the size of softballs. And I turn on the charger. A jolt sends him convulsing in the chair.

"Tsk-tsk, looks like you have just pissed on yourself."

"I believe you guys used a belt of some sort on her as well correct."

He can't answer because the electricity is still flowing on a low dose to his nipple. I take out a black leather strap and I hit him on his chest. Immediately there are gashes.

I turn off the battery charger. And he vomits all over himself.

"You really are a sissy. I hear you guys tortured her for hours. And it was an on-going thing but I am not going to be doing this for long."

"What do you mean you are not going to do this for long, are you going let me go?"

"Oh no Elijah, there will be no letting you go but I won't be the one to kill you, Oh no Elijah that joy will lay with Kayla. She killed your brother, and now she is going to kill you as well."

"Please, let me go, I will never hurt her again. I swear."

"Too bad I don't fucking believe you." I slap him hard and hear his nose break.

"You mother fucker. You will pay for this."

"Oh please, you don't even know who I am. Kayla will be here soon and she will give you what you deserve but before that, I am going to show you how it feels to be tortured."

"She will never do it. I know that Superstar will save me."

"Funny how you think you know her. Guess what? She paid me to come out here. She paid me for the drugs that killed your brother, and she is paying me to fuck you like you did her."

I pull him out of the chair and throw him on the ground.

He tries to fight but it does him no good. My guys have him held down, and I have his jeans down around his ankles.

He is begging me.

"Beg please, god beg. I love it when a little bitch begs."

"I'm sorry, I don't know your name but please tell Kayla

I am sorry. It was all my brother. He was the mastermind."

"Oh isn't that grand, you are blaming your dead brother. He can't even defend himself."

"I swear on my life that it was him."

"That is not what I hear."

I breathe in his ear. "I hear that you were worse than he was, that you took great pleasure in hurting Kayla. That it was you who also took great pleasure in raping her. That it was you who would beat her. That it was you, Elijah, that burned her with cigarettes."

And in one swift motion, I have him flipped around and I have my cigarette pressed against his neck.

He is breathing heavy and screaming each time I touch him with the cherry end of the cigarette.

"You thought I was going to rape you, didn't you? I am not like you, I don't have to rape someone to get them in bed, but I had your bitch ass scared shitless. You are no man, more like a little mouse." I flip the switch on high, and he screams in pain.

I knock him out and tell the goons to place him back in the car and make sure all traces are gone.

I send Kayla a message to tell her that he is ready.

***

It's pouring outside. I see the black car sitting on the side of the road. I tell VI to stay in the beast.

I get out and walk over to the car. He is bleeding and has bruises everywhere. Damn I see the cigarette burns along his collar bone and have to laugh because those bitches hurt.

I put a pair of latex gloves on and open his car door. He jumps at the sound and looks at me.

"Superstar, I knew you would save me, I told them that you would save me..."

I look at him with pure hatred, grab the rig, and drew back the syringe filling it with air. I move his neck so I can get to his carotid artery. I stab him suddenly and look out the window and see VI looking at me. I push the plunger, letting the air go into his vein.

He struggles, and I know he will die of an embolism.

I lean in close and tell him, "I am done being afraid of you. You can't hurt me any longer. Oh, say hello to your brother when you get to hell. Oh, the reason you didn't get raped wasn't because of me. I told him to do it, but you won't be so lucky because you are going to die. But I forgive you."

I walk away and never look back.

CHAPTER THIRTEEN

Meeting the Monster

"Life is really simple, but we insist on making it complicated."

~Confucius

When we get back inside the beast its quiet and I can see what had occurred is bothering VI.

"Are you okay?" I ask.

"Yeah, I'm fine. I never thought you had that much hatred. I saw the look on your face. You really hated him."

"He was a monster, VI. You have no idea the vile things he was capable of. For years he had a power over me and by holding that needle in his neck, I took back all that power. He can no longer hurt me or anyone else."

"I understand that Kayla, but I've never seen that look on you before. To be honest, it scared the shit out of me."

"I'm sorry, but in my defense I told you to stay in the truck."

"I know you did and I probably should have but I wanted to make sure if you needed help, I was there. I had my gun in my hand."

"Thank you for that, but I need to know if you can forget what you saw?"

"Yeah I can, but if you want me to forget, you need to tell me a few things first"

"Oh yeah? Like what?"

"Well first off, what did you do?"

"I filled his artery with air which will cause him to have an embolism."

"Okay, you are going to have dumb that down for me because I have no idea what the hell that is."

"I injected air into his artery that caused him to have a blockage. Basically I put a bubble of air into his blood supply."

"And how did you know you could do that?

I look over at her and see she is trying to figure things out.

"So what exactly are you asking VI? You know I am not just going to start talking about my past but I will answer if you ask the right questions."

"Okay, so when you were using, did you always use needles?"

"Sadly no. I snorted, smoked, and shot up."

"What is the difference? I know I sound like I'm an idiot, but I want to know."

"VI, I never thought you were an idiot babe, but I will tell you. Snorting is inhaling the powdered form of an illegal drug, especially cocaine, through the nose. I will give a run down on smoking Heroine. Heroin smokers start by attaining a rectangular aluminum foil about three centimeters by seventeen centimeters. You'll also require some kind of funnel tube to help you inhale the vapor. You can create one__"

"No! Stop! I don't need that many details. I understand," Vi interrupts me.

The look on her face makes me start crying.

"Oh Kay, please don't cry, I am just trying to figure things out, but I really don't need that much detail. I never plan on smoking the stuff."

"I know VI, it's just I looked at your face and you looked like you were disgusted. I am not proud of the path I took those years ago, but I did it and I have to own up to my mistakes. If I could do it all over again, I would but I can't. My past has made me who I am now. I am not shy about telling people I was a drug user. Hell, I will proudly tell anyone to not use drugs. Do you have any more questions?"

"Yes, how did you pay for your drugs?"

"I had money, but I didn't always use the best judgment when I was high. I slept with men for drugs. I traded sex for drugs. Hell I even stole for drugs. I am no angel," I say to her and hang my head.

"Oh Kay, I was not judging you I swear. I was just trying to get some background because the Kayla I saw a few minutes ago, I have never saw before."

"I never wanted you or anyone to know that side of me. This is my dark side. I've got the blood of Edwin on my hands, I have the blood of Elijah on my hands, and when I die, I will have to answer for my sins."

"Can I ask what it makes you feel?"

"I told you that if you ask I will answer. The euphoria of heroin is normally the first thing that hits you. The rush, coming up, whatever you want to call it."

"Can you break down snorting like you just did for smoking?"

"I can try."

"Here's what I can tell you about snorting Heroin or Black Tar. The first method, the one I call monkey water, is my preferred way. You put a bit of tar into a spoon as you would if you were prepping for IV. Then you add some hot water to the spoon, but not boiling hot. Hot water from the tap is more than adequate because it helps the tar dissolve easier. Next you mix it around in the spoon until all the tar is dissolved. I like to use a little piece of a straw to do the mixing, but it doesn't really matter what you use. Now you should end up with a spoonful of water ranging from dark brown to light orange. How dark it is will depend on how much tar and water you used."

"Now careful not to spill, bring the spoon up to your nose and snort a bit of the water. Do not try to snort the entire spoonful in one big sniff. If you do this, some of it will probably go down the back of your throat and/or just fall right back out of your nose and make a big mess. Snorting a liquid is a bit different than snorting powder, mainly because liquid doesn't stick to itself and every piece of moist tissue it comes in contact with. Also the liquid has much less resistance going up so you don't have to snort hard at all."

"The point being, what you want is it to cover your mucous membranes in your nose and sinuses. So do a little at a time until you get the hang of it. Sometimes what I would do immediately after snorting the "monkey water", is tilt my head forward so gravity helped move the solution towards my sinuses rather than just dripping out of my nose or down the back of my throat."

"If done correctly you will feel a mild burn and the onset of effects will be rapid. This method is extremely effective and not really very difficult to learn/execute. I just wanted to be detailed because I remember the first couple times I remember just railing it hard and having most of it go down the back of my throat and not getting me high lol.

"But anyway, this is the only way I did tar. In my honest opinion, the advantages of doing monkey water are it's fast to prep. You can get the dose accurate, there are no needles and track marks, and compared to snorting powder, it's a lot easier on the nose.

"The second method is called cheese. This is how you actually turn your heroin from tar into powder that can then be snorted. It's a bit more complicated than monkey water. The first thing you need is a surface to work on. You can use a plate, a mirror, a marble counter top, or a very smooth piece of plastic or glass. Really any flat, smooth, and non-porous surface will do. Wood is a no-no. I usually use a plate because it's easy to move around and clean up afterword.

"The second thing you want to do is make sure your plate is very clean and has no dents, chips, or cracks in it. If it does the tar is going to get stuck in them and it's a bitch to get it out. Also any residue on the plate is going to end up in your nose, and that's gross. If it all looks good then we can get started making our cheese. Now take your tar and place it on your plate. If the surface you're working on isn't very big try to place the tar close to the center so you have more room to work with."

"This next step is very important—"

"No! Stop! I've heard enough. I can't listen to this anymore. I understand now, and I know there's no fucking way I'd ever do that shit." Vi screams.

Now the look on her face is pure terror. I reach over and grab her hand. "This is why I never told you this stuff, Vi."

"No Kay, I wanted to know."

I look over at her and she is crying. I wipe away a tear because it's hard seeing your best friend cry. "VI, please don't cry. I can't handle seeing you upset."

"Kay, I am crying because you lived a whole life in seven years. I am so sorry that I was not there to help you"

"Oh VI, you could not have done anything. You would not have even liked me then. I was cold, had no life in my eyes. I did not care who I fucked over."

***

We sit in silence all the way until we get to the Christmas tree farm.

"Where are we?"

"I told you I didn't have a tree, so we're going to get one, and they'll deliver it tomorrow."

"Do you know what kind of tree you want?"

"I didn't know there was more than one kind."

"Oh, geez! There are all kinds."

We get out of the beast and start walking toward the lot of trees. I see a man dressed as Santa, and he is selling Christmas trees. I give a chuckle because I never believed in Santa.

"What are you laughing at?"

"Santa over there. I never had a present from Santa."

"Girl, you're killing me. What the hell did the Stanton's do for Christmas?"

"They gave us money. It was easier for them, and they didn't have to be home for that."

"That is so sad, but I understand why you wanted a huge blowout for Christmas. This is your first one."

"Yep, so let's get the biggest tree we can find. My ceilings are twenty feet high, so I think we need at least a twelve foot tree."

About that time, Santa walks over and tells us that he has the perfect tree for us. I look at him like he's crazy but who am I to judge? He walks us to the back of the lot, and there stands a tree so grand, it would put the tree at the White House to shame. I go up and touch the branches, and they're so soft. The tree has an amazing smell, and I know this is my tree.

"I'll take it!" I yell.

"Don't you want to know the price?"

"No I don't. I want this tree. Can you have it delivered tomorrow?"

"Ma'am, this tree is not cheap."

"Sir, with all due respect, I did not ask how much the tree was. I want this tree, and I am willing to pay whatever it is. I also need a tree stand. So when it is delivered tomorrow, please make sure they bring a stand that will hold it."

"I can see that I am not talking you out of this tree ma'am."

"No you aren't. So, let's ring it up. I'm exhausted."

I go and pay for the tree and the stand. He was talking like it was expensive, but it was only two hundred dollars—that included the stand.

"Come on, VI. I am exhausted and ready to get home and prop my feet up."

"Let's go, doll."

We make our way home, and by now, it's beginning to snow. I pull in to the garage, and VI and I grab a few bags before heading toward the elevator. To our surprise, Rodney is waiting.

"Are there more?"

"Oh, yes. The back of the beast is full."

I see him open the back, and I hold back a laugh.

"Holy shit, Kayla."

"We bought out the stores."

"I can see that."

"Come on. Grab what you can. I want to see them muscles work."

"I have them all, just hold the elevator."

"Okay," VI and I say in unison.

We get into the living room, and everyone is in there talking.

"Damn! Did you leave anything in the stores?" Wyatt asks.

"Nope, we bought it all."

"I'm just going to drop the bags and sit down for a few minutes because I'm dragging ass."

"Me too, Kayla. Me too."

As I drop the bags, Patrice's phone rings.

***

"Hello, this is Dr. Doyle. How can I help you?"

"Patrice, this is Seth, and I am not taking no for an answer. I will be at Kayla's in ten minutes, and we need to talk."

He hangs up the phone and Patrice looks over at me and says, "Kayla, Seth will be here in ten minutes. He says he wants to talk and is not taking no for an answer."

Rodney and Garrett both start talking.

"Fine, let him come in. I am sick of the damn phone calls, but I will not be threatened in my own home."

Within a few minutes, there's a knock on my door. Rodney goes and answers it.

"Officer Jernigan, what are you doing here?"

"That's none of your concern, but know that I will continue to be here."

"I just want to talk to my daughter."

"Come on Seth, we can talk in the office."

I walk towards the office and Patrice follows. All other eyes are looking at me like I've lost my mind.

"I'll be okay. There will be no problems, will there Seth?"

"No, Kayla there will not. I only want to talk."

I walk over and shut the office doors and tell them both

to sit. I walk behind my desk and sit in my comfy chair.

"So, Seth, you wanted to talk. Now's your chance."

"First, I want to apologize to Kayla for letting the rape go on for as long as I did. I should have put a stop to it the moment I even suspected it. I should have kept you safe, but I was too caught up in my own life and political career. I am sorry."

"What are you sorry for? That you let it happen, or that you let it continue?" I ask, crying.

"Kayla, I am truly sorry."

He tries to come and hug me, but I push him away.

"Have you lost your fucking mind? Do you think I would let you console me? You're delusional."

He backs away with his hands in the air.

"Patrice, I owe you an apology as well. I never should have raped you, and I will spend the rest of my life trying to earn your forgiveness. I never meant to hurt you. I was not in my right mind that night. I was drunk."

"And that is an excuse!" I scream, "You raped someone. You forced yourself on someone, and you think that you can say I'm sorry and it'll be okay?"

"Kayla, I know you're angry, but I am still your father."

"Ha! That's funny. A father? A father is someone who makes you feel safe, kisses you when you're hurt, and tells you he loves you. A father protects you from harm. Did you ever do any of those?"

"I will never be able to take back what happened in the past. I was wrong. I hope one day you can forgive me."

"Are you done? Did you do what you came to do? Did you get it all off your chest? Is your conscience clear?"

"Patrice, can you please forgive me? I am sorry, and if I live a hundred years, you'll never know how sorry I am. But on the positive side—"

"What positive side? You raped my mother. You're a fucking monster!"

"The positive side is you were conceived."

"Good job! You created a child that you let get hurt for years. There was sexual, mental, and physical abuse inflicted by the hands of the kids you raised as your sons. Oh, but that's right, they aren't yours. So, is that why you're apologizing? You're trying to make things right? You can go since you've cleared your chest. I will never accept your apology. You'll never receive forgiveness from me. Go fuck yourself in the seventh circle of hell until you burn to ashes and are fucking dead."

I stand to leave, but he continues, "I understand that you have every right to feel that way and say those things, but I am truly sorry, Kayla."

"Don't come here feeding me some bullshit story just to make it easier for you to sleep at night. Guess what? It will never change the past, so stay the fuck away from me and leave me the fuck alone."

I turn to walk out, but I hear him say to Patrice, "I am sorry for what I did to you in college. Forcing myself on you despite the amount of alcohol is still no excuse. I'd like you to know that the regret and guilt of hurting you or letting Kayla be hurt haunts me and has for over twenty years. It will until the day I take my last breath."

"Well, that day can't come soon enough!" I scream and walk to the door.

Patrice is frozen and appears unable to speak, so I tell him.

"I think I speak for both of us when I say this. Seth, do the world a favor and just fucking kill yourself. You have no clue what you did. Let me tell you, you raped a woman. You took her choice away. All those years of you running for office, how would you have felt if the voters took your choice away? You'd have been pissed, but then again, you may have just swept it under the rug like you did with me. You treated me like I was no one, like I was a cheap trick. You sent me away Seth, with nothing more than a check. I had no one. I had nothing. Do you know I was addicted to drugs? Do you know I sold my soul to the devil? I was always looking over my shoulder. I was eighteen and alone. I have been fighting addiction since. I even bought drugs just the other day. Did you know that? No of course not. Do you know who stopped me from shooting up? It wasn't you. It was Rodney. A man who has known me for roughly a few months. He stopped me. He found me. Where the fuck were you? I am sure you were doing what you always do, you were probably balls deep in some whore who is young enough to be your daughter. Like it would matter to you. You have a thing for raping women."

"But now all of a sudden you are sorry. And I am supposed to just forgive you?? Ha-ha you got jokes. I will tell you when I walk out of this room, my conscious is clear. I have never wanted anyone out my life more than you. You have no soul. You will fit right in hell when you get there. You are a low-life bastard who don't deserve forgiveness. Make sure you tell your son hello for me. You are not worth me wasting another breath on. I am done with this conversation and I am done with you. After today don't contact me. Lose my number and forget where I live, because you are no longer welcome here. If I see you so much as breathing the same air as me, you better act like you have no clue who I am. I wouldn't spit on you if you were on fire."

I get in his face and tell him, "You are dead to me."

I walk out before he can see me break down. I will not give him the power to make me break, and he will never see me shed another tear.

CHAPTER FOURTEEN

Self Defense

"A life is not important except in the impact it has on other lives."

~Jackie Robinson

I open the door and find exactly what I expected — Garrett and Rodney standing there without saying a word. I look at Garrett and walk into his arms.

"Did you guys get a good ear full?"

I can't be mad at them because I know they were there to help if we needed it. The only person I'm truly pissed at is Seth. I pull myself from Garrett's arms and walk toward my room, closing the door behind me. I sit down on the bed and cry. I know I should forgive Seth — my faith tells me to, but right now, I can't.

I see Garrett walk into the room through my watery eyes, and he sits on the bed beside me.

"Are you okay?"

I glare at him and say, "I'm not. He wants me to forgive him, and I know I should, Garrett, but I can't. These wounds are too deep."

"Do you want to talk about it?"

"Yes. I do."

He looks at me, his shock obvious. I can't blame him for feeling this way because I always say no when he offers.

"Where do I begin?"

"Wherever you're comfortable," he takes my hand and raises it to his lips.

I wipe a tear that runs down my face before I begin.

"All my life, the only thing I wanted was a family. I wanted a mom and dad. Well, now I have both, and I am so thankful Patrice has moved here fulltime and has started a practice. She's in love with Rodney and I couldn't be happier for her. I'm still hurt by the adoption admission, but I understand it better now. Patrice has opened her heart and life to me. She knows things about me no one will ever know and that's okay. I was hurt for a while when I found out she was my mom, but now it feels right. I can't imagine every having that bond with someone else. She is my mom, and I love her. Seth, however, is a different story. There is absolutely no connection or bond there."

"He had me my entire life. Hell, I lived under the same roof as my father all my life and he's a stranger to me. How is that for bullshit? I don't have the first clue about him. I couldn't tell you what he likes to eat, his birthday. Hell, I don't even know my grandparents. He never showed that side of himself. We didn't celebrate the holidays. The only reason I ever knew it was a birthday or holiday was because we all received money."

"But he sent me away like I was nothing. He gave me

half a million dollars to leave. The whole time I was gone, if he had reached out to me, I could have saved myself from all the hurt I put myself through."

"I became addicted to heroin and sold myself for drugs. I did things I'm not proud of. I was constantly looking over my shoulder. When I finally got clean and sober, it was because of Patrice. She helped me see myself. The entire reason I am back home is because Patrice told me it was time. It was never Seth."

"Then I came home and all was good for six months. Then all hell broke loose. I got you all mixed up in this shit. All of you would have been better if I would have stayed away."

"Kay honey, I love you, and I am so glad you came back," he interrupts me.

"How can you love me after I told you what I've done?"

"Kayla, we all have a past we aren't happy with but you've made your life better. Your past only defines you if you allow it to. So, are you going to let it? I would love you no matter what you've done. You are my reason for breathing. I think of you before I make any decisions. I think of you before I think of myself. I would move oceans to make things easier for you. How can I not want to be with you?"

"I don't want the future to be ruined because of my past. Can you accept my flaws? I'm not perfect. I'm positive I'll fuck up more times than not but I will always stay on track as long as you believe in me."

"Kayla, I love you no matter what. One day I will marry you and then we are going to have beautiful babies together. I would ask you now, but I don't have a ring."

"Garrett, thank you for believing in me and remember I want a pink diamond when you ask."

He starts laughing.

"Can we get out of here for a little while? We can take a drive and see where we end up. I want away from all this fucked up shit."

A few minutes later, we leave in his truck and drive without saying a word for the longest time. He finally breaks the comfortable, peaceful silence.

"Hey Kay, that amazing band call Last Moment is performing at Club Fuchsia. I know you love their lead singer. Would you like to go?"

"Yes, I would absolutely love to go. I kind of have a mad crush on Alex the lead singer. She is a bad ass rocker chick. I know they made a brief appearance here last month just to check on the venue. I would love to actually listen to them sing. I am not really dressed to go out though." I am in jeans and sweater and thigh high boots.

"Kay, you could wear a wool sack and you would still be stunning."

"Aww, I know you are just trying to make me smile, but its sweet."

"Wyatt and VI are meeting us there. Is that okay?"

"Duh, I can't enjoy this without my number one Bitch."

"You really love her don't you?"

I look over at him and grab his hand, "Yes, I love her. She's part of my heart, the same as you and Wyatt."

I look out the window and see all the homes decorated for Christmas. I can't wait to get the house decorated.

"Garrett, I bought a Christmas tree today, and it'll be delivered tomorrow. Will you help me decorate it? I want to make this Christmas huge."

"I will help you with anything babe. All you have to do is ask."

Before long we are at the club, and the beat of the music is hypnotizing. I watch the people dance close to each other. There are people grinding on each other then there are those couples who act like no one else is around.

"Wyatt is doing well with this club." Garrett says.

"Yeah, he is. It was a much needed staple here in Seattle. Did he tell you he is thinking of doing a teen night on Wednesdays?"

"No he didn't but I think that would be a great thing to do. He would stay busy, and they need some place to hang out."

VI and Wyatt meet us and we party the night away. Toward the end of the night, I finally hear some good news. VI and Wyatt announce they are officially a couple, and they want to see where things can lead between them. Neither liked the idea of the other seeing someone else, so they made it Facebook official.

I laugh at this because I had given her shit about it just

the other day. I have known they need it to just become exclusive. I can see the love they have for each other. It's about damn time they saw it and admitted it so they can see if they're meant to be—just like Garrett and I are meant to be. I mean, look at what we've been through, and we've made it work.

I raise my glass and make a toast, "It's about damn time you two finally saw what the world has seen for the last few months."

After, we all hit the dance floor and let loose, but before long I get an eerie feeling that something is off and something is going to happen, but I have no fucking clue what it could possibly be.

VI and I are on the dance floor while our men have a drink. We dance our asses off to the club-mix before Last Moment takes the stage.

I look over and see a woman walking toward Garrett. He tenses up.

I grab VI and tell her we have to get to the bar. She looks over and sees Reagan. The club is pretty packed, and the dance floor is where most seem to want to be. So we make our way over to the bar only to hear Garrett.

"You need to stay the fuck away from her. We're together now, and you have to fucking accept that and stay the fuck away."

I walk up with my biggest bitch face on and ask, "Is everything okay baby?" Then I kiss him with more raw passion than I planned but I really don't give a fuck.

So after we break the kiss and catch our breath, I turn to Reagan, "You need to leave."

"Oh Kayla, did you ever tell your precious Garrett what you and your friend here did to me in the parking lot last time we were all here?"

"No, I don't have to tell him everything. He trusts me, unlike you."

"Oh, so you don't think he would like to know that you and VI tased me and broke my nose."

I hear Garrett laugh.

"Are you seriously laughing Garrett? Your girlfriend messed up my face, and I have scars all down my body."

"Reagan I'm sorry, but your face was already messed up. I think I made some improvements. Now at least your nose is straight because before it was not. Your plastic surgeon needs some glasses." VI says.

I look shyly over at Garrett and he knows.

"I already knew. Wyatt has cameras you know. I have known since that night. We were in the office watching."

I look over at him stunned. He never said anything to me.

Wyatt walks over and tells her it's time to go.

"Here, let VI and I show you out." I say.

I take one arm, VI takes the other arm, and we drag her

out the back entrance so I can share a few choice words with the cunt.

When we get out back, we let go and she start swinging and ranting, "You'll never make him happy. You're not good enough."

In order to shut her up, I pushed her backward, knowing her head will hit the brick wall behind her.

"Oh Kayla, you act like that was supposed to hurt. So I hit my head on a wall. Big deal."

"Reagan, I have dealt with your smart ass mouth since we were kids, but I am over it. I want you to leave my man alone."

"Awe, that is cute. You think he is your man."

"He is my man. He sleeps in my bed every night and is in my pussy every day." I see that I am pissing her off.

"Reagan, did you know that I make his eyes roll back in his head when I have his dick in my mouth."

"You are a fucking whore. First you sleep with your brothers, then you sleep with Garrett."

"I'm the whore? You're fucking hilarious. I'm not the one who got caught with two men fucking you in Garrett's home, and I heard that they had to have surgery. Awe poor guys, hope they are okay."

She spits in my face, and I slap her. "You fucking cunt. I am so over your petty childish games. You want to fight? Let's do it."

I have her pinned up against the wall and hit her face. I hear bones cracking. Blood is running down her face. I take a step back just to catch my breath and the next thing I know, I feel a knife slicing my hip. I reach my hand down and feel a slice going up to my ribs, and then I hear a gunshot. When I turn to look over at VI, she has tears running down her face. She keeps repeating it's over. VI is still holding her gun, and it's still aimed at Reagan's lifeless body on the ground.

"I had to. She would have killed you if I didn't stop her."

I walk over to VI, feeling the blood ooze out of my side and down my body. As I get to her, I take the gun out of her shaking hands and wrap her in my arms.

I whisper, "Thank you, VI. You saved my life."

I put the gun on safety and slip it back into her purse and call Rodney to come out. When he finally arrives, I explain to him what happened.

He agrees if VI had not taken action, the bitch would have tried to kill me or would have kept trying until she got the job done.

Rodney said he would be coming to write up the report and get everything all wrapped up in a nice neat lil bow and that he doesn't think any charges will be filled because there are witnesses to prove we did not start the fight.

By this time, the guys have pinned us out side and see a dead Reagan laying at our feet with a bullet hole in the center of her head and me bleeding.

So Wyatt locks the backdoor so that no one from the club can come out back.

Wyatt leads us to a bench, where he places thirty-two butterfly bandages on my hip and side after it had been cleaned.

I put my shirt back on, and Rodney walks in to take our statements, but no charges will be filed because VI shot Reagan to prevent her from killing me.

It was all caught on tape from the cameras monitoring the peer.

CHAPTER FIFTEEN

Forgiveness

"With the new day comes new strength and new thoughts."

~Eleanor Roosevelt

We go home and have the most incredible lovemaking session either of us has ever had. Afterward, I am laying on Garrett's chest, and he has fallen asleep. He always makes me feel so loved. I enjoy nothing more than lying in his arm and thinking about how he took me so loving but so passionately at the same time. He has a way that makes me feel cherished. I know I am.

While I am having delicious thoughts of our lovemaking and all the things he did to me, my damn phone starts ringing and it doesn't stop. I don't want it to wake Garrett, so I grab it from the nightstand and see it's the police station calling.

"Hello?"

"Is this Kayla Ashby?"

"Yes."

"This is officer Jernigan's partner, Tracey Mathews, and he has been trying to reach you all morning. There's something you need to know. Please hold."

"Hello, Kayla?"

"Yes, Rodney, what's going on?"

"Seth committed suicide early this morning—around one."

"What? Seth is dead?"

"Yes, he was found by Millie. He was hanging in the pool house by some purple ropes."

"Okay, why are you telling me? I wasn't there. I was at the club. You know that."

"Millie is saying she will kill you for this because it's your fault. Kayla, Seth is your father.

"Don't you dare say that vile man is my father? Yes we share the same DNA but that is all, he is nothing to me!"

"Kayla, I am not trying to make you have feelings for him. But the truth of the matter is Seth was your father. And as his next of kin we had no choice but to notify you. Millie is here screaming it's all your fault

"How is it my fault? I haven't been there in, well, fuck, since I left. I haven't stepped foot back in that house. So explain to me how this is my concern."

"Well, there was a letter addressed to you, and I'll bring

you a copy so you can read it."

"His suicide note was written to me?"

"For the most part, but I'll explain more in an hour or so. I'm going to pick up Patrice because you'll need her shoulder when you read this."

"Why? I hated the guy. He never stopped the twins from raping me and when he was told about the abuse he just cut me a fat check to make me disappear. So, why the fuck would I care what he has to say?" I can't help but think of the last thing I said to him. I had told him that he was dead to me. I walk out of the room so not to wake Garrett. "Millie has said that she will kill you for this because it was your fault."

"Kayla sweetie, I agree, but you need to read the note."

"Okay, make it two hours, and you have a deal."

"Okay, two hours and we'll be there."

I walk back into the bedroom. Oh, God, what the hell have I done? I wished him dead, and now he was.

"Garrett honey, you have to wake up." I shove him.

"What? Is everything okay?"

"No, Seth has committed suicide."

"Kayla, this is not funny."

"Do you see me fucking laughing? Please get up. I need you to go with me."

"Go where?" He asks, throwing on a pair of jeans.

"Apparently there's a suicide note left for me. I wished him dead. Is this my fault?"

"No Kayla, only the weak kill themselves. This is not your fault. Now go get dressed, and I'll wake everyone."

I sit on the bed with my head in my hands. I can't believe he did this. Why would he kill himself and leave a note for me? My words were harsh.

"I killed my own father," I say sobbing then I realize I should say a prayer.

God our Father,

Your power brings us to birth, your providence guides our lives, and by your command we return to dust.

Lord, those who die still live in your presence, their lives change but do not end. I pray in hope for my family, relatives, and friends, and for all the dead known to you alone.

In company with Christ, Who died and now lives, may they rejoice in your kingdom, where all our tears are wiped away. Unite us together again in one family, to sing your praise forever and ever.

Amen.

I am crying over a man who knew I was being hurt. My thoughts go back to when I was younger. I do remember one occasion that I thought Seth was the coolest person ever.

I had just turned sixteen years old. I wanted to learn to drive. So I had went and asked Millie and of course she was too busy. She was planning some event for the Mayor's Ball or something like that. So I was walking back into the living room and Seth had asked me if I was okay?

"What difference does it make? I will be the only sixteen year old who doesn't know how to drive," I mumbled.

"You don't know how to drive? Kayla come on I will teach you." He grabs his keys and we go out to his blue B.M.W. He throws me the keys and says "Come on. I will teach you."

I am so excited that I scream and jump up and down.

I get in the car, and look over at him, because I have no clue what I am doing. He goes over a few rules, about checking my mirrors and adjusting my seat. He tells me to buckle my seat belt, so I do as I am told.

"Next you are going to stick the key in the ignition and turn the key."

I do as I am told, and the engine comes to life.

"Place your foot on the brake and then put the car into reverse. Slowly back out of the driveway and keep your hands in a ten and two position."

I back out of the driveway, and then he tells me to put the car in the drive position.

Again I do as I am told. Before long I am driving down the road. He tells me to make a right, and I do. I see the interstate up ahead, and I act like it is not a big thing. Before long I am driving down the coast of Seattle. We have the top off the car and we are having a good time. No talking, just listening to the radio and enjoying the drive. We stay gone for most of the day.

He even buys me lunch that day. We had seafood at some little off the wall place on the water.

It doesn't take long and my room is buzzing with people. I am numb, and I don't even hear them talking to me. I know VI is getting me dressed. I don't even care that Wyatt is in here while I am changing. She pulls out some jeans and a black long sleeved shirt. She puts some mascara on my eyes, and a little blush because she says I am pale.

I get up, but I am on automatic. I don't know anything that is going on. I am being pulled into the vehicle, next thing I know we are at the last place I'd ever come to again.

I am about to have a nervous breakdown.

I feel Patrice grab my hand and walk with me.

We are greeted by cops.

The officer says, "I'm sorry, but this is for family only."

Patrice says, "This is his daughter."

The cop then asks for Rodney.

Rodney gives a nod, and I am taken back to the pool house.

All of a sudden old images of my rape comes flooding back.

"Time to pay the piper, sweetheart." His words circled the air and sent shivers up my arm, making me nauseous.

"Please don't." I couldn't get those words out of my

mouth. It seemed like the cat caught my tongue.

Edwin then lit up a cigarette and puffed away, making smoke circles.

Gradually, I crawled to my knees and gathered all of my stuff. And before I knew it...

He clunked me in the back of my head with his fist. I tumbled over and peered at the water.

Like a caveman, he dragged me to the pool house. As soon as I was aware of my surroundings, I tried to fight him, but he was too strong. I couldn't do anything but dig my nails into him and claw at his eyes. He forced himself on top of me and burned my chest with his lit cigarette.

The burning tobacco cuts into my breast and created marks.

Every time I fought him, more marks showed.

"Stupid ass cunt." He slapped me so hard that I thought my teeth and eyeballs were going to pop out of my damn head. He continued to drag me on the red tile floors kicking and screaming, I tugged on my hair to release from his hold, but I lost momentum and dark red liquid flowed over my back, matching the tile on the floor.

I whimpered and cried. Hell, I even screamed the last time. He tossed me into the game room of the pool-house like I was yesterday's trash.

My limp body rolled. I laid on my back, stunned and mortified to what would happen next.

Edwin snapped my hair toward him and ripped it as he lifted me up. I felt like the roots were coming out of my head.

"Scream bitch, no one will help your ugly ass." He sneered.

"Stop it!" I stomped on his right foot.

"Ow, you fuckin bitch. You'll pay for that." His left hand smacked as his knuckles dented my cheeks. As blood seeps from the corner of my mouth, he then slams me into the wall. His hands wrapped around my throat. "Shut your fucking trap, you cock teaser."

"Edwin, enough!" Elijah's booming voice echoes through the hall.

"Please, Elijah," I shouted. "Help!"

Elijah strolled up to me, soothes my cheeks and grabs a hold of me.

"Edwin, get the rope cuffs," he bluntly said.

"Why do I have to get the damn cuffs?" Edwin asked as he swayed.

"Because I said so," Elijah's face was full of malice. "Now."

Edwin snagged a purple rope that had hoops at either end from one of the drawers where their father kept his sex toys.

"Please," I shouted and collapsed in Elijah's arms.

"Go ahead and scream bitch, we love it when you fight

us," Edwin said as he grits his teeth. "Just so you know the more you scream... the harder things will be for you." His voice vibrates through his throat.

I can feel the tension from here, I'm about to have a nervous breakdown. I grab my chest and start breathing heavily.

"I can't do this. I can't be here."

"Kay, we are all here with you". Wyatt says

"You don't fucking understand I scream. I can't do this. I can't walk into the pool house."

"Kayla, I want you to look at me." Patrice stops us and she grabs my face. "You are not that little girl, you are a grown woman, and you can do this."

"I can't, Please don't make me go in there. I know they will be there and they will hurt me."

With her hands on my face she says "Kayla, remember you are a survivor you are not a victim. You left. And you know that Edwin is dead and Seth is dead too. Come on grab your big girl panties and let's go."

"I am a survivor I mumble."

"Good now, come on let's go because if you don't Millie wins. She already thinks this is your fault. Don't give her more reason to doubt you."

"She will not win. I will not let her."

I start to run out but Patrice takes my hand. "It will be okay, just breath."

"I can't do this. I can't be here."

"Yes, you can. You need to face this."

"Will you stay with me the entire time?"

"Yes, I will. I'll be right here the whole time, but we have to do this."

"Okay, just hold my hand."

"I will baby, I promise."

We get to the pool house and nothing has changed. The smell of the chlorine is still very strong. I look over and see him hanging in the hallway. I hear the other cop say that he suffered and it wasn't a quick death. I overheard that he choked to death.

I can see where the chair was just out of his reach.

The medical examiner said he would have heard the blood pounding in his ears as his heart beats harder—the adrenaline surges through his body. The thoughts swimming through his head would have been guilt, anguish, and pain until he faded into oblivion. The smell is horrid. Seth pissed and shit on himself.

I look over at his neck, and it is stretched and deformed. His tongue is black and protruding and his legs and feet are swollen from the blood pooling at the lowest point causing his legs and feet to look horribly bruised.

I gasp because I was not expecting this. I thought they would have him down and covered.

Rodney walks over and hands me an envelope.

I turn away and open the envelope, and I see a neatly written letter.

To whomever finds this:

My life was not taken by anyone else's hand

Nor did it have to end, but the voices in my head

The visions of my daughter's crying eyes and sorrowful cries because of my own boys

Not in normal teases but in torture of a sexual nature. I can't stand the nightmares that I barely raised.

What has been done will scar her for life

But no one sees the pain she masks

Her innocence in tatters.

And I didn't do anything to help her

I am the worst

To see what I wanted to see in my boys

And not know the hidden truth behind my angel's eyes

I am worthless alive so these are my goodbyes.

Kayla I want you to know I am sorry. I never meant to hurt you. I hope my death will make your life easier. I will not burden you. Just know that this will be my way of taking your pain away from you.

Please forgive me. I love you my darling daughter.

Sincerely,

Dad

I am numb. I feel nothing—no hate, no revulsion, no forgiveness. I am simply numb. As I start to walk out of the room, everything goes black.

I wake up some time later with people around me, screaming. I lay still because I don't want to move. As long as I am not moving no one will know that I have woke up. I must have passed out.

Millie is now in the room, I can hear her yelling that I will pay for this.

Rodney then says we have more bad news. Elijah was found dead as well.

CHAPTER SIXTEEN

Letting the Past Go

"It's not stress that kills us, it is our reaction to it."

~Hans Selve

Millie comes charging at me, screaming curse words.

"This is all your fault. You are nothing. I knew you would end up taking everything away from me."

"What do you mean this is my fault? I have not stepped foot back in this God-forsaken house. I hated living here. I didn't kill Seth, and I damn sure didn't kill Elijah."

"Excuse me, but my husband is dead because of you. He told me what you said. You wished he was dead."

"Millie, I wish you were dead too, but it doesn't mean it would be my fault if you suddenly died."

"Kayla, I knew from the beginning you were Seth's daughter. Why do you think we got you? I knew about him raping your mother. Hell, I covered it up at the college."

"Are you insane? That's a dumb question. Of course you are. Why would you do that? How did you know about the rape?"

"Oh honey, I know about all the whores in the cock house. I know about every woman who my husband has let his cock play with."

"You're a sick bitch. Why didn't you ever tell him I was his? You could have prevented everything. The rapes, the beatings, and the deaths. Have you lost your fucking mind?" I go after her and manage to get my hands around her throat. "You crazy, fucking cunt." I am squeezing her, and then I am pulled off.

She screams she wants me arrested.

"Go ahead and arrest me," I scream at her. "All of this is your fucking fault."

Rodney gets everyone out of the room other than the family.

"Millie, I want you to know you are the nastiest person I have ever met. Your husband rapes women, and you cover it up. Then your evil sons rape and torture an innocent child. You chose her because she was mine and Seth's. So because you couldn't have a biological child with Seth, you use ours. What kind of person does that? You need help. I hope that you get the help you need." Patrice screams at her.

"Millie, I hate to tell you this but you are under arrest." Rodney tells her.

"Me? Why am I under arrest?"

'Well, I will think of something to charge you with but right now, let's just say because you covered up a crime."

"Aren't you going to arrest Kayla?"

"I didn't see a crime. I saw you provoking her, and she lashed out at you. So I see that as self-defense."

"Kayla, I swear that you will get what is coming to you."

"Tsk-tsk. Oh Millie, you threatened her in front of a cop. Keep on talking. I am sure there are more charges to add."
Rodney says.

"Garrett, I need to get the hell out of here. I've been here long enough."

"Okay honey, let's go."

We walk out of the room, and I watch as they load Seth into the coroner's van, and Millie in a patrol car.

"Babe, let's go home. I want to forget this day ever happened.

On the way home, Garrett is silent for a few minutes allowing me to gather my thoughts.

Finally I speak up.

"I knew as soon as I walked in that dad was dead. I could see that he had struggled. He died all alone. I was not there for him. How could I be so selfish? All he wanted was to be just a small part of my life, and what do I do, I tell him I wished he was dead. Garrett he hung himself with the purple ropes that held me down for years."

"It's an unnerving feeling, knowing that all I had to do was accept his apology. He tried to call me last night. I hit ignore, Garrett I hit ignore on my father's last phone call. How can I be such a monster?"

"Kay, you are not a monster you are human. He hurt you, and your instinct was to have nothing to do with him. I am so sorry sweetie. When my dad died, I felt a huge sigh of relief but to be honest I was hurt. Even though he hurt us for years, it was still hard. You always hurt in your heart when there is a death."

"This one will be harder on you because you walked in and saw him."

"I will never forgive myself for not telling him I forgive him. Now I will never have the chance."

Garrett leans over and takes my face in his strong hands, and tells me that he loves me, and that I forgive Seth, then he will know. He may not know in the physical world but in the spiritual world he will.

I place my hand in my hands and I cry silently, and say a silent prayer.

Lord, you invite all who are burdened to come to you. Allow your healing Hand to heal me. Touch my soul with your compassion for others; touch my heart with your courage and infinite Love for all; touch my mind with Your Wisdom, and may my mouth always proclaim your praise. Teach me to reach out to you in all my needs, and help me to lead others to you by my example. Most loving Heart of Jesus, bring me health in body and spirit that I may serve you with all my strength. Touch gently this life which you have created, now and forever.

Amen.

I want to go home. I am quiet the remainder of the way home. It is snowing outside and it's so peaceful. I feel a little flutter in my stomach and tell Garrett he has to pull over.

"Kay, it's snowing outside."

"I don't care, please pull over. I have my hand over my mouth."

He glides the truck to the edge of the street and before he comes to a complete stop I have the door open and I am getting sick.

He throws the truck in park and runs over and moves my hair out of the way.

"Is there anything I can do for you Kay?"

"No, just get in the truck. I don't want you to see me like this."

"Babe, I am not going anywhere. I will always help you whenever you need it."

I wipe my mouth with the back of my hand and go to lift my head and I am dizzy. I grab the side of the truck for balance.

Garrett picks me up and places me in the truck.

"Do you want me to call the doctor?"

"No I will be fine. It's just the stress of the day. I will be fine I just want to go home and decorate our house for Christmas. The tree should have been dropped off, and I want to enjoy the holidays."

"Okay honey."

We drive through Seattle, and I notice all the snow that has fallen since we have been at the house. The roads are slick, and I tell Garrett to be careful.

"It's just a little snow," he says.

We finally make it home and we slide into the garage. I hold on to the 'oh shit' handle and scream.

We get up the elevator and the biggest tree I have ever seen is there waiting on me. I call the guys in from the elevator shaft and tell them they have their work cut out for them.

"Damn Kayla, this tree is huge."

"I don't know if it will fit."

"Oh yes it will. I have twenty feet ceilings. This is a bet I'll win."

It takes them roughly an hour, but my tree is up and in the stand. My house smells like a forest, and I love it. During that hour I have all the end tables decorated. The mantle is done. The house is coming together nicely.

I go and grab the ladder so I can start decorating the tree.

I get the lights ready, and I have every strand blinking at different times.

"Kayla, are you really going to put all those lights on this tree?"

"Why yes I am Wyatt. And this tree is going to be the best tree ever."

Garrett walks in with hot chocolate.

"Oh honey, you are a life saver. I was craving that."

"I'm sorry, but did you say that you were craving something?" VI asks.

It's just a saying, but that makes me think. When was my last period?

VI sees the look on my face, and hers lights up.

"So Garrett, when are you going to make an honest woman out of my best friend?"

"What do you mean VI?"

"You know, put a ring on it." She says, doing her best Beyoncé move.

"Oh, I don't know. I am sure it will come soon."

"Don't scare him off VI. I like having him around."

"I don't think you could scare that man off if you tried."

"Let's get this tree decorated because I want to turn off all the lights and just sit and look at it."

"Wyatt or Rodney, will you please start a fire? Garrett, I need you to please get your fine ass on this ladder and start stringing the lights."

He does what I ask, and I am enjoying the view.

In no time we have the lights on the tree. It looks amazing. All you see are twinkling lights. There is not a dark spot on the tree. Everyone is having a good time. We are all sitting there making small talk while Christmas music is playing in the background. Before long the tree is decorated, and it is stunning.

"Hey, where is VI?" I ask.

"I don't know. I think she went to the bathroom."

I get up to go into the kitchen, and VI meets me.

"Kay your tree is missing something."

I look at it, but I have no clue what it's missing.

"Where is it missing something?" I ask.

"Close your eyes and stick out your hands."

"Hell no, you may have ice or something."

"I swear it's not ice."

"It's only because I love you that I will do what you ask, but it better not be anything that is going to scare me."

"Kay if it does, I give you permission to shred all my sexy bras."

Oh hell, this must be something because she is a sexy bra hoe. I close my eyes, and she leads me to the couch. I sit down, and I'm waiting. It seems like forever

"Okay Kay, you can open your eyes."

My eyes pop open, and I don't see anything.

"What am I looking at, the tree looks exactly the same?" Then slowly my eyes reach the top, and there she is. My angel is standing proud on my Christmas tree. I immediately start crying.

"You asshole, you knew I wanted her. Why didn't you tell me?"

"I saw her the other day, I knew you would fall in love with her. So I took you into that store. I had already bought and paid for it. When you went to the front of the store looking for the sales lady, I had it taken down and placed in a box. I wanted to give you something you wanted. And I knew you would want her."

I'm bawling now, "It's my first Christmas, and you just made it the best one ever. I freaking love you," I go and squeeze her.

She whispers in my ear, "There is a pregnancy test in my bathroom. Go use it."

I look at her stunned, but I nod my head.

"Hey guys, please excuse me for a few moments." I wipe my tears

I hear Garrett start to get up, but VI tells him to give me a few minutes. I hear their conversation, and they're making small talk.

I go get the pregnancy test from VI's bathroom and read the instructions. I pee on the stick and set it on the countertop. I can't tear my eyes away from it, and almost as soon as I lay it down, it shows I'm pregnant.

"Holy shit," I think to myself, "I'm going to be a mom. Oh, God, what will Garrett think? Will he be mad? Will he leave me?"

Of course I know the answers to all these questions, but I still can't help but think them. Before I leave the restroom I stick the pregnancy test inside a book. When I return to the living room, everyone is sitting around the tree, discussing their Christmas wish lists.

I know in my heart I have to forgive him, so I grab my journal and start writing. I am so hurt, the words spill out.

You did not know

Hell no one did

How could anyone know?

I kept it all hidden

Locked inside

I ran away

As soon as I could

I hid from everything and everyone

Not looking back

Letting fear rule me

I fought alone

The demons

That threatened to rip me apart

Running only masked

The reality

It never stopped

Any of the nightmares

From haunting me

Day and night

I reinvented myself though

I came back stronger

All of it

Made me

Who I am today

And now this

Why

Why couldn't you give us a chance?

You could have seen

How far I have come

We could have moved past all of this

Had an amazing future together

You robbed me of all of that

Reopened Pandora's Box

And left me

Left me to battle alone

Again

You selfish prick

It was not your fault

Damn it

Why couldn't you just talk to me?

Now you are gone

And here I am

Facing the demons

I thought

I had conquered

Time heals all

Or so they say

For me time only mends

The cracks of my broken soul

To truly be free

From all of this

I need to tell you

I forgive you

I forgive them

I forgive me

I am closing the door

I won't look back

I hope that peace finds you

Wherever you may be

I close my journal and walk into the bathroom and look in the mirror. I place my hands on my stomach and whisper, "I already love you."

I get in the bed because the day has been an emotional one. I lost the man who raised me, and then I find out I am carrying the love of my life's child. It isn't long before I fall into a sound sleep.

I wake up to the smell of someone cooking eggs, and I haul ass to the bathroom to toss my cookies. The smell is killing me. When I think I've emptied my stomach, I stand and wash my face and brush my teeth to hide the evidence.

I go downstairs, and see my family laughing and talking.

I hear Rodney in the office on the phone, and I walk in there to check on him.

"Hey Rodney, what's up?"

"Well, Millie made bond and she has a court date after the New Year. The coroner and the morgue called to ask if you had thoughts on what to do with Seth."

"Oh, wow. I didn't even think about what would happen, but shouldn't Millie make that decision?"

"No, the will was changed last month, and you are his next of kin."

"I have no idea what he would want. I think we should cremate him and have a small service."

"If that's what you want, I'll call them. I think it's a good idea because I know how hard it was for you to see him."

"Yes, it was hard. I won't lie. I've never had to make any decisions like this, so I hope they're right. Can you make all the arrangements for me, Rodney?"

"Yes Kayla, I can. I will ask your opinion each step of the way."

"Thank you for everything you do for me."

"You are so welcome. You are family, and we take care of our own."

"You are so right."

Over the next few days, Christmas is in full swing at my house. Somehow my living room has turned into Santa's drop off. There are so many presents under the tree that you can't even see the floor. I have never seen so many. There are gifts for everyone under the tree. All sizes and shapes. The stockings are full, the house smells amazing. We have thrown a couple of pine cones into the fire.

Before we know it, it's Christmas. I am so excited to give Garrett his gift. He has several, but I am most excited about the little thin box. Over the next couple of hours we have a fabulous dinner, with all the trimmings. Wyatt cooked this time. His ham was amazing. It had pineapple and cherries on top. He made ranch mashed potatoes, homemade gravy, fried green beans, and he made this mac and cheese that had seven different kinds of cheese. I was in heaven. I had three plates of food. I was starving. After dinner it's time for presents.

I have waited all my life to experience a feeling like I am feeling right now. The gifts are exchanged, and there is paper everywhere. I see everyone has a pile of gifts. I tell Garrett there is one present in the tree that he has to find.

"What do you mean there's a present in the tree?"

"Exactly what I said, doll, and look in the tree."

"Okay, let me see what we have here."

He gets up and searches all over the tree. I see him reach into the tree, and he pulls out a slender box. I get my phone ready.

"Babe, why do you have your phone out?"

"No reason. Just open your gift."

He slowly opens the box and the house is quiet. You could hear a pin drop. He opens the box, and I see him look down, then at me, and once more at the box.

"Is this what I think it is?"

"Well, it depends on what you think it is."

"I think this stick is telling me I'm going to be a daddy."

"Would you be okay if that is what it's saying?"

"Kayla, I'd be over the moon. So don't kid around with me, is this your way of telling me that we are going to be parents?"

He comes over and grabs me and pulls me up. "Babe I am serious, are we going to be parents? Have you given me my greatest wish?"

"Well I didn't do it on my own."

Patrice jumps up and looks over her shoulder and screams, "I'm going to be a grandma!"

"Yes babe that is what it is. We're going to be parents. Are you okay with this?"

His silence makes me cry.

"No honey, please don't cry. I'm excited. I've always wanted kids and now you're giving me a child."

He scoops me into his arms and kisses me.

"And you said I gave you the best present. VI says"

"Your present was second best to the present I just got"

Garrett is kissing and tears are running down my face.

We hear, "Hey now, that's how you got pregnant."

We start laughing, and I am still crying.

"Babe, why are you crying?"

"I'm so happy. Are you still going to love me when I'm fat?"

"Honey, I can't wait to see your round belly. I will love you even when you are round because you are carrying my child.

"Garrett Winters you did not answer the question. I said are you going to love me when I am fat."

"I did answer, but I'd never call you fat. You could weigh a ton and I'd think you are perfect."

"I am far from perfect. I am Damaged and I have been Broken."

"Kay listen to me I will love you for a thousand years. I love you and it's because of your past. And yes you were Broken and you may be Damaged but you are fixing yourself. And even a broken girl can be fixed."

***

Before long Christmas is over, and it's New Year's Eve. Tonight is Wyatt's Masquerade Ball. Everyone is decked out. It is a black tie affair, but you have to have a mask. I ordered our masks around Thanksgiving.

My dress is a floor length with an open back. It had a slit on my thigh. You could just barely see the top of my garter. My hair is done to perfection, and so is my make-up. Of course VI dressed me. I have not started to show yet, I don't even know how far along I am. Wyatt has ordered all bar staff to make sure there is non-alcoholic drinks for me, which is fine because that means I can drink all the cute girlie drinks because they all come non-alcoholic.

Garrett is wearing a kick-ass patterned black and white mask and is dress in black like me.

VI has a purple mask that matches her purple and black dress, and Wyatt has on a half covering mask on his left side in a black grey tone. He has a purple shirt and black slacks.

He took tonight off to spend their first New Year's Eve as a couple and to celebrate that we are all back together and inseparable.

I am dancing with Garrett and we are next to VI and Wyatt who are also dancing to an oldie but goody, Mariah Carey Always Be My Baby. As we are dancing and being held close to our men, I finally feel that life is as it should be. For once things are going my way.

The next thing I know I am being ushered outside, and it is freezing cold.

Wyatt has the peer closed off, and I see why. There is a hot-air balloon on it. Garrett takes my hand and leads me to it. He helps me in, not saying much other than it's our first New Year's, and he thinks it should be our most memorable.

When we are settled in the balloon, I look at my watch and see it's eleven-fifty. We float high above the bay as the fireworks begin.

I turn in Garrett's arms right before midnight. I want to tell him how beautiful and breathtaking it is.

From up here, he drops to one knee and opens a ring box.

"Kayla, I have been in love with since the first night we spent in St. James. There has never been another that could compare to how I feel for you. Please make my lifelong dream a reality and say you will be my forever and always and that you will share your life with me. Will you be my once in a lifetime?"

I am speechless, and all I could do was nod my head

with the biggest smile on my face. Our lips meet, and we hear
the screams of midnight.

Yes, this year will be so much better than the past years
of my life.

We land the balloon after a nice romantic ride down the
bay to see the fireworks. By the time it lands, my family is there
waiting to see the ring. I had not even looked at it until now, and
I see it's a pink diamond like I wanted.

I am over the moon happy. For the first time in my life, I
can say I am completely happy.

EPILOGUE

It has been a crazy few weeks. The holidays have come and gone. And my house is getting somewhat back to normal. Well as normal as it can be with all the construction going on. I wanted a big huge elaborate wedding, but with all the shit going on with the all the deaths. And never knowing what Millie was going to do. I told Garrett that we needed to just elope.

"Honey, it will be perfect no matter how we get married. As long as you are there, I will be fine."

He smiles and kisses my head. He has this look about him that says I am up to something, but I can't put my finger on it.

"Garrett, honey what are you up too?"

"Me, nothing." He says smiling at me.

I go about my business because right now I can't focus on him.

He hollers down the hall to be ready to go in an hour.

"An hour? Where are we going? And you know I need longer than an hour."

"I'm telling you to be ready in an hour. And I am not telling you."

I get up and go look in the mirror and do my make-up. I have no idea what he is planning so I go natural. I make an oval with my mouth and open my eyes to put on my mascara. My lashes are thick so it don't take much to make them stand out. I put on some light pink lip gloss. And just a smidge of blush.

I toss my make-up bag in my purse. I walk over to my closet, since he gave me no ideas of what we are doing, I grab a pair of skinny jeans and a sexy one shoulder top. I grab my six inch fuck me heels. I walk over to the dresser and grab a pair of the sexy panties that Garrett bought me for Christmas. These are white with light blue bows along the sides. I grab the matching bra. I spray some Wings perfume in the air and walk through. I get dressed and look in the mirror. I look over my shoulder and see Garrett standing there staring at me.

"See something you like big boy?"

"Oh yeah very much so? And I will explore it all later, but right now we have to go."

"Why are you rushing me?"

"No reason, other than we have plans. But you are not going to know about them."

I watch as he takes a blind fold out of his pockets.

"Excuse me. What are you doing?"

"Kay, have faith in me please. I want to surprise you and this is the only way I can do it."

"Oh I have faith in you Mr. Winters but I don't know about this surprise."

He grabs, my hand and kisses my knuckles.

"You will be fine, just listen to the sound of my voice."

"Okay, I will trust you but you better not do something that is going to scare me, because if that is the case we aren't having sex till the baby is born."

"Kayla I swear you will love it."

"I better."

He is guiding me through the house. I hear bags being gathered.

"Garrett, who all is here? I hear more than one person."

"Don't worry about it Kay, just listen for once in your life. No questions. Just enjoy."

He grabs my hand, and I know we are close to the front door, as I hear the alarm code being punched in.

Soon I am being placed in the beast and he says, "You need to wear the headphones as well. I want the music so loud I can hear it in the driver's seat."

He places the ear buds on my ears and immediately I am being blasted with Uptown Funk. I sit back and relax.

I feel him latch my seatbelt and start the engine.

We ease onto the road, and it don't take long and we are at our destination.

I feel him unlatch my seat belt. And he takes my music away.

"Can I take off the blind-fold now?"

"No, leave it on."

"Yes sir."

"I can get used to the sir stuff, ma'am."

"Yeah, well, if I don't like this surprise, you are going to get used to your hand."

"Dang Kay, that is harsh."

"No, you know I don't like to be scared. And there better not be anything that will jump out at me."

"Okay, I promise."

He takes me hand and leads me into a cool building. I smell candles and flowers, but I can't place my finger on where we are.

I feel the cool breeze as a door open. And then the mask is taken off my face. It takes a minute for my eyes to adjust. And when they do, I see I'm at St. James Church.

"Babe, what are we doing here?"

His face lights up and he says, "I know you said that we could elope, and you would be fine with that. But when we are old and gray I did not want you to have regrets. So I have planned everything. From the dress to your flowers."

"But how did you know?" I say crying.

"Honey, I know you. I know that yes, you would have been okay with quick wedding, but deep down you would have regretted not having the whole church wedding, so Vi and Patrice have been planning this since before Christmas."

"Are you fucking serious? How did you all plan this?"

"I have connections. Now go in that room and get ready. I will be the one at the end of the isle waiting on you."

***

I walk into the room and look at VI standing there.

"You asshole you knew."

"Yes, babe, I did, but I was sworn to not say anything."

"So, tell me what I am going to be wearing since you've picked everything out, ma'am."

"Your dress is over there, hanging on the hanger."

I walk over to the hanger and unzip the garment bag. I pull out a blush colored dress, and I gasp. It is the dress I looked at over Thanksgiving when I ordered the masks for the ball.

This dress is stunning. It is a ball-gown style dress. It has a fitted bodice that comes in at the waist and then flares out to a full, floor-length skirt with lots of volume for a more formal and traditional bridal look. I also have a Tiara. That has pink diamonds all over. I see I also have a pair of what look to be pink glass slippers.

My flower bouquet is what I pictured in my head. It is called La Vie en Rose Bouquet. Tiny butter-yellow tea roses provide the perfect foil for the myriad shades of pink found in these garden roses, spidery jasmine buds, and scabiosas with their pincushion centers.

I get into the dress with VI's help. She does my hair in a fancy up-do with wisps of hair hanging down.

"Vi, will you ask Patrice to come in here for a minute?"

"Sure, babe. I'll be right back."

I am looking at myself in the mirror, and I see my mom walk in. She looks beautiful. She has on a light pink formal dress. She looks like a million bucks. I have never seen her so stunning.

"Awe, baby, you look gorgeous."

"Thank you, Mom. I don't know how you and Vi did it, but you have picked things out that were only in my mind."

"We know you, Kay, and we knew you would regret not having the church wedding."

"Thank you so much for doing this."

"It was no problem at all, sweetheart. We love you."

"I love you all so much. Do you think Rodney would walk me down the aisle?"

"I think he would be honored."

"Actually, I want you both to walk me down the aisle, if that's okay."

"Oh baby, you made my life complete. Thank you for accepting me as your mom."

"I couldn't ask for a better person to be my mom. I am sorry I was so hurt when I found out."

"It's in the past, Kay. You have a future to look forward to."

I wipe a tear off my face, and she comes and gives me my first hug as her as my mom.

"Ladies it's time." I hear Rodney say.

He walks in the door and gasps, "Kayla, you are so beautiful. Garrett is a lucky man."

"Rodney, will you please walk me down the aisle along with my mom?"

"Oh, Kay, I would love to. Thank you for asking me. You've made my night."

Before long the music starts and I know that is my cue. Vi is down the aisle in just a few minutes. They open the doors and my eyes are filled with tears. The church has never looked more beautiful.

With Rodney on my left side and my mom on the right they walk me down the aisle to A Thousand Years by Christina Perri. It don't take long and I see my soon to be groom standing there looking at me. He has a tear in his eye and he don't even bother to wipe it away.

"You look beautiful," he whispers.

The priest asks who gives this woman to this man.

Patrice and Rodney both say I do.

He gives my hand to Garrett, and I see Wyatt standing beside him.

I am crying as the priest is talking. I don't remember anything he said till he said it's time for the Vows.

"Garret, will you please tell Kayla what is in your heart?"

"I believe in you, the person you will grow to be and the couple we will be together. With my whole heart, I take you as my wife, acknowledging and accepting your faults and strengths, as you do mine. I promise to be faithful and supportive and to always make our family's love and happiness my priority. I will be yours in plenty and in want, in sickness and in health, in failure and in triumph. I will dream with you, celebrate with you and walk beside you through whatever our lives may bring. You are my person—my love and my life, today and always."

I wipe away the tears that are streaming down my face.

He gently reaches over and wipes a tear that I missed.

"Kayla, will you please tell Garrett what he means to you?"

"You have been my best friend, mentor, playmate, confidant, and my greatest challenge. But most importantly, you are the love of my life and you make me happier than I could ever imagine and more loved than I ever thought possible... You have made me a better person, as our love for one another is reflected in the way I live my life. So I am truly blessed to be a part of your life, which as of today becomes our life together. On this day, I give you my heart, my promise, that I will walk with you, hand in hand. Wherever our journey leads us, living, learning, loving together, forever."

And we don't even wait for him to pronounce us as husband and wife. He has me bent backwards and is kissing me like there is no tomorrow.

"Garrett you have made me the happiest person in the world."

I rub my belly.

***

I am now showing, as I am about five months along. Garrett says that I am beautiful. I tell him he is only saying that to get in my pants. He laughs and kisses my belly. He sings to my belly every night. I will wake up in the middle of the night, and he is talking to our peanut.

"Babe, I have news for you."

"Oh, yeah? What is it?"

"I bet I can still shock you."

"Let's see."

"We're having twins."

"Don't joke with me."

"Honey, I swear on all things pink, we're having two

babies."

He scoops me up and kisses me. The kiss turns to raw passion.

"Babe, please make love to me."

"You don't have to ask me twice, but are you sure it's safe for the babies?"

"Yes it's safe. I asked the doctor."

I kiss down his neck and across his collar bone. I kiss down his stomach and lick the V in his hips. I unbutton his jeans and his cock jumps free into my hand. I slide my hands down his cock. I hear him hiss. He pushes me onto the bed. Starts at my feet and kisses all the way up my legs. Within seconds, he is inside me. He stops for just a minute to allow me to stretch to fit him. He starts slowly and it doesn't take long before my toes are curling, and I am screaming out his name. A few minutes later he is moaning my name as well.

He lays his head on my stomach and whispers, "Daddy loves you"

Acknowledgments

To all the Readers out there thank you from the bottom of my heart. I know that not everyone will love my work. But I hope that some do and can relate to my characters. They say that each book has a little bit of truth thrown in with a lot of fiction. Is that true? Yes I do believe it is. We put our hearts and souls into writing our books, and without readers well it would just be words on pages. From one reader to another, thank you for wanting to read my work.

"The heart will break, but broken lives on" Lord Byron.

About the
 **AUTHOR**

I was born in Tulsa, Oklahoma but moved to Pensacola, Florida in 1996. I have a huge family who I shocked them when I told them I was writing my first book. I have had a love a reading since I was young. Reading has always been my escape. I can read and be a princess or a warrior. Reading for me was always something magical. And I hope to pass that on to you all.

I am 34 years old and writing my first book. I am blessed to be the mom of a little girl named Sage who is the light of my life. {I call her Olga, and she hates it} I did not give birth to her but I choose her. I am blessed with great friends who have always had my back. I have a lot to learn in this world of writing but, so far I am enjoying the ride.

I'm very opinionated and have no filter. I speak my mind without thinking of the consequences. Does this get me in Trouble? Yes it does every single day. But I will not change. I march to my own beat. My mom says that I can be a one man band.

I am always willing to help out anyone who is in need all you have to do is ask. I never knew that writing a book would show me so much about myself. I have learned so much in a short amount of time. And I can't wait to learn more.

Website:

www.tsu.co/Authorlayla/22142148

Instagram @authorlayla

Pintrest authorlayla

Google + Layla Stevens

Pizap Layla.stevens.author@gmail.com

Tumblr @authorlayla

Twitter @authorlayla

Email Layla.Stevens.author@gmail.com

Like page

https://www.facebook.com/pages/Layla-
Stevens/697947530238039

Amazon page

http://www.amazon.com/Layla-
Stevens/e/B00MRB0TTM/ref=ntt_athr_dp_pel_1